INCANDESCENT MAGIC UNKNOWN

By Sarah Chayer

Second edition August 2023

ISBN 979-8-9886525-2-6 (hardcover)

ISBN 979-8-9886525-3-3 (paperback)

www.sarahchayer.com

Thank You

I want to give the sincerest thank you for everyone that donated to my GoFundMe to help me achieve my dream! From the bottom of my heart, thank you, thank you, *thank you* so much for everything you have done for me (including those who donated anonymously).

Reuben Avalos	Michelle Betancourt
Rafael Betancourt	Jeb Bins
Theresa Watkins-Chayer	Stephen Chayer
Michelle Cruz	Amy Gogin
Katherine Hardwick	Helena Helemo
Chris Kelly	W.R. Key
Danielle Kintz	Erin Krueger
Morgan Lindgren	Jessica Marsh
Gillianne Rekowski	Andrew Rekowski
Ashley Rooney	Lauren Garcia-Toler
Zachary Toler	Alex Wenham
Sean White	Kelly Wilson

Dédié à grandmama:

toujours dans mon cœur ♥

Chapter 1

Don't Tell

No light filtered into the cold, humid room, but through the darkness Sofia was able to make out the shapes of the men standing over her. The ropes around her wrists cut into her skin, and her bony knees dug into the cement floor. Despite her restraints, she sat upright, her chin held high.

"Who are you? What do you want?" Her words echoed through the chamber, but the three shadowy figures in front of her remained still.

"Get your hands off me," a man's voice said in the ruckus coming from the room next door.

Sofia's heart sank. "Jacob?" She shuffled, attempting to stand.

Two hands slammed down on her shoulders from behind, forcing her knees back into the cold ground and holding her in place. A hot tear spilled over her cheek.

"Fia," Jacob called back. "Are you okay? Have they hurt you?"

Before she could respond, one of the men stepped forward and struck her across the face with the back of his hand. "One more word and we start removing fingers."

His hushed words sent prickles down her spine. She dropped her head, choking silently for air.

"Don't tell them anything," Jacob shouted. A series of muffled screams followed from the next room.

A door in front of her opened, and a large silhouette appeared against a dim light, then stepped inside. Three of the men left, leaving only the person holding her down and this new, mysterious shape.

The room plummeted back into darkness as the door closed.

"You must be Sofia Hanwel." The man stopped a few feet away, towering over her. She couldn't see his face, but she could sense his grin from the tone of his voice. "You were surprisingly easy to find."

"Please," she begged quietly, her body trembling. "Please don't hurt Jacob. Everything was my doing. He wasn't involved in any of it."

After a weighted moment, the large man gradually lowered himself to a squat so they were eye-to-eye. He traced a circle in the air with his hand. A small sphere of light appeared, hovering in his palm.

She flinched from the brightness, but then her eyes widened. *They're Witcans*, she realized.

In the light, Sofia could finally make out the man's face. His eyes were dark and glinting, his hair slicked back, and his jaw strengthened with a short, trimmed beard. Under different circumstances, he would have appeared a handsome, trustworthy man.

She squirmed as she tried to move away, but the grip tightened on her shoulders and held her in place, causing her to wince.

"I'm not here to investigate your history," the man said. He reached out and squeezed her chin. The ball of light stayed in place, floating in the space between them. "I actually rather admire your work."

Sofia's shallow breaths came in pants that made her chest heave. "Then what do you want?"

He chuckled. "I just need your help finding someone. Someone I know you helped hide several years back. A young man by the name of Kye." Sofia shook her head, and the man released her jaw. "You may know him as Kurt. Kurt Carlsons."

Her heart plummeted into her gut. She swallowed hard, pressing her lips together and dropping her head to hide her face behind her blonde hair. "I don't know what you're talking about. I don't know a Kurt Carlsons."

His smirk disappeared, and he slowly rose. The blood drained from Sofia's face as he turned away.

"I don't think you are being honest with me," he said.

Sofia shrieked, scalp burning as she was yanked to her feet

by her hair. "Stop. Please. I really don't know! Please."

The hands that were entangled in her hair jerked her head back, whirled her body around, and slammed her cheek against the cold cement wall. Her jaw immediately began to sting.

The man leaned in over her shoulder. "Just tell me where I can find him," he hissed into her ear.

Sofia choked back a sob and shook her head. "I don't know."

She was pulled back. She staggered to reclaim her footing, but was shoved back into the wall again. Her shoulder crashed into the concrete, and she felt a pop. Sofia wailed, her knees weak, but her body was pinned in place against the wall. Her arm hung loosely, a severe throbbing pain swelling in her shoulder.

"This all ends if you just tell me where I can find him." He stood with his back turned as his accomplice tossed Sofia down to the floor.

She feebly tried to wriggle away, her arms still tied behind her and her shoulder stinging. A burning sensation erupted between her shoulder blades, and her flesh blazed with a scorching pain. Sofia rolled onto her side to see her captor standing over her, holding a flickering ball of fire. His pale face showed no emotion.

Her side scratched across the floor as she dug her feet into the ground to push away. The young man just watched, undoubtedly waiting for her to tire herself out.

Don't say a word. You can't say a word, Sofia told herself, whimpering as she inched away towards the wall.

"Is his life worth your own?" The taller man, still facing away, spoke softly and calmly. "Are you prepared to die for him?"

"I'm not afraid to die," Sofia muttered, finally dropping her head to catch her breath.

The younger man pulled back his hand and flung the second fireball at her. It burned into her thigh, charring her jeans and skin. The room remained quiet as she contained her cries by biting her lip. She soon tasted blood.

More commotion came from the room next door. *Jacob. I hope he's okay.*

A couple of kicks delivered into her gut knocked the wind out of her. Sofia went limp with a deep cough.

Again, the young man stepped back and waited.

They were toying with her, she realized. Sofia twisted over, and the pain in her shoulder returned. Gasping, she peered over at the taller man. He hadn't moved.

Her entire body levitated, hovering a few feet off the ground before crashing back down with a heavy thud. Then up and back down again. And again.

The man finally strutted over to her. "Where is Kurt Carlsons?"

Sofia's sobs were much weaker now, intermixed with wheezes. "I . . . don't know." She was hardly able to get the words out.

His shoulders went rigid, but with a growl he turned away and knocked on the metal door. The sound echoed for several long seconds until the door finally opened.

Two bodies shuffled through. The first crumpled to the ground with a grunt.

"Jacob," Sofia cried out. She struggled, unable to sit up, and instead began inching her way towards him.

His reply was muffled by a gag wrapped over his mouth. Jacob slowly pulled himself up, but before he could get to his feet, the towering man slammed a foot into his back and pressed him down into the floor. He held out a fist at Jacob, which began to glow a dark, ominous shade of blue.

"It's time to see whose life your wife values more." The man smirked.

Sofia moaned. "No. No, don't hurt him, please."

He watched her, and when he finally spoke again, he delivered every word delicately. "Tell me where I can find Kurt Carlsons."

A hot stream of blood poured from a wound on Sofia's brow down her cheek, but she didn't say a word.

Jacob squirmed as he tried to shout through his gag. Rubbing his face against the concrete floor, he managed to work the band out of his mouth. "Don't give them anything, Fia."

The man's fist glowed brighter, revealing the wrathful look

in his eyes.

"Wait," Sofia cried, jerking forward. Her eyes met Jacob's, and he simply shook his head. Her short, sharp breaths caught in her throat. "Jacob, I'm sorry. I'm sorry," she said through gasps.

He stared up at her with tears in his eyes. "It's okay. It will be okay."

Neither spoke for those few short seconds.

"I love you, Fia."

Before Sofia could protest further, the glow filled the entire room as the man fired a beam of blue light from his fist into Jacob's back.

Jacob released a deafening shriek. Then his head dropped as he went silent.

"No!" Sofia screamed, and collapsed forward in sobs.

The man waited, backing away from Jacob's body, before asking his question again. "Where is Kurt?"

Sofia stayed silent.

Many men came and went, but the leader stayed, repeating the question.

Hours must have passed. Sunlight crept in through a crack of the boarded-up windows. Sofia's limbs trembled, and her cheeks were soaked in blood and tears. Her eyes had swelled to the point where she could hardly see the golden light illuminating the basement room.

The tall man opened the door and peered out into the hall. "Have you found her yet?" he said to someone outside the room.

"No sign of the daughter," a woman's voice replied.

"Well, keep looking."

Thank God, Kris is safe, Sofia thought with the saddest sense of relief. With the last of her strength, she finally managed to slip out of her binds as the door closed once more.

With her one good arm, she dragged herself across the room to Jacob's corpse. Her injured arm hung to the side as she stopped over her husband's body. She moved her hair to gaze down at his face.

"Oh, Jacob." She sobbed, stroking his icy cheek. "I . . . I'll be with you soon."

Sofia lifted her chin and glared at the man as he approached. He scowled, but she was no longer afraid. She collected herself, knowing her next words would be her last. "You're not going to win. You don't stand a chance against Kurt."

Chapter 2

Frozen In Time

Kris pushed a cardboard box to the side and opened a bedroom closet filled with dusty shirts and dresses.

"You still haven't unpacked?" Brie tiptoed around the boxes to the bed.

"How can I? Look at this place," Kris murmured, dragging a finger down the sleeve of a blue blouse. *With all of Mom's stuff still here, frozen in time since the day she left this hellhole.*

"They really kept all of your mom's stuff exactly the same, huh?" Brie sat cross-legged on the mattress and gazed around at the framed photos and books that lined the room's shelves. Her eyes settled on the green messenger bag propped up against the bed, bloated as though filled with belongings. She grabbed it and peeked inside, her shoulders slouching with a deflated sigh. "Are you planning on going somewhere?"

Kris sprang over and slapped her bag shut. "It's nothing," she muttered as she carried her bag over to the closet and set it against the wall.

Brie cocked her head to one side and crossed her arms.

"Come on, Kris. As if I can't see right through you."

"It's *nothing.*"

"Running away? That's stupid. Like, where would you even go?"

Kris sighed. "Anywhere." She bent down and rummaged through a crate of books on the floor of the closet. "Live on the road. See the world. Join the Peace Corps."

"That's a little dramatic, don't you think?"

"Coming from you?" Kris shot her a skeptical look.

Brie stood up from the bed, waving her hands around as she spoke. "However bad you think this is, you have to stick it out. They're family."

"Family" that ran her mom out when she was only a teenager and never spoke to her again. "Family" that only did as much as send a couple of measly birthday cards to their granddaughter over seventeen years.

"Family isn't blood, it's love," Kris mumbled, mostly to herself. She continued to dig through the box of books.

Brie hovered over the messenger bag for a moment before returning to the bed. "Okay, whatever, just . . . just stick it out, okay? In a few months you'll be eighteen, and then you can do whatever you want, right?"

Kris wrinkled her nose at the thought of waiting so long to escape. "So, what's going on at school? How's the gang doing?" she asked, eager to change the subject.

"Ian's been asking about you. He wanted to come with today, but I told him it probably wasn't a good idea."

"Good," Kris hissed under her breath.

"You can't stay mad at him forever."

"I can, and I will." Kris flung some old books on the ground to get to the bottom of the box. "Ah!" she exclaimed, then held up a tattered paperback novel and waved it around in the air.

Brie bounced over, snatching the book and hugging it close to her chest. "Oh, thank God!"

Kris crossed the room and dropped into her desk chair.

"Ian wants to make things right," Brie continued.

"Well, tell him he can shove it. I don't need his pity."

There was a soft knock on the bedroom door. A small, aging woman took a single step into the room, carrying a plate with a sandwich and carrot sticks.

Kris's shoulders stiffened, and she spun around in her chair to turn her back to her grandmother.

"Hello. Brianna, right?"

"Briella, but just Brie's fine. We met briefly at the memorial."

"Oh, yes. Brie. Excuse me. The old melon isn't what she used to be." Her grandmother laughed.

Kris rolled her eyes when Brie laughed along.

"Kristen, I noticed you didn't have any lunch again today." Her grandmother walked over and held out the plate. "I made you a turkey and cheese."

"I'm fine," she grumbled, picking up a pen and drumming it on the wooden desk.

"Oh, okay." Her grandmother shifted her weight around before setting the plate down on the edge of the desk. "I'll leave it here for you. You should eat."

"Yep."

The air between them was heavy, and Kris could feel the old woman searching for conversation. *Just leave*, she prayed. *Please just go away.*

"Another Witcan attack on the west side of town this morning," her grandmother stated. "Put a young man in the hospital."

"Yeah, I heard about that," Brie added softly.

"It's terrifying to see the world changing around us. Those dangerous *things* hiding in plain sight."

"You can't chastise an entire race for a few bad eggs," Kris muttered under her breath.

Her grandmother turned and faced Brie, but Kris could feel her eyes pierce the back of her skull when she spoke. "There was one living in our neighborhood years ago. Right next door. Sofia used to babysit him. An evil little thing. We had to have the National Witcan Detention Agency come take care of it before he could harm her."

"He was just a kid," Kris whispered, squeezing the pen in

her hand.

"We tried warning Sofia to stay away from those monsters, but she never listened. And look where that got her."

Kris threw down the pen, which bounced and rolled across the desk.

"That's . . . awful," Brie said.

"I hope you are staying away from those things," her grandmother warned.

Kris cleared her throat. "Yeah, whatever. Is that it?"

Her grandmother dropped her head and slowly backed away. "You should eat," she said again before pulling the door almost completely shut behind her.

Brie looked at Kris, confusion twisting her brow. "She seems . . . nice," she offered, but there was uncertainty in her voice.

Kris slouched forward, her dark hair hanging over her face. She could hear her grandparents whispering to each other from the living room down the hall.

"Just like Sofia," her grandmother said. "So quick to defend those monsters—I knew we should have had child protective services intervene sooner. Sofia raised her daughter to be just as dangerously naive."

"I don't understand her compassion for them," her grandfather replied. "Especially after what they did to her parents."

Kris clenched her jaw.

"You should give them a chance. They *are* trying," Brie murmured, nodding toward the bedroom door.

Kris blew raspberries. She shuffled her finger around on the touch pad of her laptop to wake the screen. "I'm only here because of guilt."

She scanned her social media profile, and the feed was flooded with news stories.

WITCAN ASSAULTS AT ALL-TIME HIGH, SAYS NWDA

MAN HOSPITALIZED AFTER ALTERCATION WITH WITCAN GANG

UNIVERSITY OF CHICAGO: 13 STUDENTS INJURED IN WITCAN ATTACK

"They chose to open up their home to you," Brie protested, twisting the book around nervously. "They are trying to make amends . . ."

Kris stopped scrolling.

HUSBAND AND WIFE FOUND SLAUGHTERED: NWDA INVESTIGATING

Attached was a photograph of her parents, taken last Christmas. Her mother's wavy blonde hair framed her fair, dimpled face, and her father's dark brown hair was pushed to the side to reveal his kind eyes. They were sitting on the living room couch, dressed in ridiculous holiday sweaters they'd picked out for each other, smiling and laughing. So young. So happy.

So alive.

Kris slammed an elbow down on her desk and swiveled away, staring out the window into the fenced yard. "Me being here has nothing to do with me," she said, resting her cheek against her fist. "They could have taken me in because they loved me, or—or they wanted to get to know me. Not because it will ease their conscience for cutting my mom out of their lives."

She could sense the cold, negative energy in the air, but she didn't turn around.

Brie sighed and motioned toward the bedroom door. "I should probably go." She paused and looked back at Kris. "I'll see you tomorrow? For lunch?"

Staring blankly at the tree branches rattling in the wind, Kris swallowed the lump in her throat and then faced Brie. "Yeah."

"Don't do anything stupid," Brie added, her eyes darting over to the messenger bag by the closet. "You should unpack. Make this a home and not, like, you know . . . a tomb."

"Yeah, sure," Kris said flatly.

Brie hesitated at the door, then nodded and left, leaving the door open a crack just as Kris's grandmother had done.

Kris pressed her forehead into her palm. *I should have known something was wrong. I should have said something. I should have done something. Maybe if I had, Mom and Dad would still be here. Everything would be fine.*

A memory of the strange phone call her mom had made to

someone the day before her parents had gone missing kept replaying in her head. Her mother had used an old flip phone, one Kris had never seen before. She'd paced nervously around her bedroom and closed the door without explanation when Kris came to check on her.

Or if Kris had been home, maybe she could have stopped it. Maybe she could have saved them.

She opened her eyes and stared at the sandwich beside her. Her stomach churned, but not from hunger.

She bent down and retrieved a small plastic bag from a nearby box. She dumped out the earrings and slipped the sandwich inside, then tucked it into her messenger bag. The glint of a pocketknife inside the bag caught her attention. Kris picked it up and flicked open the blade. Flipping it back and forth, she stared at her reflection in the metal. She lowered the knife and looked up at the many boxes stacked and scattered around the room. Her eyes burned with defeat.

Maybe Brie was right. Maybe she should stay . . . There was no going back. No getting her parents back.

She walked over to the nearest cardboard box, and the knife punctured the top of it with such force that half of Kris's fist punched through as well. She ripped it out and set the blade aside, then tore back the cover with both hands. Inside was a bunch of unfolded T-shirts, surprisingly undamaged by the knife.

Kris walked over to the dresser and opened the top drawer,

which was already filled with her mother's old clothes. She'd
have to find somewhere to put them later—she couldn't bring
herself to get rid of them. She held up a floral black tank top
trimmed with lace. Without much thought, she brought it up to
her face and gave it a long sniff. Beyond the stench of dust and
old wood, Kris could still smell her mother. She spread the shirt
out on the bed, smoothing out the wrinkles and admiring it.

Her eyes darted to her bag, then back to the shirt. But Kris
shook her head and returned to the dresser. She scooped out the
rest of the shirts, put them in a pile on the bed, and began
stuffing the contents of the first box into the dresser.

One box down, many others to go.

She used the pocketknife to slice open the next box: old
stuffed animals, a fleece blanket, random knickknacks from her
childhood. Kris pulled out a stuffed monkey, squeezed him in
her hands, but quickly put him back in the box and pushed it
aside.

Kris turned to the next box, taped up heavily across the top.
She pierced a corner with the blade and shimmied it along, but
in the struggle, she sliced her finger open against the cardboard
edge. She yelped, dropping the knife to the floor with a loud
clatter, and instinctively put her finger to her lips. The bitter taste
of blood filled her mouth.

She examined the inch-long cut along her pointer finger as it
swelled with fresh blood. *Smooth. Real smooth. That's an omen if I
ever saw one.*

She sighed, her gaze settling on a silver locket on top of the dresser. It belonged to her grandmother. Her other grandmother. The one who actually cared. The locket had been handed down to Kris's mother, and then to Kris when she'd turned sixteen.

Her finger tingled, but a weird sensation enveloped her. She stood up straight and clasped her chest over her heart at the familiar feeling. The warmth in her chest trickled out into her shoulder and down her arm until it collected around the cut on her finger.

No. No, no, no. Not again.

The slice on her index finger burned hot for a moment, and Kris could only stare wide-eyed as the beads of blood retracted beneath her skin and the cut closed itself up. It took only seconds, then the warm feeling in her chest faded away. There was no more pain. No more blood. No cut, scab, or scar.

It's not possible. It was a dream. Last time had been a dream—no way this is real!

Kris's heartbeat throbbed in her ears as she studied her finger. The bitter taste lingered in her mouth, and a small smear of blood collected in the creases of her hand. There was no denying that there had been a cut on her finger only moments before.

It was the rollerblading accident all over again.

Kris looked at her elbow, remembering the gash she had opened up while rollerblading a few months back. She had experienced a warm feeling in her chest back then too, and her arm had completely healed by the time she'd returned home.

But that hadn't been real either. That had been a dream, or something . . .

She traced her fingertip over the healed flesh, then her gaze settled on the pocketknife. Kris hesitated but eventually reached down and picked it up.

This is crazy, she insisted before digging the tip of the blade into her fingertip until it drew blood. Kris winced and squeezed her finger to express a large crimson droplet.

Her laptop hummed behind her. The screen was still displaying her social media feed, littered with stories about the recent Witcan attacks.

NWDA INVESTIGATING WITCAN STUDENT ATTACK AT UIC

A blurry cell phone photo showed a young man in a lecture hall. His fists looked like they were glowing green.

Kris trembled as she stared at the drop of blood, which eventually dribbled down her finger and dripped off her knuckle to the floor. She chuckled to herself. *See? Nothing. You're just losing it.*

Then the rush of warmth swept over her again, starting in her chest and traveling down to her fingertip, faster than before. The thin stream of blood slithered back up her finger, and the small prick closed up. Completely healed.

Kris gasped, stumbling backwards until her back crashed into the bedroom door and slammed it shut. *No. No way. No freaking way.* She shook out her hand and studied it again. Impossible.

Her grandmother's footsteps approached, her slippers gliding over the hardwood floor. Rattled, Kris pushed her back firmly against the door and fumbled to lock it as she scrambled to collect her thoughts.

She couldn't be a Witcan. She couldn't be . . .

Her mind drifted back to a time when she had fallen out of a tree as a child, but she had no recollection of hitting the ground, almost as though she'd stopped in midair. And a time when she swore she'd heard words that Brie had not spoken. And the way the volleyball had curved mid-serve during a game, allowing her team to get the winning point.

Was all of that real? Had she made those things happen?

Memories came flashing back, rapid fire, overlapping each other.

Her grandmother's footsteps grew closer. "Kristen?"

Kris's heart sank. They couldn't find out. She had to get out of here.

She lunged across the room, snatched up the messenger bag, and stuffed the pocketknife in her back pocket. Her eyes settled on her mother's old shirt, still laid out on the bed. She grabbed that and pushed it inside, as well as the locket.

"Are you okay?" her grandmother said from the hall. "I heard your door slam."

Kris snatched her cell phone from the desk and a half-empty water bottle from the nightstand. Her hands shook as she whirled around to the window.

"Kristen?"

Do or die. Maybe literally.

She grabbed the bottom of the window and jerked on it with her whole body, forcing it open a little more with each yank until there was enough space to fit through.

The doorknob jiggled. "Kristen? Are you in there? Unlock this door."

Heart pounding, she squeezed the strap that crossed her chest and breathed in deep. Her grandparents would never accept her if they knew what she had just done. There was no going back.

Kris kicked one leg over the windowsill, dipped under the glass, and slipped outside into the yard. The instant her feet touched the grass, she ran.

Chapter 3

Do Or Die

Kris rested her hands on her knees, leaning forward to catch her breath, and she managed a small grin. She couldn't believe she'd done it.

She glanced back over her shoulder, but the rural street was quiet. No cars, no cyclists. Her eyes followed the long road to her right that stretched far into the trees. Small houses dotted either side of the street, poking out between the foliage.

Kris dug her water bottle out of her bag and scarfed its contents down in seconds, then cursed herself for not refilling it. She turned her attention to the zigzagging road ahead. The houses were much larger and spaced farther apart. The budding, early-summer trees hung overhead, casting some shadows in the already dimming daylight.

As she started down the quiet street at a brisk pace, she told herself she couldn't turn back.

While she walked, Kris examined her finger. There was nothing left of the gash. If not for the dried blood still collected in the creases of her knuckles, there would be no evidence it had happened at all. She reached into her pocket and squeezed the folded knife.

This whole thing was unbelievable. It was just a ridiculous dream.

Kris kicked a stone off the road into the ditch. "Witcan," she muttered, then laughed at the thought. She couldn't be a Witcan. She would have known. There would have been signs. She would feel it. Right?

She remembered the warm, tickling sensation she had felt in her chest just before her finger inexplicably healed itself. It was oddly familiar, like something she had experienced before, but this time it had been stronger. As though with purpose.

"So now what, Kris?" she asked herself with a long, deflated sigh.

A chilly breeze rushed by, rattling the leaves loudly and filling the evening air with a soft ambience. It calmed her for a brief second, but the worry returned just as fast.

What would she do now? Should she call Brie and tell her what happened? Should she get her involved?

Kris scoffed. Brie would never believe her. Or worse . . .

She scuffed her sneaker over the asphalt while kicking another rock away. Maybe she hadn't planned this out as well as she'd thought. It wasn't like she could just hop on a bus or get a cab. Or check into a hotel.

She thought about her grandmother's snide remarks. Her grandfather's bigoted statements. The story of the eleven-year-old neighbor boy they had reported to the NWDA. Her mom had said she never saw him again.

Kris looked back over her shoulder, down the empty road. She had to press on. If she went back there . . . If they found out what happened, what was to stop them from turning her over to the NWDA too?

A cold feeling in her gut prompted her to look forward again. Not far ahead, a woman stood with her back turned as she stared up into the tree branches.

Kris stopped dead in her tracks, examining the woman's wavy blonde hair and small frame. Her heart was thudding so heavily that she feared it would burst out of her chest.

That looks like . . .

She released the knife in her pocket, and her arms hung at her sides. She stood perfectly still, her eyes glued to the woman ahead of her. The sky-blue sneakers with the electric-purple highlights. There was no denying those shoes. Kris had seen them before many times, placed neatly on a shoe rack—right by the front door of her home.

How?

She hesitantly took a few steps closer. Her throat felt tight, but Kris finally stopped a few feet away and waited for the woman to turn around. She wanted to speak, to say something, but no sound came out. She could only stand there, anxiously waiting to see the woman's face.

Kris was dizzy with conflicting emotions. Her hands were sweaty, her veins pulsed, her jaw was tightened to the point of physical pain. But the pain meant it was real. It wasn't a dream.

After what felt like hours, the woman began to turn, in a moment so slow Kris swore time had actually stopped.

Her stomach twisted and her knees nearly buckled. She blinked back tears, staring deep into the blue eyes that faced her.

"Mom?"

Chapter 4

In The Flesh

Kris stared, wide-eyed. Her jaw hung open.

Her mother was standing in front of her in the flesh with arms held out for a hug. With that welcoming, kind smile she knew so well.

"How is this possible?" Kris took a couple of steps closer, but then immediately moved away again. "Am I dreaming? Is this just a messed-up dream?"

"Not a dream, honey," her mother said, beckoning her closer.

Kris stayed rooted in place, her eyes welling with tears as she sucked in sharp breaths. "But you're dead. I . . . I saw you. I *buried* you."

Her mother lowered her arms and began to close the gap between them. "I know. I'm so sorry, sweetheart. But it was the only way." She glanced around, her shoulders hiking up in alarm. "It's not safe here. We need to go."

Kris felt a stone drop into the pit of her stomach. Her skin prickled with itchy unease.

Something wasn't right. Something was making her hair stand on end.

She jammed a hand into her pocket and traced her finger over the pocketknife. She took several strides back, studying her mother's face and searching for some sign that her intuition was wrong. The woman looked and sounded exactly like her mother. But the way she inched closer, the way her fingers waved elegantly with each word, the way she kept dropping pet names.

Kris pinched her lips together to keep them from trembling.

The woman looked at her, confused. "What's wrong, honey?"

Kris swallowed hard and blinked away the tears. "If you really are my mother, then what was the last thing you said to me? The day you disappeared?"

"I told you that I loved you and that everything was going to be all right." She moved closer.

Kris gasped as the woman's eyes flickered brown, then black, before back to blue, and she felt a heavy weight in her gut. She slipped the knife out of her pocket, holding it out of view behind her back. She shook her head, and her mother's face twisted into a scowl.

"You aren't my mother." Kris fought the sob stuck in the back of her throat, flicked open the knife, and held it out toward the woman in front of her. "So, who the hell are you?"

A hand reached out from behind and grabbed her wrist.

Kris whirled to find a man with dark hair wearing a black hoodie clasping her forearm. He pulled her hand closer and reached for the knife. Panicked, she snatched the blade with her free hand and swung wildly at him. He released her arm and ducked away.

"Back off," she shouted, taking another swipe through the air with the knife.

Kris looked back at the woman just in time to see her mother's face morph into that of a stranger. Her blonde waves shortened and darkened into a chocolate pixie cut. The bright blue eyes distorted into narrow, black irises. This new woman smirked as she rushed forward with an outstretched palm.

Who was she? *What* was she? How did she make herself look like her mom?

Kris didn't have time to process her thoughts as an invisible force struck her in the chest and threw her backwards. She yelped and crashed hard on her back, the wind knocked out of her. The knife slipped from her hand and clattered against the asphalt. Her vision was fuzzy as she tried to regain her bearings, and she managed to roll over and push herself up to her knees.

Witcans.

Through the blur, Kris's eyes zeroed in on the open pocketknife just out of arm's reach. A hand swiftly snatched it up.

"No." Kris cleared her head quickly, standing up to rush the man now holding the knife.

She was grabbed from behind and her arms were pulled back.

"Got her," the woman shouted. "Where the hell is Shay?"

Kris thrashed, kicking about to free herself. "Let go of me!"

The man pointed the blade at Kris, but the squeal of car tires caught the attention of all three. The woman released Kris and dove out of the way, narrowly escaping a red sedan that drifted to a screeching halt just in front of her.

Kris staggered and slapped both hands down on the hood of the car to keep from falling.

The driver's side door was thrown open, and a young man with messy brown hair leaped out. His eyes were fixed on the dark-haired woman in a glare, and he didn't even acknowledge Kris.

He clapped his hands, and as he pulled them apart, a sparking purple ball appeared between his palms, flashing and flickering like lightning. With a grunt, he hurled it at the woman. Before she had a chance to react, it hit her in the chest, launching her off the road and sending her tumbling down into the ditch.

This man was Witcan too? Were they following her?

Kris darted around the car and crouched below the hood.

"Kye!" The man holding Kris's knife dashed around the car and charged at the young man. His fists were glowing a deep shade of indigo as he wound them up.

The driver ducked under the first few punches, then thrust an open palm into his attacker's back. The man with the knife was thrown against the open car door, slamming it shut.

Kris panicked and dropped to her knees to hide entirely behind the car. She clutched a hand against her chest. As she heard the chaos continue, she pressed her eyes shut. *Wake up, wake up, wake up.*

A loud crunch of leaves nearby startled her, and she opened her eyes to see that the woman was on her feet, striding out of the ditch. Her fists were glowing bright red as she glared at the driver, who was still occupied in a one-on-one struggle in the middle of the empty street.

I have to help him.

"Look out!" she yelled. Without thinking, Kris pounced up and extended both hands towards the woman. She sensed an energy resonate in her chest, vibrate down her arms, and stretch beyond her fingertips. Despite the distance between them, Kris felt herself push the woman, and watched in astonishment as the woman did in fact topple backwards into the gravel on the side of the road.

The driver whipped his head around, meeting Kris's eye with a look of astonishment. He looked familiar, but she couldn't place his face.

His assailant slashed the knife through the air, ripping through the young man's sleeve. He cried out, clutching his shoulder. Blood spilled through his fingers as he moved away.

The man with the knife seized his opportunity. Grabbing the driver by the throat, he squeezed hard as his hand began to glow blue again. The driver fought back and struck his attacker's arm to no avail. The dark-haired man held tight.

Kris sprinted around the car, grabbed at the knife again, and tried to wrestle it away.

"What the—?"

Something struck her across the face, but she maintained her grasp of the blade as she fell. She pulled the man over with her. Although the concrete shook her head, Kris didn't let go, finally slipping the knife away.

The driver rushed up and kicked the man in the skull. It knocked him out cold.

Kris inched away, clamping down hard on her elbow as the pain from her not-so-graceful fall set in. She met the young man's eyes again.

"Get in the car," he instructed Kris, pinching his shoulder wound.

Her head was still reeling, but she nodded and scrambled to her feet with knife still in hand. The woman came at her again. Kris held out the knife, preparing to defend herself, when the woman lifted off the ground and hovered for a moment in surprise before spiraling through the air into the trees several yards away.

The young man stood behind the open car door and lowered his arm with a deep breath. "Get in," he barked again.

Who was this guy?

Despite her hesitation, Kris climbed in.

Chapter 5

Kurt

Tires squealed as the car pulled a sharp U-turn and rocketed down the road.

Kris sat on her hip, her eyes fixed on the scene in the rear window as they sped away. She couldn't believe what she just saw.

"Who were those people?" she asked, sliding down into the passenger seat when she could no longer see them.

The car's dashboard was completely clean, not a speck of dust. The mat at Kris's feet was clear of dirt, and even the car door was free of garbage. Yet the driver's hair was tangled, his jeans wrinkled, and his T-shirt now stained with fresh blood.

"They're part of a Witcan cult. Witcan supremacy extremists." He peeked under his hand and checked the gash on his arm.

"You know them?"

He groaned, wrinkling his nose. He steered with only his right hand; his left was still clasped on his bloodied shoulder. "We're not strangers," he said flatly.

"Well, thank you . . . I think," she stammered, looking at him from the corner of her eye. "For, uh . . . saving me."

He smirked and shook his head.

Kris sat up as he turned down a street, and all the air escaped her lungs. "Where are you going?"

"*You're* going back home."

"How do you know where 'home' is? Were you following me?" She made a big gesture of turning toward the door and grabbing the handle.

"Don't be stupid," he grumbled, shooting her an agitated glance. "You're not jumping out of a moving car."

"Answer the question."

"I've been checking in on you, making sure you're safe. Trying to keep *them* off your trail." He motioned with his arm but flinched and squeezed his shoulder again. "But then you had to go and run away."

"Stop!" Kris shouted, stomping her feet on the floor of the car. "I have, like, a thousand questions, but first and foremost, I am *not* going back there. I don't know who you think you are, but you cannot make me."

He scoffed and stole a glimpse out the window to his left. "I'm Kurt," he finally said.

She waved unenthusiastically. "Kris."

"I know."

I know? She gave him a curious glance, playing the words over in her head again.

"So, tell me, Kristen: What was your big plan when you ran away from home? Where exactly did you think you were going?" She didn't miss the thinly veiled layer of condescension in his voice.

"First of all, just because I lived there does not make that place my home." Kris slid her messenger bag onto her lap and crossed her arms with a pout. "But I don't know. I was just trying to get out of town and figure the rest out from there . . ." She let her voice trail off, realizing how juvenile it sounded.

After a long sigh, Kurt checked over his left shoulder before pulling another U-turn. "You can stay with me for a few days until you figure it out."

"How do I know *you're* not a Witcan supremacy extremist, or a murderer or something?"

He laughed. "I wouldn't have risked my life imposing myself in your little stand-off back there."

Kris frowned. "Fair point."

A long silence passed between them.

"I've seen you before," she said.

"Yeah?"

"Yeah." Kris fidgeted with the closed pocketknife in her hand. "At the funeral."

"Oh." Kurt's shoulders tensed, and he gripped the wheel so firmly his knuckles turned white. "I didn't think anyone saw me."

She shifted her attention to the scrape on her elbow. It had stopped bleeding, but it still stung. "Did you know my parents?"

Kurt gritted his teeth. "Fia and I are old friends."

"You mean 'were'?"

The image of her mother's face morphing into that of a complete stranger was burned in her brain. She felt sick thinking about it. How had that woman been able to make herself look like her mom? Did she know her mom too? Were they the ones who killed her parents?

Kurt turned onto the highway and picked up speed, checking his rearview mirror every few minutes. The repetitive motion annoyed Kris, but she bit her tongue and said nothing, instead playing back the skirmish in her head over and over.

She had felt something back there, like a jolt of caffeine rushing through her chest. Like when she'd healed herself. Kris raised her hand, studying the place the cut had once been, before dropping her hand back into her lap.

Soft, ambient guitar music played in the car. It calmed Kris's racing heart until she noticed a large, blotchy scar around Kurt's right wrist and forearm. A burn mark, perhaps?

"So, why did you run away?" he asked, breaking her train of thought.

She shrugged and stared down at her canvas sneakers. "Didn't want to wait around to see what those strangers would do when they found out—I mean, if they thought I was a . . . you know . . ."

"A Witcan?"

Kris released a sharp breath and slammed her head back into the headrest, saying nothing.

They turned off onto a deserted country road. A dense wooded area walled off one side of the street. The other was wide open with season-ready farmlands. The sun kissed the horizon, bathing the air in a golden glow.

Things should be peaceful.

Kris glanced at the blood dripping from Kurt's hand. "Your shoulder."

"I'm fine," he muttered, squeezing harder on his arm.

Without so much as a thought, Kris bent forward and rummaged through her bag for a T-shirt. "Here." She lightly touched his hand, trying to get to the laceration.

"I said I'm fine."

She motioned to the blood seeping through his fingers, the scarlet droplets dappling the gray car seat and center console. "You're not fine. You're bleeding all over your car. So, unless you want a giant mess and a jacked-up shoulder, I suggest you let me help."

Kurt turned his head quickly, glancing between the road and the blood stains. "Anyone ever told you that you are irritatingly stubborn?" he grumbled under his breath.

Kris smirked. He cared more about the cleanliness of his car than he did his own health.

He eventually lifted his hand to expose the slash through his sleeve and arm. Though the sight of the cut and heavy bleeding made her feel faint, Kris promptly pressed her bunched-up shirt against the wound. Kurt recoiled at the initial contact, his muscles tense.

"You should go to the hospital," Kris mumbled, taking in a deep breath to fight the dizziness.

"I'll be fine." He wiped the blood from his hand on his shirt, then peeked over at Kris, giving her a quick once-over. "Are you okay? You fell pretty hard back there."

She giggled to herself, then immediately felt awkward. Her scratched-up elbow seemed trivial compared to Kurt's shoulder. "It's nothing. Just a scrape."

She leaned closer to apply more pressure to his arm. He winced, but he said nothing.

A familiar melody started. The plucking of guitar chords filled the car, and Kris perked up. "Oh hey, 'Sacrifice.' I love this song."

Kurt raised an eyebrow. "You know Dragonfleye?"

"Just the one song," she admitted with an uneasy smile. She fought the urge to sing along as she eyed the scarring around Kurt's wrist.

"This is it," he said softly, turning into the woods and following two dirt tire tracks into the trees.

Still holding her shirt against Kurt's arm, Kris stared out through the windshield at the path cutting through the shaded woods. The leaves were still budding on the branches, and through them she could make out a meadow up ahead, which almost glittered in the evening sun.

Wow.

But as they got closer, a sinking feeling settled in Kris's gut, like the sensation of going over the highest hump of a rollercoaster, only to come barreling back down to earth. Her vision became cloudy until everything was white. She blinked, trying to clear her sights. What was happening?

She turned to look at Kurt, but he was no longer there. She could still feel his shoulder, but Kurt, the car, the trees—they were all gone.

Where was she?

Kris felt the crunch of grass beneath her sneakers. *What the . . . ?*

Sure enough, through the heavenly glow around her, a patch of grass had appeared beneath her feet and was slowly spreading outward.

"Not so tough now, are you, Goddess?"

Kris turned towards the man's voice. The sound was fuzzy, but she could make out a group of men circled around something in the field. As she moved closer, the figure of a woman curled up in the grass came into focus. Her hands and ankles were tied with rope, and through the long, dark hair that hung over her face, a ball of fabric stuffed in her mouth was visible.

One of the men grabbed her wrist and viciously removed a silver ring from her finger. "You're nothing without your precious ring."

Everything moved in a flash before Kris's eyes. Fire, blazing beams of colored lights, punches, kicks, screams, tears. The woman's body was thrown around like a rag doll as the men beat her to a bloody pulp.

By the time Kris could process what was happening, the mysterious woman was barely conscious. Her black hair had been cut. Her flesh was slashed, bruised, and burned. Yet she was attempting to stand, getting so far as to sit up.

"Stop it, please!" Kris pleaded. She tried to run to the woman, to help her, but her strides never took her any closer.

"You have more fight than I thought," said one of the men, promptly kicking the woman over again and spitting on her.

Another man stepped forward and whispered something to her before rearing back a blade as though prepared to stab her through the chest.

No. No, no, no. Kris spun away, raising her arms to cover her ears and pressing her eyes shut so tight that they hurt.

After a moment, she opened her eyes again. All she saw was the silver ring they had removed from the woman's finger, lost in the tall grass. Beautiful engravings of vines and flowers twisted around the band and cradled a polished emerald.

Kris's head abruptly snapped back, and she was in the car again, facing Kurt. They were driving down a dirt road, surrounded by tall grass. A small cabin sat on the opposite side of the meadow.

What just happened? Was any of that real? Who were those people?

Kurt hadn't seen any of that, Kris quickly determined, as his eyes were focused on the path ahead. She scanned the meadow, taking in the surrounding trees. This looked like the field she'd just seen. In her head. Had all of that happened here? That woman?

"Are you all right?"

"What?"

Kurt was now staring at her. "You're white as a sheet."

Kris wiped sweat from her forehead and shook the hair from her face. "Oh, it's nothing." She gestured to the drying blood on his sleeve. "It's just the blood. Makes me feel faint."

The car stopped just in front of the cabin and Kurt turned off the engine.

"Wait." He moved her hand away and examined his shoulder. "What the . . . ?"

Kurt's shirt was still torn and stained with blood, but his skin was completely healed, no sign of injury.

Kris shrunk into her seat, holding her bloodied shirt against her chest. She had done it again.

In that moment, she heard Kurt's voice in her head, despite his lips not moving: *How is that possible? How did she do that?*

Chapter 6

The Cabin

Kris hid the pocketknife behind her bag as she got out of the car, and she continued to eye Kurt while he slid out of the car on his side. He turned his attention from his healed arm to her.

He opened his mouth and started to speak, then chuckled to himself and closed the car door. "I can't believe this," he mumbled, rubbing his neck as he circled around the car.

Kris scanned the small cabin in front of her. The wooden siding. The small picture windows. The porch swing. The vegetable garden along the side of the cabin. *Looks cozy. Not like the lair of a serial killer, right?* Her shoulders relaxed, but her grip on the knife remained tight.

Kurt motioned for her to follow him up the steps to the front porch. His eyes were narrowed as he looked her up and down. Why was he giving her that look, like he didn't trust *her*? She was the one following a stranger to a secluded house in the middle of nowhere.

He held the door for her to go inside.

She walked in and looked around. "This is . . . quaint."

Several couches in a living room to the left were turned towards a small fat-back TV. On the right was a hardwood dining room table, with five matching chairs and a single mismatched one. Between the countertops and some mounted cupboards from the ceiling was a space to look into the kitchen on the other side.

"This is home," Kurt said with a shrug.

Kris trailed behind him, twisting the strap of her bag and admiring the framed photographs of flowers and winter landscapes that lined the walls. "Are we safe? I mean, those people aren't going to find me here, right?"

"No, we're safe here, I promise." He motioned to the kitchen.

Kris stepped into it and eyed the clean countertops. The window above the sink perfectly framed the setting sun through the trees.

"How long you lived here?" she asked.

Kurt gestured towards the bathroom on the left as they headed to the back of the house. Kris poked her head in and spotted a large tub with a checkered shower curtain and faux-marble counters. Nothing but a lit scented candle and a cup holding a single toothbrush sat atop the vanity.

"A few years," he replied with no inflection.

"Alone?" Kris paused in the hall, absorbed in a photograph of tall autumn trees that stood immersed in dense fog, all reflected on a calm lake.

"Mostly."

She discreetly slipped her knife in her bag. "Do you get lonely?"

He shrugged. "Not really."

A few steps away, Kurt opened one of the three doors at the end of the hall and held it for her. She stopped in the doorway and peered in. Inside were two twin beds, each made up with red, plaid comforters. The walls were also adorned with assorted framed photographs of raindrops and sunsets.

"Is there something wrong with me?" Kris asked quietly, hiding her face with her hair.

"What do you mean?"

She shrunk away, her posture collapsing in on itself. Kris wrung and tugged at the canvas strap that hung off her shoulder. "Never mind." She brushed past him into the room.

Kurt pivoted awkwardly in place and pushed back his messy brown hair. "Look . . . There is probably a lot we should talk about. But you should rest first."

"Sure."

Kris put her bag on the nearest bed and sat. She immediately felt a crushing weight pulling her down, like she was sinking through the bed, through the floor, into the earth's crust.

Kurt tensed, as if sensing the change in the room's air, and he backed away into the hall. "Just let me know if you need anything."

He barely got the door shut before she flopped over on the bed, burying her face into the pillow.

~

Kurt pushed his back against the wall just outside the guest room door, which muffled Kris's cries on the other side. Pressing a hand to his forehead, he took a deep, angry breath in. After a few more hearty inhales, he turned to his shoulder, pulled back the ripped and blood-stained sleeve, and examined his now perfectly healed skin.

That couldn't be a coincidence.

He went to the kitchen in a few long strides, snatched an old mobile phone off the counter, and flipped it open. Kurt's hands trembled while he dialed.

Pick up. Pick up.

The phone rang a few times before someone answered. "Hello?"

"Hey, Larsen, it's Kurt," he whispered into the receiver. He glanced down the hall before carrying the phone to the front door and going out onto the porch.

"Hey. You okay? You sound frazzled."

"It's been a wild afternoon." Kurt lowered himself onto the swing and clenched his fist to control the shaking.

"Is it about Sofia?"

Kurt took a sharp gulp of air, his foot tapping rapidly on the wood of the porch. "It's about her daughter, actually."

Birds flew overhead, and their calls echoed through the meadow. Their silhouettes fluttered across the pink-streaked sky.

"What about her daughter?" Larsen said.

Kurt pinched the bridge of his nose and closed his eyes. *This is unbelievable*, he told himself again, shaking his head.

"Kurt?"

"Yeah?"

"What about Sofia's daughter? Is she okay?"

Kurt chuckled to himself, his gaze pinned to his arm. "I think she's Annona."

Chapter 7

A Gift

The faint strumming of a guitar woke Kris from her sleep. She rolled over, pulled the blanket to her chin, and opened her eyes. Glancing around, she saw the extra bed under the window, the nightstand beside her littered with wadded-up tissues, the framed photo of a raindrop clinging to the rim of a bright green leaf.

Her mind slowly pieced together the events of the previous day. *Oh, right. It wasn't all a dream.*

Kris's head throbbed, and each musical strum vibrated in her skull like a violent shake. She needed an aspirin. Or six.

She kicked the comforter aside, still wearing her jeans and T-shirt from the night before. She dumped the contents of her messenger bag out on the bed, picking out her mother's floral tank top and a pair of shorts.

While she changed, she zeroed in on her cell phone, powered off since leaving her grandparents' house. Kris adjusted her shirt and stared at her phone for a long moment before turning it on. The multiple buzzes notified her of many missed messages. Most were calls from her grandparents, with some from Brie and one voicemail that made her chest burn. She knew she shouldn't listen to it, but she lifted the phone to her ear anyway.

"Kris, hey. It's Ian. Brie called. She told me you ran away. I'm just . . . I'm worried. I hope you're all right. Anyway, when you get this message, please call me. I miss you—"

She ripped the phone from her ear and jabbed at the screen to delete the voicemail, then stuffed her phone into the back pocket of her shorts, ignoring the many texts and missed calls from Brie. Kris also equipped herself with the pocketknife before opening the bedroom door just a crack. The guitar chords grew louder as she stepped into the hallway.

Through the front window, she could see Kurt on the front porch. He gently rocked back and forth on the porch swing, plucking and strumming at an acoustic guitar. The sound called her in, and the closer she got to the entrance, the lighter her head felt. She stood at the screen door, listening.

Kurt slapped a hand over the strings and whipped his head around, spotting Kris. He had bags under his eyes.

"That was beautiful," she said softly through the screen, nodding towards the guitar. She crossed her arms as she leaned against the doorframe.

He sat up and rested the guitar against the railing. "It's just a silly hobby," he muttered. "How did you sleep?"

"I slept fine. Did *you* sleep?"

Kurt laughed, moving his hair from his eyes. "Insomnia."

Kris stared down at her arms and pursed her lips. "Thank you again. You know, for helping me yesterday. And for letting me crash here."

He stood up from the swing, planted both palms on the railing, and looked out across the field. The early-morning sun illuminated the dew that clung to the tall grass, giving the entire meadow a mystical glow.

"You're welcome," Kurt said faintly.

Kris pushed open the screen door and stepped out onto the porch. It was much chillier than expected, and goose bumps ran up her arms and legs. "So, why were you following me, anyway?" She watched the way he studied the dewy field. She could read the tension in his lips, but his pale eyes were calm, moving slightly as they panned across the meadow.

"I promised Sofia I would look after you."

"How exactly did you know my mom?"

Kurt leaned forward on his elbows, his face warping with silent contemplation before he spoke. "Fia found me a few years back. She brought me here. Gave me a home."

"Was she . . . you know . . . ?" Kris trembled, unsure if a result of the cool breeze or her nerves. She stepped up beside Kurt and peeked at him for a moment but then cast her eyes down.

"Your parents aren't Witcan, if that's what you're asking."

But if she were Witcan, wouldn't that mean her parents were too?

Before she could speak, Kurt went on. "Happens more often than you'd think," he said quietly, tracing a finger over the head of the guitar that rested next to him. "It's not always genetic."

If it wasn't genetic, then how? Divine intervention?

She fiddled with her necklace as she admired the yellow beams of sunlight erupting behind the trees. "Are your parents Witcan?"

Kurt cleared his throat and turned away. "Are you hungry?" He picked up his guitar and marched past her inside the house before she even had a chance to respond.

What was that about?

Kris followed him but stared from the hall, mouth hanging open. He was pulling out ingredients from the fridge and piling them on the counter.

"What are you doing?" she asked.

Kurt slapped a pan on the stove, retrieved a bowl from a cupboard, and cracked some eggs inside. "Making breakfast. Do you like bell pepper?"

She opened her mouth to speak, but her phone buzzed in her back pocket. "Yeah, whatever," she mumbled to him, then slipped into the dining room to check her phone.

A call from Brie.

She bit her lip and let the phone ring for a few seconds. Taking a deep breath, she answered. "Hey."

"Oh my God. Finally! I've been so worried."

Kurt paused in his chopping efforts and peeked at her from under the kitchen cupboards. "You kept your phone?"

Ignoring him, Kris backed away into the living room and out of his line of sight. "I'm fine. Don't worry," she said to Brie.

"Why did you run away? I told you not to. Your grandparents have been calling, like, everyone. I was so worried something had happened. Why didn't you answer any of my calls?" Brie's voice was so shrill that Kris had to hold the phone away from her ear.

She sat down on the couch, hunching forward and rubbing her head. "I'm sorry. I just . . . I need some space. After everything."

"Where are you?"

Kris looked around at the mismatched living room furniture, the swing on the front porch, the trees out across the meadow. "I'm . . . I can't say. I mean, I'm safe. I'm fine, but . . ."

"Kris . . ." Brie said softly.

Kurt cleared his throat, and Kris turned. He stood outside the kitchen, looking down at her with his lips pressed in a frown.

"I should go," she said. "I'm sorry. I love you."

Before Brie could protest, Kris hung up. She remained still, her elbows propped up on her knees. *I'm sorry, Brie. I wish I could tell you where I am. About what happened. What I did.*

"What?" she said to Kurt, who was still watching her.

He nodded at her phone. "You shouldn't have brought that here. The NWDA can use cell phone signals to track you."

Kris rolled her eyes and pushed off the couch to her feet. "Well, according to the NWDA, I'm not a Witcan, so they aren't looking for me."

"Not yet." Kurt threw up his arms as he spoke. "But they have an algorithm. They recognize patterns to identify potential Witcans, and it won't take long for them to put two and two together that the sixteen-year-old runaway orphan from an area with escalating Witcan altercations is a Witcan."

Kris recoiled, and her arms broke out in goose bumps again. They were going to come looking for her? She'd thought that if she got out and went on the run, she'd be safe.

"Even Fia knows," he said. "She recognized the signs long before she and I even met."

She held herself tightly, staring out the window as the morning sun grew brighter. Her mom had known? Why hadn't she said anything?

Kurt looked back at the kitchen and scratched the back of his head. Kris could smell oil burning on the stove.

"I need you to understand the risk you're taking by keeping that phone here," he said, and gestured towards the kitchen. "I have to tend to breakfast."

Kris frowned while twisting the phone around in her hands. She traced every edge of it before stuffing it into her back pocket and walking into the kitchen. Neither of them said a word as she gently took the knife from Kurt to chop the bell peppers, while he returned to the skillet and cooked the sausage.

"I'm not sixteen, by the way," she said, stealing a glance at him as she diced the vegetables. "I'll be eighteen in December. You?"

He stirred the meat around in the pan. "Twenty."

Kris carried the cutting board over to him, and he motioned for her to add the chopped peppers to the pan. She stared at his shoulder for a long moment, and then the scar on his forearm.

"So, can you not heal yourself?" she asked. She returned to the counter and cut into the onion. Her eyes immediately began to sting.

Kurt shook his head. "It's a rare skill. A birth-given gift. It's not something that can be learned. You're the first healer I've ever met." He looked at her as she wiped a tear from her cheek. "You okay?"

"Just the onion," Kris replied with a forced laugh.

He chuckled, taking the knife. She stepped back and watched him masterfully chop up the rest of the onion in only seconds.

"Have you known about your regenerative abilities long?" he asked.

Kris shook her head. "I didn't realize it until yesterday after I cut myself by accident, and it healed almost instantly. And then your shoulder last night . . . It's bizarre."

Kurt offered her a soft, sincere smile while he walked the cutting board over to the pan to add the diced onion. "It's a gift many wish they had."

"Like those weirdo cult members?"

His posture went rigid mid-stir. "Yeah, probably."

"We both knew I was going to bring them up eventually." Kris washed her hands and leaned against the counter, watching Kurt flip the contents of the frying pan around. "That woman who attacked me yesterday. She was able to make herself look like my mom."

He kept his back to her, but the tension in his shoulders was evident. "Shapeshifters can imitate physical appearances. It's like your healing ability, albeit not nearly as rare."

"She had to have known my mom, right? To be able to mimic her appearance and her voice?"

Kurt didn't answer and instead poured the beaten eggs into the pan, silencing the sizzle.

Kris waited for his response but eventually got impatient and wandered over to stand beside him. "Why were they looking for me?" She leaned over to catch his eye.

"Their cult is known for targeting lost or homeless Witcans to recruit. They must have been looking for new members."

"You said they're supremacists?"

"Yeah, their leader, Tynan, promises to rid the world of the NWDA and humans."

Kris fiddled with her hair as she watched him cook. "How's the psychopath going to do that? Some wacky curse, or something?" She snickered.

"Something like that," he muttered. The omelet broke when Kurt tried to flip it, so he sighed and mixed everything together as a scramble instead. Still standing over the stove, he looked back and extended a hand. The bag of shredded cheese lifted off the counter and shot across the kitchen right into his open hand.

"Whoa." Kris stood up straight with a wide smile. "Can . . . can you teach me how to do that?"

"What? Telekinesis?"

"Yeah."

"No." After adding cheese to the eggs, Kurt sealed the bag and sent it back across the kitchen. This time, the fridge opened and the bag tucked itself right inside the shelf of the door.

"Why not? Let's assume I *am* a Witcan, and those weirdo cultists come after me again. Shouldn't I know how to defend myself?"

"Don't worry, I'm sure you will have your pocketknife." He laughed.

Kris crossed her arms. "I'm serious."

"God, you're stubborn."

"What if I—"

"I said no." Kurt opened a cupboard and retrieved two plates, then pushed scrambled eggs onto each one. "Grab some forks."

Kris clutched her stomach as it rumbled and glanced down the hall to her room.

Kurt carried the plates to the dining room. Her stomach growled again, so she obliged and searched the kitchen drawers for silverware.

She scarfed down her breakfast. Both avoided the other's eye, and neither said a word.

Chapter 8

Larsen

Kris glanced back at Kurt as she put her empty plate in the sink. She knew she should say something, but what?

He turned the sink faucet on, his shoulders rigid.

"I'm gonna go . . . I don't know . . . clean up, I guess?" she murmured, slowly backing away into the hall.

Kurt pivoted toward her, his eyes down and his mouth opened as though he were about to speak. Instead, he sighed and turned back to the sink.

"Yeah, that's what I'll do." Kris spun on her heels and headed back to her room.

Once she shut the door, she picked up her empty messenger bag from the floor and started stuffing the pile of clothes inside. *This is so stupid. I shouldn't be here. He clearly doesn't want me here.*

With everything back inside the bags, Kris let out a heavy breath. She sat down on the edge of the bed and took out her cell phone, then scrolled through the many, many texts Brie had sent since the night before.

Clutching her phone to her chest, she flopped back onto the bed and stared up at the ceiling. She couldn't go to Brie, she realized. Brie's parents would immediately send Kris back to the Grand-Hellhole. Or report her if they found out what had happened. That she might be a Witcan. *Ugh.*

She closed her eyes to try to relax. How had she gotten here? How had her life unraveled so fast? A month ago, everything was so normal.

Kris lifted her phone and stared up at the text messages from Ian. They went back over the last month, and she hadn't responded to a single one.

I know you blame me for what happened, the most recent message read. *I think I blame myself a little too. I'm so sorry about your parents. Sorry for what I did. Sorry for how I ended things. Sorry I screwed up the best friendship I've ever had. I hope someday you can forgive me. I miss you, Skittles. I hope you're safe.*

Kris read the message over and over. She found herself starting to type a reply, but quickly deleted it.

She rubbed her eyes. She had never felt this alone in her life, and wished she could talk to Ian, but she was still so angry with him.

A floorboard creaked in the hall just outside the room. Kris rolled over and spotted a shadow dancing around under the door. Like someone pacing back and forth.

After a minute, there was a gentle knock.

"I didn't mean to snap at you." Kurt's voice was barely audible through the door. "I'll be outside . . . if you want to talk."

The footsteps disappeared back down the hall, followed by the squeak of the screen door opening and closing.

Kris relaxed into the bed again. She studied the ceiling in silence for a long moment before finally sitting up and pushing the messenger bag aside.

Outside, she found Kurt crouched down in the middle of the field, almost completely hidden in the tall grass. He held a large black camera up to his eye and took a photo of the dewdrops on a white wildflower. Kurt lowered the camera and stood up, half turning toward Kris. His eyes, however, were fixed on the camera, which looked like the old type that still used film.

It looked like her mom's.

"I'm sorry if I freaked out a little before," he said as he fidgeted with some of the camera settings. "It's not personal, I just . . ." Kurt released a heavy breath.

"You don't want me here. I get it." She motioned back to the cabin. "You've got your own life. Your own problems. You certainly don't need my baggage dumped on your doorstep, so I can just be on my way and get out of your hair—"

"That's not what I'm saying." Kurt's voice wavered for only a second. "Fia certainly didn't need my baggage, but she went out on a limb. She gave me that chance."

Kris looked away, tucking her dark hair behind her ear. "Look, I don't need another person in my life just using me to right their own wrongs or whatever."

"I'm just trying to do the right thing here."

She swung her arms out to the side with a nervous laugh. "You don't owe me anything. Let's just say your debts are paid up or however you want to put it, and we can both just walk away like none of this ever happened."

"You think those guys aren't going to come looking for you again?" Kurt scoffed and stared her down as he walked past her towards the cabin. "That's pretty ignorant."

Kris crossed her arms, chuckling to herself before hurrying after him. "You said they were probably just looking for new recruits. I'm sure there are plenty of feeble-minded Witcans eligible for their brainwashing. Why would they go through the trouble of pursuing me?"

Kurt stopped at the base of the steps and fiddled with the camera. Kris could see the gears turning in his head as he carefully considered his words. He was thinking up a lie.

"I have no doubt they would take interest in your healing abilities," he finally mumbled.

"Uh-huh." She glared, shifting her weight to one hip. "And they would know that how? What aren't you telling me?"

Kurt rubbed his brow and closed his eyes, then spun away again. "I think that's enough for today."

"No." Kris strode forward. "What else do you know?"

He squeezed his camera but was keeping his face hidden, shifting his feet as he stayed quiet.

She swallowed the lump forming in her throat. "Those Witcans who jumped me yesterday. That cult. They're the ones who went after my parents, aren't they?"

He slowly nodded, refusing to meet her eyes. Before she could ask any follow-up questions, Kurt disappeared into the house.

Kris crept up the stairs and collapsed into the porch swing. Why would they have gone after her parents? Were they looking for her?

Are Mom and Dad dead because they were trying to find me?

The thought shook her to the core.

~

The news anchor on the living room TV was talking about a Witcan attack at a university in Chicago. A student had opened fire on a class, flipped desks and chairs, and thrown classmates across the room. Some reported that he had created and manipulated fire, causing serious damage to the building. No casualties, but several hospitalized for injuries.

Kurt mindlessly scrubbed the kitchen counters and noticed Kris leaning against the screen door. Dark clouds had rolled in.

The air was humid and heavy with an impending rain, yet the birdsong still echoed through the meadow.

Kris nibbled on her thumbnail with eyes glossed over. She looked serene, lost somewhere far away.

Kurt stopped cleaning and wandered out into the hallway. "Hey."

Life returned to Kris's green eyes as her head perked up.

"You all right?" He inched forward, wiping his hands against the sides of his pants.

She dropped her hand so her arm rested on top of the other across her stomach. "I'm fine," she said in a hushed voice.

He leaned against the frame of the front door directly across from her. He forced a smile and crossed his arms as well. "You don't seem fine."

She glanced at him through the hair that hung over her face. He tried to make his smile inviting, though it was clearly a product of his own discomfort. He kept any hint of condescension out of it.

Kris rested her head against the doorframe. "I'm just . . . trying to piece together the shambles of my life." Though she kept her face hidden, Kurt could still read the energy radiating off her, could hear the weight in each word. "I don't expect you to understand." She traced her finger over a stitched-up hole in the screen door.

Thunder rumbled faintly in the distance.

"I, uh . . ." Kurt clenched his jaw and stuffed his hands in his pockets, shuffling around in place. What the hell could he say to that? She was expecting words of encouragement. He had to say something. "I'm sorry," he finally said. He started to reached out to touch her shoulder, but promptly decided against it.

Kris nodded with a huff. "Yeah. Everyone's sorry. A lot of good it does." Without another word, she pushed open the screen door and plopped down on the porch steps.

Kurt stood there, replaying the conversation in his mind. He could feel the gravity of her emotional state. Like a black hole. Her shoulders rose and fell with each intense breath. Kurt paced back and forth, debating whether to go outside.

You'll make it worse. Just give her space, he finally decided, and retreated back to the kitchen.

~

Kris rocked on the step. Inside, she could hear Kurt return to cleaning the counters. The house was already immaculate, but she was sure that cleaning was a great way to avoid talking to her.

She stared down at a small stone in the dirt just in front of the steps, and she found herself focusing on it more and more. The rumble of thunder grew closer, and the knot in her stomach continued to twist.

She'd been so stupid to think he would care, so stupid to run away. To get in the car with a stranger. To think she could make it on her own.

Kris's breathing became heavier as her thoughts continued to spiral, but she sat up a little taller as her gaze still lingered on the rock. It was a jagged white stone, no bigger than a bottle cap, barely an arm's length away. She let her mind go blank as she extended a hand, her fingers flexed out in every direction.

She squinted and tucked in her chin, focusing all her energy on the rock. *Come on. You can do this. It should be easy, right?*

Kris gasped for air, realizing that she had been holding her breath. She dropped her arm and stared at her hands. Her nose crinkled with disappointment.

"Try again."

Kris yelped at the voice and jolted back, her spine slamming into the porch step just behind her.

A small, slender young man stood in front of her with a duffle bag over his shoulder. His bright red hair and face full of freckles almost glowed with his warm smile.

"Where did you come from?" she asked, clapping a hand over her chest to slow her heart rate. Kris hadn't even heard him approach and there were no vehicles parked out front except for Kurt's car. Had he walked here?

"Didn't mean to startle you," he said with a laugh. He glanced down at the rock, then back at her. "Come on. Try it again."

Kris looked him up and down. Who the heck was this guy? Another Witcan?

She tentatively stretched out her hand again.

"Breathe," he said.

Duh.

Focusing on the rock again, she took a long, deep inhale. The warm feeling in her chest returned, and her breath caught. Unlike the previous times, the sensation seemed to flicker like a flame in the wind. The muscles in Kris's arm tightened as she tried to force the heat into her hand as she had before.

Breathe.

Kris released a long, drawn-out puff through her lips. She felt the familiar tingle roar in her chest for a second, fire down the length of her arm, and reach out through her fingertips. She felt the rock before she even saw it move.

It bounced an inch off the ground and rolled in the dirt once it landed, but Kris lowered her arm with a smile, even though her muscles were suddenly throbbing and a mild headache was setting in.

Holy smokes. She'd actually done it.

"I'm Larsen," the young man said with his hand out.

Kris stood up, swiftly dusting dirt off the seat of her shorts, and gave his hand an awkward shake. "I'm Kris." Once standing, she noticed he was much shorter than his posture suggested, standing only a few inches taller than her.

Another roll of thunder. The rumbles were getting louder.

"It's a pleasure to meet you," Larsen said, flashing a genuine smile. "Is Kurt around?"

Kris jerked her thumb over her shoulder toward the front door. "Cleaning."

On cue, the screen door swung open and Kurt emerged. "Hey."

The tone he used when he addressed Larsen was so different—so warm and welcoming—that Kris did a double take. He hurried down the steps and gave Larsen a hug before looking back at her with a smile that couldn't be contained.

"Kristen, this is my friend Larsen." Kurt's whole face lit up as he patted Larsen on the back. "I figured he could help."

Kris gave the newcomer another once-over. Tan slacks, a dark blue polo shirt, and brown dress shoes. His limbs were scrawny and his hair neatly combed.

"Help with what exactly?" she said.

"Whatever you need," Larsen explained as Kurt took the duffle bag from his hand. "If you want to talk, if you want to learn, if you want to assemble a plan for schooling or housing."

Kris watched Kurt step aside and glance up at the darkening clouds. He motioned to the door. "Why don't you two talk? I'll go put your bag in your room."

She turned toward him as he passed by, her chest raising with a sharp inhale, but he went inside and her shoulders deflated.

Larsen followed, holding open the screen door for her. "Let's chat inside before this rain starts."

Kris nodded and trudged up the porch steps. Once inside the living room, she turned off the TV before dropping onto the sofa.

"I heard what happened to your parents," Larsen said, eyes darting down the hall. He took his shoes off by the door before entering the living room. He lowered himself into the recliner and sat up tall. "I'm so sorry for your loss. That's a horrible way to lose a loved one."

Kris stared down at the hardwood floor, grappling with the question that burned in her mind. "Is Kurt just pawning me off on you?"

Larsen snickered. "Be patient with him."

She slouched, pulling a knee up to her chest and hugging it.

When Larsen spoke again, his voice was much softer. "Kurt has some trust issues. And he is still struggling with loss himself."

"So . . . what? He sent you in to fulfill my emotional needs?" She could sense that Kurt was listening. She didn't know exactly where in the house he was, but she could feel him hanging on every word.

Larsen turned away and scratched the back of his head. "I just want to help. Help you. Help Kurt. I lost my parents when I was very young, so I know what you're going through."

"Oh."

A loud crack of thunder was soon followed by the gentle trickle of raindrops on the roof. The soothing sound filled the house, and after a moment the heavy downpour began.

"What happened?" she asked. "To your parents, I mean."

Larsen leaned over as far as he could and peered down the hallway. He hesitated, tracing his fingers over his watch before finally speaking in a hushed tone. "They were killed. As were Kurt's parents. When we were just kids."

Kris jolted upright. Her jaw hung open while she tried to find the right words to say. "That's horrible, I'm sorry."

A door slammed at the end of the hall and they both jumped. Kris leaned back on the couch to gaze down the dim hallway. Kurt's bedroom door was closed.

"Is he . . . ?"

"Kurt doesn't talk about it." Larsen shifted around in the chair. "I probably shouldn't have told you."

She stared down the hall, trying to ignore the nausea in her gut, but she finally turned back around.

He offered a weak smile and looked out the window. "Like I said, be patient with Kurt. Try not to take it personally."

"He doesn't seem to want to talk about my parents either."

"We all cope with grief differently."

Kris nodded and focused on the sound of the storm. The rain was still coming down hard, filling the house with an ambient white noise she found relaxing.

"I was fortunate enough to have access to some great counselors at Salman Sanctuary—it's a Witcan reserve in Michigan—but Kurt just internalized everything."

She glanced down the hall at Kurt's closed door. The feeling of guilt weighed on her chest.

"What about you?" he asked.

Kris sank deeper into the couch to the point that she was lying down on her side, but she could still watch the rainstorm outside. "What about me?"

Larsen offered a comforting smile. "How are you handling things?"

She laughed as she rolled onto her back and pressed her palms into her eyes. "I'm keeping it all together, can't you tell?"

"So, humor?"

Kris looked back at him and smirked. "What are you, my therapist?"

He motioned to her. "You *are* lying on a couch."

"Touché." She giggled, turning onto her side again and propping her head up. "I don't know." Kris sighed and fiddled with the seam of the couch cushion.

Larsen stood to look out the front window as a bolt of lightning lit up the dark sky. "Internal reflection is important, but sometimes just talking through stuff out loud can help clear things up in a whole new way."

Kris scoffed. "I don't think talking is going to fix my problems."

"You are dealing with a lot of big life changes. Something as small as talking things out can fix more than you know."

Over the sound of the rain on the roof, she heard Kurt's door open again. She didn't look up, but she could feel his presence at the entrance to the living room.

"I'm going to be staying here with Kurt for the next couple months, at least until classes start up again in the fall," Larsen said. "I'll be here whenever you want to talk, or even if you don't want to talk but you don't want to be alone."

Kris twisted her head to peek out at him from behind the cushion. Out of the corner of her eye, she could make out Kurt leaning against the wall, hands stuffed inside his pockets, staring down at the ground.

"Thank you."

~

Kris breathed in deep and then out again before opening the dresser drawer. There were a few shirts and sweatpants folded on one side, but there was still plenty of room.

This could be home.

She removed the unfolded pile of clothes from her messenger bag on the bed and stuffed them into the drawer.

Kris nodded, smiling to herself as she slid the drawer closed again.

At least for now, this feels like it could be home.

Chapter 9

Cade

Kris sat up abruptly in bed and gasped for air. Her head whipped around, taking in the room and trying to place herself. Kurt's house, she reminded herself. She clasped a hand to her chest as she tried to steady her breathing. *In. Out. It was just a nightmare.*

Her throat felt dry and her hands were trembling. She tapped the screen of her cell phone on the nightstand. Nearly three o'clock in the morning.

The rain had finally let up, so the house was completely silent except for gentle music coming from somewhere outside the room. Kurt's guitar?

Her heart was still racing as she climbed out of the bed and tiptoed out of her room. The front door was closed, but light shone from the porch. She crept through the house, past Larsen's closed door, and arched her neck to gaze out the living room window. Sure enough, Kurt was sitting on the swing, plucking at the guitar. A small ball of light hovered beside him.

He was still up? Did he ever get any sleep?

Kurt stopped playing when Kris stepped onto the porch, still in her pajamas. "Hey."

"Hey," she replied, pulling the door shut behind her. "You up already, or up still?"

He smirked and ran his hand down the neck of the guitar. "Both. It's like this most nights."

"What are you playing?"

"I was just trying something out."

Kris leaned against the railing on the far side of the porch. She stared at the floating orb of light and admired the way it glistened off the guitar. She gave a half smile. "Can I hear it?"

He pushed the hair from his face and met her eyes. He studied her, perhaps judging how serious she was, before pressing down on the guitar frets. His fingers moved elegantly from string to string while he plucked the chords.

Kris took a deep breath in, mesmerized by his talent. As she stood there watching Kurt pick away at the guitar, she felt the increasingly familiar warmth in her chest. Her heart pounded as fire enveloped it. She put a hand on her chest and smiled. The melody filled the humid night air so beautifully that Kris was on the verge of tears.

"That was incredible," she said once Kurt stopped playing, and the heat in her torso evaporated.

"Thanks." He bowed his head, but she caught his smile.

He lifted the guitar off his lap and slid over on the swing so there was room for her. He leaned the guitar up against the railing as Kris took a seat. They sat in silence, listening to the crickets out in the rain-soaked meadow.

"I tried to learn guitar," Kris stated, rubbing her arms. "When I was younger. Begged my mom for years to let me take lessons, and when she finally agreed, I almost immediately decided it was too hard and quit." She let out a nervous giggle and tucked her hair behind her ear. "She wasn't too happy with me."

Kurt chuckled.

"Did you take lessons?"

He grinned and shook his head. "I'm entirely self-taught. Never actually played anything for anyone before."

"Well, I feel privileged that I was your first audience." Kris laughed and gazed out into the darkness. The meadow was spooky at this hour. No lights. No moon. No stars. Just blackness.

"You and Larsen seemed to really hit it off," Kurt said. He touched the glowing orb and moved it around through the air before releasing it again to hover in place.

Kris nodded, fiddling with a strand of hair. "Yeah. I think so. He seems like a real stand-up dude."

"Stand-up dude," he mouthed to himself, snickering.

"Seems like you two really care about each other." She watched him from the corner of her eye. "He talks very highly of you."

"He's family," Kurt said without hesitation. "He's always been there for me. Even when I didn't want him to be." His posture stiffened and his eyes went wide for a moment before he looked away. He cleared his throat and continued before Kris could speak. "It's late. You should go back to sleep."

What just happened? He flipped again.

Kris stared at him, trying to get a read on his facial expression, but he kept his head turned away. She slapped her hands down on the swing and pushed herself up to the door, but she stopped before grabbing the handle. "Why do you do this?"

"Do what?"

Kris rolled her eyes. "You know what I'm talking about. *This.*" She circled a finger around in the air. "Every time we start having an actual conversation, it's like you shut off. What are you so afraid of?"

Kurt dropped his head. His lips were pressed together tightly as though holding back a response.

"Are you so afraid to be vulnerable? To show some humanity?" When he still didn't answer, she stomped back over to him and threw both arms out. "Are you really that much of a coward, Kurt?"

He stood so fast that Kris hopped back, startled. His jaw clenched and his blue-gray eyes flashed. "You don't know the first thing about me."

"So then tell me!"

Kurt's face twisted as he scoffed. "Do you really not get it? Are you *that* ignorant?"

"God, why did you even bring me here?" Kris clasped her hands over her face. "If you so badly want nothing to do with me, then why didn't you just leave me be? Why not just let those weirdo cult people take me?"

He took a long stride toward her, and Kris recoiled. "*I'm* the bad guy because I didn't let a murderous cult kidnap you? Do you hear yourself?"

She jabbed a finger into his chest. "You didn't have to interfere."

"I promised Sofia I would look after you," Kurt growled under his breath, swatting Kris's hand away. "And it would have been so easy, too, if you had just stayed home. But no. You had to run away, like a child."

"You are in no place to judge my actions."

"You want to leave? Fine, then go." He twisted away, slamming his hands down on the porch railing and staring off into the night.

"Is that why you put up your walls? Because you think I want to leave?" Kris leaned over the banister to look him in the eye.

He turned his head away and remained silent.

She let out a bitter laugh. "Right. Can't talk about that either."

A broken breath seemed to catch in Kurt's throat, and Kris felt a pang in her chest. His anger appeared to be rapidly dissolving. She reached out to touch his shoulder, but he jerked it away.

"Don't."

Kris flinched and held her hand awkwardly against her chest.

"Just go to bed." He kept his head down, hair hiding his face.

Without another word, she disappeared inside the house.

~

Kris dried the clean dinner plate with a towel and held it out to Larsen to put away. "Did you know my mom?"

Larsen went rigid. He turned his head ever so slightly toward the dining room, where Kurt was clearing off the table. "Not personally," he finally replied in a hushed tone, putting the plate away in the cupboard. Kurt cleared his throat in the next room, and Larsen stepped closer to Kris. "Your mother was well known among Witcans as somewhat of a hero. She sheltered many Witcans over the years, gave them a safe place to stay, helped them hide from the NWDA. She was a strong advocate for Witcan-Human Coexistence."

Kris dried her hands with the dish towel and tossed it on the counter. "Really?"

Kurt was suddenly behind her, snatching the wet towel and hanging it on the handle of the oven. Larsen backed away as he eyed Kurt's reaction.

Kris watched Kurt meticulously smooth out the damp kitchen towel. "My bigot grandfather mentioned that my mom used to attend some anti-NWDA rallies back in the day, which they grounded her for. Other than that, I had no idea she was involved in any of that stuff." She slumped back against the counter and stared down at her feet. *I wish she had told me.*

"Fia didn't want you involved," Kurt whispered, back turned to her.

Kris whipped her head toward him in surprise. She nibbled on her thumbnail, waiting for Kurt to say more. He peeked over his shoulder and glanced between Larsen and Kris. He opened his mouth but then closed it.

Larsen stood up straight, a startled look on his face.

"What?" Kris asked.

Then she heard it. The revving of an engine. It sounded like a motorcycle, and it was getting louder.

Larsen pressed his lips together and shot Kurt a look. "You didn't."

Kurt shrugged, then forced a smile. "Sorry. I didn't think you would show up if you knew he was coming."

Kris leaned over the kitchen sink and gazed out into the field. A motorcycle rocketed down the path, throwing up a cloud of dirt behind it. "Who's that?"

When she could no longer see the motorcycle from the kitchen window, she followed the two of them to the front porch.

The rider pushed the kickstand down with his foot and pulled off his helmet, revealing a young man with a shock of blond hair down to his shoulders. He shook his locks from his face and offered Kurt a smile, which immediately vanished when he noticed Larsen.

"Oh, great. The nerd is here," the motorcyclist muttered in a raspy voice. He rested his helmet on the handlebars and unzipped his black leather jacket, then grinned at Kris. "Who's the hot girl?"

"Excuse me?" Kris parted Kurt and Larsen and stepped forward, a scowl on her face. She was prepared to tear into this stranger, but Kurt put a hand on her shoulder and eased her back.

"What is he doing here?" Larsen growled. "I thought you weren't talking to him anymore." He turned towards Kurt but spoke loud enough for the rider to hear.

The man approached the steps and slipped off his ratty backpack to remove his jacket. Elaborate tattoos of roses, flames, and what looked like an abstract panther of shattered glass decorated his left arm. "I'm sober now, so don't get your panties in a bunch." He shot Larsen a quick glare before focusing his bright blue eyes on Kris again. He pushed back his long blond hair with a confident smirk, and Kris caught a glimpse of a large scar across his forehead.

He held out his hand toward her. "Don't believe we've had the pleasure. I'm Cade."

Up close, the stink of cigarettes and beer burned in Kris's nose. She crossed her arms and looked down at his hand, but refused to shake it. "Kris."

"Sober, my ass. You reek of beer," Larsen fired back.

Cade gave Kris a wink. "Just the occasional drink."

She shifted her weight. "Before driving? Real responsi—"

"It's good to see you," Kurt cut in, slapping a hand on Cade's shoulder.

"It's great to be back." Cade scanned the meadow before looking back at the house. "If not for the nerd and the sassy hot chick, it would be just like old times."

"Seriously?" Kris grumbled, looking to Larsen.

He rolled his eyes and shook his head.

Kurt pulled open the screen door and held it for everyone to enter. Cade bowed his head, motioning to Kris to go ahead. She glared and stepped back.

"You first," Kris said. She twisted away awkwardly.

"Your girlfriend is feisty." Cade laughed, shooting Kurt a finger gun as he went inside. "I like her."

"Not my girlfriend," Kurt called after him.

"I can't believe this," Larsen said as he followed Cade inside.

Kris and Kurt were left standing on the porch. She shot him a withering look while his eyes expressed a silent plea.

"Who the hell is this guy?" she hissed, jerking a thumb into the house.

"He's an old buddy of ours. Cade's a good guy. Just give him a chance."

Kris scoffed. "Like I have a choice." She charged past Kurt into the cabin.

Cade had tossed his backpack and jacket onto the table and was wandering around the dining room. Larsen was sitting cross-legged on the couch, making no attempt to hide his disgust.

Kris leaned on the back of the couch with arms folded over her chest. "So, what brings you here, Cade?"

"Blew all your drug money, so you're back to taking advantage of Kurt?" Larsen asked.

Before Cade could respond, Kurt stepped in. "I called him. I asked him to come."

Cade pulled out a chair at the table and sneered at Larsen. "I've been clean almost a year now." He flicked open a lighter and then snapped it shut again.

"So you invited him to show Kristen what not to do with her life?" Larsen spat.

"Enough," Kurt said.

Kris slid a step away from him.

"Can we just be adults? Please?" Kurt insisted, looking from Larsen to Cade.

Larsen and Kris locked eyes for a moment. She recognized his posture. The way his feet tapped on the floor with irritation. The way his eyes darted to the door, then back.

His shoulders finally relaxed. He stared down at his lap, grinding his teeth for a moment before nodding. "Fine."

Kurt then turned to Cade and held out a hand in waiting.

Cade chuckled and rolled his eyes. "Yeah, whatever, man." He draped his tattooed arm over the back of the chair. "Right, Larsen. We're good?"

Larsen shifted around uncomfortably, looking from Kurt back to Cade. "Yeah, we're good," he muttered. "But if I find out you're still using, I'm gone."

"Then we won't have a problem," Cade said. He stood from the chair, dragged his bag and jacket off the table, and jutted a thumb to the hallway. "First room on the right?"

"Yeah," Kurt said.

"Don't you touch *any* of my things." Larsen sprang up and darted down the hall after Cade.

Cade ducked into the bedroom. "Well, now I have to touch everything."

Kurt sighed, rubbing his eyes, then leaned back against the couch next to Kris. They were both quiet for a moment. She could hear Larsen bickering about "his side of the room" from down the hall.

"Old friends, huh?" Kris asked, staring down at her feet as she dug her toe into the floor.

Kurt nodded, his face hidden in his hand. "Since we were kids."

"Look, about last night . . ."

"I don't want to talk about it."

"What's really going on here, Kurt?" she asked under her breath, motioning towards the bedrooms. "How many more 'old friends' should I be expecting?"

He planted both hands on the back of the couch to prop himself up. "Just Larsen and Cade."

"Is this just so you can avoid talking to me?"

Kris watched him from the corner of her eye. Kurt shook his head, his lips pressed together tightly. Quiet. Thinking.

"I think Tynan is searching for you," he finally said, standing up taller. "I thought having some extra help—"

"So instead of just teaching me how to use *my* powers, you thought it would be better to potentially endanger your friends' lives to 'protect me' from some evil guy that may or may not be hunting me down."

"Can you dispense with the attitude, please?" Kurt snapped, giving her a quick look before turning away again. "I'm trying to be responsible."

"But I'm not your responsibility." Kris pushed off the back of the couch and threw up her arms. She whirled around to Kurt, trying to keep her voice down. "I'm not a child. You're not my guardian. I don't need you coddling me."

She kicked the screen door open and marched out into the field.

~

Kurt groaned as he flipped over the back of the couch so his head dangled off the front and his feet hung in the air. He clapped a hand over his face.

"She's fiery, isn't she?"

Kurt lifted his hand to see Larsen leaning with his elbows behind the couch. He laughed, dropping his head down again. "You could say that."

Larsen sighed and rounded the armrest, then sat next to him. His lips were tightly pinched as he fidgeted with his watch. "I overheard some of it last night too. You can't keep treating her like a ward. She needs you to be a friend."

"She doesn't need another friend. That's why you're here," Kurt murmured, pivoting to sit up correctly on the couch. "She's seventeen. She needs guidance. She needs discipline."

"Discipline?" Cade laughed from where he leaned on the wall and looked down at them. "Nah, not discipline. Y'all got a *whole* different kind of energy going on up in here."

Kurt groaned and slouched forward, gesturing as he spoke. "She's so stubborn. And frustrating. She gives me so much attitude, it drives me up the wall. I don't know what she expects from me."

Cade snorted. "I have an idea."

"Shut up. You're not helping," Larsen said with a glare. He pushed an open palm in Cade's direction. Though several feet apart, Cade stumbled back from the shove, still chuckling.

Kurt stood up and circled the living room before sitting down again. "I don't know what to do. I don't know how to tell her. Or if I even *should* tell her."

"You have to tell her, Kurt," Larsen said.

Cade nodded and stepped into the living room. "Dude, you just have to rip off the bandage and deal with the aftermath." He fiddled with his lighter again.

Kurt wrinkled his nose and gazed out the window into the field. Sitting out in the tall grass, Kris had her back turned to the house with shoulders slumped forward.

"She's not going to believe me," he said under his breath, watching her pluck a blade of grass and flick it away.

"Just talk *to* her, and not down to her," Larsen said. "She trusts you. Otherwise, she wouldn't still be here."

Chapter 10

Graveyard

Kris stood outside, looking up at the house. Pale blue painted siding with accents of white, tall bow windows, a porch that wrapped around the side and connected to the garage, black Spanish tiles on the roof.

She clutched the strap of her book bag as she ascended the steps to the front door. "Mom's going to kill me," she muttered to herself. She gripped the handle, but she stood there staring at the gold door knocker. *Everything will be fine. You've got this.*

Kris finally pushed the door open and entered the house, tiptoeing past the living room.

"Mr. Irving called this afternoon."

She spun around. Her mother stood from the living room couch, her hands on her hips and a flat expression on her face.

"He said you got in another physical altercation with Julia today at lunch."

Kris slipped her backpack off her shoulder, holding it in front of herself like a shield. "I can explain."

Her mother scoffed and threw her hands up in the air as she turned away. "You can't expect to 'explain' your way out of assaulting your classmate! This is the third time this year. Clearly the anger management counseling didn't help."

"She called Brie a slut." Kris stomped her foot. "She wouldn't apologize, so I may have pushed her, then Ian got involved . . ."

Her mother stood still in the middle of the living room, arms crossed. Her facial expression remained unchanged. "I'm sorry she said that, but violence isn't the answer. It's never the answer. You should know better by now."

Kris dropped her bag on the floor beside her. Her eyes welled up as her mother crept up closer, staring down at her.

"I've never been more disappointed in you," she whispered. Her eyes, though narrow with anger, were also tearing up. She moved past Kris and headed up the stairs to the second floor.

Kris stared down at her feet. She had just been trying to do the right thing. She had to stand up for Brie.

Her cell phone beeped in the back pocket of her jeans. It was a text message from Ian: *Can you come over?*

Kris looked up the stairs, then back at her phone. *I don't think I should*, she typed back. *My mom is really upset about the detention. She didn't say I was grounded, but I think it's implied.*

She carried her backpack to her room and tossed it onto her bed.

Her phone buzzed again. *Please? It's important.*

Kris sighed, stuffed her phone back into her pocket, and returned to the front door. She squeezed the handle and pulled the door open, but on the other side wasn't the sun-filled front lawn. It was a cold, dark room that smelled. The floor was wet, slapping beneath Kris's shoes as she moved farther inside.

A small, narrow beam of light shined through a sliver in a window near the ceiling. It was a basement, she realized.

As her eyes adjusted to the dark, Kris recognized that two bodies lay on the floor in front of her. Her breath caught in her throat, and tears spilled out of her eyes. "Mom? Dad?"

She slowly got down to her knees and reached out toward her mother's bloodied face. There was a large gash on her forehead, dried blood caked all the way down her neck. Kris's hands were trembling so fiercely that she had to clutch her arms against her chest.

Kris choked back the sobs. "Mom . . . I'm so sorry." She clapped a hand over her mouth, trying to control her cries.

Her mother's eyes snapped open, already fixed directly on her. Kris screamed as she stumbled, falling back and pushing away.

"You failed us, Kris." Her mother spoke so softly that Kris could hardly hear her words.

"What? I don't . . . I didn't—"

"You let this happen. You could have saved us."

"No. No, I didn't know . . . I . . ."

Kris tore her eyes away and threw herself down on the floor. "I'm sorry. I'm sorry. I'm sorry," she cried out over and over, each time a little louder, until she was shrieking.

"Kris?"

She pushed herself up, panting. Her vision was blurry, and it took longer than usual for her to collect herself and recognize her surroundings. Sunlight poured in through the window, reminding Kris that she was still in her bedroom at the cabin.

"Kris, are you okay?" It was Larsen's voice on the other side of the door.

"Yeah," she lied as she wiped sweat from her face. "Just a bad dream."

She flung the blanket away, turning to plant her feet on the floor. Hunched forward, she breathed in deeply. Her head was ringing, but even after clearing her eyes, the room still looked fuzzy.

Kris reached for her cell phone, immediately remembering how she had reached out for her mother's face, and her hands began to shake. She squeezed her hands together, forcing breaths in and out more aggressively. *It was just a dream. It was just a dream.*

When she finally picked up her phone, she saw it was almost noon. She'd slept away the whole morning. As she changed out of her pajamas, Kris couldn't get the words from her dream out of her mind.

Her chest was still pounding when she left the room.

Larsen stood outside the closed bathroom door, towel in hand. He offered her a big smile. "Just barely get to say 'good morning' to you today."

As she approached, Kris could hear that the shower was running. "Sorry, I never sleep in this late."

"Don't worry about it. Rest is important right now."

Kris clutched her arm, twisting side to side.

"You sure you're okay?"

She shrugged, dropping her head. "Yeah. Yeah, I'm fine." Her palms felt clammy as she glanced toward Kurt's closed bedroom door. "Is Kurt up?"

Larsen pointed over his shoulder toward the front door. "He's in the garden. Wait." He gently touched her shoulder as she tried to walk by. "What's wrong?"

Kris's throat started to close up. She tightened her jaw and kept her eyes down. "Just a rough night," she managed to get out. "Bad dreams."

He gave her arm a squeeze but moved aside so she could pass. "You don't always have to be tough, Kris."

"I'm fine."

The fresh air washed over Kris as soon as she stepped outside. She stood on the porch, taking in some deep breaths.

Her heart was still racing as she descended the stairs and trudged through the grass to the side of the house.

Kurt was on his hands and knees in the garden, ripping weeds from the soil. He sat up as she approached. "Late start this morning."

Kris nodded, hugging her arms close.

He stood and removed his gardening gloves. "Something wrong?"

"Can you take me into town?" she asked quietly.

Kurt's posture changed immediately, becoming more rigid. "Why? What do you need in town?"

Kris did her best to maintain a strong, sturdy tone as she tried to swallow the lump in her throat. "I want to visit my parents."

He stepped back, waving his hands back and forth. "No, absolutely not."

"I just want to talk to them."

"That's way too dangerous. Tynan would be expecting you there."

Kris shook her head. "I just . . . I had . . ."

"I'm sorry, but no." He turned away and stood with his fists on his hips, then looked up to the partly cloudy sky. "It would be foolish to leave at all. Definitely stupid to go to the one place Tynan knows you will go."

"Please."

"No."

After scowling and blinking incessantly to keep her eyes from filling with tears, Kris stomped back inside.

Larsen followed her as she rushed by him to her room. He closed the bedroom door behind him. She collapsed onto the bed and buried her face into the pillow as he sat down on the edge of the bed.

"I just wanted to visit their graves," she grumbled, clutching the pillow. "I just wanted to talk to them."

"Kurt is only trying to protect you," Larsen whispered. "If he said no, you should trust him."

She rolled to her side and traced her finger around on the sheets. "The last thing my mom ever said to me was that she was disappointed in me. I let her down, and now I can never make it up again."

"Your mother loved you more than anything. She fought to make this a better world for you."

Kris scoffed. "I failed her. It's my fault. If I had *just* stayed home, if I hadn't left, maybe I could have saved them."

With a sigh, Larsen rested his elbows on his knees. "You can't change the past. Even if you had been there, Tynan likely would have taken your life too."

"Well, maybe he should have." She plunged her face back into her pillow.

"Don't say that."

"I know, it's a terrible thing to think," she mumbled. "It just keeps coming back to me, more realistic every night. I keep reliving that last moment over and over again." Kris sat up and pulled her knees in tight. "I thought visiting their graves might help me start to gain some closure. I haven't been to see them since the funeral."

Larsen nodded, then stood up and opened the bedroom door, checking the hallway. "I can take you. I can get you there and back in minutes."

"Wait, are you serious? How?"

He held out his hand towards her. Kris hesitantly took it and stood up.

"I can teleport through physical space. It's a rare gift, like the healing abilities you have."

Her eyes lit up. "Wait, really?"

Larsen gave a firm nod and held up his free hand. "We have to be fast and we have to be careful, okay? And do not tell Kurt, or he will flip."

"Yeah, of course." Her heart thudded against her rib cage as Larsen took her other hand.

"I've never teleported with someone else before, full disclosure," he said quietly, closing his eyes. He took a deep breath in and exhaled. "Don't let go."

Kris squeezed his hands tighter.

She felt it first just behind her eyes. What started off as a nagging discomfort increased when the room began to spiral around them, smearing together like wet paint, until the feeling progressed into a full-blown pain erupting inside her skull. She couldn't keep her eyes open as the pain grew worse. Her knees became weak, and she felt herself collapsing, but she made sure not to release Larsen's hands.

A whirlwind blew around her, howling for a moment before dying down almost immediately, leaving a hum in her ears. Though her head was still throbbing, Kris pulled her eyes open to watch a yard of tombstones gradually come into focus around them. When Larsen let go, he stumbled back, then staggered to regain his balance.

Kris caught him. "Are you all right?" She walked him over to the fence.

Larsen chuckled and pushed his hand against his forehead as he gripped the top of the wooden rail. "That was exponentially harder than traveling alone." He stood up straight. "But I'm fine."

"Are you sure? You can rest a moment."

He shook his head and took a few steps into the graveyard. "We shouldn't be here any longer than necessary." He scanned the stones on either side of the narrow gravel road. "This is the correct cemetery, right?"

Kris nodded, stepping up beside him and pointing up the incline ahead. "They're up on the hill."

They walked in silence. Her body trembled with nerves while Larsen continued to survey their surroundings. Fortunately, the graveyard was empty of visitors.

Kris paused near the top of the hill, her eyes focused on a line of trees along the path to the left. That was where she'd seen Kurt for the first time, at the funeral.

Larsen hung back, allowing her to guide him off the road between some tombstones. She stopped in front of a wide stone plaque with two names side by side: Sofia Angel Hanwel and Jacob William Hanwel.

"I'll give you a minute," he whispered, and took several steps back.

Kris kept her hands clasped against her chest as she stared down at the dying flowers resting at the base of their tombstone. *I should have brought fresh ones.*

She lowered herself to the ground and touched the crunchy petals of the white peony bouquet. Before she even realized it, the familiar warm tingle traveled down her arm, vibrating through her already trembling fingers. The dried, wilted flowers renewed—their bright white color returned, and the petals bloomed once more.

Kris stifled a cry and pulled her hand away. The bouquet looked just as it had the day she'd left it there.

She clasped her hands in front of her face and closed her eyes. *Mom. Dad. I miss you both so much. I hope . . . I really hope that, wherever you are now, you don't feel the pain or misery you experienced in your last moments here on this earth. I hope you are together. I hope you are still making each other laugh. I hope you are happy.*

Her chest felt strained as she rested a hand on top of the cold headstone. Shivers ran through her entire body.

I'm sorry I wasn't able to protect you. For not being there when it happened. I hope you are still watching over me.

Kris wanted to cry, but as she sat before the stone and stared down at her parents' names, she felt nothing. Like it wasn't real. Like it was all an elaborate dream, or a sadistic prank, and she would turn around and see her parents standing just beside her.

I really miss you.

Kris snapped back to reality when Larsen let out a sharp gasp. She turned to find a man standing behind him, a large hand wrapped around Larsen's neck. His fingers were nearly touching as they constricted, and his eyes were bright red, like nothing Kris had ever seen. The sight of them immobilized her.

Larsen's entire body was tense as the color drained from his face. It took a few seconds for his eyes to lock onto hers. "Run," he managed to say.

Kris took a couple of steps back. She couldn't run. She couldn't leave him here.

"Run," he said again.

She didn't have the chance to decide. A force threw her up in the air, and she flailed as she crashed down into a tombstone. Her shoulder clipped the side of the stone, which toppled her over. Her head knocked hard on the dirt, causing her vision to distort.

"Larsen," she called out in her confusion.

As she tried to stand, a pair of hands grabbed her by the arms and pulled her to her feet. She knew it wasn't Larsen, but she was too disoriented and couldn't put up much of a fight. Once she stood upright again, Kris could see a young man with short brown hair gripping her upper arms.

"I've got her," he said.

More cult members?

Kris tried to pull herself free. "Let go of me!"

A blow struck the side of her head, and her body went limp. Her ears rang, her legs felt weak, and the man holding her had to scoop her up and carry her in his arms.

"Xan! What did you do that for?" he shouted.

The world drifted in and out of darkness, but Kris fought to stay awake. She could see a third man, this one with golden hair.

"She was going to attract too much attention," the man called Xan muttered before looking over at Larsen. Even in her daze, Kris could see a startled expression seep into his eyes.

"Red, release him," Xan said.

"Tynan said to dispose of anyone else," the red-eyed man protested.

"I know what he said. But I recognize this one. I can make him talk."

Red released Larsen's neck, and he crumpled to the ground. His eyes slowly opened, adjusting to take in the young man now squatted over him. "Alex?" Larsen said.

"Shay, take Red and the girl back," Xan barked to the man holding Kris. A wicked grin played across his face. "I'm going to have a little conversation with Larsen here."

"Don't you dare hurt him," Kris murmured, unable to muster the strength she'd intended to use in her voice. She tried to push away from her captor, but he held on tight.

Before she could say anything else, the ringing in her head grew louder, like a drill burrowing deep into her brain. As the cemetery began to swirl around her, Kris realized she was teleporting again.

"No. Larsen!" she called out before everything plummeted into darkness.

Chapter 11

Leverage

"I have to say, I never expected to see you again, much less directly in my crosshairs."

Larsen's neck burned. He felt like his flesh had been singed and the nerves and muscle underneath had been electrocuted. The feeling was slowly returning to his fingers as he struggled to prop himself up in the grass. He tried to focus on the face in front of him.

"Alex." His voice was weak, and it wavered as he spoke.

Alex smirked. "After Chicago, I figured you would be in the wind again." He pushed Larsen's arm, causing him to collapse back into the ground.

Larsen managed to get to his knees, and he rubbed his neck as he gasped for air. "What are you doing here? Why were they calling you Xan? Where have you taken Kris?"

Alex stood and wandered over to Sofia and Jacob's headstone. He ran his fingers across the polished stone and then kicked the bouquet of flowers with such force that all the petals fell off along its trajectory across the graveyard.

"I warned you this would happen," Alex huffed, whirling back to Larsen as he began to stand. "I can't believe my luck that you would just appear right here. Where I've been stationed for weeks. *With* the girl we've been searching for." He laughed to himself before delivering a blow across Larsen's cheek with a glowing green fist. "You've known him all along, haven't you?"

Larsen spit out a mouthful of blood into the grass and swiped his hand across his lip, smearing blood down the back of it. "Known who?"

Alex's lips pursed as he glared down at Larsen. "You know we've been looking for Kurt Carlsons. Why else would that coward have sent you here instead?"

Kurt?

Alex approached and swung another punch, but Larsen raised his arm to deflect. He staggered away, holding on to a stone cross to balance himself. "What do you want with Kurt?"

"That's none of your concern. But either you or the girl will tell us where he is." His eyes flashed as he reached out towards Larsen's raw throat. "And I would much rather it be you."

Without thought, Larsen squeezed his eyes shut and disappeared from the graveyard in a whirlwind.

~

Cade tapped the ash off his cigarette over the railing into the grass and looked inside, where Kurt was pacing vigorously between the dining room and living room.

"You sure you don't want me to just go look for them?" Cade asked him again. He took a long drag of his cigarette and let the smoke circle around his head. "The graveyard can't be that far."

Before Kurt could answer, Cade heard a thud in the lawn just behind him.

Larsen was kneeling in the grass, panting to catch his breath.

"Dude, Kurt is pissed at y—" Cade's grin disappeared the instant he saw the bruising around Larsen's neck and the blood spilling from his lip. "Oh shi—Kurt," he called into the house, flicking the cigarette and jumping over the porch railing to Larsen. "What did you do? What the hell happened?"

Cade grabbed Larsen by the arm and heaved him to his feet.

The screen door burst open and Kurt appeared beside them a moment later. He took Larsen by the other arm and helped guide him to the porch steps to sit. "What happened? Where's Kris?"

Larsen wiped blood from his chin, his eyes dancing around and out of focus. They finally settled on Kurt. "Tynan isn't after Kris. He's tracking you."

"What? Tynan is looking for you?" Cade asked.

Kurt clasped both hands behind his head and stared out across the field. He took a deep breath and whirled back to Larsen. "You have no idea what you've done. You should have just listened to me."

"He's going to make her talk, Kurt," Larsen explained, carefully rubbing the handprint on his neck. "By any means necessary."

Kurt dropped his arms. "Kris is a pledge trinket," he mumbled to himself before jabbing a finger in Larsen's direction. "This is *your* fault."

Larsen opened his mouth to speak, but Cade cut him off. "Hey, hey, hey. I hate the nerd too, but this is not the time for literal finger pointing." He put a hand on Kurt's chest and lightly moved him back. "Your girl's life is in danger."

Kurt bowed his head as he nodded. "You're right. I'm sorry," he said, and held out his arms. "Tynan's not going to kill her. As far as he knows, he needs her alive as leverage, but we need to get her out of there."

Larsen pulled himself to his feet with the stair railing. "Alexander would have left the cemetery by now. We have no way of knowing where they took her."

Kurt clenched his jaw. "I know where he took her."

Kris's head was still ringing when she finally came to. *What . . . happened? Where am I?*

She pushed herself to sit up on the cold floor. A light touch of her cheek made her wince as a sharp pain fired across her skin. She tried replaying in her mind what she could remember. She'd been at the cemetery with Larsen when three guys jumped them. One of them had stayed back with him. *Oh God, I hope he's okay.*

Kris crawled through the dark room, reaching out blindly to feel for a wall. Voices came from somewhere, and though she couldn't understand what they were saying, she recognized the tone of the red-eyed man from the graveyard.

She had to get out of here.

Kris bumped a wall of jagged rock. Holding on to it with both hands, she pulled herself to her feet and moved along the stone wall, hoping to find a door. There had to be a way out.

Her hands finally fumbled over what felt like a handle. She wrapped both hands around it and jerked, which caused it to jiggle but not budge. She pulled on it harder and leaned back with all of her weight. The handle gave way, and Kris toppled backwards, crashing on her back.

A large silhouette came into view in front of her from the doorway. A tall man with broad shoulders and muscular arms.

Behind him floated a glowing orb, finally casting some light into the small room.

He glanced over his shoulder at another person standing behind him. Kris recognized the young man who had grabbed her at the graveyard. "I specifically ordered for her not to be harmed."

"That was Xan," the young man said. Kris racked her brain, trying to remember his name. She thought they had called him Shay.

"Where is he?" the man in the doorway shouted. His voice boomed in the small space, echoing off the rock walls of the rounded room. Kris flinched and shuffled away.

"He hung back," Shay explained. "He has her friend back at the graveyard. He said he could get some information about Kye."

Even in the dark, Kris could see the grimace on the man's face.

"I'll deal with your incompetence later." The man stepped into the room, the ball of light bobbing along behind him. Once cleared of the door, he slammed it shut.

Although her heart was racing, Kris slowly got to her feet. He killed her parents. Now only a few feet away, she stared deep into his dark eyes.

"Tynan, I presume. That's a stupid name," she said. Though her hands shook, she stood her ground and held her chin high.

He grinned. "Oh good. You've got spunk. Just like your mother."

Kris's jaw tightened, and she balled her fists at her sides. "Don't you dare talk about my mother."

Violence isn't the answer. Violence isn't the answer, she kept reminding herself.

Tynan took a step forward. "I'm trying to find Kurt."

"Kurt?"

"I know you had an encounter with him the other day, and I know he has been hiding you since. If you help me find him, I will let you go."

"You're after Kurt?" Kris asked again, clutching her arm. "Why?"

He smirked as he held his hands behind his back. "He didn't tell you?"

"He told me you're a murderer," she blurted, and backed away. She slipped a hand into her back pocket. "He told me you killed my parents."

Tynan turned to the side and touched the ball of light with his finger. It nearly doubled in size, casting a long shadow behind him. His dark eyes were illuminated now. "All your parents had to do was give me Kurt. They put his life before their own. Before yours. Are you willing to die for him too?"

Her heart plummeted deep into her stomach, and she felt sick. Kurt was the reason her parents were dead? They died protecting him? Shivers ran down her spine. That was why Kurt hadn't wanted her to leave. Why he had been so distant. He knew Tynan was trying to find *him*.

Kris stared down at her dirty sneakers, shaking her head gently. She kept coming back to the night on the porch. The serene, genuine moment. Kurt hadn't wanted her to stand between him and Tynan. He'd been trying to protect her.

"Is he really worth any of this trouble?" Tynan pressed on.

Kris wrapped her fingers around the knife in her back pocket. Her mind raced, but suddenly every scowl, every sarcastic remark, every condescending comment from Kurt was gone. If her parents had stood right here, brave and ready, then she wasn't going to budge either.

"Or what about your friend back in the graveyard? Is his life worth more to you than Kurt's?"

Kris shot him a glare and squared her shoulders. "Don't you hurt him," she hissed through clenched teeth.

Tynan turned his back, but she could still feel his grin enveloping the room. "I could spare him, depending on your cooperation."

Kris flicked open her pocketknife and charged at Tynan. She let out a guttural cry, stabbing the knife through the air towards his back with all the strength she had. But only inches away, her body froze mid-swing.

What was happening?

She tried to force her arm forward and push with all her might to drive the knife into Tynan's back, but she couldn't move. He chuckled, and Kris was dropped onto her side on the floor. She scrambled to get a hold of her pocketknife as it skidded away. Getting to her feet, she again jumped at Tynan, who effortlessly stepped out of the way. With as little as a wave of his hand, Kris was thrown backwards onto the floor once more.

"Your cute little knife won't help you here." He peered down at her as she clutched her shoulder in pain.

Kris got to her knees, squeezing the knife handle until her knuckles turned white. She glared up at him. "You don't scare me."

With a wicked half smile, Tynan sauntered over to the door and gently knocked. "Send in Red."

The door opened, and the red-eyed man from the graveyard came in.

"Our guest needs a little motivation," Tynan said.

Red nodded and Tynan left, pulling the door shut behind him.

Kris held out her knife. "Don't touch me."

He grabbed her forearm, and she was immediately immobilized by the fire, the sting, the pain that followed. All of it collected where his hand met her skin, and it spread through her entire body, radiating through her muscles, vibrating her bones.

She cried out and dropped the knife almost instantly. Kris fell to her knees as her eyes began to burn. Her pulse raced, her heart spasming uncontrollably with an irregular rhythm. She screamed, but no sound came out. Every last drop of her strength felt like it was being absorbed.

Red may have only held her arm for a few seconds, but it felt as though hours had passed by the time he released her. Kris collapsed on the ground, breathing hard and fast. Her arm was bright red and still burning, while her fingers tingled with pins and needles. She watched helplessly as Red bent down and scooped up the blade.

"No. No, please." Kris attempted to sit up, but her arms felt like rubber. "It was my father's. Please."

Red carried it over to the door and knocked. When Tynan returned, Red handed the knife to him. "Could use this as her trinket, if you're interested."

Tynan held it up, examining it in the light.

Kris coughed and managed to prop herself up on one elbow as she fought to regain her strength.

Tynan watched her struggle with an amused expression, then crouched in front of her. "I admire your tenacity. I see a lot of Sofia in you."

"Don't you *dare* speak her name," Kris growled between coughs and pants. She looked up at him and was met with her own knife held against her throat. Her breath escaped her lungs.

"I see a lot of Kurt too," he whispered. "I can see why he would take a shine to you."

She swallowed hard, holding up her hands and staring down the knife. "Just go ahead and do it, because I'm not telling you anything."

A flicker of anger flashed across Tynan's face. It wasn't the look that scared her. It was how quickly it had come and gone.

He stood again. "Send in Flint," he called to the door.

"Bring it on," Kris said, putting a hand on the wall to slowly stand.

She recognized him immediately. Flint was the Witcan man who had jumped her and Kurt the day she ran away. And as he stepped into the light, she noticed the deep purple ring that circled his eye where Kurt had kicked him.

The door wasn't even closed when Flint rushed her, slamming his glowing indigo fist across Kris's already bruised cheek. The blow knocked her down with more force than a typical punch, but he still hit her again. And again.

Everything faded in and out as she looked up at Flint, head throbbing. Her mouth tasted like blood, so she spat a mouthful at him. "What else you got?"

Flint grabbed her by her ponytail, jerked her up to her feet, and threw her back down on the ground. Kris shrieked, unable to catch herself, and she crashed down on her collarbone. She felt it all the way down to her finger as she lay there panting.

Come on, get up, get up, she kept telling herself.

The ringing in her head slowly transformed into the plucking of guitar strings. A beautiful, soothing melody filled her mind as she remembered the night on the porch when Kurt had played for her. Something about those chords and the effortless way his fingers glided over the strings resonated with Kris. Just as it had then, her heart warmed.

The pain in her shoulder slowly dissipated, then the sting in her cheek, and finally the vibrating in her skull.

"Yeah, bet you assholes can't do that," Kris said as she sat up and glared at Flint.

But he was staring at her with a bewildered expression, blinking for a few seconds before looking back at Tynan.

Tynan stepped forward; his jaw hung open. "I don't believe it." He and Flint exchanged glances.

"Believe it," Flint insisted, holding out a hand towards Kris. "She's Annona."

Kris balled her fists and held them up in front of her. "What's Annona?"

"Kye led us to her," Flint whispered to Tynan. "*This* is how we find Calosant."

This is stupid, Kris thought, but lunged forward anyway in an effort to snatch the knife from Tynan's hand. Tynan caught her by the throat, stopping her in her tracks. He constricted his grip, which lifted Kris into the air. She gagged, wheezing, as she clutched his wrist with both hands to try to free herself.

Their eyes locked. His dark brown irises zeroed in on hers, unmoving as he burrowed into her soul.

I can't breathe.

Kris swatted at Tynan's arm and kicked her legs frantically, but he held on tight.

"Sir," Flint said quietly, watching her face.

Tynan said nothing, just continued to glare as he tightened his grasp.

"Tynan." Flint's warning came louder this time.

With a grunt and his hand still locked around her neck, Tynan swung Kris down on her back, pinning her against the floor. Everything ached, but she continued to squirm in her attempts to pull herself free of his grasp.

"Don't ever test me again," he growled, then finally released her.

Kris gasped, taking in such a huge gulp of air that her back arched off the floor. She coughed and wheezed while clutching her chest and wiggling around on the ground.

Tynan turned toward the door. "Clear out," he said to Flint.

Kris didn't even hear the door open and close, but through the blurs she watched the ball of light dissolve, leaving her in darkness once again. She dragged herself over to the wall, wrapped her arms around her legs, and hugged her knees.

Kurt . . . My mom and dad died for you. To protect you. She shook her head with such force that she knocked her forehead against her kneecap, and her body trembled against the cold stone wall. She didn't know why Tynan was looking for him, but she wouldn't let her parents' sacrifice be in vain. Even if it meant . . .

Kris chuckled to herself and sniffled, fighting the pain in her throat that was itching to become tears. The last thing she wanted to do was to die here. Alone.

Be brave, Kris kept telling herself as her hands continued to shake. *You're going to make it out of this place. Kurt won't let you die here . . . right?*

Chapter 12

The Bunker

Kurt and Larsen climbed out of the car.

"This is a terrible idea," Kurt heard Cade mutter as he stepped off his motorcycle and hurried over to them.

The three stood on the side of the road and stared down the hill into the thick brush of the forest.

"How do you even know she's here?" Larsen asked.

Kurt jutted his chin forward. "Tynan's bunker is just down there."

"He'll be expecting you."

He nodded slowly and kept his eyes focused on the trees as he took a few cautious steps down the slope. "I need you guys to hang back. I'm going in alone."

"What? He's going to kill you," Cade said, and started after him.

Kurt held up a hand, stopping him in his tracks. "No, he needs me alive, but he might not show restraint with you. That's why I need you to stay here."

"Kurt," Larsen said.

Glancing over his shoulder, Kurt could see that Larsen's hands were shaking. Kurt held his breath for a second before letting it out again, trying to slow his own heart rate. "If things go sideways . . . if I don't make it out . . . get Kristen out of there. At any cost." He exchanged a look with Larsen before continuing down the hill.

Kurt pushed through the underbrush and entered the woods, shaking his head at this whole situation. He ducked under a low branch and scanned the area. He was getting close, could feel Kris's presence getting stronger, could sense her pain and anguish.

Be brave. You're going to make it out of this place. Kurt won't let you die here . . . right? He heard Kris's voice in his mind.

I won't let Tynan hurt you, Kurt thought. He vaulted over a fallen tree, his pace quickening as he recognized the tree stump in front of him. The entrance was around here somewhere.

He kicked around dirt and pine needles, searching the ground. An oval-shaped stone about six feet across protruded out of the earth. He crouched down to open the hatch, and his heart sank as he felt a familiar presence draw near.

A shadow cast over him. "Well, well. Fancy seeing you again." A woman's voice, calm and menacing.

Kurt slowly raised his hands, fighting to keep them from shaking.

"Stand up. Turn around."

His breaths were short and fast, but he kept himself collected as he stood and turned to face the young woman. Her fists glowed red.

"You've got balls just waltzing in here, especially after attacking Flint and me the other day." She cracked a wicked smile.

"I'm just here for Kristen," Kurt whispered, meeting her dark eyes. "No one needs to get hurt, Night."

Her face softened. She nodded and looked off to the side before turning her attention back to Kurt, with lips curled up in a snarl. "That's where you're wrong."

She delivered a punch to Kurt's face, throwing him down to his knees. A wipe of his chin revealed that the blow had opened a cut on his bottom lip. His head was ringing as he clambered to his feet again.

Night kept her fists up and nodded towards the stone. "Open it."

Kurt planted both hands on top of the large slate, which vibrated under his fingertips. The stone slid back, revealing a staircase down into the earth.

"Go." She grabbed his shoulder and forced him onto the steps.

Raising his hands again, he descended the stairs into the darkness. He could hear Kris sobbing now as he entered the bunker. Tynan better not have hurt her.

A kick to his back propelled him forward down the steps. Kurt tried to catch himself, but his wrist gave out and he crashed onto the floor, a fit of laughter behind him. His head bounced off the rock and his vision went black for a moment. Before he could stand on his own, two sets of hands heaved him to his feet.

"Tynan has been expecting you."

Kurt's vision was still cloudy, but he could see light spheres appear around him as he was guided down the dim corridor to the left. He struggled to raise one foot after another, but his captors seemed content dragging him along.

Kris's broken breaths and puffs of pain grew louder, and when the door at the end of the tunnel opened, Kurt could see why. Tynan was holding Kris in front of himself like a shield. He twisted one of her arms behind her, hyperextending her shoulder. With his other hand, Tynan held Kris's pocketknife up against her throat so close that a small line of blood tarnished the blade.

Her green eyes were turned up to the ceiling, her lips pressed shut as she clearly tried to control her breathing and keep her neck extended as long as possible to avoid the knife.

Kurt's mind cleared at the sobering sight. "Let her go." He tried to pull free, and a kick in the back of the leg forced him to his knees.

"I must say, I'm impressed," Tynan said with a grin. "You were not easy to find." He loosened the knife against Kris's throat. "I had to get creative."

Kris immediately took a deep breath in. "You murderous piece of—"

Tynan twisted her arm. "Shh. The grown-ups are talking."

Kurt locked eyes with Kris, and he shook his head, jaw clenched. "You got what you wanted, okay?" He glared up at Tynan. "I'm here. You got me, now just let her go."

Tynan hesitated but released Kris's arm, flinging her to the floor as he did so. She cried out as she crashed into the ground.

"Truthfully, I *was* going to let her go," Tynan said as he slithered closer to Kurt. He smacked Kurt's cheek several times, then pointed the pocketknife toward Kris's balled-up form on the floor. "But then I realized you found Annona."

Kurt licked the cut on his lip, rolling his head up to meet Tynan's eye. "You can't keep us here." He pulled against the two people holding him again and let out a roar as he failed to break free.

"Well, the good news is I don't need you anymore."

Tynan wandered back to Kris and dug his foot into her side, then pushed her over on the floor. Like a cat playing with its next meal. "Tell me, Kye." He stepped on Kris's injured shoulder and slowly shifted his weight onto it. Her scream became louder as he leaned into it.

"Stop it," Kurt shouted, watching Kris's face twist in agony.

"Tell me why this girl matters so much, but you let her parents suffer such a grueling, excruciating death."

Kurt coughed when his breath caught in his throat.

Tynan leaned back for a minute, taking his weight off Kris to leer at him. He held the knife out in Kris's direction. "You let Sofia die. And she was *so* important to you, wasn't she?"

Kurt screamed, jumping to his feet, and he managed to throw the guards back this time. He charged Tynan, clapped his hands together, and formed a large flickering ball of fire once he pulled them apart. He lobbed it in Tynan's direction, who side-stepped and easily avoided it. Fists now glowing a pale green, Kurt took a couple of swings at Tynan, who was always one step ahead in his dodges and deflections.

"Must we really go through this again?" Tynan said. He thrust an open palm into Kurt's gut and sent him onto his back.

"You are not allowed to talk about Sofia," Kurt said through clenched teeth as he shot to his feet.

Before he could rush Tynan again, Red grabbed a hold of Kurt's arms and pinned them behind his back. Kurt squirmed, but his fight was diminishing rapidly as he fell to his knees.

~

Still holding her shoulder, Kris rolled away. She watched Kurt, terrified, remembering how much pain she'd felt when Red had touched her skin. She had to help him.

Tynan stood over Kurt with her blade, and he made sure Kris was watching before jabbing the knife into Kurt's side.

"No!" she yelled. Without a thought, she extended her arm.

Time seemed to almost halt.

Her open hand began to glow, and it erupted in a flash as a white beam of light fired from her palm at Tynan. Kris and Tynan both had the same wide-eyed shock as the shining ray stretched across the room. Just before it struck him, he raised his arm, and a translucent blue wall appeared in front of him. The beam reflected off the shield into the stone wall, but the force of it pushed him back so that he skidded on his heels and barely retained his balance.

Kris turned her glowing hand towards Red, the beam following the movement. He dropped Kurt and ducked away before she hit him.

The beam flickered out as she gasped, and she stood there bewildered. How had she done that?

"Kris!"

Larsen appeared in front of her. He reached out a hand and grabbed her wrist, then turned his attention to Kurt. The shapeshifting woman who had previously attacked Kris and Kurt ran at him, rearing back her red-glowing fist, but she was thrown to the ground as Cade sprinted into the room.

"Get Kurt and Kris out of here," Cade told Larsen.

Red lunged at Larsen. Kris raised her hand, trying to summon the light again. Nothing happened. Larsen spun his hand through the air and formed a small turquoise ball in his palm, which he threw at Red. The ball burst when it came in contact with his knees, spilling a gel-like liquid down his shins and over his feet before solidifying into a thick layer of ice that rooted Red in place.

Larsen pulled Kris along as he dashed over to Kurt. Kurt was on his knees, both hands pressed into the gash in his side. Blood pooled underneath him, and his face was sickly pale. He was losing too much blood.

Kris clasped her free hand over the wound. "Kurt, I'm so sorry," she said through sobs.

In the background, she could hear Larsen calling for Cade. When she looked up, Tynan was rushing them, a wild look flashing in his eyes. Kris pulled against Larsen's grip and tried to move in front of Kurt to shield him, but the bunker blurred, causing Tynan and the others to disappear.

Kris blinked, confused, as she was suddenly staring out into dark woods.

"Let's get Kurt in the car. Now."

Larsen and Cade hoisted Kurt from the roadside grass and led him to the car. The back door swung open on its own. Kris stumbled as she got to her feet, knees trembling, and followed. Cade laid Kurt down in the back of the car, where his blood smeared across the seats.

"Wait." Kris grabbed the car door before Cade could swing it shut. Without a word, she slid into the backseat alongside Kurt.

Larsen stumbled around the car to the driver's side, and Cade ran back to his motorcycle. Kris slammed the car door shut, then turned her attention to Kurt. Her heart raced as she carefully moved his hands and lifted his shirt to reveal the inch-wide laceration in his abdomen. Scarlet blood oozed out at an alarming rate.

Larsen turned so harshly onto the road that it threw Kris back into the window and slammed her head into the headrest. But she hardly noticed. She pulled herself closer to Kurt again and pressed her hands against the wound, ignoring the hot blood that seeped between her fingers.

"Kurt, stay with me," she kept saying. Her nerves were shot, and her entire body trembled.

"Just breathe," Larsen reminded her.

One long, deep breath in. One long, deep breath out.

I can do this. I have to do this.

Kurt's breaths were shallow and labored. He managed to open his eyes a sliver, peering up at Kris with blue-gray eyes.

Her pulse raced, but the warm sensation wasn't there.

Breathe in. Breathe out.

Kurt reached out and touched Kris's hand, making her jump. He gave her a small nod of encouragement, and her chest immediately burned as the heat trickled down her arms to her hands. As she held Kurt's weak gaze, she could feel the warm blood seep back through her fingers. The gash in his side gradually started to close itself up.

Kris's head weighed heavy. Every muscle in her body felt strained, pushing every last ounce of strength she had. Her hands began to burn, and a slow pain crept up each finger and crawled up her wrists. Her head was pounding, and Kris ached to let go, but she held on until she could feel that the wound had healed entirely.

With a heavy gasp, she collapsed back in the seat and let her head drop into the headrest. She panted as she waited for the pain to dissipate.

"Are you okay? Is Kurt all right?" Larsen looked over his shoulder at them, jerking the whole car to the side as he did so.

"Just watch the road," Kris cried out as she grabbed the passenger seat in front of her. She clasped her chest with a sigh. "He's fine. He's going to be fine."

Kurt, eyes unfocused and on the cusp of unconsciousness, twisted his head and looked up at her. He offered her a faint smile, which almost immediately vanished. "You should have listened to me."

His eyes fluttered shut, and Kris shifted to the edge of the seat, pressing her body against the window.

She closed her eyes and hugged herself. "I'm sorry," she whispered.

The car was silent the rest of the drive back to the cabin.

Chapter 13

Annona

Kris's cell phone was ringing with an incoming video call. In a daze, she reached over and fumbled around the nightstand to answer it.

Brie gave an enthusiastic wave. "Good morning, sunshine."

Kris dropped her head back into the pillow and rubbed her eyes. "Hey," she said, then yawned.

"I'm so glad you answered. I was worried you were ignoring me."

"No, not ignoring you. Just . . ."

"Where even are you? I can't believe you're still in bed. Are you okay?"

Kris pressed her eyes shut as she tried to process the rapid-fire sentences. "I can't tell you where I am."

"Your grandparents have stopped calling around. They assume you aren't coming back."

"I'm not," Kris said, and sat up abruptly. The fresh memory of being jumped at the cemetery the day before really bolstered the idea. "I'm never going back there."

Brie shook her head and offered a forced smile. "I don't understand you sometimes, Kris, but I trust you. And I'm glad that you're okay. Like, wherever you are."

"I miss you."

"I miss you too." Brie pretended to hug her phone. "Am I going to see you next week?"

Kris's eyes widened. "Your birthday. Oh my God, Brie, I forgot."

She waved a hand off to the side. "Oh no, don't even worry about it. I mean, after everything that's happened, I'm not even, like, having a party or anything. But I was hoping I could at least see my best friend. What do you say?"

Kris dropped the phone as her hands began to shake, sending it clattering on the wood floor. She quickly scooped it up again. "I . . . I don't know, Brie. I don't think I can show my face over there."

Before Brie could protest, a shrill voice echoed on her side of the camera. "Briella! Where did you get that phone? You are grounded from all electronics!" Brie gasped just as the call was disconnected.

Kris sat there, mouth hanging open. *Oh jeez, what did she do this time?*

Dazed, she got up to get dressed, and she recalled the previous night's events. She shouldn't have gone to the cemetery. Tynan's men would have killed Larsen if he hadn't escaped. They would have killed Kurt too.

Because she wouldn't listen.

Kris picked up the silver locket from the dresser and hooked it behind her neck. She kept remembering the look Kurt had given her in the car. Encouraging and supportive, but also terrified and disappointed.

She knew she should go talk to him. To apologize.

Kris put her cell phone in her pocket and rummaged through her things in search of her pocketknife. A sharp pain enveloped her chest when she realized it was still in Tynan's possession.

There was no getting it back now. She couldn't return to that place.

She walked out of the room to a quiet house. Cade was doing sit-ups in the living room, but she saw no sign of the others.

"Kurt and Larsen still asleep?" she asked, opening the front door. She gazed through the screen at the beams of sunlight piercing the cloudy sky.

Cade slapped his hands back, propping himself up on the floor while he caught his breath. "Yeah, but I'm not surprised after they both went toe-to-toe with that red-eyed guy."

Kris brushed her fingers over her arm. She swore it started to burn at just the thought of Red's grasp. "It felt like I was going to die when he grabbed me."

Cade stood up and wiped sweat from his brow. "Apparently he can absorb your life force, your energy, through skin-to-skin contact. I've never seen anything like it."

Kris crossed her arms and leaned against the doorframe, lost in thought.

"How about you? You okay?"

She scoffed and rolled her eyes. "That's a little arbitrary given the state of things."

"Yeah, I guess it is." Cade took a long drink from his water bottle before tossing it over his shoulder onto the couch. "You seem like you're handling things pretty well, though."

Kris chewed her bottom lip. Her eyes fixed on the porch swing as it lightly swayed in the breeze. "I almost got Larsen and Kurt killed . . ."

"Look, don't worry about those guys," Cade said, waving a hand toward their closed bedroom doors. "They went in knowing the risks."

"But they were only in harm's way because of *me*. Because of a stupid decision that *I* made." She sighed and bowed her head.

"If it makes you feel better, Kurt isn't angry with you. The nerd's the one who should have known better."

"Larsen," Kris corrected.

Cade laughed. "What? You got a little thing for him?"

Kris scowled at him. "He's my friend. And I thought he was *your* friend too."

Cade groaned and leaned back on his elbows. "More like a parasite. But he's freaking *Jesus* in Kurt's eyes. Can do no wrong. Well, until yesterday."

"Oh, like you're so virtuous," Kris mumbled, looking him up and down. "Claiming sobriety with beer on your breath."

Cade raised his hands in front of him. "Whoa, no, I'm far from flawless. But I own my mistakes. I don't redact large chunks of my past, or enable my friend's self-destructive behavior while lying about my own unhappiness." He flicked his gaze down the hall, then crossed to the dining room. "I've faced my demons. And I've survived."

Kris eyed the tattoos covering his arm as he dug into the pocket of his leather jacket, which was hanging on a chair. He removed a cigarette with his lips and put the pack back in his jacket.

"You can judge, but at least I'm honest." Cade gently pinched Kris's chin with his thumb and forefinger, offering her a wink as he passed her and stepped outside.

She stared down the hall for a moment longer before following him to the porch. "Hey, can I ask you something?"

Cade breathed out a large puff of smoke. "Is this it? Are you coming on to me?"

"What? No."

"Because I have some serious qualms with my friend's girlfriends hitting on me," he said, cracking a grin.

"Not his girlfriend," Kris grumbled as she waved the smell of smoke away. "Also, definitely *not* what's going on here."

"I'm just messing with you. So serious."

"What's Annona?"

Cade shook his head. "Uh-uh. Nope." He slunk away and gave a nervous chuckle. "I am not the one to ask."

"They called me Annona. Twice. I just want to know what it means."

"I really think that's a question better suited for Kurt," he insisted, backing himself into the corner of the porch.

Before Kris could pry more, Kurt pushed open the screen door.

"Hey, Kristen, why don't we talk," he said quietly, offering Cade a nod.

"Oh, thank God," Cade whispered.

Kurt waved for her to follow him as he started down the steps. "Walk with me."

Kris nodded and trailed behind him.

They walked side by side through the tall grass, a couple feet of space between them. He opened his mouth, but Kris spoke first. "How are you feeling?"

Hands stuffed in his pockets, Kurt shrugged. "I've had better mornings. Had worse, too."

"I'm so sorry. I should have listened to you. I almost got you killed—"

"I'm fine. Don't worry about me." He rubbed the nape of his neck and kept his head down as they walked. His eyes looked tired. "I get why you went. I just . . . You shouldn't have had to endure any of that."

Kris wrapped her arms around herself and stared down at the grass. "Did you know? That Tynan went after my parents trying to find you?"

"I had suspicions."

A gust of wind blew by and rustled her hair. She tried to collect it as it fell across her face, but a small strand tangled around her necklace.

"Oh shoot." Kris craned her neck, trying to free her hair from the chain.

"Here." Kurt inched closer and fidgeted with the silver necklace.

Kris's heart raced every time his fingers brushed her skin. Heat rushed to her cheeks, and all she could do was quietly stare.

"There," he whispered, finally freeing the necklace from her hair. He ran his fingertips over the locket against her chest, a look of recognition in his eyes. He then stepped away again, clearing his throat loudly.

He took a few more strides forward and Kris followed, tucking her hair behind her ear and glancing away.

"I should have told you sooner, but I didn't know how to bring it up," Kurt said as he scuffed his feet over the dirt.

Kris said nothing and waited for him to continue, one arm wrapped around her waist and her shoulders hunched forward.

"A long time ago, there was an ancient city—a sanctuary—for all Witcans called Calosant," Kurt explained, his eyes cast down. "It was protected by a woman, often regarded as a goddess. She was incredibly powerful, and also the only one in history with the ability to heal others, not just themselves." Kurt lifted his gaze just enough to study Kris's face. "Until you. You are the only other Witcan who has *ever* possessed powers of rejuvenation that extend to others."

Kris grabbed a chunk of her hair and nervously twisted it around her fingers. "Oh. Wow."

"Her name was Annona. She disappeared. Presumed dead. Without Annona to keep Calosant safe from invading humans, the city was eventually abandoned and sealed away, but many prophesied that Annona would be reborn. Like a Second Coming kind of thing."

He offered Kris an awkward smile. A gust rattled the tall grass, but they remained quiet.

"You think *I'm* Annona?" she said, pointing to herself with eyebrows raised.

Kurt nodded slowly, but his brow furrowed in a look of both sympathy and fear. "At least, part of you is."

"You realize how weird that sounds, right?"

He stifled a laugh. "Yeah. I'm well aware."

"I'm a nobody. How can I be some reincarnated Witcan ruler?"

"*Protector.* Annona was a *protector.* And I wished it weren't true, but there's no denying it after you conjured a white beam last night."

Kris clutched her arms around herself to keep her hands from shaking. Her entire body trembled as she forced a smile.

Kurt held out a hand, palm up, and it began to glow with a pale green light. "Your inner light is a reflection of your soul. Your truest self. And in all of Calosant's stories passed down over generations, Annona's inner light was always white."

She shook her head. "Okay, let's assume it *is* true and I *am* Annona. What does that mean?"

Another gust blew by, pushing the clouds across the sky so a ray of sunlight could reach the earth below.

"It has been prophesied that Annona would return and reopen Calosant. Inherit her Mina Ring once again to deliver all Witcans from a world of fear and prejudice."

Kris stopped in her tracks and blinked wide. She nearly laughed. "Wait, what? What does *that* even mean?"

Kurt motioned with his head for her to continue walking. Though shaking, she obliged.

"The Mina Ring was Annona's ring, a gift forged for her by the Elders of Calosant. Legend has it, the ring amplified her magic. Made her stronger. Enhanced her reach. It allowed her to feel Witcans the world over."

Kris paused for a moment. The vision she'd had when Kurt first brought her here, when she saw that poor woman get beaten and killed. The men had mentioned a ring. One of the men had ripped a ring off the woman's finger and called her "goddess."

Had she seen Annona? Had that been her death?

Kris nibbled on her thumbnail as she played the images over in her head again.

"Some believed Annona would end the war with humans. Others believed it meant removing humans from the picture all together."

She hadn't even noticed Kurt was still talking, and she jerked her head up in surprise.

They were at the border between the meadow and the woods. The clouds had rolled in again and the wind was picking up. The breeze sent a chill down Kris's spin.

She stopped and stared into the woods. A small bird gripped the bark of a tree trunk and pecked the wood before bouncing to a new spot. When it noticed Kris watching, it cocked its head, blinked, and fluttered off.

Why had those men killed Annona? What could she have done to deserve such a violent death?

"You're quiet." Kurt looked back at her, eyeing her suspiciously. "Kristen?"

"I'm fine," she insisted. She shivered as the wind whirled around them, and hugged her arms tight. "It's just . . . why me?"

"I don't know."

Panic rose in her chest. "What does Tynan want with me? I don't know anything." Kris cleared her throat and turned away.

"You would be able to harness the Mina Ring's full power."

"To eradicate all humans?" she asked, voice weary.

Kurt spun around to face her, and she jumped back. "Look, I'm sorry," he said.

She blinked. "For what?"

His eyes darted all around, as if unable to focus on Kris. "I know I'm a little . . . rough around the edges. Cade has made that abundantly clear." His chest heaved with a deep breath. Only then did she notice he was trembling too. "I didn't want to get you involved. With Tynan, or this Annona prophecy. But isolating you here was unrealistic, and not providing you with some basic self-defense training was irresponsible."

Kris shrugged, opening and closing her mouth as she struggled to find a response.

"I just wanted you to know. And, I, uh . . ." Kurt sighed. "I wanted to take you up on your request for training. You know, if you are still interested."

She couldn't contain her smile. "Really?"

He bobbed his head with brow furrowed. "For self-defense *only*."

Kris held her hands together behind her back, blushing with a restrained grin. "Yeah, okay."

"Okay?"

"Yeah. Let's do it."

Chapter 14

Lesson One

"Lesson one: telepathy."

Kris sat in the grass facing Kurt, bouncing in anticipation. "You want me to read your mind?" she asked, suppressing a laugh.

He rubbed the back of his neck and pulled a face. "I mean, no, but it will have to do."

"So, teach, what do I do?" She tucked her hair behind her ear, then fiddled with her necklace.

"I'm going to think of a question. I want you to read my mind to hear the question, and then respond telepathically."

"Oh sure, that sounds easy."

"Just give it a shot." Kurt's shoulders relaxed, but he gave her a suspicious look. "Please don't be intrusive, okay? Just the question."

Kris nodded and Kurt closed his eyes, sitting up tall.

Okay, read his mind. Can't be that hard, right? I've done it before . . . by accident.

She squinted and studied Kurt's face: the strain in his jaw, the slight curl of his lip, the way his eyelids twitched when his eyes shifted.

What are you thinking?

The wind rustled the grass around them, but he remained unmoving. Kris jutted her chin forward, concentrating hard.

Kurt opened one eye, and a crooked smile lit up his face. He tapped a finger against his temple. "If you're struggling to focus your telepathy, then direct contact may help."

"Are you sure?"

He lifted Kris's hands by the wrists and held her fingers against his forehead.

"Okay . . ." Kris said. Why was her heart racing so fast? She felt shaky, but took a deep breath in. She closed her eyes, letting the connection of her fingertips to either side of Kurt's head speak to her.

Behind her closed eyes, she saw only darkness, until some sort of mist began to move in and cloud the vast emptiness. Was she inside Kurt's mind?

The world outside fell quiet. Kris couldn't even hear the wind. She pressed forward, the mist twisting around her. An echo, barely audible at first, reverberated in the air, and it became clearer the farther forward she moved through the darkness.

Just ahead stood a wall that wavered like fluid but was rigid like glass and shimmered like diamonds. Light refracted off it, despite no discernible light source.

Kris extended a hand to graze the mysterious barrier and was surprised to find it warm to the touch. Once she made contact with it, the echo sounded again, this time clear as day: *What's your favorite color?*

Kurt's voice. It wasn't resonating in her ears, but instead Kris could feel it in her mind. Like it was her own thought.

She gasped and opened her eyes. *I did it!*

Kurt's eyes were still closed, but a smile lit up his face. Kris moved her hands away, before remembering she had to respond. She bit her lip, the answer tickling her tongue.

She lightly rested her fingers on Kurt's temples again and closed her eyes. Her breath caught at finding herself already at the translucent wall. The mist seemed to be spinning away from her.

A hardwood floor materialized on the other side of the refracting barrier. Kris put a hand on the wall again, just as she had before. She leaned close to it, her lips only inches away, and whispered. *Maroon.*

The palm of a hand appeared on the other side of the shimmering, shifting wall. She stifled a cry and jumped back.

Why maroon? Kurt's voice echoed through the barrier.

Kris steadied herself and smiled. Her eyes followed the wall, but it extended out in all directions as far as she could see. She bounced closer, returning her hand to its surface again.

When I was younger, I was on a summer soccer team, and our jerseys were maroon. Her words echoed around her as a form slowly appeared behind the palm on the other side. *I wore that jersey all the time. We sucked, no one would ever show up for practice, but we had a lot of fun. That's how I met Ian.*

Kurt's figure was blurry but now recognizable on the other side. *Who's Ian?* he asked.

She stepped back and removed her hand from the barrier.

Her eyes snapped open, and she was sitting in the meadow again. She dropped her hands into her lap, looking away as Kurt opened his eyes.

"Why'd you stop?" he asked quietly.

Kris twisted her hands together and bit her lip. "I didn't mean to tell you that. About Ian. The thought just popped into my head; I didn't know you would hear it."

Kurt bowed his head with a grin. "You don't have to be embarrassed."

She hunched forward and buried her face in her hands.

"You don't have to talk about it if you don't want to."

"Ian is . . . He's my ex," Kris grumbled through her hands. Her face burned. "We were friends for a long time, then we dated for almost two years. He, uh . . . He dumped me about a month ago."

"Oh."

Kris peeked through her fingers. Kurt's spine straightened and his smile vanished.

"Yeah," she muttered, allowing her hands to slide down her face and fall into her lap again.

"That's . . . I'm sorry."

Kris forced a laugh. "Well, now it's your turn. I told you something super personal, so now it's your turn to share."

His face flushed, and he shook his head. "I don't think that's a very good idea."

"Come on. I'll practice telepathy."

Despite the apprehension on his face, he closed his eyes.

Keeping her hands in her lap, Kris did the same. She was surrounded by darkness again, but she hurried forward through the mist and searched for the crystal barrier. As she ran, a wall suddenly rose just before her and she skidded to a halt.

Behind it, a blurry world formed, starting with Kurt's hand against the shimmering divide. Though the image beyond was fuzzy, it looked like the living room of the cabin.

Kris put her hand against the barrier as well.

What do you want to know? Kurt asked.

She chuckled nervously to herself as she shuffled her feet. *Did you have a first love?*

Through the crackling barrier, she could make out Kurt's bowed head. He was quiet for a long moment. *Yes.*

Kris bit her lip, itching to pry. *Tell me about it.*

Kurt stepped back for a moment and circled his side of the barrier before returning. *Not much to tell. I fell hard and fast. She wanted more than I could offer her, so I didn't stop her when she wanted to leave.*

Kris rested her second hand on the barrier. *Do you regret it? Letting her leave?*

He disappeared behind the wall again, back turned to her. The divide became denser, making it harder to make out his figure on the other side. She waited for a response, but it never came.

Out of the darkness behind her came a breeze that tickled the nape of her neck, and she turned. Not too far ahead stood another foggy, shimmering wall, only this one was flickering.

A distant scream made her heart stop.

Kris took a few steps towards the barrier. The closer she came to it, the louder the sounds grew, a buzzing cloud of multiple distorted voices and cries.

Kristen, stop! Kurt's voice echoed from somewhere else, freezing her in her tracks.

She stared at the flashing wall in front of her and couldn't make out what was on the other side, but the muffled cries and voices continued.

She opened her eyes. Kurt was hunched forward, face hidden.

"What was that?" Kris asked, moving her hair from her eyes. "I heard screaming."

"Nothing," he mumbled as he stood. He held out his hand to her. "We should take a break. Get some lunch."

She remained rooted in place, nibbling her bottom lip, unable to get the screams out of her head. All the noise behind that barrier in Kurt's mind made her blood run cold.

What was on the other side? Were those memories?

What was Kurt hiding?

Chapter 15

No More Running

"So, do you want to explain what happened yesterday, or do I need to pry?" Larsen said over the noise of the television. He adjusted his shirt and smoothed out the wrinkles as he entered the living room.

Cade and Kurt sat on opposite couches and looked up as Larsen turned down the volume of the nightly news.

"What do you mean?" Kurt asked, rubbing his eyes.

Larsen remained standing with his hands in his pockets. "Why was Tynan hunting you? How did you know the location of his bunker?"

"Oh." Kurt kept his face hidden when he finally spoke. "I crossed Tynan's path some years back. He believed I was the 'first key' to finding Calosant. Said I would be the one to lead him there."

"You know the location of Calosant?" Cade asked, leaning closer.

Kurt shook his head.

"Then why would he think that?"

"More importantly, why does he want to get into Calosant?" Larsen said.

"I think we all know why," Cade muttered, nodding to the television screen.

The three stopped and stared.

"Thirty-three confirmed dead and more injured in a terrorist attack at the Des Moines National Witcan Detention Agency facility tonight," the anchorwoman said while images of a dilapidated building and injured agents flashed in the background. "Eyewitnesses say the raid was led by a group of Witcan extremists who broke into the compound, freed detained Witcans, and collapsed the building, trapping many NWDA agents inside . . ."

Larsen crossed his arms and dropped his gaze. "How much does Tynan know?"

"As far as I know, he has no leads." Kurt leaned back into the couch, staring up at the ceiling. "All that's known is that there are five keys. Five clues left by Calosant's Elders that will guide him to its location and allow him to reopen the gates. He will comb the earth looking for those keys. For Calosant. And now that he knows Kris is Annona, he will never stop looking for her either."

"If the Mina Ring does in fact enhance a Witcan's magic and reach, and Tynan finds it . . ." Larsen motioned to the death count on the TV. "We're talking about genocide on a global scale. It will be this, but everywhere."

"Is that such a bad thing? Eliminating the NWDA?" Cade said with a shrug, despite the wavering doubt in his eyes as he stared at the news.

"He would be killing thousands."

Cade shot up from the couch. "And *they* are killing too many of us every day."

"You can't fight fire with fire," Larsen said, taking a stride forward and giving Kurt a pleading look. "We have to do *something*."

Cade snorted. "You want to intervene? Did you forget how they kicked your ass yesterday?"

Larsen flinched and rubbed the bruise around his neck.

"Even if we stop Tynan, it will never end," Kurt muttered, squeezing his hands together. "There will always be someone else chasing that power."

"So, what? We just let it happen?" Larsen asked. "Just leave thousands to die at the hands of that sociopath?"

"We can find Calosant first."

All three of them jumped at Kris's voice. She stood at the end of the hall, clutching a damp towel.

Kurt shook his head. "If we found even *one* of those keys, Tynan would stop at nothing to obtain it from us."

"We find Calosant, and we destroy the Mina Ring."

Kurt stood and crossed the room to the window. He stared outside for a long, quiet moment, then turned back to them.

"Larsen's right," Kris said. "We can't stand by and let Tynan get away with this. We have a responsibility to do something."

Cade shook his head. "Even though the NWDA—"

"I know what they've done," Kris cut in, hugging the towel close to her chest as the anchor read off statistics. "I know what they're doing, but killing them doesn't make us any better. They're still people. They don't deserve to die."

Cade cleared his throat and bowed his head. The anxious tapping of his foot accompanied the news anchor's words.

"I think Kris is right," Kurt said.

She reared back her head, eyes wide, and a subtle smile curled the corners of her lips.

Larsen dropped his arms to his sides, looking between the two of them.

"I'm done hiding." Kurt eyed the living room around him. "The stakes have changed."

"You realize that racing Tynan to Calosant is a suicide mission, right?" Cade said.

Kris locked eyes with Kurt. He offered her a small, sad smile and a firm nod.

"I don't expect any of you to—" Kurt began.

"I'm with you," Kris said, stepping closer.

Cade shrugged. "Me too. What have I got to lose, right?"

Larsen looked away for a moment before turning back to Kurt again. "Are you sure you want to do this? I mean, I have your back, I always will, but Tynan already tried to kill you once."

Kurt nodded. "No more running. I'm ready."

~

"So, when do we get to the really cool stuff?" Kris asked, leaning back on her hands in the grass. "Like the fireballs and moving stuff with my mind."

"It's called telekinesis." Kurt held up a hand to his brow to block the sun from his eyes. "And you can learn it when you're ready. You have yet to master balancing the mental and physical spaces."

Kris threw her head back with a groan.

"Come on," he said. "One more time."

She sighed and sat up again, keeping her eyes open and watching Kurt as she entered the dark world in her mind.

A heavy fog enveloped her as she stood outside another shimmering crystal barrier. Kris passed her hand just above the surface of the wall, which glowed as her hand approached. Doing so made her head pound, and her eyes yearned to shut.

"It's hard to choose what to focus on," she mumbled, fading between the meadow and the world in her mind.

And that's why you aren't ready for telekinesis, Kurt said. As his voice echoed, the wall illuminated, and suddenly propelled forward at her.

Kris stumbled back but caught herself. She watched as the barrier jerked closer again. *What's happening?* she asked. *What are you doing?*

Push back.

She backed away, catching her breath. *Push back?*

Though uncertain, Kris extended both arms to plant her hands on the barrier. It jolted against her, but she held her ground, preventing it from moving in closer. But it kept pushing harder and Kris's heels started to slide back.

You've got this, Kurt told her from the other side of the wall.

Kris took a deep breath and thrust both hands forward, able to shift the barrier back ever so slightly. With a grunt, she pushed a little harder and watched in amazement as a new layer seemed to spread from her palms over the shimmering barricade, making it thicker and more opaque. The third shove was easier, allowing Kris to force it back several feet. She could feel herself physically panting, but she remained in the telepathic void.

Well done, he said.

A familiar sound caught her ear, causing her to step back from the barrier.

It's the screams again! she told him.

Kris turned on her heels and darted through the darkness toward the sounds. The world around her gradually morphed into a tunnel, and it didn't take long for her to recognize the room at the end of the corridor.

It's Tynan's bunker.

Kris, stop, Kurt called, a flicker of panic in his voice.

Cries of agony were coming from inside the room.

She'd heard those screams yesterday, she realized, as she slowly approached the closed metal door. *Whoever it is, they need help!*

Kris could feel Kurt calling her in the distance, but she couldn't ignore the cries from inside. She grabbed the door handle and started to push the door in. The scream was much louder—a man, crying out in pain. The sound twisted in her gut.

Stop! Kurt shouted.

Before she could enter the room, a thick barrier formed in front of her, jolting forward and forcing her away. Kris lost her footing and stumbled backwards, the back of her skull cracking against the rock floor. The impact broke her concentration.

Kris blinked, the meadow slowly returning to focus. Kurt was now standing with his back to her. His shoulders heaved with deep breaths.

"I told you to stop," he said.

She climbed to her feet, head still ringing despite not physically hurting herself moments ago. "Was that you screaming? Is that a memory?"

"It's none of your business. I told you to stop."

Kris's brow wrinkled. "I heard someone in pain, someone who needed help, so I acted on it."

"It wasn't your place. I extended my trust, and you betrayed it." Kurt walked away toward the cabin.

"Trust is a two-way street," she countered. She rushed around him, cutting him off. "What did I see in there?"

His hair hung over his face and hid his eyes, but she could see the scowl on his lips. "We're done for the day," he grumbled as he marched past her.

She watched him walk away and held out her hands in a choking motion before clutching both closed fists against her head and twisting away.

"That was difficult to watch."

Kris gasped, then put her hand to her chest with a breath of relief. A few feet away, Larsen stood with his hands in his pockets.

"You saw that, huh?" she said.

He nodded and ambled closer, rubbing his neck. "He's really trying, you know."

Kris brushed her hands over her jeans to clear any dirt left from sitting in the grass. "I wasn't trying to invade his privacy. It was just instinct."

"He'll be fine. Don't worry." Larsen massaged his neck again.

"Does it still hurt?"

He gave a nervous laugh and dropped his arm. "No. Just can't stop thinking about it."

"You knew that guy, right? Not the red-eyed guy but the blond one. Xan?"

Larsen peered across the field to the cabin, then slowly nodded. "Alexander. We went to school together. We used to be close."

Kris nibbled her nail. Her phone vibrated in her pocket, but she ignored it. "Did you lose touch?"

Larsen scoffed. "It's complicated," he said quietly. "I wanted to hide that I was Witcan. He didn't. Makes perfect sense, looking back now, that he would end up working with Tynan."

"Was it hard seeing him again?"

"Always is."

The sun was getting lower, casting orange light across the meadow. Kris found herself intoxicated by the bright colors streaking across the sky, until her phone buzzed again. She had two social media messages from Brie.

My mom saw some old texts I sent to Dylan, so she took away my phone and laptop, the first message read. *Joke's on her, I still have my old phone. And thanks to the miracle of Wi-Fi, I can use social media on it.*

Kris scrolled to the second message. *Can I please see you for my birthday? I miss your face! Plus, it's the last week of school, which means next week we will finally be seniors! More reason to celebrate.*

"Everything okay?" Larsen asked.

"It's my best friend's birthday next week," she mumbled. She held her phone close to her chest in thought. "I want to visit her, but after the cemetery . . . I don't want to risk putting her in any danger."

"You could meet your friend somewhere else?" he said with a shrug. "Meet her somewhere discreet. Where Tynan wouldn't know to look for you."

Kris studied Larsen suspiciously. "Why aren't you fighting me on this? After the other day?"

He stole a glimpse toward the cabin and cracked a sad smile. "If someone matters so much you are willing to accept any and all risks just to see them, then do it. It's important to seize whatever happiness you can find in this world."

Kris looked back at the cabin. "Kurt's going to be angry," she whispered.

"Probably. But some things are more important."

She smiled and unlocked her phone. *Remember where we had that double-date picnic for Labor Day last year?* Kris typed. *I'll meet you there. Next Monday at 2 p.m.*

Chapter 16

Balance

Kris poured herself a bowl of cereal as Kurt emerged from his bedroom. "Are you still mad at me?" she asked.

"What do you think?" he grumbled; his voice dropped when Cade opened his door. He awkwardly scratched the back of his head and watched his friend from the corner of his eye.

Cade looked between the two of them, cracking a smile. He placed a cigarette between his lips and strutted to the front door for his morning smoke.

"Why can't you just tell me what I saw?" she asked, stuffing the cereal box back into the cupboard.

"Do you not understand what you did?" Kurt loomed over her, his pale eyes glistening with a twitch of anger. "You were in my *head*. You were entering areas that even *I* won't visit."

Her heart pounded. Kris wanted to look away, but the focus in his eyes kept her trapped. "I'm sorry," she finally said. "I shouldn't have snooped, but you shouldn't hide stuff from me either."

He scoffed and wiped a hand across his face. "You know what, forget it."

"Kurt." Kris trailed behind him into the hall, but he continued outside.

She leaned back against the wall, knocking her head against it. She knew he wanted to trust her, but how was she supposed to trust him when he was clearly hiding a bunch of skeletons in his closet.

She rolled along the wall back into the kitchen. As she poured milk into her bowl of cereal, the screen door opened.

"Can I give you some advice?" Cade said.

"Why not?"

"Let it go."

She eyed him as she slipped into a dining room chair. "I expected some ridiculous comment like 'just kiss and get it over with' or something."

"Nah." Cade laughed and stretched his arms. "I mean, unless you *want* to kiss him."

"Ha, no thanks." Kris emphasized her words with her eyebrows.

"When Kurt is ready to start digging into his history—*if* he is ever ready—he will come to you."

But what if he never opens up?

"Pick your battles," Cade said. "Especially if you still plan on asking him to take you to visit your friend next week."

Kris froze with a spoonful of cereal at her lips. "How do you know about that?"

He smirked. "I'm perceptive."

"Well, I don't care what Kurt says about it, I'm going with or without him."

"Good for you, showing some of that backbone. I love it."

"I mean, you show enough for all of us . . ."

Cade chuckled. "If you need a ride to visit your friend, I'll take you. Don't let Kurt scare you into his hermit lifestyle."

He slipped on his leather jacket and picked up his helmet from the coffee table in the living room. He was already on his motorcycle, speeding out of the meadow, by the time she was washing her bowl in the sink.

No way Kurt is ever going to trust me. I don't understand what he's so afraid of. What could he have possibly gone through that was so bad he blocks it out of his own memory?

~

Kris sat out in the grass and leaned back on her palms. Her eyes shut as she basked in the morning sun with music playing on her phone to soothe her nerves.

Bobbing her head with each beat, she sang along quietly with the man's gentle voice over the calming strum of guitars. An angelic sound. "Are you ready to face the world with your hand in mine? Did you know that I would wait forever and a lifetime?"

A crunch in the grass made her eyes snap open. Kurt was standing a few feet away, his camera held up to his face.

She jerked upright, fixing her hair and fumbling with her phone to stop the song. "What are you doing?"

"You looked so peaceful," he replied with a crooked smile, then lowered his camera. "I couldn't resist."

Her cheeks burned. "You can't just sneak up on someone and take their photo like that . . ." Her voice trailed off as Kurt raised an eyebrow. "Yeah, okay fine, I see your point," she grumbled, getting to her feet.

He scoffed and fiddled with his camera. "I thought about what you said, though. And I need you to trust me. That's the only way this is going to work."

"Look, I'm sorry, okay? It won't happen again."

Kurt cleared his throat, examining the meadow around them. "How about a break from telepathy? How about we take a stab at telekinesis?"

"Really?" Kris took a long stride forward.

"Yeah. Let's go inside. We'll start small."

~

Kurt lined up three pencils on the dining room table before slipping into the chair at its head. He eyed the empty chair next to him and nodded slightly. It slid a few feet away from the table towards Kris.

"That's so cool," she said as she sat down.

"Telekinesis is going to be more challenging than telepathy," Kurt explained, extending a hand over one of the pencils. Without him even thinking about it, the pencil lifted off the table and hovered just beneath the palm of his hand for a few seconds, then lowered back down. "You need to be aware of your surroundings. You *need* to have that balance of the physical and mental spaces like we were working on yesterday."

Kris beamed and sat up in her seat. "Okay."

She held out her own hand just as he had done, focusing on the pencil nearest her. He couldn't help but smile at the look of concentration on her face. *I really should have trained her sooner.*

Kris let out a long breath. The yellow pencil rattled against the table before finally rising into the air. She closed her fingers around it and chuckled. She rotated her hand so her palm was facing upward, then slowly unrolled her fingers to expose the pencil. With a squint and a twinkle in her green eyes, Kris gave a slight grin. Her cheeks were glowing.

Kurt's mouth hung open as he watched the pencil levitate just above the palm of her hand. It may have only been a few short seconds before it tipped and bounced back down on the table, but it seemed nearly effortless.

"Good," he said, resting his arms in front of him. "Again."

Kris repeated the action. Each time, she was able to hold the pencil up longer. After letting it float for nearly a whole minute on her fourth try, she let it drop to the table.

"All right, I've mastered that." She brushed her fingers over her shoulder with a laugh. "What's next?"

Kurt motioned to the other two pencils still left untouched on the table. "How many can you control at once?"

He watched her try, and couldn't take his eyes off the adorably competitive smirk Kris wore on her face. She would grin when she lifted a second pencil in the air, then grunt when it fell. After a few failed attempts, she picked up a pencil with her fingers and flung it back down again. The eraser bounced off the table.

"Don't be discouraged. You're doing well," Kurt said, catching the pencil before it rolled onto the floor.

She pressed a hand against her forehead. "My head's spinning. It's harder trying to split my focus like that."

He wiggled his eyebrows. "You wanted a challenge."

"I know. I just need a sec."

"That's fine," Kurt said, captivated by a strand of dark brown hair falling in Kris's face that swayed with each breath she took.

"You never told me your favorite color."

"What?"

Kris brushed the hair from her face and shot him a smirk. "The other day when we were practicing telepathy. You asked me my favorite color, but I never heard yours."

He laughed and tapped his fingers on the table for a moment. "Red."

"How about this?" she said, perking up and leaning forward.

Kurt matched her posture.

Kris pointed at each of the pencils on the table. "For every one I can control, you have to answer a question. For every pencil I drop, you get to ask *me* a question."

His eyes narrowed, and a slight smile curled his mouth. "You just can't stop prying, can you?"

"If telekinesis is *so challenging*," she said, hunching farther forward, "then you should have nothing to worry about."

Their faces were only inches apart. Kurt's palms became sweaty, but he didn't let it show and instead nodded slowly. "Okay. Okay, you're on."

"Okay."

They both leaned back, mirroring each other's smirks.

Kris immediately turned her attention back to the pencils. The first lifted off the table, and she held up a finger while not averting her eyes. "What's your favorite food?"

He looked up to the ceiling as he considered his words. "Roasted chicken and vegetables."

"Yum," she mumbled, her eyes shifting between the levitating pencil and another on the table. The second one wobbled at first as it rose, before hovering vertically. "That's two." She held up two fingers.

"Is this a hustle?"

"A deal's a deal. Who's your favorite musician?"

Kurt ran a hand through his hair. "Dragonfleye."

Kris raised a hand, trying to use it to stabilize the two pencils in the air as she shifted her focus to the third.

"Struggling?"

"No," she muttered. The pencil rattled around on the table, and one dropped and rolled to the floor. "Damn it."

"That's one," Kurt teased, holding out a finger just as Kris had. He bowed his head in thought. "What did you want to be when you were a kid?"

They continued for a while, going back and forth. Kurt could only stare at her, impressed, until she eventually managed to balance all three pencils in the air at once.

"Got any more pencils?"

Kurt chuckled and looked around. "I can grab some silverware . . ."

His car keys, at the edge of the table, jingled as they lifted and dropped.

"So floppy," Kris said.

The keys hit the table a second time.

"That counts as two," Kurt said. "Most embarrassing moment."

"Okay, but this answer counts for two, then." Beads of sweat were forming on Kris's forehead, a tight scowl on her face as she concentrated. "I had to go to anger management counseling last year because of recurring fights with this girl in my class." She struggled for a few minutes before finally lifting the keys. "Bam! How you like them apples?"

Kurt leaned back in his chair, snatching an apple from the kitchen counter. He set it on the table in front of Kris. "Impressive."

"Are you a dog or a cat person?" she asked.

"Neither, but I guess more so cats."

"What?"

He shrugged. "I don't like dogs."

"How can you not like dogs?"

"NWDA K-9 nicked me when I was younger."

"I guess that would be pretty traumatic," Kris muttered, fumbling to lift the apple. "Goddamn, this is hard."

"That's the point." Kurt crossed his arms on the table and offered her a reassuring smile. "I will say, I'm impressed. I thought it would take longer to get you to this point."

Kris let out a grunt. The keys crashed down first, followed by all three pencils, leaving the apple teetering. She planted both hands on the table with a heavy pant. "I forgot to breathe," she whispered, her face glowing bright red.

He stood up. "Take a break. I'll grab you some water." As he passed, he patted her on the head, then leaned in close to whisper in her ear. "That counts as four."

"Yeah, yeah," she grumbled, waving a hand at him.

Kurt opened a cupboard in the kitchen and retrieved a glass. "What's your favorite subject in school?"

"I really enjoyed an astronomy class I took last year."

He was filling a glass in the sink when he heard a thud against the floor. He peered under the cupboards into the dining room. "What are you doing?"

Kris giggled and hunched her shoulders. "I was trying to lift the table."

"Don't overdo it." Kurt rushed into the dining room. "You're going to hurt yourself."

She blew raspberries and took the glass from him. "If your muscles aren't sore, you aren't pushing hard enough. How is this any different?"

"You still owe me three."

She stared at him over the rim of the glass as she sipped, and held it close to her lips when she spoke. "What else do you want to know?"

Kurt shuffled his feet, considering his question. "Are you still in love with Ian?"

Kris coughed up a gulp of water. "Wow. No idea you were going to go there," she rasped, trying to clear her throat.

He said nothing as he waited.

"I don't know." She clutched her chest. "Spent so long being mad at him, I don't know what I feel anymore."

"Was he your first boyfriend?"

Kris flicked her hair from her face and looked at him skeptically. "Are there a lot of Ian questions?"

Kurt crossed his arms and shrugged. "Just curious."

"Yes, Ian was my first boyfriend. You get one more question. Make it a good one."

He dropped his head and cleared his throat. He opened his mouth, but quickly closed it again. "Forget it. Let's break for now. We'll pick it up again after lunch."

"What? No, this won't stand. We had a deal, and you get another question."

Kurt grinned. "All right . . . favorite pizza topping?"

Kris scrunched up her face with a mischievous smile. "Pineapple."

"That's disgusting." He laughed and walked away.

"Nah, it's really good. I'll take you to Filippelli's sometime. Best pizza in the state."

Kurt's hands started trembling, so he stuffed them in his pockets and turned back to her, returning the smile. "Okay, fine. You've got a deal."

Chapter 17

Bad Timing

Kris held out her plate as Kurt cut a piece of lasagna for her.

"So training is going well?" Larsen asked, serving himself.

"Kris is improving," Kurt said. "We're fine-tuning her telekinesis."

Kris nodded. "Kurt won't let me try any of the cool stuff until I 'learn the basics.'"

"Well, good," Cade said as he entered the dining room. He cracked open the beer can in his hand. "Don't need you burning down the house or something."

"Where did you get that?" Kurt asked, pointing with his fork.

"I hid a stash so you wouldn't dump it." Cade took a long sip and plopped into the seat next to Kurt.

"I don't like you having alcohol in my house."

"It's *beer*. It's fine."

Kurt and Larsen exchanged glances but continued to eat.

"So, Cade, you're still living in Indianapolis?" Larsen asked between bites. "They have a good rehab center there?"

Cade picked at his lasagna and shot Larsen a grin. "I think what you need is hypnotherapy, not rehabilitation. But no, I've got a place in northern Indiana now. Got a sweet gig working at the local motorcycle dealership."

Larsen eyed him from across the table as he ate. "And how much are you embezzling from this job?"

The playful look in Cade's eye disappeared for a moment, but he shook it off. "I'm making an honest living, nerd. Paid for my motorcycle with my own paychecks and everything."

Larsen scoffed and continued with his dinner.

Kris ate quietly. Her phone buzzed in her pocket, and she knew it was Brie messaging her again about tomorrow. She peered around the table, her chest thumping. She opened her mouth to speak, but Kurt spoke first.

"You like your job?" he asked Cade.

"Oh, hell yeah. I get to work with my hands, I get a sweet discount on parts from the store, plus I've got a thing going with the receptionist."

"Oh, I didn't know you had a girlfriend."

Cade howled with laughter. "No. No, no. Not a girlfriend. She can't tie this down." He flexed an arm muscle and raised his eyebrows at Kris.

She stared at him. "Is that supposed to impress me?"

"So, you're just stringing this poor girl along with zero intention of committing to her?" Larsen dropped his fork on the ceramic plate and gestured with both hands.

"I told her point-blank I'm not a relationship guy. But I tell you, these smoking-hot 'nice' girls are like putty. I'm irresistible to them. Right, Kris?" He winked at her.

Kris looked around the table, shrugging. "Am I supposed to be part of that demographic? Do you expect me to swoon?"

Cade chuckled, taking a big bite of pasta.

As silence enveloped them again, Kris eyed Kurt across the table. She had to say something. She'd put it off all week.

She set her fork aside and cleared her throat. "Tomorrow is my best friend Brie's birthday, and I'm going to see her at North Rapids."

Kurt's head jerked up. "You serious?"

"It's a discreet location. I've only been there once before. Tynan won't think to look for me there—"

"You're actually serious."

"I would appreciate if you would give me a ride there, but if not, both Larsen and Cade have volunteered separately to take me."

Kurt looked between the two of them.

Cade sat upright, pointing to Larsen across the table. "Hey, didn't you want to show me—"

"Literally anything?" Larsen blurted.

"Yep."

"Yep."

They both jumped up and sprinted down the hall to their room.

Kurt stared across the table at her. "Do we really need to go over this again?"

"I know you think it's dangerous," Kris said. "You don't have to remind me what happened last time, but that was different."

Kurt clasped a hand over his eyes.

"Tynan knew to look for me at the cemetery, and I was unsuspecting. But this place is like thirty minutes away. It's secluded and quiet. He would have no idea to look for me there. Plus, I've had some training. I'm more aware of my surroundings—"

Kurt dropped his hand in his lap. His hair hid his face.

"Brie is my family," Kris said quietly. "I haven't seen her in weeks. I've had to hide so much from her, I feel like I'm losing myself . . ."

He remained silent, shoulders rigid and held high with tension.

"I'm asking you as a formality. I'm going one way or another."

"By conspiring with my friends behind my back?" Kurt lifted his eyes just enough to meet hers.

She shrugged. "I would rather *you* take me, but I knew how you would react."

His face was expressionless as he stared off toward the hall. Kris waited for him to consider his answer.

After a few seconds, he turned back to her. "I have ground rules."

She recoiled but smiled ever so slightly. "Okay."

"I will drive you and wait nearby while you're with your friend. You are to remain within a designated area and a set time limit." He counted each rule on his fingers.

Kris nodded, smiling a little bigger. "Okay. Agreed."

Kurt leaned forward and jabbed a finger into the table. "And if you or I observe *anything* suspicious, then we turn back immediately."

~

"Anything suspicious?" Kris twisted around in her seat. "Can we move forward now?"

Kurt was parked on the side of the street, scanning the woods. "Can't be too careful," he mumbled before finally putting the car in drive again.

Her legs bounced, and she tapped her feet frantically on the floor. Her heart was pounding. "The turn's right here," she said, pointing to the road on the right.

"You excited?"

Kris flipped her phone around in her hand. "You have no idea. Can't wait to pretend I'm just a normal teenager again." She sat up taller and poked her finger on the window. "Here! Pull over. The trail is behind there."

Kurt pulled into the dirt. "Don't touch the window. You're going to get fingerprints all over it."

She ignored him as she unbuckled her seat belt and snatched her messenger bag from the floor. "Okay, I'll meet you back here in a couple hours—"

"Wait, hang on." Kurt gently touched her shoulder. He undid his seat belt and twisted around to the back seat. When he leaned back again, he held out a small rectangular gift wrapped in flowered paper.

"What's this?" Kris asked, taking it from him.

He shrugged. "You mentioned she enjoys books, and I know you weren't able to get her something . . ."

As she stared down at the present, she pressed her lips together to try to contain the smile threatening to take over her face. "That's . . . That's really sweet of you," she whispered.

Kurt beamed and gave the steering wheel a squeeze. "I'll be close. You know, if you need anything."

She nodded. She sat there studying the twinkle in his eyes for a moment. *Should I hug him? Would that be inappropriate?* She decided against it, finally opening the car door and sliding out.

"Be safe, okay?"

Kris bent down to peer inside the car. "You too."

Her cheeks were still burning as she slipped between the shrubs to the dirt trail that ran parallel to the road. She draped her messenger bag over her shoulder and tucked the gift inside.

Why is he being so cute today? Oh God . . . Kurt is cute? When did that happen?

Kris hit herself in the forehead with her palm. Was she crushing on him?

She scuffed her foot across the path, kicking dust up in the air as she walked. The sound of the rapids grew louder, and the white caps appeared through the branches. A little farther down the trail, Kris cut through the trees to the water's edge.

A few feet below, the river splashed over the rocks and roared as it rushed downstream. On the small ledge between the trees and the water was a wooden picnic table. She traced the old wood of the table with her fingers before plopping down on the bench. The entire table tipped, rocking back with the motion, and she had to quickly lean forward again.

Like Kurt would be interested in you. He did ask a lot of questions about Ian, though. Why would he do that unless . . . ?

"Kris!"

She jumped, and the picnic table teetered again.

Brie hopped out from the trees and threw her arms out as she bounded over. Kris barely had time to stand before Brie gripped her in a giant bear hug. She jumped up and down in place, giggling.

"I missed you, I missed you, I missed you," Brie gushed, squeezing tighter. "I might never let you go."

Kris returned the hug. "I missed you too, Brie-bear."

Brie laughed and stepped back. She pressed her lips together, flashing Kris with puppy-dog eyes. "It's my birthday, so you can't get mad at me."

Her heart dropped. "Why?"

A figure emerged from the trees behind Brie. Kris immediately recognized the tattered band tee, styled blond hair, and sun-kissed complexion.

"Hi, Kris," he said, setting down a small cooler.

Kris's shoulders deflated, and she shot Brie an annoyed expression. "Why is Ian here?"

Brie wandered over, taking Ian by the sleeve of his T-shirt and guiding him closer. "You two need to talk. I love you both and I hate seeing you two miserable like this."

Kris looked him up and down and shook her head. "I have nothing to say to him."

Ian shrugged and gave her a sad smile. "Can you just hear me out, Kris?"

"Please?" Brie said, bouncing up and down. "Do it for me. It's my birthday."

Kris frowned with arms crossed and looked down at the rushing water below. "Fine."

Brie clapped her hands and grinned from ear to ear. "Yay! Okay, I'll be over there, definitely *not* eavesdropping, whenever you guys are done." She started toward the picnic table.

"Oh wait, hang on." Kris opened her bag and fished out the gift. "Here. Happy birthday."

Brie's eyes lit up as she squeezed it and knocked on the surface of the present. "It's a book," she said before ripping open the wrapping paper. "Ooh, *Song of Midnight*. I'm going to start chapter one." She danced over and sat on top of the table, opened the book, and started reading.

Ian stepped closer to Kris. "It's great to see you." He tried to touch her hand, but she panicked and pulled her arm away.

"Why are you here? What is there to even talk about?"

"Kris, you've been ignoring me for over a month. Your parents died. You ran away. I've been so worried about you. I still *care* about you."

She kicked a rock off the ledge into the water and shrugged. "If you cared so much, then why did you do it?"

He sighed, putting his hands in the pockets of his athletic shorts. "I messed up. It was stupid and selfish, and there is nothing I can say to make up for that."

"I told you I wasn't ready, so instead of waiting . . . You know what? I really don't want to get into this again. I came here to see Brie. To celebrate her birthday, not to dig up this mess."

Ian grabbed her arm as she started to turn away, spinning her to face him.

"What the hell?"

"I should *never* have cheated on you," he said, holding her shoulders. His blue eyes gazed longingly into hers. "I can say I'm sorry a million times, but it will never be enough. I want you back. Just give me another chance."

Kris couldn't contain the smile that slowly crept across her face, but then an image of Kurt flashed in her mind and her heart skipped a beat. Her stomach churned, and she turned away. She tucked her long hair behind her ears. "Ian."

He hesitantly stepped up beside her as they watched the river rage for several seconds. "Is it bad timing? Or are we . . . done?"

She shook her head. "I—I don't know."

Ian laughed quietly to himself. "I can't believe how much I messed things up. I'm such an asshole, aren't I, Skittles?"

Kris cracked a small smile. "Yeah. You really are."

"I'm not giving up on you. On us. I will do what it takes to earn your trust back. But can we at least be back on speaking terms again? Like if I text you, can I expect a reply?"

She scrunched up her face. "Sure."

They stared at the water, and after a minute, Ian playfully punched her shoulder. "Come on. Let's go wish the Brie-bear a proper happy birthday."

Kris glanced through the trees in the direction Kurt had parked, before following Ian back to the table.

"How's the book so far?" she asked Brie as they approached.

Brie tucked a scrap of the wrapping paper between the pages and closed the book. "Only a few pages in, but I'm hooked." She set it aside and looked between the two of them. "So . . . ? Are you guys getting back together?"

Kris and Ian both laughed nervously.

"It's complicated," he said, setting the cooler down on the table.

Brie's face fell. She turned to Kris as though demanding an explanation.

Kris stepped over the bench and sat down. "Don't worry. We'll be civil."

"I can't believe this table is still here," Ian said as he sat down across from her. "I thought for sure someone would have moved it back."

Brie climbed down off the table, sitting next to Kris on the bench.

"So, for starters . . ." Ian opened the cooler and gave Brie a mischievous grin. "For the birthday queen." He lifted out a plastic tiara studded with rhinestones and lined with pink feathers.

Brie gasped, clapping and holding out her hands. "Oh my God. Adorbs! Gimme, gimme, gimme." She grabbed the tiara and tucked it on top of her head. With a grin, she framed her face with her hands. "How do I look?"

"Gorgeous," Kris replied.

"Secondly," Ian continued, reaching into the cooler again, "we are finally seniors, and we need to celebrate."

Kris's stomach churned when Ian pulled out a half-empty bottle of spiced rum.

"Oh, heck yeah," Brie cheered.

"Will's of-age friends hooked me up," he explained as he set the bottle on the table in front of Kris. He rummaged through the cooler for a few cans of cola and red plastic cups.

Kris stared at the gold liquid as it swished around. "I . . . I don't think I should . . ."

"And voilà, a little something extra for the birthday queen." Ian tossed Brie a tiny pink bottle.

"Exotic Berry Super Premium Vodka," Brie read off the label. "Ooh, that sounds delicious." Kris breathed in harshly as Brie twisted off the cap and held the miniature bottle under her nose. "It smells fruity."

Ian poured rum into two of the cups, and Kris swiftly clapped her hand over the third.

"I don't think I'm going to partake," she told him quietly.

"What?" Brie kicked one leg over the bench to sit sideways and face Kris. "But we need to celebrate."

"It's just . . . I don't like rum."

Brie held out the mini pink bottle. "Here, have some of this, then."

Kris stared at it, and the artificial fruit smell was so pungent that it burned her eyes. "I think I'll just have soda."

"Come on, really?" Ian held out the bottle of rum. "Just a little bit. It won't hurt."

Kris shook her head, grabbing a can of soda. She poured a little bit into her cup, then held the can out to Ian. Ian and Brie exchanged a look, but he put the cap back on the rum and set it aside.

"Well, I'm not going to pressure you into it, but it's here if you change your mind," he said.

Brie tipped her head back, downed the pink bottle, and topped it off with a "woo." Ian poured some cola into each of the cups with rum and handed one to Brie.

"To seniorhood," Ian announced, and held up his cup.

"To seniorhood." Brie tapped hers against his.

Kris followed by holding up her cup as well. They each took a sip, and she swirled the dark soda around. Her palms felt sweaty as she watched Ian gulp down the rest of his drink.

"So, what have you been up to, Kris?" he asked as he refilled his cup. "Where have you been hiding out? Brie has been super mysterious about it."

"I told you, she wouldn't tell me," Brie insisted, adjusting her tiara before looking back to her. "Where *have* you been staying?"

Kris traced her finger along the rim of the cup. "A friend of my parents had a spare room, so I've been crashing there. Off the grid."

"Why off the grid, though?" Ian asked.

She opened her mouth to speak, but Brie interrupted her. "Kris, please come back with us. We won't make you go back to live with your grandparents, but it scares me not knowing where you are or who you're with."

"Brie, I really appreciate it, but we both know your parents would immediately send me back there."

"Then come live with *me*," Ian offered. He set his cup aside to sit on top of the table. "My parents adore you. They liked your parents. They would be more than happy to help you out."

Kris held up her hands. "I'm fine. Honestly. I'm safe. I'm— I'm happy. I'm recovering."

"Kris," Brie said, slouching forward dramatically, "we pry only because we care. Who is this person? How do you know they aren't a murderer or psycho or something?"

Kris giggled, nudging her in the arm. "Obviously I asked him before I moved in."

"Wait, *him*?" Ian interjected with a nervous laugh. He rocked back and forth on the table. "You're living with a guy?"

"Uh . . ." *Probably shouldn't have mentioned that.*

"Are you blushing?" Brie cried out as she poked Kris's cheek.

"What? No!" Kris jerked her head back and pressed her fingers against her face.

Brie inched closer. "Oh my God, you are! Seriously, who is this mystery man?"

Kris took a long sip of soda, eyeing her friends over the brim of the plastic cup. "Just a guy," she whispered into the cup.

"Are you two . . . ?" Ian gestured with his hands.

"No." She laughed and shook her head. Then, realizing she was smiling, she straightened her face and spoke in a more serious tone. "No. No, we are not involved. Totally platonic."

"Totally platonic, like you and I were 'totally platonic'?" Ian said.

"Just trust me, okay? So how about we just change the subject? How did you both do on finals?"

Brie downed her cup and shrugged. "This conversation is far from over, but I did not do well in algebra. Barely passed. My mom is making me retake it next year."

Ian flicked a leaf off the table. "Pretty much Bs across the board, but I made first-string forward for fall soccer."

"That's awesome," Kris exclaimed.

Though she was watching Ian's mouth move, she suddenly felt herself standing in the dark world, a cloudy barrier behind her.

Hello? she called, resting a hand on the wall. The crystals refracted, waving and twisting in the ripples from her touch, and became more translucent.

Kurt was standing on the other side, his hand also flexed against the barrier. *I sense another Witcan,* he told her.

Sitting at the picnic table, Kris tried as hard as she could to look casual as she turned her head and scanned the woods on either side of the river.

Do you think it's one of Tynan's goons? Kris asked. She didn't hear or see anyone else.

Kurt shook his head and flicked his eyes up to meet hers. He didn't look worried. *I walked your perimeter. There's no one else nearby.*

Kris's heart dropped into her stomach. Her eyes darted between Ian and Brie. *Wait, are you saying it's one of them?*

He nodded slowly. *I can't say which specifically, but yes. One of your friends is a Witcan.*

~

Kris gave Brie one last tight hug goodbye.

"Thank you so, so much for coming today. And thank you for the gift," Brie gushed.

"I missed you so much," Kris said, finally letting her go and stepping back.

Ian carried the cooler as he slipped between the shrubs to the dirt hiking trail. "You sure you don't need a ride back into town?" he asked again. "It's really no trouble. You can ride with us."

Kris smiled and shook her head. "Thanks, but I've got a ride waiting for me."

"Is it the guy?" Brie asked with a smirk. "Can we meet him?"

Kris clapped her hands together, interlocking her fingers. "I don't think so. Not this time. He's, uh . . . he's really shy, so."

"Okay fine, but I'm meeting him next time." Brie tapped the tiara on her head as though it proved her authority.

Kris laughed. "Okay, sure. Drive safe, guys." She waved as she turned away to head down the trail.

As she walked, she found herself fixating on what Kurt had said. Could Ian or Brie really be Witcan too? Would it not be obvious? Would she have not noticed it herself over the years?

She squeezed the strap of her messenger bag. Just ahead, through the trees, she could see Kurt's car.

"Kris, wait."

She turned over her shoulder and watched Ian jog after her. "What is it?"

She didn't have time to react as he wrapped his arms around her waist, lifted her off her feet, and gave her a passionate kiss. The familiarity of his lips made Kris's chest burn. When he set her down again, her cheeks were on fire.

"Ian, I . . ."

"Just something to think about," he whispered, offering her a smile. His face was flushed too. "I'll see you around." And just like that, he disappeared back down the path as quickly as he'd come.

Kris touched her lips with her fingers. As she made her way through the underbrush, she found Kurt leaning on the hood of his car, arms crossed.

"Oh," she gasped, shrinking back to catch her breath. "Did you—"

"So that's Ian?" Kurt stood up straight, lips pressed together in a tight smile. "He seems nice."

She gestured behind her. "I didn't—"

"Come on." He gestured to the car and went around to the driver's side. "We should go."

A nagging sensation itched in Kris's stomach as she climbed into the car. *Why do I feel guilty? It's not like Kurt and I are together. It's not like I cheated on him. Or on Ian.*

She let her hair hang in her face as they drove off, and she twisted the strap of her bag.

Kurt said nothing. They rode home in silence.

Chapter 18

Unfocused

"Y ou're unfocused. Again." Kurt shook his head as the branch dropped back into the grass.

Kris panted as she leaned forward on her knees. "I'm trying."

Kurt was standing near the base of the steps, leaning back against the porch. His arms were crossed, and though he kept his face blank, she could read his sour energy.

"The other day you were balancing four objects with relative ease," he reminded her as she fumbled to lift the branch telekinetically again. "You've taken a huge step back."

She put her hands on her hips, kicking at the ground in defeat as she paced. "Yeah, I suck. You don't have to tell me."

"You just need to focus."

Kris marched back and forth through the grass, her head down. She sighed loudly, then pivoted towards Kurt. "Look, about Ian—"

"I already told you, it's none of my business."

A few days ago, he wouldn't stop prying about her relationship with Ian. And now he wouldn't even let her bring it up.

She puffed up her chest and tried again. "I didn't know he was going to be there."

Kurt held up his hands. "Kris, just stop, okay? I don't care." He took his weight off the porch and motioned to the branch on the ground a few feet away. "We're here for training, and if you can't focus, then let's just call it a day."

Kris scoffed, reaching to touch his shoulder. "Kurt, I'm trying to talk to you. Can you stop being such a robot for, like, one second and listen?"

He extended his hand and the jagged tree branch, about four feet long, fired out of the grass and launched across the meadow. It shattered on impact when it landed near the trees.

"We're done for today," he muttered, turning toward the front door.

"Stop it." Kris charged forward and slammed a hand into Kurt's chest to physically obstruct his path. She pulled her hand away in panic when her finger brushed against something hot.

He took a step back. "Don't do that."

"What was that?" Kris cried, looking up from her hands.

"What was what?"

She reached out again and rested a hand against Kurt's chest. Something small and round was tucked under his shirt. It was warm, heating her hand through the fabric. Without a thought, she identified a thin string hanging around his neck, and she lifted a small silver pendant about the size of a nickel out from under Kurt's shirt. It was hot against her palm.

"What is this?" Kris asked as she turned it over in her hand. There was a small engraving of two interwoven loops on the back.

Kurt stood over her, staring down at the pendant in her hands. "It's an heirloom," he finally said. "Passed down for generations."

The pendant felt like it was gently buzzing against her skin. "It's resonating," she said, looking up at him. "Do you feel that too?"

His breaths grew short, and he pressed his lips together and shook his head. "It's from Calosant."

Kurt cleared his throat, and Kris suddenly realized how close they were standing. She dropped the pendant against his chest and took a small step back, cheeks burning. "Sorry."

He wrapped his hand around the pendant and peeked down at it. His eyes shifted side to side, and she could tell he was deep in thought.

She gently touched his hand. "Look, Kurt—"

"I have to talk to Larsen." Kurt pulled the necklace over his head and held it tightly in his hand. "Just sit down and relax. Get your head straight. We'll try again tomorrow."

"Done with your training already?" Cade asked as he entered the living room with a half-eaten apple in hand.

Kris dropped her phone in her lap and sank deeper into the couch. "Kurt says I'm 'unfocused' and need to 'get my head straight.'" She made air quotes with her fingers as she mocked the words.

Cade vaulted over the back of the couch and landed beside her. "Do you think you're unfocused?"

She glanced down the hall to Larsen's closed bedroom door. She could hear him and Kurt talking quietly inside. "You could say that."

"You've been a little off since you visited your friend the other day." He took a bite of his apple and talked with his mouth full. "Did something happen?"

Kris fiddled with her phone, scrunching up her face but saying nothing.

"Kurt's been acting strange too. I know it wasn't a fight, or I would have heard about it by now. So, what did you do?"

It had been a few days, but Kris could still feel Ian's lips on hers. Thinking about it made her stomach twist. "I don't know if I can talk about it with you," she mumbled.

Cade snapped off another bite of apple and raised an eyebrow. "Come on, what did you do? Now I have to know."

The bedroom door opened. She pushed herself off the couch to face Kurt and Larsen as they filed into the dining room.

"Kurt and I are going to Chicago," Larsen told them, slinging a backpack over his shoulder. He had Kurt's pendant in hand. "We'll swing by my apartment and grab some things, then go to Salman Sanctuary to see if my old Witcan history professor can tell us anything about this."

"Cade, you're in charge," Kurt said as he pulled on his sneakers. "Neither of you are to leave the house."

"So, can I smoke inside?" Cade asked with a snide smile.

Kurt rolled his eyes and tightened the laces. "No smoking inside."

"But you said I can't—"

Kurt shot him a glare. "Don't leave the *property*."

Kris inched closer to Kurt and slid her hands into her pockets. "Be safe," she whispered, leaning in so only he would hear.

"You too," he said, avoiding her stare.

Kris shrunk back when he turned away to face Larsen.

"We should be back in a couple hours," Larsen said.

He put a hand on Kurt's shoulder, and in a blink, they vanished from the dining room.

Cade twisted around on the couch. "Wow, that tension." He rested his stubbly chin on the back cushion and flashed Kris puppy eyes. "You *want* him."

"Shut up." She threw herself down into the recliner, rocking with the motion.

"I know what you need." Cade sprang to his feet and darted to his room.

Leaning back in the chair, Kris clasped a hand over her eyes. *Oh my God, what is wrong with me?*

The clinking of glass made her look up. Cade sashayed into the room carrying two stacked shot glasses and a bottle filled with golden liquid.

"Oh no, what is that?" Kris asked. She crinkled her nose but sat forward anyway.

"When I'm in an emotional crisis, Lady Tequila is the cure." He set the items down on the coffee table.

"I'm not in an emotional crisis—"

"You have too much on your plate," Cade declared as he opened the bottle and took a whiff. "You need to let go."

"I don't know, Cade. I don't drink."

He filled both glasses anyway. "In that case, let me see if Kurt has limes."

He disappeared to the kitchen and started rummaging through the fridge. Kris allowed herself to slowly slip from the chair to the floor and inch closer to the table.

"God bless you and your selection of fresh produce, Kurt," Cade said. Kris could hear him fumbling with knives.

She lifted the bottle and sniffed it. The smell burned fire through her nose all the way down her throat. Peeking over to the kitchen, she picked up one of the shot glasses and took a tiny sip. She immediately started coughing, spilling tequila on her jeans and across the coffee table as she returned it to its place.

"Jesus hot sauce Christmas cake, that's poison," Kris exclaimed, pressing a hand to her mouth.

"Nah, that's good stuff." Cade returned with a saltshaker and a bowl of lime wedges. "I only buy premium tequila. None of that bottom-shelf shit."

"I don't think I can drink that."

He plopped down on the floor next to Kris and held out his palm. "Give me your hand."

I've made a lot of stupid decisions lately. What's one more, I guess? She reluctantly complied. He dabbed one of the lime wedges on the back of her hand and sprinkled a little salt on it.

"Great. I'm all seasoned for roasting," Kris said, taking the lime he held out to her.

He chuckled and slid her shot closer. "So here's what you do. You lick the salt, down the shot, and bite the lime."

"Salt, shot, lime," she repeated to herself. Her hands were trembling as she picked up the shot glass again.

"Cheers." Cade held his up and licked the salt off his hand, then swallowed the tequila in one swift gulp. He turned to Kris as he bit down on his lime, nodding for her to follow suit.

"Screw it." She licked the salt, put the glass to her lips, and tipped back her head with the shot. Her throat felt like it was closing up and she nearly choked again, but she forced herself to swallow it despite how much her eyes burned.

"Lime. Lime," Cade reminded her.

Kris sank her teeth into the slice. The acidic juice oozed over her tongue, rinsing the burning sensation down her throat.

"Was that so bad?" he asked, pouring himself another shot.

"It burns," she rasped. She set her chewed-up lime wedge on the table and eyed the spilled tequila. "Kurt's going to kill us if we don't clean that up."

She stood and turned to the kitchen to get a rag, but Cade grabbed her arm and pulled her back down.

"Don't worry. It's fine," he insisted, then did another shot of tequila. "Kurt told you to relax, didn't he?" He slammed his glass back down, knocking over the saltshaker. Little white grains scattered across the coffee table, and Kris sucked air in through her teeth. He refilled her glass and slid it in front of her. "Here. Have another."

"I need a minute." She looked at him as he threw back his third shot of tequila. "I thought you were sober. How are you still drinking so much?"

Cade bit down on a lime, sucking out the juice before flinging it down in front of him. "I'm off the heavy stuff, and I cut back on alcohol."

Kris swallowed hard as she felt her shot coming back up, but she kept it down. "*This* is a cutback? You just slammed three shots in less than five minutes."

He laughed. "I was a huge wreck, Kris. You don't even know." He rested an arm on the edge of the table, turning his body to better face her. "I had several disgusting addictions, and they took me to some very dark places. Kurt gave me the benefit of the doubt and let me crash here for a while. I was completely strung out, going through some nasty withdrawals. I stole one of his guitars and sold it for heroin, so he kicked me out."

Kris jerked her head forward, her jaw hanging open. "Oh my God."

Cade drummed his fingers across the table before tapping Kris's shot glass closer again. "My lowest was when I crashed a stolen car into a school. It was late at night. No one was there, so thankfully no one got hurt." He brushed back his hair to reveal the scar across his forehead. "It's a miracle I lived. My blood alcohol content could have killed me alone."

She gasped and shook her head. "Wow. No wonder Larsen didn't want you here."

He smirked. "Yeah, he knows all my dirty history. Thinks I'm a bad influence on Kurt, a bad influence on you, blah, blah,

blah." He made a talking gesture with his hand and rolled his
eyes.

Kris laughed as she picked up her shot glass and focused
hard on not spilling. "I mean, he's not wrong."

"Oh please, you need this," Cade insisted, handing her a
lime.

The second shot went down smoother than the first. Her
chest felt warm and her cheeks were definitely glowing.

"So . . . are you going to tell me what's going on between
you and Kurt yet?"

Kris chewed on her lime, contemplating, then grinned.
"No."

"Oh, come on. What do I gotta do?"

"It's weird, dude," she said with a laugh, tossing the chewed-
up lime next to her shot glass. "I don't know you that well. It's
weird to be sharing intimate details with you."

"Intimate?" Cade perked up. "Did you two kiss?"

Kris rubbed her hands over her face. "No. Kurt doesn't
want to kiss me."

"So you tried to kiss him and he turned you down?"

"Oh my God, if it will make you stop talking . . ." She
motioned for him to pour another round. He obliged and they
each took another shot.

"My best friend, Brie, surprised me by bringing my ex-boyfriend with her the other day." She waved her hands around as she spoke, and her words were beginning to slur. "He kissed me, and I'm pretty sure Kurt saw. And now Kurt is acting all weird and distant. I mean, *more* than usual." Kris traced a frowning face in the spilled salt. "Which is so stupid because I didn't even *want* to kiss Ian. But now Kurt won't talk about it, and I'm pretty sure I blew it."

"Wow. It's worse than I thought." Cade let out a quiet laugh. "You are so head over heels for him."

She tried to hide her smile as she punched him in the shoulder. "Oh, shut up. I am not."

"You are. And that's okay. So what's the plan? How do we fix this?"

Kris shrugged, licking the salt off her finger. "I don't think there is any fixing this."

Cade picked up the tequila by the bottle's neck as he stood, then took a swig. "I refuse to believe that."

Then Kris sat slumped back against the couch snacking on stale crackers.

"Kurt has no chips in this house," she said when Cade came back inside with a waft of cigarette smoke. "Can you believe that?"

Cade took a bite of the cracker and spit it out across the living room. "Ugh, these are awful. Why does he do this to us?"

Kris laughed and jammed another cracker into her mouth with a shrug. "He thinks he's my mom or something. She wouldn't buy chips either. Didn't like having candy in the house. Soda was only for *special* occasions."

Cade blew raspberries as he sat on the floor next to the coffee table. He spilled tequila while he tried to pour himself another shot. "Your mom sounds adorable. You're adorable. It must be hereditary."

She scoffed. "You're drunk."

"Also hereditary," Cade said, lifting his shot glass in the air and licking the salt off his hand.

Then Kris was in the hallway. The walls suddenly tilted and she staggered into the bathroom doorframe.

He snorted. "You cannot hold your liquor."

Steadying herself against the wall, Kris pivoted to the kitchen. "I told you I don't drink," she slurred, staggering over to the sink. Instead of getting a glass, she cupped her hands under the running water and brought it to her lips to slurp up.

"We need pizza," he said.

Kris groaned as she zigzagged back into the living room. "I wish, but Kurt said we can't leave."

In a blink, she was beside Cade on the couch. She traced her fingers over his tattoos, admiring all the detail. "Never thought I would like tattoos," she mumbled. "But yours are pretty cool."

Cade smirked and flexed his bicep. "Oh yeah. It gets all the rich little daddy's girls excited. Good girls love bad boys."

She slapped his shoulder. "Oh, shut it."

"No, I'm serious. They think I'm this lost, broken boy. And they think they can be the one to 'fix' me. Then they brag about it to their friends, like I'm one of those internet videos of an abused puppy being adopted."

Kris scrunched up her face in confusion. "You're telling me this whole thing you have going on—with the drug abuse and the leather jacket, the motorcycle, the earring—is all an act just to get naive girls to sleep with you."

He pouted with a dramatic shrug. "Not entirely, but I play it up. I lean into their fantasy."

"And it works?"

Cade leaned in close with a seductive smile. "You tell me."

Kris found herself on the floor, leaning over the coffee table. She looked around, confused. How had she gotten there?

Cade lay on his back on the couch, flicking his lighter open and shut. "If you weren't here, like if none of this had happened, what would you be doing right now?" he asked.

Kris slouched forward and began drawing pictures in the tequila and salt with her fingers. "Swimming."

He snapped the lighter shut and contorted his neck to look at her. "Swimming?"

"And hiking. Campfires. S'mores. Midnight swims."

Cade sat up, raising an eyebrow. "Skinny dipping?"

"No, perv. Camping with my parents. At Lake Lampyridae."
Kris rested back against the couch and scrolled through old
photos on her phone. She stopped on a family photo. Her
parents stood on either side of her, smushing their cheeks
against hers. Behind them, the lake reflected the late-afternoon
sun.

"Wow," Cade said. There was a sincere pang of sadness in
his voice, and it resonated in Kris's ear.

Tears stung her eyes. "I miss them so much." She dropped
her phone in her lap and buried her face in her hands. Cade's
hand rested on her shoulder, but she couldn't stop crying once
the floodgates opened. "I keep waiting to wake up from a bad
dream," she slurred, sniffling loudly. "Waiting for Mom and Dad
to appear and tell me everything is going to be all right. How am
I supposed to go on like this?" Her words rapidly changed into
incoherent babbles.

"Oh no. She's unraveling." Cade stood up from the couch
and grabbed Kris's phone from her lap.

She didn't even fight him and instead let her hands drop,
staring down at them in defeat. They were wet with tears.

Cade swiped through her phone until soft music began to
play. It was a Breathing Oceans song. One of her favorites.

He set the phone aside and held out a hand to her. "May I
have this dance?" he asked in a goofy voice.

Kris sniffled again, wiping her cheeks dry and forcing a laugh. "Sure."

She let him heave her to her feet and wrap his arms around her waist. With the height difference, she could just overlap her hands behind his neck as they swayed gently to the music.

"No more crying on my watch," Cade said, his fingers lightly brushing up and down on Kris's back. She rested her cheek against his chest, comforted by the back rubs.

The next thing she knew, Kris was leaning against the wall outside the kitchen and Larsen was holding a glass of water to her lips, urging her to drink. Her eyelids felt heavy, each blink taking several seconds for her eyes to readjust again. Through the window above the kitchen sink, she could see it was dark outside.

What time was it? How long had she been drinking?

Kurt was yelling in the living room, but with the ringing in her head, she couldn't understand what he was saying. *He must be mad about the mess.*

"I'll clean it up," Kris muttered, and she tried to turn to the living room.

"No," Larsen said, moving her back toward the hallway. "You're going to bed."

Suddenly Kris was standing at her bedroom door. Kurt stood before her with a bewildered look in his eyes.

"What the hell is wrong with you?"

"Was just trying relax," Kris slurred. Her voice cracked, and she realized she was crying again. "You says relax, so Cade helping me relax."

He motioned for her to go into her room. "You're drunk."

"Why don't you like me?" She wrapped both arms around her head and collapsed into a crouched ball on the floor. Hyperventilating, she tried to breathe through her moans and sobs.

Her head jerked up off the pillow when she came to. Her mouth was dry and her eyes ached as they searched the darkness around her.

"Kurt?" she whispered.

In the little bit of moonlight entering through the window, Kris could make out a figure sleeping on the bed across from her. She began to sit up but immediately reclined again when both her head and her stomach turned on her. Clutching her gut, she turned over to face the wall.

"I'm a screwup," she mumbled before falling back to sleep.

Chapter 19

Screwup

The creaking of the floorboards echoed in every corner of her brain and woke Kris from her slumber. Blinding sunlight poured into the room, but through it she could make out a figure standing from the bed beneath the window—fluorescent orange hair and a slender build.

"Sorry. I didn't mean to wake you," Larsen whispered.

With one eye barely open, Kris pulled herself off the mattress to sit up. "Why are you in here?" she asked, moaning and rubbing her eyes.

"You got sick last night after your little row with Kurt." He tiptoed across the room, picked up a waste basket from the floor in front of her bed, and moved it to the side.

Kris suddenly pulled her blanket up against her chest, and her whole face flushed.

Larsen followed her line of sight to her tequila-soaked jeans in the middle of the floor. His cheeks turned red as well. "Yeah, I, uh . . . I couldn't get you to keep them on."

She yanked her blanket completely over her head. "Oh my God," she squealed.

"No funny business, I promise. I didn't even look."

Kris flopped over, burying herself in the bed. "Not helping."

"I'll go get you some water," Larsen murmured.

I made a mess of Kurt's living room. I threw up in the garbage. I took my pants off in front of Larsen. I had a fight with Kurt.

Kris pressed her face as far into the pillow as possible and tried to ignore the pounding in her head. She couldn't even remember huge chunks of the night . . .

She reached out from under her blanket, tapping around the nightstand in search of her phone. It wasn't there. Goddammit.

Kris peeked out. The bedroom door was closed, so she clumsily slipped out of bed and got to her feet. The instant she stood up, she felt sick, and snatched the garbage just in time.

She wiped her mouth with her tank top and pressed a hand against her forehead. Still squinting in the bright sunlight, Kris stumbled over to the dresser and fished out a pair of black shorts and a Breathing Oceans T-shirt.

I should just seal this room shut and never leave again, Kris thought when she realized she put her shirt on backwards and had to twist it around. *It's about the only dignified thing I can do at this point.*

She caught up with Larsen in the hall, who was carrying a glass of water and two pain relievers. "Here," he said, and he wouldn't look her in the eye as he held out his offering.

"I really don't want to." Kris's stomach churned as the smell of tequila and cleaning products filled her nose.

"It will help."

It didn't. She nearly threw up the water, but fought to hold it down.

"I need to find my phone," she said.

Larsen slipped his hand into his back pocket and pulled out her phone. "You asked me to take it away. Before you did something you would regret."

"Oh God." Kris let her hair hide her face as she wrapped her fingers around her phone. She ducked past Larsen but saw that the bathroom door was closed, so she rushed outside. She rammed open the screen door, threw her torso over the railing, and vomited into the grass.

"I'm surprised you're up." Kurt's voice came from the swing.

Kris squeezed the banister and pressed her forehead against her hands. "I feel like death," she muttered between gags.

Kurt strummed his thumb over his guitar strings before leaning forward. "I hope it was worth it. My living room rug reeks of alcohol, and my coffee table is permanently stained. But at least you two had fun."

She groaned, rocking her head gently from side to side. "Oh, shut up. You're the one who told me to relax."

Kurt set his guitar aside and stood up. "I thought you were more mature than this."

"Well, I'm sorry I'm such a disappointment." She spit into the grass and wiped her mouth with her wrist.

It was quiet for a moment. Kris had to look back to confirm Kurt was still there. Her chest tightened at the grimace staring back at her.

"I don't understand you sometimes," he said.

Kris's laugh was cut short by a deep gag. "Yeah, *I'm* the enigma here," she muttered.

He took another step forward. "Don't you care? About . . . about training? Finding Calosant?"

She leaned against the banister and rubbed her eyes as they began to tear up. "Of course I care."

"Then why don't you act like it? It feels like you don't take this seriously. Like you don't take *me* seriously."

Kris took her weight off the railing and hugged her arms around herself. The wood beneath her bare feet was beginning to warm up as the sun crawled higher into the sky. But she was still trembling. "You're so cold sometimes," she said under her breath, sniffling.

"Come on, don't cry." Kurt sighed and beckoned her closer. "Come here."

Kris slouched forward, head still down. She kept her arms clutched tightly as Kurt embraced her, then sobbed into his chest. "I'm sorry. I'm such a screwup."

"You're not a screwup." He rested his chin on her forehead and gave a small laugh. "You might *screw up* from time to time, but you're not *a* screwup."

The smell of lemon filled Kris's nose, and her head instantly felt lighter. She carefully unfurled her arms to wrap them around Kurt.

"Why do you always have to push my buttons?" he whispered to her.

She hunched her shoulders. "I don't know," she admitted. The nausea was rapidly disappearing as she felt the familiar spark in her heart pumping through her body.

Kurt lightly rubbed her back and chuckled. "Well, then stop it."

Kris cracked a small smile, hugging him just a little tighter.

~

Kurt waited outside the bathroom door until it finally opened.

Cade jolted back. He slapped one hand on his chest and the other on the counter to regain his balance as he stumbled. "Jesus

Christ, dude," he grumbled, rubbing his eyes with his thumb and forefinger. "You scared me sober."

"You think this is a joke?"

Still clasping a hand over his face, Cade shook his head and took a step. "No."

Kurt lurched forward, cutting him off before he could leave the bathroom. He jabbed a finger into Cade's chest, his other hand clenched in a fist at his side. "If *anything* like last night happens again, then you are gone. We are *done*. Do you understand me?"

Cade dropped his hand and squinted as if trying to focus. He teetered back and forth as he slowly nodded. "I understand. Won't happen again."

Kurt looked him up and down. "Good." He side-stepped to allow Cade to exit the bathroom. "Go lie down, sober up. And then I want you to dump out every last drop of alcohol you have in this house."

~

Kris sat on the porch steps, waiting for Kurt to return so they could start training again. Hunched over her phone, she scrolled through her messages from the night before. She had sent several nonsensical messages to Brie, and one somber reply to Ian.

I still care about you, and maybe somewhere deep down I do still love you. I'm sorry I put so much blame on you for my parents' death. I know it wasn't your fault. I guess it was just easier to blame you. Kris took a sharp breath in, pressing her fist against her lips as she continued reading the message she had no recollection of sending. *There is no going back now. No putting everything back in the box. I'm sorry.*

I love you, Skittles, Ian had replied several hours later. *I will always love you. And whoever he is, I hope he makes you happy. I hope he treats you better than I did.*

Kris shut off her phone and clutched it against her chest with a sad smile as the screen door screeched open.

"Ready?" Kurt asked, resting a hand on her shoulder.

She nodded, pulled herself up using the railing, and tucked her phone into her back pocket. "Yep. Let's do this."

Chapter 20

The First Key

Sun was spilling in, casting half the room in yellow light. It illuminated the bed, with the covers smoothed of wrinkles and the sides tucked under the mattress. A small stack of hardcover books sat on the nightstand, the spines flaking and weathered with age.

The shaded half of the room was littered with dirty socks and T-shirts. The blanket hung off the bed, balled up on the floor. A muddy pair of biking boots was thrown carelessly in the corner. A couple Polaroid photos of friends were tacked to the wall just above the bed. Several half-empty packs of cigarettes lay scattered throughout the mess, and one bottle of hair product rested on the end table.

Larsen sat up perfectly straight at the desk in the corner, scrolling through internet articles on his laptop. Every few clicks, he would lean over and scribble some notes in his notebook, then return to his keyboard.

The bedroom door flew open, and Larsen glanced back to see Cade wiping sweat from his brow.

"Still wasting time with that?" Cade said.

Larsen turned back to his computer. "Someone has to," he mumbled, stretching his arms over his head. "Some of us care about the lives at stake. So unless you know something I don't know . . ."

Cade hovered behind him. "I bet I know a lot of things you don't know."

"Then tell me what you make of this." Larsen snatched Kurt's pendant from behind his laptop and slapped it down on the edge of the desk.

Cade picked up the small silver pendant with two fingers, holding it closer to his face to examine. "What is it?"

"It's Kurt's," Larsen explained, twisting to the side in his chair. "Passed down in his family. Turns out a few of these were distributed to the last remaining families in Calosant hundreds of years ago before the city was abandoned and sealed off. It's supposed to help guide us back someday."

Cade held it in his palm and traced his thumb over the engraving with a confused expression. "Why Solomon's Knot, though? What does that have to do with Calosant?"

Larsen stood up to inspect the charm again. "What's Solomon's Knot?"

"This symbol. It's popular in Celtic art and culture."

"How can you possibly know that?"

Cade sneered. "My roommate Whitney is Irish, and she has it tattooed on her—"

Larsen swiped the pendant from his hand and turned up his nose. "You're gross." He dropped back into his chair and returned to his laptop.

Cade laughed, then leaned down over Larsen's shoulder. "Try searching 'silver Solomon's Knot.'"

"It's not silver. Silver would have tarnished," Larsen realized out loud, passing his fingers over the pendant again. "It's platinum."

~

A wooden dining room chair stood in the field a few feet away from Kris. As she extended her hand, the chair ascended from the grass and slowly hovered upward. It tipped and twisted, fighting gravity as it levitated higher and higher until it was about five feet in the air.

"Now bring it down. Carefully," Kurt instructed from behind her.

The muscles in her arm pulsated and Kris flexed her fingers apart. Her telekinetic grasp on the chair was slipping. In her mind, she clutched the back of the chair with both hands, struggling as she delicately lowered it.

She took a large gulp of air when she finally got the chair back on the ground gracefully. With her fists on her hips, she threw her head back.

"Catch your breath, then try again," Kurt said.

"Oh my God, how many times do I have to do this?" Kris grumbled, straightening her spine. "I've been lifting this chair for hours."

Kurt sauntered by and adjusted the placement of the chair. "We're building your speed and precision. And you aren't supposed to be complaining."

"I know." She threw her arms up. "It's just boring."

"That's still complaining," he pointed out, flashing Kris a crooked smile as he stepped around her. "Come on. Again."

She held her hand out and narrowed her sights on the wooden chair again. *If I do this quickly, then I won't have to do it anymore.*

It's not a race, Kurt's voice said, ringing through her head.

The chair jerked into the air, then eased upward. Kris let out a long, slow breath and lowered her arm, allowing the chair to sink back down into the grass.

"Better."

"Do I have to do it again?" Kris asked, her shoulders slouching forward.

"Kurt!" Larsen marched out onto the porch, waving his arms with a grin on his face. "I found the first key," he exclaimed as he skipped down the steps into the grass.

Cade pushed his way through the screen door behind him, his hands in his pockets. "Excuse me, *we* found the first key."

"It's at Platinum Rock," Larsen continued, uncharacteristically ignoring Cade as he held the pendant out to Kurt. "It's a historic landmark. A cliff on the shores of Solomon, Maine."

Kurt took the pendant from Larsen and slid the twine over his head so the necklace hung on his chest once again. "I'm speechless."

"What's in Maine exactly?" Kris asked, slinking forward. She clutched her arm, watching Kurt's smile from the corner of her eye.

"I don't know specifically," Larsen confessed with a subtle shrug. "But it will lead us to the next clue. We'll be one step closer to Calosant."

Kurt pushed his hair back from his face. "That's incredible. When can we go? Can we go now? Can you take us all?"

Kris looked to Cade, then tore her eyes away. *Guess Kurt doesn't trust leaving me alone again.*

"I should be able to get us close," Larsen said, his head bobbing around as he spoke.

"Okay, cool. Day trip," Kris joked. She raised her fists up and shook them in sarcastic celebration.

Kurt's smile didn't fade, and he didn't even turn his head to acknowledge her. "Let's go. Let's do it."

"So weird seeing you excited to leave your cocoon," Cade said.

Larsen held out both arms, and Kurt linked his around one. Cade yanked his hand away, choosing to circle around to hold Kurt's other arm instead. Kris closed the space between Cade and Larsen, and she pressed her eyes shut.

"Here we go again," she mumbled as the pain pounded her skull.

The world felt like it was collapsing in. The sound of the songbirds distorted, morphing into crashing waves. The air became sticky and humid, and the smell of salt water and pine filled Kris's nose. She squeezed Cade's and Larsen's arms when the dizziness kicked in, but she refused to open her eyes until she suddenly felt her feet slide out from under her.

Kris screamed, twisting her body to keep from landing on her face as she slipped down a ditch. Mud lathered the back of her shirt and jeans. Rocks and pine needles scratched her arms until she abruptly stopped by slamming against the trunk of a pine tree. Water droplets rained down on her from the branch above.

Cade laughed. "Nice landing, nerd," he shot at Larsen, punching him in the shoulder.

Evergreens and flowers surrounded them. The ground was rocky, but the patches of dirt were soft from being saturated with recent rain. Kris clambered to her feet, using the tree to stabilize herself. She flicked her grimy arms out to the sides.

Kurt stifled a laugh as he carefully descended the muddy slope and side-stepped down to her. "Are you okay?"

"Of course this would happen to me," she griped, rotating her arms to examine the dirt that coated her hands.

"Come on." Kurt gave her a gentle smile and softly wiped mud from Kris's cheek with his thumb. "It's not that bad. We'll clean you up when we get back."

"I definitely have dibs on the shower," she said. She took Kurt's hand and let him pull her back up to where Cade and Larsen were waiting.

"I'm sorry." Larsen brushed mud off Kris's arms and back. "I was basing my entry on photos, not experience. I didn't know where we would appear."

"It's fine," she mumbled, plucking pine needles and grass from her hair. "Let's just find your thing and get out before I fall in some poison ivy or off a cliff or something." She slapped her hands back and forth against her pants and shook her bangs from her face. "So where are we going?"

Larsen motioned with his arm, then led the way through the branches. "We head north along the coast. Watch your step."

"Too little, too late."

Kris continued to dust herself off as she followed Kurt. He held a low-hanging branch aside for her to pass between some pines. Beyond the trees, she could finally see ocean waves rolling towards the rocks on the shore down below. They walked through the dirt along the top of the ridge.

Between stealing glances at the water, she cautiously stepped around puddles. The sun was dipping closer to the horizon, filtering the world in golden rays of light that danced across the ripples on the water.

"How much farther is this Platinum Rock?" Cade called from the back of the line. His foot slipped off a rock into a puddle, and he grumbled as he kicked muddy water from his boots.

Larsen pointed to a wooden railing just ahead. "That's the hiking trail. It loops around Platinum Rock, so it should only be like a half-mile hike to the cliff."

The ocean cut inland, circling off a small bay area lined with jagged red rocks. The shore became steeper as it looped toward the inside of the inlet where the waves had eroded the rocks at the base and left a cliff hanging over the water.

Kurt pointed to the cliff. "That must be it."

As Larsen reached the edge of the hiking trail, his body passed through the wood railing. Kris did a double take as Kurt did the same. The railing was still perfectly intact.

She stopped on her side of the fence. "Whoa, when do I get to learn *that*?" She immediately rolled her eyes and said, "When you're ready" at the same time Kurt did.

"No complaining," he warned, turning back to watch Kris struggle to get her leg over the railing.

She hopped down onto the hiking path, and Cade climbed over as well.

He lifted his leg and brushed off his black boots. "I did not wear the right shoes for this."

"Me either," Kris said, kicking out her canvas sneakers. "And I have decent hiking boots back at the granddevils' place too."

"I don't want to teleport closer," Larsen explained as he followed the trail towards the cliff. "This is a popular landmark. I don't know what the tourist situation will look like down there."

Kris squinted. From where she stood, she couldn't see any figures by the cliff, but it was getting harder to tell as the daylight dwindled.

Kurt and Larsen walked alongside each other, so Kris lagged behind them with her hands in her pockets. A breeze blew over her from the ocean, bringing with it a comforting mist. She closed her eyes and breathed it in. *I could live by the ocean*, she thought with a slight smile. *Maybe someday.*

The stench of cigarettes woke her from her daydream as Cade released a cloud of smoke into the air around them. She pulled the top of her shirt up over her nose and glared at him.

"You have to stop," Kris said with a groan, her voice muffled through her T-shirt.

Cade leaned in close as he took a long drag of her cigarette.

"Don't you dare," she said, pushing on his chest to back him away.

He turned over his opposite shoulder and breathed out the smoke, then chuckled. "So serious."

"Wish I brought my camera," Kurt said from ahead of them. "This place is something else." He paused and leaned over the railing that separated the trail from the rocks. He stared down at the waves crashing against the shore, spraying water in all directions.

"It's beautiful, that's for sure." Kris seized the opportunity to admire the ocean shores as well.

"Let's keep moving," Larsen insisted, nodding towards the cliff. "We're losing daylight."

Kris flashed Kurt a smile, but he turned away and continued up the trail. Her cheeks burned as she dropped her chin to her chest.

As the cliff grew closer, she could see that it was entirely gated off. A couple was taking photos through a chain-link fence, but other than that, the area was completely devoid of visitors.

Cade sighed. "There's no one here. We could have definitely teleported closer."

"A little exercise is good for you and your blackened lungs," Larsen fired back.

Kris stopped in her tracks, squaring her shoulders back and straightening her spine. She rested a hand on her chest as she felt a zing that left her short of breath.

Cade paused and looked back at her. "You okay?"

She scanned the cliffs ahead. She didn't see anything, but in her mind, in the dark world, there was a light. It was small, but still penetrated the blackness.

"I—I think I can feel it," Kris said. "At least, I feel something."

Charging forward past Kurt and Larsen as they slowed, she was surprised to find her feet carrying her so quickly down the hiking trail toward the chain-link fence that separated the path from the cliffs. One defined point jutted out over the water, and her heart was leading her to it. In her mind, the light was burning brighter, and everything else seemed to melt away.

The two tourists were gone by the time she reached the fence. Kris ran along it, her eyes glued to the tip of the bluff on the other side. She locked her fingers around the fence and shut her eyes. The world wasn't as dark, and the glow ahead was gently pulsating, expanding outward. Calling to her.

A strand of light spiraled out towards her as Kris reached out a hand. It circled her arm like a ribbon and twisted around her, yet she felt calm.

"I think I feel it too," Kurt whispered from somewhere nearby.

Kris opened her eyes, but she could still see the ribbon of light waving faintly in front of her, beckoning her towards the cliff. "Do you see it? The light?"

Now standing next to her, he shook his head. "No. But I can feel it." He put a hand on her shoulder. "This may hurt."

Before Kris could question him, Kurt pulled her forward into the fence. Her breath caught in her throat. As her skin touched the fence, it burned and tingled. She watched in astonishment as her arm phased straight through the metal wires. She lost feeling in her hand when it happened, as though it had been separated from her body entirely.

The sensation continued up her shoulder as Kurt pulled her through the fence. Every muscle in her body ached, like the cells were being torn apart and reassembled on the other side.

Her heart throbbed in her chest and her skull was ringing, but finally she was through. Kris dropped to her knees in the grass, panting and coughing. She fell forward on her hands and strained to calm her spasming heart rhythm.

"You'll be fine," Kurt said, resting a hand on her back. "Just keep breathing."

"Never mind. I don't want to learn how to do that." She wheezed and clutched her chest with each raspy breath. She twisted her torso to look up at him, and then at Larsen as he walked through the fence, completely impervious. "That was horrible. How are you fine right now?"

"Practice." Larsen lifted a hand to block out the sun as he gazed back at the hill behind them.

Kris shook her head and slowly stood. "I don't know. I think I would rather go another round with Red than intentionally do that to myself ever again."

"It gets easier," Kurt said, brushing some of the dried mud off her shoulder.

The fence rattled as Cade dropped down from the top. He looked back at it. "Not worth it."

A chilling breeze blew over the bluff, but it didn't affect Kris. The light was still waving, calling her closer, and it felt warm. Without a word, she moved forward onto the rocks and carefully placed her feet to keep from slipping. She crouched near the edge, then peered down over the cliff at the waves crashing down below.

"Kris, please be careful," Kurt said from behind her.

"Whoa, Nelly," Larsen muttered.

The world in Kris's mind was no longer dark, as the light completely enveloped all of her surroundings. She felt safe, despite standing at the tip of a fifty-foot drop into roaring ocean waves.

"It's here," Kris said. She kicked back her legs to lie on her stomach at the ridge, then reached down to slide her hand over the rock. She extended her arm, her fingertips tracing a smooth surface. "It's in the face of the cliff."

With her eyes closed, the light suddenly condensed in her mind to a diamond-shaped object just beneath her hand. It resonated from her fingers through her whole body. Kris wrapped both hands around it and effortlessly lifted it.

Hovering out in front of her over the ledge was an oblong shield, pointed at the top and bottom with a notch on each side.

Cade let out a low whistle. "It's a shield?"

Kurt reached out, taking a hold of the straps on the inside of the shield and releasing it from Kris's telekinetic grasp. "Got it."

Kris let out a breath, realizing only after she let go how much she was expending herself. Cade held her arm to help her to her feet, then clapped the dirt off his hands.

Though the shield was heavy, Kurt's posture lifted. His eyes danced about the inside of it in a look of confusion and awe. The face of the shield was decorated with elaborate engravings that circled the center and around the outer edge. The crest at the top contained a polished brown gem that almost seemed to glow. Kris grazed it with her fingers, astonished by how smooth it was, considering the length of time it had been exposed to wind, rain, and ocean waves.

"Okay, great, we got it," Cade blurted, backing away towards the fence and motioning for the others to follow. "Let's just take it and get out of here."

Kris nodded. "Yes, please. I need a shower."

Kurt's head jerked up and his eyes cleared. "Yeah," he said flatly. Slipping an arm through the straps, he carried the shield over to Larsen, who was waiting near the chain-link fence.

The land was getting dim as the sun disappeared behind the trees. They searched the trails around them leading up to the bluff, and there was no one around.

"We can teleport from here," Larsen said, putting a hand on Kurt's shoulder.

Kris linked arms with Larsen and looked back at the cliff one last time. The waves out on the ocean looked so calming, and the salty smell of the air relaxed her.

Wish I could put all of this in a bottle and save it for another day, Kris thought as the world around began to blur together. *Someday.*

Chapter 21

Sacred Place

Kurt set the shield down on the dining room table and brushed his fingers over the surface, then examined his hand. "Look at how clean it is."

"That makes one of us," Kris muttered, kicking off her dirty sneakers by the cabin door. "I'll be in the shower."

"Hey." He took a few steps after her as she started down the hall, and she turned to him. A pine needle had tangled itself in her hair, and he found himself staring at it for far too long. He cleared his throat, scratching the nape of his neck. "You did good today."

Kris bowed her head with a smile. Her cheeks turned pink as she brushed her dark hair behind her ear. "Thanks."

He waved awkwardly and turned back to the dining room, but he glanced back and caught Kris's eye as she was closing the bathroom door. *That was smooth. Why did I wave?* Kurt snapped his head forward to the dining room again, where Cade and Larsen were both leaning over the shield, elbowing the other for space.

He slipped in the spot between his friends to study the shield.

Larsen traced a finger over a long string of symbols etched along its base. "It's encoded."

"Do you know the language?" Kurt asked, examining each character individually.

Larsen shook his head and frowned. "I'll do some digging, but I've never seen anything like this."

"Why would the Elders make this so complicated?" Cade crossed his arms and leaned against the table. "Can't it just say 'go here' in plain English?"

Kurt sighed, rubbing his eyes. "They didn't want just anyone stumbling across Calosant. It's a sacred place, you know?"

"The important thing is that we have the shield and Tynan doesn't," Larsen said. "Puts us one step closer and him one step further away." He snatched a pen and notepad off the kitchen counter and started scribbling down the symbols. "I'll see what I can find out, but I expect it will take a while to crack without a cipher."

"How long?" Kurt pressed.

Larsen shrugged with his entire arm. "I mean, I have to scour the internet for symbols I've never seen before, or try to interpret them myself . . ."

"How long?" Kurt asked again. "If you had to guess."

Larsen rested on his elbows and sighed. "With any luck, a couple weeks."

~

Kris rubbed her hands together as a bead of sweat trickled down her temple. Despite the clouds, the late-morning air was hot and humid, and each breath felt like suffocation. A fire raged in her heart, and she tensed her muscles, trying to force it down into her hands. The hairs stood on her arms as the flames flickered under her skin.

"Slowly," Kurt said.

Kris carefully pulled her hands apart, the rush of heat collecting in her palms. At first, there was only a spark, but it flashed and then spiraled into a blazing ball of fire. She gasped in surprise, but her smile quickly vanished when the fire winked out again.

She dropped her arms with a groan. "Not that I'm complaining, but can we call it a day on fireballs?" Kris wiped sweat from her face. "It's just too hot for this."

Kurt gave her shoulders a squeeze. "You're doing great. Just give it a few more tries, then we'll break for the day."

She rolled her head back and choked on the muggy air. "But I'm not getting it, and this heat isn't helping at all. I feel like this is a waste of time."

"How long did it take you to master guitar?" he asked, stepping back and crossing his arms with a smirk.

"I didn't."

Kurt jabbed a finger in her direction. "Exactly. Because you didn't practice."

Kris rolled her eyes up to the cloudy sky again. "Fine."

"You got this."

Letting out a long breath, she limbered up by shaking out her arms. "Fine, fine. Let's do this."

She locked eyes with Kurt for a second, and her heart leaped out of her chest. In that moment, Kris forgot all about the humidity.

She clapped her hands together and focused again. It didn't take long for her to call up the fire inside herself and channel it down to her hands. The fireball flickered twice, then puffed out.

"Damn it," Kris growled. She shook out her limbs again and bent her knees, grounding herself. "I can do this."

She shut her eyes and huffed heavily on the thick summer air. In her mind, the world wasn't as dark. She could see the glow from the shield nearby, pulsating, calling to her. Each flash of light made Kris feel a little stronger. Breathe a little clearer. The light grew brighter, encompassing her and embracing her, and it smelled sweet in a way she couldn't describe.

There was something emerging in the distance through the white light. It looked like columns. Kris squinted hard to make it out, hesitantly sneaking forward.

With each step, the ground became more solid, and it changed into a slick path of silver stone. The pillars ahead took shape, and she recognized she was staring at some sort of structure: a towering building with columns suspending the front. Everything else was still fuzzy, blurred by the glare of the bright white light.

Kris started running towards it, but it never seemed to get any closer. What was this place? Calosant?

She looked down at the rocks beneath her feet, then back up at the building far ahead, studying the silhouette of its ridges. Her chest burned, hotter than it had before.

This is it, Kris told herself, opening her eyes again. *This is what I need to make that fireball last.*

She felt the heat in her hands and started to pull them apart as they began to glow.

"Wait, Kris—"

Before Kurt could say anything else, Kris's hands lit up, and a white beam of light blasted out from between her palms. The look of terror on Kurt's face was like nothing Kris had ever witnessed. He threw himself down into the grass, narrowly avoiding the ray of light that fired across the meadow.

She ripped her hands apart with a grunt and the beam vanished. Panting, she turned her hands around, but the glow was gone.

Kurt pushed up to his hands and knees. His back heaved rapidly with each breath.

"I'm so sorry," she cried, staggering over to him. "I don't know how that happened." She bent down to help him up.

"Don't touch me." He swung his arm and flung Kris backward. She lost her balance, falling back on her hands. "I'm sorry," he wheezed while slowly climbing to his feet. He kept his back to her as he stood.

Kris sat in the grass, bewildered, as Kurt sprinted to the house and disappeared inside without another word.

~

Kurt kept his head down as he entered the living room where Cade and Kris were watching TV.

"Hey," Kris said, immediately sitting up when she saw him. "Are you okay?"

He shot Cade a curious glance before looking back at Kris. "Can I talk to you?"

She looked at Cade, confusion on her face, but pulled herself off the couch. "Sure."

Kurt motioned for her to follow him to the front porch. The air outside was still sticky and humid.

"I'm so sorry about earlier," Kris said, hugging herself. "It was an accident. I obviously wasn't trying to hurt you. I don't even know how I did that . . ."

He held up a hand and offered a little half smile as he leaned back against the porch railing. "I know, I know. I'm fine. It's okay."

Kris shuffled over to the swing and slumped down into it. She stared at her feet while gently rocking herself forward and back. "I still feel bad, though."

"I didn't handle it very well," he admitted, turning to look out across the darkened meadow. The clouds overhead blocked out any light from the moon and stars. "Beams are very advanced and extremely dangerous. They're . . . essentially, they're a manifestation of our truest selves. Our truest intent. Inflicting damage on a spiritual level by ripping a soul apart, bit by bit." He laced his fingers together and rested on his elbows. "They can be lethal."

The swing continued to creak behind him. Beyond that, all Kurt could hear were the crickets out in the field and the TV quietly playing inside. Neither he nor Kris said anything for a few minutes, letting the evening absorb them.

Finally, Kris stood up from the swing. "Well, I'm still struggling with fireballs, but I'll get there." She nudged Kurt's arm as she leaned forward on the railing beside him. "I told you I would prove to you that I'm serious, and I am."

He smirked. "Well, good. We can try again tomorrow morning. And maybe you don't try to kill me this time."

"Ha. Funny."

The smile that curled her lips was intoxicating. Kurt couldn't pull his gaze away. And she watched him staring too.

A buzz broke the silence and Kris jumped back. As she pulled her cell phone out of her pocket, her smile vanished. "It's Ian."

Kurt cleared his throat and pinched his lips into a smile, but his posture deflated. "Go ahead. Answer it."

Though apprehensive, Kris accepted the call, whirling around to face away from him. "Hey," she said quietly into her phone.

He could hear the voice on the other line, but he couldn't understand what was being said. Kris's shoulders went rigid a moment later, and he knew something was wrong.

"What?" She gradually turned back to Kurt, her face white as a sheet.

"What's wrong?" he mouthed to her.

Her lip trembled as her eyes welled with tears. She stumbled back until her spine hit the railing. "Brie's been arrested by the NWDA."

Chapter 22

National Witcan Detention Agency

"Calm down. Catch your breath," Kurt was saying as Kris circled the dining room.

"How am I supposed to calm down?" she shouted, waving her hands around before finally locating her sneakers beside the living room couch. She plopped onto the floor, stuffed her feet into her shoes, and fumbled with the laces as her hands shook. "I have to go. I have to save her."

Cade stood from the couch at the same time Larsen appeared in the hallway.

"What's going on?" Larsen asked.

Kris jumped up and moved for the front door.

"Kris's friend has been detained by the NWDA," Kurt explained, blocking the door as she tried to pass.

"Oh no." Larsen hurried into the room and tried to comfort her, but she shrugged him off.

She moved to slide by Kurt, and he shifted to keep her from reaching the door. She glared up at him. "I have to help her. Please don't try to stop me."

"Storming out into the night on foot with no idea where you're going or what you're going to do if you get there isn't going to help your friend." He squeezed her shoulder and forced her away from the door.

"I don't care! I can't just sit here and do nothing."

"Then let us help you," Cade said, inserting himself between the two of them.

"How?" Kurt slapped his arms down at his sides. "We have no idea where the NWDA would be holding her."

Cade looked between Kurt and Kris. "There's an NWDA facility about an hour north of here just outside of Rockford. It's the closest one to Greenville, and where they would likely have taken her. Plus it's understaffed, which means it's minimally guarded."

"Then that's where I'm going," Kris said, tying her hair back in a ponytail. "Brie is my family. I can't let anything happen to her."

Kurt took a long, deep breath in and stared into her eyes. "Larsen," he said without looking away.

"I can take us there. I just need to know where I'm going."

Cade pressed his palm against Larsen's forehead and closed his eyes. Larsen gasped, then raised his head with a look of recognition on his face.

Kris's heart pounded in her chest. *I'm coming, Brie.*

"Anything we should know before doing this?" Larsen asked Cade as they circled up.

"Yeah. Don't get shot."

~

A ten-foot cement wall and a sturdy iron gate separated Kris from the asymmetrical building illuminated by spotlights against the black sky. NATIONAL WITCAN DETENTION AGENCY was written just above the doors. The first floor was lined with ceiling-tall, tinted windows, but the floors above were solid walls.

Two SUVs sat parked outside what appeared to be the main entrance, but there was nobody in sight. No movement.

"They keep prisoners on the upper floors," Cade whispered from their hiding spot in the trees near the gate.

Kurt looked up and down the cement wall. "How do we get in there? There must be cameras and motion detectors everywhere."

"I can go," Larsen said. "Scope things out."

"So that, what, we can just waltz up to the main entrance?" Cade hissed, shooting him a glare.

Larsen hit him in the shoulder. "Then what's your brilliant idea, smart guy?"

"Stop it," Kris snapped. "This is no time for bickering."

"Kris is right." Kurt motioned to the roof. "There must be access to the roof for helicopters. Do you think we could get in from there undetected?"

Cade nodded. "That would be more discreet."

"But we would still need to determine what cell your friend is being kept in," Larsen said. "I would need to access the files at the front desk."

Cade put a hand on Larsen's shoulder. "I'll go with you."

"I'll go with Kris," Kurt said.

Kris held on to Larsen, thankful that the headaches from teleporting were getting easier for her to deal with after each trip. They seemed to be going away faster too.

Now standing on the darkened roof, the four rushed across to the door as silently as possible.

"I don't see any cameras," Kurt whispered as they approached the roof door.

Kris's heart hammered and her mind raced. *I'm coming, Brie.*

"Buckle up." Kurt grabbed her by the wrist and phased through the door.

Kris hardly had time to even process the pain of passing through the steel door. Once inside the stairwell, she stumbled to regain her footing. Kurt held on to her arms to stabilize her. All she could focus on were the calluses on his fingertips and how rough they felt against her skin.

Larsen joined them, pulling Cade after him.

"God, I hate that feeling," Cade muttered, pushing a hand against his forehead.

"What's your friend's name?" Larsen asked Kris as he looked down the stairwell to the floors below.

"Briella Wright," she replied in a shaky voice, then spelled it out. Her limbs were trembling so fiercely that she had to clutch Kurt's shirt to hold herself up.

"Calm her down," Larsen said to Kurt. "Cade and I will get to the front desk to find Briella's file. I'll let you know what we find."

Kris watched the two of them creep down the stairs. Dazed, she tried to follow, but Kurt held her back.

"You need to breathe," he whispered to her. "We can't go rushing in without clear heads."

She nodded, taking deep breaths in and out. "I can't stop shaking."

Kurt's hand lightly brushed Kris's and he offered her a small reassuring smile. "We're going to get your friend, okay? She's going to be all right."

A few more deep breaths. Her heart was still pounding, but Kris slipped away, staring down over the railing. She could hear a door close several floors below, and it echoed through the cement stairwell.

"Have you had a lot of interactions with the NWDA?" she asked, trying to take her mind off things.

"More than I care to admit."

"Oh good. That's comforting."

What felt like hours passed in the dimly lit stairwell, and Kris continuously fiddled with her hair.

"What's taking them so long?' she croaked, pushing her back against the cold wall.

"They're just being cautious. No alarms have sounded," Kurt reminded her. His head jerked up. "She's in cell B216. Come on." He waved for her to follow as he started down the steps.

As they descended, voices echoed from a floor below. Kurt looked back and put a finger to his lips. He continued to press on, sneaking quietly down the stairs.

"Did you hear Hurbor is on site today?" one of the people said. "He's interrogating that old Witcan we brought in the other day."

"He's conducting an interrogation himself? Isn't that a little beneath him?"

The voices slowly faded, followed by the clank of a door shutting.

I think they're gone, Kurt told her. *She's on the second floor in the B wing. Let's go.*

Still crouched, Kris crept down the first flight of stairs. Her hands trembled, so she held them close to her chest while she searched the ceiling for security cameras.

As they turned to descend the next flight of stairs, she froze. She put a hand on Kurt's chest to stop him, then nodded to a security camera in the top corner. The camera was twisted so its lens was pointing to the wall.

Larsen must have already adjusted its position, Kurt told her.

There was a door on the landing labeled "4," so they climbed down the stairwell two more stories until they reached the second floor. They passed a couple more security cameras, also turned away to allow them to slip past.

Kris peered through the window of the door to the second floor. The corridor was mostly dark, but she could see it was lined with steel doors. Each one had a light above it, some solid red and some flashing, but she couldn't see any guards.

Kurt grabbed her wrist before she could touch the door handle. He gave her a stern expression and shook his head. *Two men down the hall headed this way*, he told her. *Let's wait for them to pass.*

She strained her neck, trying to locate the men he spoke of. She couldn't see them, but was suddenly able to identify two sets of footsteps reverberating down the hall. Kris dropped to a crouch away from the door when the shadows approached.

What if they come in here? she said.

Kurt motioned for her to get behind him, his eyes glued to the narrow window just above him. She obliged, pushing herself against the wall behind the door.

Just trust me, he said, and held a hand back as though to shield her.

With each step closer, Kris's heart sped up. The door handle turned, and her whole chest sunk into the pit of her stomach. Two heavily armored soldiers dressed in full SWAT gear shuffled into the stairwell, closing Kurt and Kris in the corner behind the door.

Oh God. She grabbed Kurt's arm and gave it a squeeze.

Kris clapped a hand over her mouth to keep from gasping as both men went limp and folded over onto the landing. *What did you do?* she asked Kurt.

"They're just asleep," he whispered out loud. He put a hand down on the floor and inhaled deeply. "We don't have long."

Kurt stepped over the armed guards, removed their long guns from their shoulders, and unclipped a key card from one of their belts. He slipped the guns over his own shoulder and opened the door, searching both directions before motioning for Kris to follow. Once in the hall, he pressed his hands together, then created a ball of fire between his palms as he pulled them apart again. He held the fireball against the door handle until it warped and melted, and then he waved the fire out of existence.

Kris tiptoed over to the nearest door. A255. She looked back at Kurt as he set the guns down next to the sealed door. *This is the A wing*, she told him. *The B wing must be on the other side.*

They rushed as quietly as they could down the hall to the right. Kris stopped and stared up at a blinking red light, then down at the door beneath it. There was someone trapped in here. In all these doors.

Kurt looked back at her and must have noticed her focused expression. *Kris, no, we don't have time for them.*

"There are other people suffering too," Kris hissed, tracing her fingers over a key card slot alongside the door. She held out a hand to Kurt. "I can't leave them here."

"They're going to raise the alarm."

"Then they can help us fight."

Kurt hesitated but slapped the key card into the palm of her hand. She swiped it through the reader, and the steel door slid open. Kris jolted back in horror.

A woman, bloodied and beaten, stood with her wrists cuffed to the wall and arms outstretched on either side. The thick metal band clamped around her neck blinked red, just like the light outside the door, and a thin plastic tube connected the band to a medical bag on the wall. Her eyes opened a sliver, a dazed expression on her face as she tried to focus on Kris in the doorway.

"I'm going to get you out of here," Kris told the woman softly, and she stepped inside to examine the small square room.

To the right of the door was a panel with a series of buttons. She pressed the large red button at the bottom of the panel, and the metal choker around the woman's neck snapped open and slid off with a loud clunk against the floor. Kris noticed a tiny puncture mark on either side of the woman's neck, a trickle of blood dripping down from each.

The woman took a deep gulp of air, her eyes suddenly widening. She locked eyes with Kris. "Press the top blue button."

Kris turned back to the panel and pushed the blue button in the top-right corner. The woman dropped to her knees as the shackles around her wrists opened as well. She squatted on the ground for a moment and rubbed her wrists, but she offered Kris a teary-eyed smile when she looked up.

"Thank you," she mouthed.

"I have to free the others," Kris whispered. "I need your help."

The woman nodded and followed her out into the hall.

Kris handed the key card back to Kurt. "I need you to open all the doors."

He glanced at the doors around him.

"Trust me," she urged with a bob of her head.

Kurt's lips were pinched and his brow furrowed, but he darted to the nearest door and swiped the key card anyway. As the door opened, the woman from the first cell hurried inside, pressing buttons on the panel and freeing the Witcan inside.

Kris, we don't have enough time, Kurt warned.

She closed her eyes. In the dark, two long lines of small red dots faded into existence and extended forward on either side of her: the buttons in each of the cells to release the cuff around the respective Witcan's neck.

I can do this.

In her mind, Kris hit a sprint, extending her arms out as she ran to hit the red buttons. The rows seemed to continue onward forever, but when she finally reached the end of the line, she turned around. She took a few deep breaths as the red dots changed to blue buttons that would release the arm restraints.

Her head pounded, and in reality, Kris could feel her knees getting weak, but she brushed it off. She took off running back down the line again, hitting every blue button she passed.

Keep going, Kris told herself as the buttons began to flicker and her pace slowed. She panted, and even in her mind she collapsed to her knees.

She crawled forward, slapping the nearest button. On her hands and knees, she pulled herself along to the next in line and reached up a weak arm to swat at it.

I've got your back, Kurt told her.

Through the darkness, Kris saw him running toward her, pushing each blue button as he approached. She smiled up at him as he stopped and pressed the last one beside her.

Come on.

Kris opened her eyes and found herself kneeling on the floor of the dim hallway. It was filling up fast with escaped prisoners, each helping the next in line. As a door would open, a person would immerge, already freed of their shackles. They moved quietly back the way Kris had come, to a stairwell at the far end of the floor.

Beyond them all, Kurt waved her over from much farther down the hall. She rushed over to him despite the tremble in her legs, slipping between the ever-growing crowd.

"Larsen and Cade are clearing the third floor. Fourth floor is vacant," he whispered to her. "We have to get over to the B wing and find your friend. We're running out of time."

An explosion outside rattled the whole building.

Kris clutched her hands over her ears and instinctively dropped to a crouch. "What was that?"

The deafening sound of alarms filled the hallway as emergency lights on the walls started flashing.

Kurt grabbed her by the wrist. "We have to move. We're not alone."

Chapter 23

Cell B216

The wail of alarms vibrated through Kris's skull as she and Kurt raced down the corridor to the B wing. Soldiers shouted from the floor below, and the sound of gunfire rang out.

The hall opened up to a large atrium once they neared the main entrance. They dropped below the railing and hid from the chaos they could hear coming from the first floor.

"Witcans," one of the men shouted into his radio. "Three of them. At the main gate."

"Someone get Hurbor down here now."

Through the now shattered glass at the front of the building, Kris could see the burning remnants of the NWDA SUVs smoldering and pouring black smoke into the night sky.

She peeked through a space in the banister down to the first floor, where a small group of soldiers was huddled behind the front desk while reloading their guns. In the flashing lights, Kris couldn't quite make it out, but it looked like they were loading their guns with silver darts.

Kurt gently pulled on her arm, and they continued forward in a crouched position until they reached an area where a sign hanging overhead read "B Wing."

More gunshots rang out. Kris flinched at the sound, but kept moving toward the series of doors ahead.

B201.

B202.

B203.

A stairwell door just ahead flung open, and a soldier ran out onto their floor. Kurt skidded to a halt, holding out an arm to brace Kris.

"More Witcans on the second floor!" The man pointed his gun at them, and Kris's heart dropped.

The rifle was ripped from his hands before he could fire, and he fell forward to his knees. Cade stood behind the man and had delivered a punch to the side of his head, knocking him out cold. Larsen threw the gun to the ground, and Kris clasped a hand to her chest.

"Lucky we're here to save your asses," Cade said.

"B216, let's go," Larsen called over to them. "Some of Tynan's men are here."

"What?" Kris cried.

Footsteps echoed from behind them.

"No time," Kurt told her, taking her by the wrist again and running.

Cade stopped outside a steel door. "Here!" He swiped a key card, and the door jerked open.

Kris darted inside before Cade, and her throat tightened at the sight inside. Strapped down on a gurney was a sickly pale body that looked like Brie's. Kris took in her injuries: a series of scratches up both arms, a large welt on her forehead, a red ring under one of her eyes.

A metal cuff circled Brie's throat, just like it had on the other prisoners. Her eyes were closed, her breaths small and weak.

"Oh God, Brie."

Kris kicked over the chair in front of her to get to the gurney. The metal band clicked, then snapped open as Cade pressed a button on the panel near the door, and Kris yanked the device away. They unhooked the straps, freeing Brie's arms and legs.

"Kris?" The sound was weak as Brie turned her head; her eyes barely opened.

"Don't worry. I'm getting you out of here," Kris said, blinking back tears.

Brie sniffled. "How did you find me?" She tried to lift her arms to sit up, but couldn't call upon the strength to do so.

"Kris, they're coming," Kurt warned from the hall.

Kris squeezed Brie's hand and pinched her eyes shut. Though feeling weak herself, she summoned the warm sensation in her heart. The cuts on Brie's arms barely began to heal when a loud bang interrupted her.

There was a series of gunshots fired in the corridor. Larsen cried out, clutching his shoulder as he and Kurt ducked into the room. Blood spilled out from beneath Larsen's fingers. He pressed his back against the wall, his breaths ragged.

"Come out with your hands up!"

An angry scowl warped Kurt's face. His fists glowed green as he leaped out into the hall and charged towards the soldiers.

A shiver ran up Kris's spine as the men screamed in terror. She helped Brie sit up, but Brie's head hung loosely against her chest.

"She's not walking out of here," Cade said. He hunched forward with his back to Brie. "I'm going to need you to hang on."

"Okay," Brie wheezed.

Kris assisted her forward onto his back, tucking her legs around his waist and wrapping her arms around his neck. Brie winced as one of the cuts opened up again and a gentle stream of blood seeped down her arm.

Another scream echoed from the hall. Larsen leaned against the doorframe, crimson slowly darkening his shirt. "Kurt. Stop," he called.

Cade heaved Brie higher onto his back as he stood. "We have to get out of here."

Kris peeked her head out into the corridor. She choked when she saw two bodies sprawled across the narrow hall, blood pooling beneath them. She dropped to her knees beside the closest one and put her fingers against their neck. A breath of relief escaped her when she felt a pulse.

Not too far ahead, Kurt had used telekinesis to pin a third man against the wall. His outstretched hands glowed a deep green, and his eyes flashed as he closed in on his target.

"No. Kurt, stop," Kris pleaded, dashing toward him and inserting herself between him and the NWDA agent.

"Move." Kurt kept his arms raised in front of him.

"No."

"You've seen what they've done."

She stretched her arms and shielded the man behind her. "I won't let you hurt him. You're not a killer, Kurt."

His shoulders relaxed ever so slightly, but before he could say anything else, a gunshot rang out and Kris's body was thrown forward. She crashed down hard on her elbows, but the sting in her side was worse. She clutched her waist with both hands, breathing in sharply. Hot blood oozed from the wound.

Over the wail of the sirens, Kris could hear the soldier cry out as he slammed into the floor. Kurt was looming over the man, who scrambled to grab the handgun nearby. Kurt kicked it away, sending it skidding across the tile, and the man whimpered as he dragged himself away on his back.

"Stop," Kris said again. Still clasping a hand over her wound, she got to her knees and extended her other hand. She reached out telekinetically to grab Kurt by the shoulder and pull him away.

Larsen hunched over her and struggled to pull her to her feet while still pressing a hand to his bloodied shoulder.

"Please," the agent on the ground pleaded, backing away from Kurt with a horrified look in his eyes.

"Stop," Cade yelled as he hurried over with Brie on his back. "That's Hurbor."

The man squinted at him, studying his face until his eyes lit up with recognition. "You . . ."

Cade stepped up beside Kurt. "He's the director of this whole thing."

Kurt held out his glowing fist. "Good."

"Don't," Larsen said as he and Kris tried to steady themselves against the other.

Hurbor raised an arm and shielded himself. "Killing me would only prove me right. It would prove to the world that you really are monsters."

Cade looked back at Kris and Larsen, then back down at Hurbor. "You don't deserve to live," he growled with a firm shake of his head. "But fortunately for you, my friends don't think you deserve to die either." He stomped down on Hurbor's shin with his steel-toed boots. The man's shriek echoed louder than the ringing alarms.

Kris cringed and buried her face into Larsen's chest for a moment before looking up again.

Cade motioned for them to fall back, then looked down at Hurbor. "Count your blessings you get yet another day."

Hurbor launched forward, clutching his leg and crying out in pain.

Cade guided Kurt back over to Larsen. They each put a hand on Larsen's shoulder, and the five of them disappeared from that godforsaken hallway.

Chapter 24

Wounds

Kris's energy was drained after healing the gunshot wound on her waist. She leaned over the table on her hands, panting hard.

"You're lucky that jackass pulled the trigger so quickly," Cade muttered as he wiped the blood from his hands on a towel. He offered it to Kris, who promptly shook her head. "Had he taken a second to adjust his aim . . ."

"Yeah," Kris grumbled, rubbing a hand over her healed skin.

Larsen sucked air in through his teeth as he hunched over the kitchen sink. Despite his best efforts, blood dripped off his elbow onto the hardwood floor.

Kris circled into the kitchen. "Here." She tried to move Larsen's hand to see the wound, and his whole body recoiled.

"It hurts," he whimpered.

"I can help, but you have to let me."

Larsen nodded slowly, blinking back tears. Still clasping his shoulder, he used his other hand to undo the top few buttons of his shirt. Kris helped him carefully pull his shirt down over his shoulder.

She immediately felt sick to her stomach at the hole ripped in his flesh and the blood still pouring out. Turning her head away, she stared into the blackness outside the kitchen window, then rested a palm on the wound.

Though still lightheaded from healing herself, Kris concentrated. The warm feeling had mostly faded, but she coaxed as much strength as she could from her heart. Her fingers tingled so much they began to go numb, and her vision became cloudy. She couldn't keep holding on.

Kris held the corner of the counter to keep her balance, but her knees buckled beneath her. Larsen breathed in sharply, catching her as she fell.

"I'm sorry. I'm sorry," she said as Larsen hauled her back to her feet. There was still blood smeared on his shoulder, and a small break remained in the surface of his skin from the bullet wound.

"Don't be sorry. You've put yourself through hell tonight. You should rest."

Kris nodded, allowing him to guide her to the hall. But when she looked out to the porch and saw Kurt sitting there, hunched over on the front steps, her heart dropped. She couldn't go to sleep without talking to him. About what had happened back there.

"Cade, can you check on Brie?" she asked as she staggered toward the front door.

Cade nodded slowly, saying nothing as he went down the hall to Kris's room.

Larsen gently touched her arm and looked at her with a plea on his face. "You don't have to do this. I can handle him."

Kris swallowed hard, clenching her jaw. "I want to."

Kurt didn't look up as she walked out onto the porch. She didn't say a word, just shut the screen door and sat down on the top step, leaving some space between them.

The crickets filled the dark, muggy night with their song. In her daze, it sounded far away. The clouds parted for a brief moment, and Kris caught a glimpse of the stars before they were quickly swallowed up again.

Kurt sat up, but he kept his head down. "Are you okay?" His voice was hushed and raw.

Kris nodded, running a hand over the tattered hole in her shirt. It was still cold with the drying blood. "Physically, at least. Can't say much about my mental state."

He cleared his throat. "I wish you hadn't seen me like that."

"Me too." She bit down hard on her bottom lip and pinched her hands together. A shiver ran up her spine as she remembered the anger she'd witnessed in Kurt's eyes. The hatred. The bloodlust.

"I don't know what happened. They shot Larsen, and I just . . . I just snapped."

She hugged her arms around herself to calm her shaking. "Fight or flight, right?" She realized she was trying to convince herself more than she was Kurt.

"I should have picked flight."

"You saw Larsen get hurt and it triggered something primal. It wasn't a choice. You can't beat yourself up over it."

Kurt scoffed and then shrugged. "You risked your life to save those Witcans back there. You stood up to *protect* the man responsible for all the pain and suffering the NWDA has caused . . . You didn't even think twice about it, did you?"

Kris shuddered at the image of Kurt's death glare when she had blocked him from attacking Hurbor. *If I hadn't stopped him, would Kurt have killed him? Is he still wishing he had?*

He sighed, curling over his knees again. "How's Brie?"

"She's resting now. She'll be all right."

Another long silence in the humid night air.

From her peripheral view, Kris could see his shoulders jerk upward every few inhales and hear the breath catch in his throat. She was relieved to see some remorse. Some grief.

She turned her body towards Kurt and lightly touched his wrist. He moved his head just enough to peer over at her from the corner of his eye.

"Why are you so forgiving?" he said. "How can you sit there so calmly after what I did?"

Kris brushed her hair from her face, anxiously tapping her feet on the steps. "I don't know. I believe in you, I guess," she whispered with a quiet laugh.

He slowly sat up and twisted to face her, and the fire was back again. Her chest burned as Kurt's eyes flicked down to her lips. He leaned in towards her, his crystal-clear blue-gray eyes studying Kris with a look of longing. Her heart raced and she found herself inching forward as well, but his posture suddenly deflated as he turned away with a long exhale.

"You should get some rest," he told her quietly.

Kris swallowed hard. She could feel her face glowing red as she reflexively nodded in agreement, but paused before she could stand. Despite his efforts to hide, she could see Kurt watching her through a part in his hair, and she just couldn't contain it anymore.

Screw it.

Before she could second-guess herself, she leaned in and planted a peck on his cheek.

"Good night," she said, moving quickly to the screen door.

Kurt touched his cheek and bowed his head. "Good night."

~

Kris entered the room, and Cade looked over at her. Brie was balled up in the bed by the window, breathing softly in her sleep.

"How's she doing?" Kris whispered, rubbing the goose bumps on her arm despite her entire body feeling like it was blushing.

He stood up from the edge of the bed. "She's fast asleep. They did a real number on her."

She crouched next to the bed and swept Brie's blonde bangs from her face. Her forehead was still swollen and bruised. "I can't believe anyone would have done this."

"The B wing is used for interrogation and experimentation," Cade said quietly, crossing his arms and turning his back to Brie. "They're still trying to isolate an identifier. A unique blood type or gene or something, to test the population and identify all Witcans from humans."

Kris blinked back tears.

"You still want to protect those people?" he asked in a flat tone.

She slowly nodded. "We don't get to decide who lives and who dies."

Cade hesitated before putting a hand on her shoulder.

"I can't believe Brie is Witcan." Kris's voice cracked. "How did she even end up there?"

"We read her file while trying to locate her cell . . . Her parents called her in."

"Oh God." She buried her face into the mattress to muffle the sob.

Cade patted her back. "You should get some sleep."

Sniffling, Kris looked back at her bed across the room and shook her head. "I want to be here when she wakes up. I don't want her to feel scared or alone."

"Fine."

Cade marched across the room, grabbed her bed's frame, and dragged it around the nightstand across the floor. Kris ducked out of the way when he went around to the other side and pushed the two beds together.

"There," he said, stretching his back. "You'll be by her side, and you can get some sleep."

Kris threw herself into his chest and wrapped her arms around his torso. After a moment of hesitation, he hugged her back.

"You're exhausted. Go to bed," he insisted, stepping back and holding her shoulders.

"Thank you," she mouthed, unable to make the words. She slipped underneath her covers and slithered over to the edge of her mattress to face Brie.

Cade turned off the light and closed the door behind him without another word.

Kris lay there for a long time, her eyes slowly adjusting to the darkness. She could make out all the half-healed cuts on Brie's arm. The discoloration under her eye. The red ring and puncture wounds around her neck.

This is what Mom stood for, Kris remined herself, sniffling again. *To put an end to this violence.*

She dug into the pocket of her jeans to retrieve her cell phone. While dialing, she rested a hand on Brie's wrist and watched the wounds dissolve into nothing.

The other line picked up after only two rings.

"Hey." Ian's voice was twisted in grief. "Are you okay? I tried calling you back."

Kris cleared her throat. "I'm fine."

"My parents and I have been calling NWDA representatives all night, just trying to get a hold of someone—anyone—and get Brie released. She's not dangerous." His voice cracked, and Kris bowed her head.

"Ian, it's okay. Brie is safe. She's with me."

The call was quiet for a long moment. "What . . . what does that mean? Kris, what did you do?"

She rolled onto her back and blinked tears from her eyes. "The less you know, the better. I just wanted you to know Brie was safe."

He let out a small gasp. "That's why you ran away." Another pause. "You know I don't care if you're a—"

"I know." Kris pressed her eyes shut. "It's best we keep our distance, though. At least until things die down. I don't want to get you in any trouble."

"I'm sorry, Kris," Ian whispered. "This is so unfair."

"Life isn't fair. But at least I know I'm not alone."

~

"Kris?"

Kris was still half-awake the next morning when she heard Brie's hushed voice. Brie lay on her side, a cascade of blonde curls framing her face on the pillow and her blue eyes blurred with tears.

"Hey," Kris whispered, forcing a smile, although her eyes were clouded too. She could see every twitch in Brie's face as she fought to keep it together.

"I was so terrified that the rescue was all a dream," Brie said, her voice cracking. "I thought I was going to wake up and still be back in that room. I can't believe you came for me."

Kris pulled herself right up to the edge of her bed, as close to Brie as she could get, and rubbed her friend's arm. "I will always come for you, Brie-bear."

Brie's eyes widened and she lifted her head off the pillow. "You got shot," she said. Guilt twisted her brows.

Kris pulled back her blanket as she sat up to reveal the bullet-torn, blood-stained hole in the side of her shirt.

Brie gasped, then reached out in confusion. "I don't understand . . ."

Kris sat cross-legged on the edge of the mattress, and she gave Brie a small smile. "There is so much I have been needing to tell you."

Chapter 25

Cursed

"**H**i."

Larsen jumped and choked on his cereal. He had been flipping through his notebook, trying to interpret the series of symbols on the shield, when the high-pitched voice caught him off guard. He pounded his fist on his chest as he coughed, looking over his shoulder at Kris's friend at the end of the hall.

"Sorry," she said, wincing and holding both hands against her chest. "I didn't mean to startle you."

"It's fine." He took a long drink of water to clear his throat.

She inched closer. "You must be Larsen."

"Yes, h-hi," he stammered, awkwardly pushing his chair back from the table to stand. He held a hand out to her.

"I'm Brie." She took his hand and gave it a weak shake, but she had a broad smile on her face. Her blonde curls bounced with the motion.

"It's nice to meet you, Brie. Officially. How are you feeling?"

"I mean, freaked," she said with a shrug, then clapped her hands loudly together in front of her. "Everything happened so fast. I'm still processing it all."

A door opened from down the hall, and Brie looked Cade up and down as he approached. He tucked a cigarette between his lips while balancing a motorcycle helmet beneath his arm.

Cade stopped beside her and gave her a once-over as well. Her dishwater-blonde hair fell in loose, messy curls around her blushing face, but he seemed more captivated by her long legs.

Larsen had to keep himself from groaning at this exchange.

"Cade, right?" Brie asked, holding out her hand and tucking in her chin. "I'm Brie."

Cade looked at her hand and smirked as he retrieved a lighter from his pocket instead. "Nice to see you on your feet."

"Thank you for rescuing me," Brie said, lowering her hand to clench her fists behind her back. She looked from Larsen back to Cade, her big doe eyes fixed on him. "I don't remember a lot about last night, but I remember you."

Cade grinned. Holding his lighter in the palm of his hand, he gently pinched Brie's cleft chin with his thumb and index finger. "Anytime."

Larsen rolled his eyes.

"I'm heading into town to grab some supplies," Cade said, walking backwards to the door. "You need anything?"

"Dish soap—" Larsen started.

Cade raised a finger. "Not you, nerd." He laughed, then gestured to Brie. "I was talking to the lady."

She giggled as she gripped the bottom of her shirt and held it out. "Some clothes that aren't Kris's?"

Cade squinted. "What do I look like, your personal shopper?"

"You better not be hassling her, Cade," Kris called from the hall. A moment later, she stepped up beside Brie and ran her fingers through her tangled hair.

"Would I do that?" He shot Kris a wicked smile.

"Just introducing myself," Brie assured her.

Larsen scooped up his now soggy bowl of cereal from the table and carried it around to the kitchen sink.

"Need anything in town?" Cade asked Kris.

"We need dish soap," Kris replied, turning to give Larsen a smile.

Cade backed through the screen door while lighting his cigarette. "I'll be back. Don't miss me too much."

Brie giggled and nudged Kris with her arm.

"Thanks," Larsen said. He squeezed the last of the dish soap onto the rag and wiped his cereal bowl clean.

Kris dragged herself to the kitchen to retrieve two bowls of her own from the cupboard. Her eyes looked heavy, as though she could barely keep them open.

"How's your little puzzle coming along?" she asked him, serving cereal from the box on the counter.

"No record of those symbols anywhere online, but I found a short cipher on the shield for some letters. Now I'm just trying to determine the rest of the alphabet. It's . . . challenging, to say the least."

"Well, let me know if I can be of any help," Kris offered.

Brie picked up her bowl. "So, where's this Kurt?" she whispered to Kris with a twinkle of mischief in her voice.

Larsen swallowed hard and hastily hung the kitchen towel back on the oven. "Kurt's outside tending the garden. He wants to talk to you once you're done."

Kris's cheeks flushed. She picked up her own bowl of cereal, giving him a nod before following Brie to the dining room to eat.

~

Kris rounded the house to the vegetable garden with Brie clinging tightly to her arm. Kurt was hunched over a bush, plucking strawberries from the plant and placing them in the bowl by his feet. He held an arm up to block the sun as they approached.

"Good morning." He brushed his dirty hands against the sides of his jeans as he carefully backed out of the garden.

"Hey," Kris replied, her cheeks glowing.

Brie waved and bounced in place. "Hi, I'm Brie. Officially."

"Kurt. It's nice to meet you. Officially," Kurt replied, pushing his brown hair from his face. "I wish it were under better circumstances."

Brie squeezed Kris's arm. "Thanks for saving me last night. And for letting me crash here. And for looking out for Kris."

Kris pulled her arm gently and shot her a look.

"I . . . do what I can," Kurt said, looking between the two of them.

Kris could feel that more words were about to boil to the surface with Brie, so she jumped in before she could say anything more. "Training today?"

Kurt wiped off his hands again. "Brie, would you mind if I spoke to Kris a moment?"

Brie giggled, giving Kris's arm one last squeeze. "Sure. I'll be inside if you need me."

Rays of sunlight danced across the meadow and poked through the clouds as they rolled by. A large wispy cloud blew across the sky overhead, and a cooling wind followed it. The breeze was welcomed, and this was the first morning in a while that the humidity didn't immediately overtake Kris.

"Larsen told me what happened. What they read in Brie's file back at the detainment center." Kurt took a few hesitant strides forward. "How much does she know?"

Kris looked over her shoulder to confirm Brie had left. She twirled a strand of hair nervously around her fingers as she spoke. "I'm sure she suspects her parents reported her, but she hasn't said anything." She turned back to Kurt. "What were Tynan's men doing there?"

"I don't know. Larsen says it was a small crew. No way they were there for us."

"So, are we still on for training today?"

"I think you should take a day off," Kurt said. "You put yourself through a lot last night and—"

"I don't want a day off." Kris strode forward and stood tall as she stared intensely into his eyes. "Between Tynan and the NWDA, and now that Brie's involved . . . I can't afford to slip up."

They stood face-to-face, only a couple of feet apart. Kurt's jaw was clenched in a failed effort to keep his lips from curling into a crooked smile. He gave her a firm nod.

"Okay."

~

Brie turned away from the TV and kneeled on the couch to peer through the front window as Cade pulled up on his motorcycle.

Outside, Kurt and Kris paused from creating fireballs in their hands and wandered over while he removed his helmet. Kris had a serious expression on her face, her arms crossed tightly as she spoke to Cade. Brie wished she could hear what they were saying.

Cade unzipped his leather jacket before opening a saddlebag on the back of his bike to retrieve a few plastic bags. He looked back at the house, and Brie sank down in her seat.

Kris formed another fireball between her palms and pulled it back as though she were about to lob it at Cade. He laughed, raising his hands up in surrender while still clutching the bags.

Over in the dining room, Larsen was mumbling to himself and dragging a pencil along his notebook pages. He rubbed his brow with his fingertips in deep, agitated concentration.

Brie slithered off the couch and sauntered up to him. "Need some help?"

Larsen dropped his pencil on the page and rubbed his eyes. "Just trying to decode something." When he looked up at her, his face turned bright red and he slouched down in his chair.

Brie hovered over him and hunched to read his notes. "Was this the code on that shield Kris told me about?"

Larsen gently slid his chair to the side, leaning away from her. "Yeah—yes. I, uh . . . I found some of the letters, but trying to figure out the rest."

The screen door opened.

"I got your precious dish soap," Cade grumbled. He set the bags and helmet down on the dining room table, then crouched down to untie his boots.

"*Our* dish soap." Larsen stood and backed away. He opened the first bag closest to him. "This bag is just filled with clothes."

Cade stood up abruptly and slapped Larsen's hand away. "That's for Brie."

"For me?"

Cade held the bag out to her. "Nothing fancy. Just hit up a thrift shop on my way back."

Brie opened the bag with a grin. On top was a folded pale pink polka-dotted sundress. "I was mostly kidding," she said, rummaging through the bag before shooting him a large smile. "But thank you. That was so sweet of you."

Larsen dug through another plastic bag. He lifted a six-pack of beer out and scowled at Cade. "You're not supposed to have alcohol."

Cade laughed, taking the cans from Larsen's hand. "It's just beer."

"Don't you have to show ID to buy alcohol? Aren't you worried about the NWDA tracking you? Hurbor got a good long look at your face last night, after all."

"Pfft, let him try."

"He seemed to already know you," Larsen mumbled. He shot Cade a skeptical look as he picked up the bags.

Cade shrugged and removed his boots with just his feet, then kicked them against the wall by the door. "I may have tried to kill him a few years back."

Brie balled up the plastic bag of clothes and cradled it against her chest. She took a step away from them.

Larsen wrinkled his nose and turned to the kitchen. "Yeah, right. You tried to kill the director of the NWDA?"

"I should have killed him then," Cade muttered, removing his leather jacket. When he caught Brie's wide-eyed stare, he offered her a coy smile.

"Well, I think I'll go shower. Try on what you bought," Brie announced, and flashed Cade a return smile before turning on her toes. She bounced over to the bathroom, feeding off his stare, and closed the door behind her.

~

"So, you and Kurt?" Brie asked, flipping over onto her stomach so her feet fluttered back and forth in the air. "What's going on there?"

Kris let out a laugh and sat down on the edge of her bed. "You're funny." She pulled the socks off her feet and threw them in the dirty pile by the door. The thought of kissing Kurt's cheek a few nights before crossed her mind, and her own cheeks flushed.

Brie started braiding a few strands of her hair. "I couldn't understand why you didn't immediately get back together with Ian. But *girl*, you are crushing on Kurt like nothing I've ever seen."

"We're just friends."

Brie pulled a face. "Right."

Kris stared up at a framed photograph above her bed, a silhouette of a daisy against a soft yellow sky, the sunrise piercing through the spaces between the petals. She imagined the way Kurt would have had to crawl and contort in the dewy grass to get that shot. *It's amazing how he can take something as ordinary as a daisy and make it so beautiful. So magical.*

"Where do we go from here, Kris?" Brie asked, breaking Kris's train of thought.

"What do you mean?"

Brie stared down at her braid, then started to unravel it again. "I mean, there's no going back home . . ."

Kris sighed, unfolded her crossed legs to rest her feet on the floor, and leaned forward. "Well, there's living on the road, traveling the world. We can build a house in the mountains and be lonely hermits together. There's that Witcan sanctuary Larsen told me about in Michigan." She offered a small smile. "All good options."

Brie twiddled with her hair, keeping her head down. "It's not fair for our lives to get robbed by this." She held out her hand. It glowed a pale pink for a moment—and only a moment—before fading again.

Kris considered her next words. "I prefer to look at it as life offering us a new beginning, rather than ending the last chapter. We've been given an opportunity."

"Everyone hates us," Brie muttered. She rolled onto her back and stared up at the ceiling. "The world, the NWDA, they want us dead. We're not blessed, we're cursed."

Kris pulled all her hair to one side with both hands and twisted it. "Turns out my mom was a huge advocate for the coexistence of humans and Witcans. There are people out there fighting for our rights. People like my mom." She peeked over to see if there was any change in Brie's mood.

Brie craned her neck to look over at Kris.

"And I'm going to fight too," Kris said with a slow nod. "I'm going to do everything I can to change this world so that no one ever has to go through what you did."

~

The bedroom was pitch black, the night deadly silent.

Kris's eyes flashed open as she stared blankly ahead, unblinking. She slowly sat up, flung the blankets aside, and stood in one long, fluid motion. Her gaze was glassed over as though she were completely unaware.

She opened the bedroom door and walked quietly through the house. Barefoot, she opened the front door, pushed open the screen, and entered the chilly, witching-hour air.

A figure stood in the middle of the field. Calling to her. Beckoning her. Kris's expression remained unchanged as she descended the steps into the grass, wandering out into the meadow towards the mysterious shape.

~

Kurt was hunched over his desk, furiously scribbling away in a notebook, when he thought he heard the front door open. He removed an earbud and sat up straight, listening.

Over the sound of his music, he heard nothing.

That's strange.

He turned off the ancient CD player on his desk and stood from his chair. A prickle traveled up his spine, and the hairs raised on his arms.

Something was wrong.

Kurt opened his bedroom door a crack and peered out. Kris's room door was ajar.

He eased out into the hall and scanned the room. Brie was asleep, but Kris's bed was empty.

"Kris?" he whispered, turning to the front of the house.

The door was open.

His heart sank. Tiptoeing, Kurt rushed outside onto the porch. He squinted and scanned around in the darkness. "Kris?" he called.

She had just been here. He could still feel her.

Kurt followed his instincts and traced her steps into the grass. He could see her footprints dragged through the dew for several feet, and then the trail went cold. He spun in a circle, but the feeling was gone. Kris's aura had faded, and there were no more footprints in the tall, damp grass.

He pulled his shaggy hair back, breathing heavily. "Kris!"

Chapter 26

Wake of Destruction

The calls of songbirds woke Kris. Why were they so loud?

Dazed, she opened her eyes slowly, and it took a moment for her vision to adjust to the sight of the forest surrounding her.

What . . . ?

She was lying in a patch of grass in the shade of the canopy, an army-green bomber jacket draped over her. Kris hurled it aside, slid away through the grass, and scrambled to her feet.

Realizing she was still in her pajamas, she looked down at her bare feet before scanning the woods around her. The trees stretched on in every direction. How had she gotten here?

"Kurt?" she called out. Her voice echoed through the woods, but there was no reply. She cupped her hands around her mouth. "Kurt!"

The dark world in her mind was empty. No matter how far she traveled, there was no sign of the shimmering, translucent wall she had grown so familiar with. She couldn't even reach Kurt telepathically.

Kris wrapped her arms around herself, shivering. She hesitated and then took a step in each direction, unsure which way to go. *How do I get out of here?*

She stared down at the green jacket, and after a short debate with herself, snatched it up from the undergrowth. She shook it off and draped it over her shoulders, hugging it tightly around herself.

Through the branches, she could make out the twinkle of sunshine, the sun still low in the sky. If that was east, then she knew which way was north. If she followed it until she found a road or something familiar . . .

The crunch of dead leaves behind her made her stomach drop.

Kris whirled around, both fists raised. A young man wearing a white, ribbed tank stood a few feet away. He had ashy brown hair and a thin beard, and he laughed as he held his hands up in mock surrender. "Whoa, easy."

She immediately recognized him as one of Tynan's goons from the cemetery. The teleporter.

Panicked, Kris lunged forward and swung a fist at him, but he leaned back and easily avoided it. The bomber jacket slipped off her shoulders into the dirt.

"I'm not going to hurt you—"

She threw another punch, blowing past his head as he bobbed away. In one swift movement, he withdrew a short, thin chain and looped it over both of Kris's fists, then pulled on it to trap her wrists together in front of her.

"What the—? Let go." She jerked her arms back, trying to slip free, but the chain pulled tighter. The metal cut into her skin.

"I just need you to relax and listen to m—"

"Relax?" Kris tried to pull her hands apart again, but he wrenched back on the chain. "Relax? You have me in chains!"

She charged at him and reached for the chain, but he twisted it around his palm until it was pinched tight against Kris's wrist.

"Where am I? Why did you bring me here?" she said. Trying to back away, she stumbled over the bomber jacket and crashed down on her hip.

"I'm trying to save you." He grabbed her arm and started to heave her to her feet.

Kris dug her nails into his hand, and he cried out, dropping her again. "Did Tynan put you up to this?"

He cocked his head to the side with a smirk, then threw down the chain at her. "Really? You just assume everything is about him?"

Kris ripped the chain off her wrists and rubbed them. They were red and bruising already. "You relinquish your identity when you sell your soul to a cult," she spat.

He laughed, checking the scratches she left in his skin. "Well, you're not wrong." He held a hand out to her. "I'm Shay."

"Yeah, I remember you." She glared up at him as she continued to soothe her wrists, but didn't accept his help.

He crouched down beside her and crossed his arms. "You have no idea what you've gotten yourself into."

"Speak for yourself," Kris growled at him. She clutched her hands close to her chest.

"Kye, Kurt, whatever you want to call him, he's dangerous," Shay insisted. He picked up the bomber jacket and shook the dirt off, then offered it to Kris. "There's destruction in his wake you can't even imagine."

"What's that supposed to mean?"

She studied his brown eyes. They were clear. Genuine. But she made no motion to take the jacket, so Shay shrugged and draped it over his arm.

"Where he goes, death follows."

Kris stared at his feet as he stood balancing on his toes. "You could say the same of Tynan," she retorted, shooting him a glare.

Shay tilted to the side. "At least you know what you get with Tynan. I'm curious, how much has Kurt told you about his past?"

She clenched her jaw.

"I lost my little sister because of him," Shay said.

Kris's shoulders tensed. "What do you mean?"

"My sister, my little Star Eyes." His voice rang with grief as he dropped his head and squeezed the jacket in his hands. "She lived with him for a brief time. He used her and cast her out. And when the NWDA came down on her, he left her to die."

She shook her head. "Kurt would never do that."

"Kye's not as squeaky clean as he would have you believe. He has history with Tynan that you don't want to get in the middle of."

"Why do you keep calling him Kye?" A shiver traveled up her spine, and goose bumps raised on her arms.

Shay watched her and held the jacket out again. "I couldn't save my sister, but maybe it's not too late for you."

Now.

Kris thrust both her palms towards him. The telekinetic energy traveled through her arms, providing extra power to the shove to his chest. He cried out in surprise and fell back into the leaves.

The instant his back hit the ground, she took off. Her bare feet scratched and scraped through the brush, sticks, and rocks, shooting pain up her legs, but Kris kept running.

Shay appeared in front of her, arms outstretched to catch her in a bear hug. "Are you always this reluctant to accept life-saving advice?"

Kris tried to stomp on his feet, but he was quick to shift them out of the way each time. "I am when I'm being kidnapped."

He lifted her up in the air. "For God's sake, this isn't a kidnapping. I'm just removing you from a dangerous situation."

She raised a knee into his groin. Shay cried out, releasing her and dropping to the ground. "What the hell?"

"You aren't allowed to start calling the shots in my life. You people are the reason I'm *in* this predicament at all."

"I had nothing to do with what happened to your parents," he insisted, his voice strained with physical agony. "I couldn't save them. I couldn't save my sister. I'm just hoping that maybe I can save you. Before Tynan or Kye kills you."

Kris backed away, still scowling. She clapped her hands together and then pulled them apart slowly. A rush of heat spiraled in her chest and down her arms, collecting in the palm of her hands until a large, flashing ball of fire formed. "I have no reason to trust you."

She lobbed the fireball in Shay's direction. He rolled away, crouched in the dry leaves. "What the hell is your problem? You're—"

Kris didn't let him finish, quickly forming another fireball to throw. Another miss.

"This area is dry; you can't just start throwing fireballs. Everything will go up in flames."

Before she could cast another, Shay raised both his arms and extended a telekinetic force towards her, catching her off guard. She stumbled backwards as her heel tripped over a large branch. Kris didn't even have a chance to catch herself as the back of her skull collided with a tree trunk.

"Whoa, hey!"

Everything was fuzzy; her vision doubled. Kris tried to prop herself up, but the ringing in her head was deafening. She could feel every step Shay took, his feet echoing through the earth, but his voice was far away.

Oh God, my head. The world was moving slowly around her in blurry white flashes as she dipped in and out of consciousness. *Kurt. I need to get home to Kurt. I'm not going out like this.*

She could feel Shay lift her in his arms. He was saying something, but through the haze, she couldn't fully understand him.

"Just think about what I said," she heard through the fog. "I'll be close by."

~

Kris was heaved off her back to sit up, and her eyes snapped open as she gasped. Kurt and Larsen were each hovering over her and holding one of her shoulders.

"What happened?" she asked, shaking her head in confusion. She looked past the two. Brie and Cade were running across the meadow toward her.

"We should be asking you," Larsen said, giving her shoulder a squeeze. "You disappeared in the middle of the night. We just found you out here."

Kris rubbed the back of her head, suddenly remembering her fall. Her skull wasn't ringing anymore. Had that all been a dream? Had any of that actually happened?

"I . . . I'm not sure," she grumbled, pressing her fingers against her eyes in deep contemplation. Her wrists were red.

From the chain, she realized, and she stood to hide her hands behind her back. *So it was real? Shay was really here?*

"Oh, Kris, thank God. I was so worried," Brie said as she approached. "Where were you?"

Kris opened and closed her mouth, thoughts firing back and forth in her mind. If Shay had really been here, then he could tell Tynan where she was hiding. But he could have also just taken her to Tynan directly. Had he been telling the truth? Or had he been trying to manipulate her?

"Kris? You okay?" Cade asked.

Larsen bent to look her directly in the eye. "You look exhausted."

"I'm fine," she said quietly. She caught Kurt's skeptical expression. "I guess I just . . . I must have been sleepwalking."

Brie reared back her head. "Sleepwalking?"

Sleepwalking? Really? That's how you want to handle this? Kris scolded herself, but she pulled a confident face and shrugged. "Must be the stress."

"Well, if that continues, we're chaining you to the bed," Cade said. "You gave us a scare."

"I was worried you left," Brie said.

Kris forced a smile as she rubbed her wrists behind her back. They burned. "It's fine. I'm fine. I'm here, let's just let it go."

Larsen offered to help her to the house, but she declined. As they all started toward the cabin, Kurt grabbed her by the shoulder to stop her.

He leaned over and peered around Kris's back to her hands. "What happened to your wrists?"

"What?" A prickle climbed up her spine, and her shoulders stiffened. "My wrists?"

Kurt held out a hand as though requesting verification of her arm.

Before complying, Kris concentrated and pushed the warm sensation in her chest down to her wrists. They grew hot for a brief moment, then the feeling dissolved. When she put her palm up towards Kurt, the red marks around her wrists were completely gone.

He took her hand and gently turned her arm to examine all sides. He kept his head down but eyed her with a skeptical look. "My mistake," he said flatly, before turning away.

Kris's heart pounded. Did he know she was lying? What would he do if he knew the truth? That one of Tynan's men had found them.

She reflected on some of the things Shay had said. About a wake of destruction following Kurt. She remembered the vengeful look in his eyes back at the NWDA facility. *He was determined to kill that man. Would he have actually gone through with it if I hadn't stepped in? Is Kurt really as dangerous and violent as Shay suggested? What more don't I know?*

Chapter 27

The Shield

Kris set the laundry basket down in front of the washing machine and glanced over her shoulder into the open bedroom behind her. Larsen was lying on his back across the bed, notebook held up in the air over his face, vigorously scratching out lines with his pencil. He traced over a few more lines, then groaned and slapped the notebook down on his face in defeat.

"Still struggling with the cipher?" she asked. She scooped up a handful of dirty laundry from the basket and stuffed it into the machine.

"I don't get it," Larsen grumbled, sliding the notebook down his face and holding it against his chest. "Every time I think I have it figured out, it just turns into gibberish."

"You should step back. Go take a walk, get some exercise, watch some TV. Clear your brain. You've been staring at that thing for nearly two weeks straight."

"Don't remind me. Meanwhile, there was another raid in Tennessee last night. Another twelve NWDA agents dead."

"You can't possibly blame yourself for that—"

Giggles from the living room caught her attention. She leaned back and peered down the hall to where Brie was leaning over the back of the couch, twirling her hair, and whispering something to Cade. He sat next to her, but when he caught Kris watching, his smile vanished and he slid farther away from Brie.

What on earth is Brie doing?

Kris started the washing machine, thumped the empty basket down on top, and closed the hall closet. She turned her attention back to the living room, where Brie had shifted closer to Cade again.

"You should take me for a ride sometime," Brie whispered to him.

"On my motorcycle," Cade blurted to Kris, backing away again as she approached.

"Right." Kris squinted at him and crossed her arms.

Brie flicked her blonde curls over her shoulder and shot Kris a mischievous smile.

Cade patted his pack of cigarettes into the palm of his hand. "Ladies," he said, dismissing himself as he slipped past both of them toward the front door.

Brie chuckled and watched him walk away, then spun back to Kris. "Oh my God, he is *so* cute."

Kris's face twisted with disgust and confusion. "Cade? Seriously?"

"Yeah. I just want to grab him and lay one on him."

"Brie, no, don't do this."

"Do what?"

Kris craned her neck to see a puff of smoke through the screen door. She lowered her head and dropped her voice quieter. "You always fall head over heels for the worst guys, and then they break your heart."

"This one's different," Brie said, shaking her head. "Cade isn't one of those jerks."

Kris wrinkled her nose. "Cade's my friend and I love him, but he's a player. A manipulator. He doesn't want a relationship."

"But maybe I can change that. Maybe I can be the one to fix him."

"Oh my God, I can't believe he was right," Kris muttered under her breath. She pinched the bridge of her nose and shook her head.

Kris turned away and headed to the bathroom to brush her teeth. Brie followed closely behind with a spring in her step.

"So, you training with Kurt again today?" Brie nudged Kris's arm. "Any excuse to get a little closer to him, huh?"

She elbowed Brie in the ribs and stole a glance down the hall, sighing in relief that Kurt wasn't there. "Shut it. It's not like that. And you should join us, do a little training of your own."

Brie's face turned white and she shook her head.

"Why not?"

"Kris, I don't . . . I'm not . . ." Brie pulled a face and looked away.

"What?" Kris started brushing her teeth.

Blonde hair covered Brie's face, and she looked the most insecure Kris had ever seen her. "I just want to be normal, Kris."

She stopped brushing. *Be normal? If only it were that easy.*

~

Kurt leaned over the shield on the desk in Larsen and Cade's room, gliding his fingers over the engraved symbols around the shield's border. He didn't look up as Larsen entered the room.

"Still no luck decoding it, I'm guessing?"

Larsen sighed. "Not yet." He picked up his notebook from the desk and dropped into his chair, shoulders slumped.

Kris poked her head through the doorway, and her eyes locked onto Kurt. "Ready for training?" she asked, fiddling with a strand of hair.

"Yeah." Kurt patted Larsen on the back.

Brie stepped past Kris into the room, a thin, tight smile on her face. She leaned over the notebook and studied the scribbles. "Oh, hey!" She jabbed a finger over Larsen's shoulder into the pages. "That's French. *Côtellete* is French."

"What?" Kris and Kurt said at the same time, looking at her in a moment of confusion before diving into the notes as well.

Larsen glanced at Brie and then back at his writing. He started writing furiously and muttering to himself.

"This one must be *écoutez*," Brie said, pointing at one of the unfinished words. "It means 'listen.'"

Larsen stared at her for a long moment before offering her a gentle smile. "You know French?"

Her eyes lit up. "You want my help?"

Kurt nudged Kris in the arm. "We'll leave you two to it. We'll be outside training. Holler if you find anything."

Kris trailed behind him as they went into the hallway. Kurt noticed her give a curious glance toward his bedroom at the end of the hall, where his door was opened just a crack. His stomach tied itself in knots, and with a jerk of his head, his door pulled shut all the way.

She looked at him, confused, but quickly flashed a smile. "All right, we going to continue working on ice stuff today or what?" She hurried past him to the screen door.

He looked over his shoulder one last time at his closed bedroom door before following Kris outside.

Kris's fingers felt cold, even in the summer sun, while she concentrated to form a bright turquoise orb between her hands. The sphere grew bigger as she pulled her palms apart, and once it was about the size of a grapefruit, she hurled it with both hands toward the mannequin about twenty paces away. The ball crashed into its chest, erupting into a gel-like liquid and then crystallizing into a clear sheet of ice.

Kurt nodded in approval and stepped up behind her.

"I'm getting the hang of it," she said between breaths. She turned to Kurt with her hands on her hips. "What's next?"

He was unusually quiet, examining the ice on the decoy as little droplets of water began to drip off in the early-afternoon sun. He twisted his hands around in silent contemplation.

"Kurt?"

His head snapped up, his eyes finally focusing again. "What?"

Kris crossed her arms, her brow furrowed. Something was off with him. "Is everything all right?" she asked.

He dropped his gaze and shifted his weight around for a long moment. He released a long sigh, then closed the space between them. "I want to show you something."

Kurt raised a hand so that his fingertips barely touched her temple. She was instantly in the dark world, standing in front of the crystallized fluid barrier, only this time it was dark on the other side. She didn't see the cabin, or even Kurt's silhouette.

A hand extended out through the barrier, palm-side up, ripples radiating across the shimmering wall.

What was going on? Was this a trick?

Her pulse quickened as she apprehensively placed her palm into the open hand. It gave Kris a gentle tug and pulled her through the barrier into the darkness on the other side.

It took a moment for her eyes to adjust to the dimly lit hallway before her. There were dusty photos on the wall of people she didn't recognize. The floors were scuffed and scratched with age.

Where am I?

Alone, Kris peered inside an open door to her left. Clothes lay scattered all around the floor. The shelves were bare and coated in years of dust and cobwebs. The one thing that did grab her attention was the word *Dragonfleye* written in cursive on a gray T-shirt hanging on the bedpost.

An echo called out, beckoning Kris towards the stairs at the end of the hall. She stopped at the top of the staircase and looked down at the damage below her. Several of the steps were broken, collapsed in. She put her hand on the banister, then quickly backed away when the railing lit up beneath her palm. The glow lasted only a second before fading.

Kris lightly touched it again. The banister was cold, even when it glowed.

She descended the stairs, carefully avoiding the broken steps as she made her way down to the first floor of the house. Floorboards were torn up, tables and chairs overturned, light fixtures ripped out of walls. The living room curtains were scorched and still smoking. A closet door in the entrance was smashed in, and the front door lay on the hardwood floor, cracked.

What had happened here?

Kris tiptoed around the door towards the entrance, following the echo outside. Beyond the front door, she found herself in a dark tunnel made of rock.

Tynan's bunker.

She traced her hand along the stone wall as she walked. Like the banister in the house, the wall illuminated beneath her fingertips in a line of light that faded as Kris moved ahead.

Something grabbed her by the ankle. She shrieked as she fell forward to the rocky ground. Before she could stand, more hands extended out of the darkness, clutching her arms and legs. Fingers locked around her, pulled her down, and pinned her against the floor. A hand clasped around her throat, squeezing until she couldn't breathe.

Distant voices quietly hissed at her, and it took her a moment to understand what they were saying: *golden child*, over and over.

Kris kicked and squirmed as she pried the hand off her neck. Its fingernails clawed her skin, but she managed to pull herself free and scramble away to her feet. She put a palm to her chest, breathing in deep. As she slowly backed away, she rubbed her neck and started to search the dark corridor around her, but the hands had vanished.

What *was* that?

The echo was getting louder. Kris could hear the tone of Kurt's muffled voice as she continued on.

The bunker changed. Trees sprouted out around her, and she was trudging through a heavily wooded forest. Shrubs and branches scratched her legs while she walked.

A gunshot rang out, and Kris felt something whiz past her side. Startled, she looked back. Shadows were running at her at top speed, and without much thought, she sprinted through the trees, swatting branches from her path. She could feel the figures behind her closing in, could hear distant barking.

Another gunshot sounded as something fired just over Kris's shoulder. She didn't stop running until she burst from the forest.

She tumbled down a short slope. Water splashed up in her face as she caught herself and clambered to her feet.

She was standing at the bank of a small creek. Up ahead was a concrete bridge that connected a hiking trail over the water. The bridge was tall enough to walk under.

And it was where the echo was coming from.

Kris shivered and clutched her arms as she approached the bridge. Two blurry figures stood under it.

Mom?

It was indisputable that one of them was her mother, with her short blonde waves and small frame. She was standing under the bridge and peering out into the surrounding woods.

There was a boy crouched behind her with his back pressed against the cement pillar of the bridge, struggling to catch his breath. And even though his hair was much shorter and his figure much more toned, Kris immediately recognized him too.

Kurt must be a teenager, she thought as she slowly drew closer.

"What do you want? Why did you bring me here?" the young Kurt asked Sofia, shooting her an annoyed look. He squeezed the baseball cap in his hands.

"I just saved your life," Sofia said. Her blue eyes searched the woods. "NWDA agents have been crawling this area."

"I'm not scared of them. Any of them attack me, I'll kill them."

Kris inched forward again, mouth hanging open as she looked between her mother and Kurt. He would kill them?

Sofia turned and squinted at him. "I don't think you would. I saw you save that little girl and her mother."

He put his hat back on and pulled down on the bill to hide his face. He cleared his throat quietly. "You don't know me."

Now that's the Kurt I know.

Kris reached out a hand, stopping short before touching her mother's face.

She won't feel it, Kurt's voice said. *This is only a memory.*

She wiped a tear from her cheek and lifted her head at the sound of sirens wailing not too far away.

"I'm Kurt," the young Kurt finally said, shuffling to sit in the dirt.

"I'm Sofia."

So this was when they'd met.

Kris waited for what felt like hours, watching her mother pace until the sirens finally died down. The woods were getting dark as the sun began to set.

Sofia turned back to Kurt. "Do you have somewhere to go?"

He adjusted his cap and stood. "Yes, my guardian is waiting for me."

Sofia nodded, looking him up and down, then held out a piece of paper with some scribbles on it. "Well, if you ever need a place to go, give me a call."

He took the torn piece of paper, and his shoulders relaxed as he breathed in deeply. "Why are you doing this?"

She offered a smile and set a hand on his shoulder. "It's not a fair world we live in. You're just a kid. And you have a good heart."

Kurt chuckled, shaking his head. "You don't know me."

Her expression didn't change as she gave his arm a gentle squeeze. "I think I know you better than you think I do. Be safe out there, Kurt."

Kris stood there, her heart beating hard in her chest while she watched her mother leave in one direction and Kurt in another.

If Kurt was as tough as he'd claimed, or as dangerous as Shay had suggested, why would he have stayed there? Why would he have accepted help from a stranger, a human, and let them walk away knowing his identity?

Kris blinked and stepped back in the field. Kurt dropped his hand to his side and kept his head down as he took several deep breaths.

"I want us to be more honest with each other," he said in a hushed voice.

She clutched her trembling hands behind her back. "I would like that." She scanned the trees along the edge of the meadow.

"That being said," he said, eyeing her curiously, "is there anything you want to tell me?"

Kris's chest became tight. Did he know about Shay? Had this all been just a ploy to get her to talk?

She shook her head, struggling to maintain normal posture. Her thoughts were racing as she tried to decide whether to admit what happened, but she ultimately decided against it. "No."

Kurt's eyes narrowed for a moment as he watched her.

He's not dense. He knows something is up, but I'm not going to tell him. Not yet. At least not until I know more.

"Okay." Kurt backed away. "I guess, if you ever have anything you want to get off your chest . . . let me know."

Kris nodded along, then scowled to herself as she turned her head away. *God, you're scum*, she told herself.

Kurt motioned to the mannequin out in the grass. The ice had completely melted. "Let's go again, then."

She searched the trees once more, but there was no one there.

As Kris formed another ball of ice in her hands, she pictured the dilapidated house she had seen in Kurt's mind. The hands in Tynan's bunker. The people who chased and shot at her in the woods.

Were those also memories? Or were they just distorted, disturbing thoughts haunting his mind?

Chapter 28

The Journal

"Listen to the northern chop; sharp spray against the thirteen floors; cradled in braided casket; dirk and winding on Natives' shores."

As Kurt removed the casserole from the oven, Kris retrieved five dinner plates from the cupboard and handed them to Brie, who set them around the table.

"What does that mean?" Kris asked Larsen, glancing over her shoulder at him.

He waved his notebook around and practically danced in place. "Well, *dirk* refers to a dagger. The *thirteen floors*, *northern chop*, and *spray* all refer to the Scarlet Islands, a cluster of thirteen small islands in Lake Superior just north of Wisconsin. Based on the references to blades and the original use of French in the translation, we think the next clue is on the shores of Épée Island."

Kris collected the silverware, glasses, and water pitcher while Larsen rambled on with his explanation. She watched Kurt carry the hot casserole dish to the dining room, but a flicker of light in the darkness outside caught her attention. She leaned over the kitchen sink and scanned the darkness, but she couldn't see anything.

What was that? Am I seeing things?

"I'm impressed," Kurt replied, brushing his hands off on his pants. He offered Brie a smile. "Thank you so much for your help."

Brie slid into an empty seat at the table. "Oh, it was nothing. It's the least I can do after all you guys have done for me. And for Kris."

Kris shook her head and hurried around to the dining room as Cade pulled open the screen door and kicked his boots off in the entrance.

"So, we have the next lead. That's exciting," Cade said, dropping into the chair across from Brie. He looked around the table with a wicked grin. "Should we go? Maybe take a little midnight skinny dip in Lake Superior?"

"It's late," Kurt replied. "We'll go in the morning."

Brie flashed Cade a crooked smile. While it made Kris uncomfortable, the real knots in her stomach were from the darkness outside. She stared out the front window into the black night, suddenly aware of how easily someone could be outside looking in, watching the five of them eat dinner.

"I'll be close by." The words Shay had said played back in Kris's head. Her hands shook as she held out her plate to Kurt for a piece of casserole.

Maybe that light had been Shay. Was he still around, watching her? Kris eyed the blinds, overcome by an intense temptation to close them, but there was no way to do so without raising suspicion.

If she were to leave tomorrow to go find that key, what would Shay do? Follow her? Use the opportunity to search the cabin? Steal the shield? Would he hurt Brie?

Kris cleared her throat. "I think I'm going to sit this one out. I would rather stay here with Brie, just in case."

Kurt studied her. "That's a good point. I better stay back too. I would hate for something to happen and I wasn't here to help."

She could feel his eyes burning into her. *He doesn't trust you, and why should he? He knows you're keeping something from him.*

"Great, so I have to go with Larsen alone?" Cade grumbled with a mouth full of casserole. "This trip is going to suck."

Kris didn't hear much else of the dinner conversation, too lost inside her own head. She continued to steal glances outside as her mind began to spiral. *I just need some proof. Something that shows definitively if Kurt is as dangerous as Shay says. If I can find that, then I will know if I can trust him or not.*

She thought back to the way Kurt had closed his bedroom door that morning. He always kept his door closed. Whatever he was hiding in there might be enough to tell her what she needed.

Kris realized that everyone had begun to clear the table except for Kurt. While Cade, Larsen, and Brie were in the kitchen putting away the leftovers and washing the dishes, Kris absentmindedly began to stand.

Kurt touched her arm, leaning in as close as he could over the table and keeping his voice hushed. "I know something is going on with you." His pale eyes shifted as he examined her face closely. "Please just tell me."

Kris couldn't look him in the eye.

He's giving you the chance, just take it, she screamed at herself. But the uncertainty continued to bubble just beneath the surface.

"It's nothing. I'm fine," she insisted, quickly scooping up her plate and retreating to the kitchen.

~

He attacked those men and tried to kill Director Hurbor at the NWDA facility.

Kris stood by the front door, watching Kurt out in the field. He was hunched in the grass with his camera, following a bumblebee from flower to flower.

He keeps some memories buried away, even from himself. He left Tynan to kill Mom and Dad. He left Shay's sister for dead.

Cade and Larsen had already been gone for about an hour, searching Épée Island for the next clue to Calosant. Brie was curled up on the couch, flipping through the pages of a book she'd snagged from Larsen's room. She was especially quiet that morning.

Kris looked up at the dark clouds overhead, grateful to be inside for a change. She glanced back at Kurt's bedroom door. What proof could she possibly expect to find that would sway her one way or another?

Just tell him what happened with Shay. He will either get angry because Shay is telling the truth and Kurt is in fact dangerous and violent, or he will get angry because you've been lying to him and you think he's some kind of murderer or something.

Kris pulled a face and scanned the woods at the edge of the meadow, as though she expected to see Shay just standing there.

Either way I lose.

"How long are you going to stare at him?" Brie's question immediately brought Kris back.

"What?"

Brie was sitting up, clutching the book to her chest. "You've been just standing there watching him. Go talk to him."

Kris scoffed and stepped away from the door. "What are you talking about? I didn't . . . I mean, I wasn't—"

Brie snickered as she stood up. "I'm going to go take a bath. Give you two some *alone* time."

"What? No, it's not like that." Kris trailed after Brie, who just giggled and closed the bathroom door behind her.

She stood in the hallway, staring at Kurt's closed bedroom door. The tub was already running by the time she made up her mind. She would go in, look around. If she didn't see anything suspicious, then that would be that and she could let this whole thing go. And she'd tell Kurt everything. And he would hate her . . .

Kurt's bedroom walls were covered in foam squares and cardboard. The blinds were pulled shut. The bed was perfectly made without even a single wrinkle in the comforter. His guitar leaned against the bed, and on the nightstand beside it was a notebook.

The desk in front of her was completely organized. Books neatly stood on the desk shelf. A cup was filled with pencils and pens, and there were no loose pages or papers. A large device took up half of the desk. It looked like an ancient, old-timey camera suspended and pointed down to a large square platform. Something for photography maybe? It kind of looked like the thing the photography class used in the art room at her school.

The dresser by the door was clean as well, all the drawers pushed in neatly, and nothing on top except for a few bottles of cologne and some framed photographs.

Immaculate, Kris thought as she made her initial inspection of the room.

She started with the notebook on the nightstand. Upon picking it up, she found a photo of herself, sitting out in the meadow, head back, eyes shut. She remembered that day when

Kurt took the photo. Her shoulders slouched in a moment of uncertainty. She shouldn't be going through his things.

But she shook her head decisively, flipping through the pages of the notebook anyway and scanning the lines. *"I only wish I could be the man that you see." "Abandon the hurt, the shattered, and broken; I'll sing all the words I left unspoken."* Lyrics.

She carefully returned the notebook to the page it had been on and replaced it on the nightstand on top the photo before opening the drawer. It was filled with more notebooks and some booklets about guitar. Nothing of note, so she turned to the desk. She found plastic film canisters, stacks of blank photo paper, and other photography equipment.

In the back of one of the drawers, Kris came across a thick wad of cash. She flicked through it briefly. *There must be thousands of dollars here. Where did he get this? Why does he have it?*

But the thing that jolted Kris's interest was a leather-bound journal buried under a pile of folded jeans in the dresser. It was worn and flaking with age. Was this his diary?

An elastic band secured the pages, and once she undid it, a folded piece of paper slipped out and floated under the desk. *Shoot.*

She got down on her hands and knees and reached under the desk to retrieve the page. While still kneeling on the hardwood floor, Kris unfolded the paper.

Kurt,

I'm so sorry to leave you like this, with just a note. But I know you would ask me to stay. And we both know I can't, despite how much I wish I could. The time that I spent here, the moments I shared with you, they were the greatest moments of my life. The thought of leaving you breaks my heart, but there is too much this world has to offer. Too much to see and to experience that I would never get the chance to if I stay. So until we see each other again, take care of yourself.

Nina

Kris read the letter over and over. It was so weird to imagine Kurt having such a normal relationship with someone. A romantic relationship. And yet, here was proof that this girl, Nina, had a serious relationship with Kurt. It must have destroyed him when she left.

Finally, she folded the letter up again and returned to the journal. She started flicking through the pages, scanning for Nina's name to find the appropriate page to return the letter to.

But a different name caught her attention instead.

Her eyes widened as she read through the page, then flipped to the next, and then the next.

"Tynan took me scouting today. We found two new recruits."

"During training today, Tynan lost his patience with me. He threw me against the floor and strangled me until I surrendered."

"I took a life today. Tynan had me be the one to kill the NWDA agent we captured. I feel sick."

The pages went on and on with entries about Tynan. About fighting. About torture. About killing.

Kris curled up in a ball as she leaned against Kurt's bed. Her hands were cold and shaking, and the heavy weight on her chest constricted her lungs, leaving her gasping for air.

Kurt had worked for Tynan? He'd killed NWDA agents. He'd killed Witcans. She couldn't understand.

There was a creak in the hallway floorboards heading towards her. Kris jolted upright.

Oh no.

Kris pushed herself up to her feet, snatched the letter that was still on the floor beside her, and stuffed it in a random page of the journal. She only just slid out the dresser drawer when the bedroom door opened.

"Kris?" The look of panic on Kurt's face quickly changed to one of annoyance. "What the hell are you doing in here?" His eyes dropped to the journal in her hands, and a horrifying expression of rage twisted his face. "What did you do?"

Kris pointed the journal at him. "You worked for Tynan? You were part of his cult. Why have you been keeping this from me?"

He snatched his journal from her hand and clutched it at his side. "You have no right—*no right*—to be in here. Snooping through my things." His voice was rough with a brewing anger like Kris had never heard, but the words she had just read were still hot on her mind.

"You've been lying to me this entire time. You *knew* Tynan. You knew what he was after. Not only did you know the horrible things he has done, but you . . . *you* did those unspeakable things yourself!"

"You don't know the first thing about me, or any of the horrors I've gone through," Kurt said, lunging toward her.

"I trusted you. My mother trusted you," Kris cried. Tears spilled over her lashes as she backed away. "My parents *died* protecting you, and you are no better than—"

Kurt squared up, pointing a glowing green hand to the door. "Get out!" His voice boomed so loud that Kris swore it shook the entire cabin. "Get the hell out of my house!"

She pushed past him and sprinted for the screen door. She snatched up her sneakers but didn't waste any time putting them on. Instead, she carried them as she ran outside, across the meadow, and down the path through the trees to the road.

A little way down the cracked and damaged country road, Kris dropped down in the gravel, fumbling to put on her shoes while her entire body trembled. She buried her face in her hands, sobbing.

"That asshole," she said over and over.

"I tried to warn you."

Kris spun around in the gravel and saw Shay emerge from the trees. She swiped her fists across her cheeks in an attempt to erase the tears. It took a moment to get to her feet as he slowly approached.

"I told you he's no good."

She didn't back away, allowing him to close the distance between them. His soft brown eyes actually looked sympathetic.

Kris cleared her throat and straightened her shoulders. When she spoke, she did so with authority. "Take me to Tynan."

Chapter 29

Puppet Master

The blur of teleporting slowly refocused, and Kris could see a living room forming in front of her. Shay squeezed her arm hard so hard that she winced, and she twisted away from him.

"Sir," Shay called into the house. "I have a delivery for you."

Kris's heart raced as she scanned the room, suddenly recognizing where she was. The house she'd seen in Kurt's mind. In his memory.

The damage to the house had been recovered. The couches were dusty but right-side up. The curtains were no longer scorched. The door to the entrance closet had been removed and the front door replaced. Heavy footsteps rang out from the stairs on the left, which had been repaired but were still in rough shape.

Was this Tynan's house? Was this where Kurt lived too?

Tynan appeared at the top of the stairs. He was wearing a tight-fitted T-shirt that emphasized his biceps, and his curly black hair was slicked back. His eyes gleamed when he saw Kris.

"Well, this is a surprise," he said as he started down the stairs.

Shay yanked forward on Kris's arm and flung her toward Tynan. "I found her wandering the streets. She specifically requested to be taken directly to you."

Kris stumbled to catch herself, then stood up straight. "I want to join you," she said, keeping her shoulders squared up to Tynan as he stopped in front of her. "In exchange for some answers."

He grinned, but it was surprisingly not as sinister as Kris had anticipated.

Movement at the top of the stairs caught Kris's attention as the shapeshifting woman with short black hair descended the steps. She stopped beside Tynan, her arms crossed and her hip cocked to the side. She looked Kris up and down and chuckled.

Tynan turned to Shay and gave him a nod. "Take Night home."

"Yes, sir."

Hearing the servitude in Shay's voice made Kris squirm.

As she passed, Night slammed her shoulder into Kris, who stumbled. Night laughed, and Kris glanced over her shoulder to catch one last glance of Shay before he disappeared with Night.

"I must say, I am impressed yet again by your boldness," Tynan said, turning from Kris to head into the living room. He raised two fingers in the air over his shoulder and motioned with them.

Kris gasped as her chest lurched forward and dragged her feet across the hardwood floor. Tynan eased himself into the large armchair beside the fireplace, looking up at her once she skidded to a stop in the middle of the living room.

"I will entertain your request. What is it you want to know?" He tilted his head with a sly smile.

Kris took a couple of deep breaths and tried to straighten the millions of thoughts circling her mind. "Did Kurt work for you?"

Tynan nodded slowly. "I took him in when he was a child, and I raised him as my own."

Her stomach churned, and she took another deep gulp of air. "How did he come to be in your care?"

Tynan crossed his legs, leaning back as though to emphasize his casual answers to the questions. "His father was a fortune-teller. Rumors circulated that he had a vision of Kurt entering Calosant, so I had to ensure that he would be able to guide me there when the day came. I had Red dispose of his parents so he would have nowhere else to turn."

Kris's body recoiled ever so slightly, but she fought to keep her sturdy posture. "He was a child. You murdered his family for a chance of finding an ancient, abandoned city?"

"He led me to you, didn't he? His family was collateral damage. My life's work, my mission, my duty . . . They were bigger than a couple of human-sympathizing Witcans." He made a gesture with his hand for Kris to continue.

She shook her hair from her face and blinked ferociously to clear the tears that had started to fill her vision. "Why do you want to get to Calosant?"

"When I was just a child, a fortune-teller showed me a vision of a free world. A world *I* would bring about. I would lead our people from a life of death and fear."

"By opening Calosant?"

Tynan smiled with a gentle tilt of his head. "By acquiring the Mina Ring, an article forged by the Elders of Calosant themselves to enhance Annona's power. A power I can harness to eliminate all of the NWDA. Permanently."

"Couldn't you do that without the ring?" Kris asked, clenching her fists to keep them from trembling.

Tynan grinned, a wicked twinkle in his eye. "The NWDA's operation has expanded exponentially. I could take out one facility at a time, but they will continue to grow, continue to retaliate." He gave a smug shrug. "With the Mina Ring, I would have the power to reach out across the country and destroy all NWDA facilities at once, saving thousands of lives."

"Is that why your men were at the NWDA facility in Rockford a couple weeks ago?"

Tynan's eyebrows raised. "I'm honestly impressed that you even know about that."

"I was there saving my friend. Answer the question. Why were *your* men there?"

"I sent some of my team on a rescue mission myself. A dear old friend had been captured, and his talents were required."

Kris paced in a small circle, grappling with the question on her mind. Finally, she turned back to him. "Why did you kill my parents?"

Tynan leisurely stood from his chair and towered over Kris. "I hadn't intended to kill them. I thought they would give up Kurt in a heartbeat. Had you been home the night we came, as planned, I'm sure your parents would not have hesitated to save *you*."

Kris slumped forward, her breath catching in her throat. She panted heavily as she fought to keep the tears away.

If I had stayed home instead of going over to Ian's, Mom and Dad might still be alive . . . But Kurt would be dead. Or Tynan's slave.

After a moment, she stood tall again. "Why did you take my pocketknife?"

Tynan smirked and motioned with his head for Kris to follow. Her knees were weak and shaky, but she trailed behind him up the stairs. In the hallway, she stole a glance into the bedroom on the left, remembering the Dragonfleye T-shirt she had seen in Kurt's memory. Through the crack in the door, Kris could see that there were still piles of clothes coated in dust.

Tynan guided her into the home office at the end of the hall. Lined up across the surface of the desk were random items, each resting on top of a small pile of either sand or salt. She immediately saw the pocketknife on the end, beside a vintage wristwatch.

He picked up the closed knife, keeping his back to Kris as he twisted it around. "For members to join my mission, I require a sacrifice. They must give up the item dearest to their heart. A pledge trinket." He turned over his shoulder to show off Kris's knife. "It discourages desertion, as they will not want to leave without their prized item."

Kris's eyes darted down to the piles beneath each item. "And the salt?"

Tynan grinned as he carefully returned the knife to its original place. "An ancient charm I have mastered, which allows me to use an item of great importance to . . . encourage subordination."

"You mean mind control?" Kris said, stepping away.

"It's not foolproof. It simply makes the end user more susceptible to suggestion."

She eyed the watch next to the knife. Something about it resonated with her. Called to her. She eventually motioning to it with her chin. "Did you control Kurt?"

Tynan followed her gaze to the watch and scoffed. "I used it to keep him in line."

"Did he know about it?"

"You have a lot of questions." He leaned back against the desk and crossed his arms, emphasizing his muscles. "You realize I don't have to answer any of these."

"Did Kurt know you were using *that* watch to control him?" Kris asked again in a firmer tone.

"It felt safer to keep that information from him."

All the horrible things Kurt did . . . maybe it wasn't him. Maybe it was all Tynan pulling the strings like a puppet master. If the watch was still here, that meant Kurt was stronger than the mind control. At least in his desire to leave.

"Are you going to control me?" she asked.

Tynan rested a hand on top of the pocketknife and traced the edges with his fingertips. "I would rather not," he finally said. "But I also don't fully trust your sudden change of heart."

Kris nodded slowly and met his gaze. "I understand. What would you have me do?"

"Kneel."

Without a thought, she lowered herself to her knees and sat back on her heels. She was breathing heavily, her pulse racing as she stared dead ahead for what felt like several minutes. Tynan stepped forward and used the sole of his boot to deliver a kick into the side of her skull.

Kris cried out and fell over from the force of the blow. She gasped, clutching the side of her head as she sat up. The inside of her cheek burned and her mouth filled with blood. She could also feel a steady trickle from her nose as her vision got fuzzy.

"Let's see those healer abilities up close," Tynan murmured, squatting down in front of her to stare her in the face.

Kris took a deep breath in, focusing her energy on the wounds. It was difficult while her head was still ringing, but she was able to summon the strength. The taste of blood gradually disappeared and her nose grew warm as it healed.

"Incredible," he said before standing up again. "Rise."

She climbed to her feet and faced him as she awaited her next instruction.

"From this point forward your name is Elle, signifying your rebirth into our cause."

That's why they call Kurt "Kye." It was the name Tynan gave him.

"Where are the keys to Calosant?" he asked. "I assume Kye has been hunting them."

Kris nodded. "We found a shield," she said, voice quavering, "which led us to the next clue on some island in Lake Superior. They are recovering it as we speak."

Tynan pressed his lips together and bobbed his head. He looked impressed. Surprised, even. "He's been hard at work to ruin my plans, I see."

I can't believe I just told him that.

He leered at her. A menacing smile twisted his mouth as he slithered forward. "One . . . last . . . thing . . ."

"Yes, sir?" Kris asked, her posture stiffening.

Tynan loomed over her, and his dark eyes seemed to almost flash as he spoke. "I need you to bring Kurt Carlsons to me."

~

The sharp steel blade measured about eight inches in length and had a gold handle. Polished garnets were embedded in the gold, as well as in the blade.

Cade held the dagger tight in his fist, Larsen's hand clasped firmly on his shoulder, as the cabin's dining room slowly came into focus around them.

Brie leaped off the couch in the living room once she saw them. "Oh, thank God you're here," she whispered, racing toward them.

Larsen's heart sank. "What is it? What's wrong?"

Brie's blue eyes darted down the hall and back again. She clutched her arms, hugging herself and trembling. "Kris and Kurt had a *huge* fight. I was in the bath. I heard them screaming at each other, and when I got out, Kris was gone."

"What?"

Cade took several long strides to the door and scanned the meadow.

"Where's Kurt?" Larsen asked, putting a hand on Brie's shoulders in an attempt to calm her.

She gestured down the hall to his bedroom door. "He hasn't come out," she hissed under her breath. "I was too scared to check on him."

Larsen patted her shoulder and guided her back into the living room. "It's okay. I'll go talk to him. Just sit down and catch your breath."

They had a fight? Larsen wondered as he hurried down the hall to the closed bedroom door. *What happened? Where would Kris have gone?*

He twisted the doorknob slowly and poked his head into the room.

Kurt was sitting on the floor with his back against his bed. His face was buried in his hands, and a journal was open on the floor in front of him.

"Kris read my journal," Kurt mumbled before Larsen could even speak. "She read about all the worst things I've ever done. All the people I've hurt. She read the letter from Nina."

Larsen closed the door behind him and approached hesitantly.

"I screamed at her, Larsen," Kurt continued. He dropped his hands into his lap, staring dead ahead into nothing. "God, it was terrible. She must hate me." He peeked over at him from the corner of his eye. "Is she okay?"

"She's gone, Kurt," Larsen said quietly, holding out an arm toward the door.

"What?" He got to his feet in an instant.

"We just got back, and Kris isn't here. Brie has no idea where she went."

"I've got to go after her," Kurt said, moving past Larsen and throwing open his bedroom door.

"But wait, where? Do you even know where she is?"

Kurt snatched his car keys from the kitchen counter and paused. He stared out the window above the kitchen sink into the meadow. "I think I know where she might've gone."

Chapter 30

Blood and Tears

"**I**f you're dead set on facing Tynan, then there is something you should know," Shay said. He reached into the back pocket of his baggy jeans and held his hand out to Kris.

Her heart skipped a beat. "My father's pocketknife." She took it calmly from his hand.

"Tynan doesn't know I swapped it. Do not let him know you have it. He'll think the knife in his possession is yours, and he'll use it to try to control you."

"Control me?" Kris raised her eyes from the blade to meet his focused gaze.

"Ancient magic. A Witcan can use an item close to someone's heart to manipulate them." Shay rubbed the nape of his neck and turned away. "It's . . . It was how I was able to get you to leave the house the other night."

"You controlled me?" She clutched the knife to her chest and took a step back.

She replayed the conversation with Shay again in her mind as she stared down Tynan. How far should she go in playing along?

Kris could feel the closed knife in the back pocket of her jeans, suddenly concerned Tynan might see it and wise up to what was going on.

Dark eyes narrowed as the tall man stepped in closer. "I command you to tell me where Kurt is."

Kris cleared her throat and adjusted her posture. "With all due respect, sir, he is useless. We don't need him anymore."

"Then you should have no problem killing him."

Her blood ran cold, but she maintained a straight face. "Is it even worth our trouble?"

"If you catch a mouse in a humane trap and release it outside, then it will come right back into the house. That is why I've learned to always terminate pests."

Kris dropped her eyes down to her sneakers. "I . . . I can't, sir." She didn't look up, but she could feel Tynan approaching. Her shoulders were already tensing, anticipating a strike. "I will help you get to Calosant. I will help you get the Mina Ring, but I don't want to hurt anybody."

Tynan snorted. "I saw right through you the moment you got here," he hissed. "I know you have no interest in actually joining my mission, but I would have been a fool not to lull you into a false sense of security.”

Kris’s feet left the ground as she was propelled backwards, and her spine slammed into the wall with a loud thud. Photo frames bounced off and clattered on the floor below, but her body stayed against the wall, held in place by an invisible force wrapped around her neck. Her face burned as she gasped for air.

Tynan sauntered close so that they were eye-to-eye.

“What happened to you to make you like this?” Kris muttered through the wheezes.

“I think you’re done asking questions now. I’ve entertained this long enough.” Tynan flicked a hand and Kris’s back slid up higher, scratching over the wallpaper. “Did you think you could just waltz in here and then leave with all this information?”

“Sort of.”

Tynan chuckled and then tilted his head to the side. Kris’s neck was released and her body toppled down to the floor. She coughed, clasping her hand to her chest.

“Your heart is too strong to control. I’ll just have to break your spirit first.”

“You’ve taken enough from me,” Kris shouted as she shot to her feet.

He hardly had time to react. A pulsating ball of white formed around Kris’s fist and she punched forward through the air, a glowing beam firing towards him. Tynan shot his fist out as well, a deep blue ray colliding with Kris's. They crashed together in an explosion of light, both holding the other's attack back.

"You're getting stronger. I'm impressed," Tynan said. "Just remember that everything Kurt has taught *you*, *I* taught him. You can't beat me."

"Joke's on you. Kurt didn't teach me this."

Kris flexed all her fingers and forced every ounce of strength she had into the palms of her hands. The white beam grew wider and brighter, nearly blinding as it jolted forward, consuming Tynan's beam until it was only inches from his fist.

Panic flashed in his eyes the moment before he threw himself to the side and rolled away. Her beam fired past him, striking the far wall and blasting a smoldering hole through the wood. She grinned. She had him on the ropes now.

"Don't be smiling yet," Tynan shouted. He slammed his fist into the floor, which smashed the surface and sent a rumble rippling through the house.

Kris lost her balance and slapped a hand against the wall to keep from falling. Tynan punched two blue fists in her direction, and although he was several feet away, she felt the impact of both punches. One struck her left cheek, throwing her head to one side, and the other connected to her chin and flung her back up against the wall. Her face became wet with blood, and her jaw throbbed.

As she pressed both her palms together, her fingers grew cold while she frantically formed a ball of ice in her hands. She hurled it at Tynan as he charged her. The first throw missed, but the second collided with his shoulder, solidifying as a thick sheet of ice against his chest.

He growled and thrust an open palm at Kris. She managed to avoid several hits, until a fireball struck her thigh. Kris screamed as the flames singed her skin. With a hand clasped over the burn and her arm bracing her against the wall, she formed a fireball of her own in her free hand.

Tynan effortlessly flung her fireball away and wrapped his hand around Kris's throat, squeezing hard. Any hint of admiration was long gone from his eyes, which now flickered like the deepest, darkest ring of hell.

"I warned you not to test me," he hissed.

He pushed Kris up against the bookcase and slammed her onto the shelves several times. Books toppled down with each hit. Her back stung with the pain that fired through her legs, all while she continued to gasp for air.

"You think you're so tough," Tynan said through clenched teeth directly into her face.

Kris pounded her fist into his wrist in an effort to free herself. But her limbs were numbed from the repeated crashes into the bookshelf.

She glared at him. "Your arrogance will be your downfall."

He rammed her back once more, then let her drop to the ground among the fallen books. Tynan allowed her several seconds of coughs and pants before she suddenly got an icky feeling. Like he was in her head.

In the dark void of her mind, Kris could see his figure in the distance as he approached. A faint silhouette, but she could read his scowl from where she stood.

Let's just see where you and your friends have been hiding out, Tynan's voice rang out.

Kris held out both her palms. Against her fingertips, a warm, rippling field began to grow, extending out to form a barrier like the ones she had seen in Kurt's mind.

You aren't getting anything from me, she said. She grunted and pushed her palms harder against the glowing wall, which grew more opaque as it thickened.

Tynan's form loomed on the other side. He slammed a fist against the barrier, and the force threw Kris away for a moment, but she rushed forward again to hold her ground.

You will never find them. I won't let you hurt my friends, she told him.

She slowly climbed to her feet, using the last remaining shelf to heave herself up. She and Tynan eyed each other the whole while.

He sneered. "That's right. Tire yourself out. It will only make it easier to break you."

While she held the wall in her mind, Kris's fists began to glow white at her sides. She threw telekinetic punches Tynan's way, but he managed to dodge them. The distraction was enough to ease up the hits to the barrier.

Kris lurched forward, trying to make contact, but he grabbed her by the forearm. He gave it a brutal twist that forced her to her knees with a cry. With her free hand, she delivered a fist into the side of his leg. Tynan stumbled with the punch and released her arm, but he swiftly kicked her across the face.

She was still clutching her swollen eye when Tynan reached down to grab her by the throat and drive her back into the shelves once more. He clasped his open palm against Kris's temple. "You can't hide from me."

Her head was ringing and her body was physically drained, so she closed her eyes. She was kneeling in the dark void in her mind, but she persisted anyway, pressing her palms against the barrier once more with a grunt.

Tynan slammed a fist against the other side of the wall. The barrier was beginning to falter.

She gulped for air. Kris was still pounding on his wrist as hard as she could, trying to break free as she gasped for breath. She reached out in an attempt to claw at his face, but she couldn't quite reach.

I will find your friends, Tynan's voice echoed through the wall. *And when I do, I will make you watch as I kill each and every one of them in a slow, painful, intimate manner.*

Kris pushed herself up against the shimmering divide, frantically trying to repair the cracks forming with each hit from his side.

You will watch the life drain from their eyes, and the last thought they will have is how you failed them.

Her knees were weak, but she fought to hold on. *I will sooner die than let you harm them*, she called out.

With the last little bit of strength Kris had remaining, the barrier glowed a glittering white, forming one last layer of protection as Tynan struck the wall once more.

One more hit and it would shatter, she realized. In her mind, she sank back to her knees but kept her hands against the barrier. Even in the dark void, things were beginning to fade in and out.

Her throat was suddenly released, and Kris crumpled to the ground among the books in Tynan's office. It took several desperate breaths and a long moment for her vision to return.

Kurt was standing over Tynan, striking him in the head with a green fist.

"Kurt," Kris wheezed, and she dragged herself off the floor.

Tynan slammed an open palm into Kurt's chest, which threw him off and onto his back. Once on his feet, Tynan aimed a fist—glowing a deep, dark blue—at Kurt.

Kris didn't even realize she was reacting until the large turquoise sphere had left her hands. About twelve inches in diameter, the ball erupted against Tynan's fist, splashed down his arm and across his chest, and dripped down to the floor. It froze him completely in place.

Kris heaved Kurt to his feet and the two hurried toward the hall.

"Go, go," Kurt shouted as he pulled her behind him.

"Wait!" She stopped abruptly, darted back into the room, and snatched the watch from Tynan's desk.

"Get back here, you little *rat*," Tynan's voice boomed.

They sprinted down the stairs to the open front door.

"Don't look back, just go," Kurt said, stepping aside to escort Kris out first.

They darted into the darkness outside toward his car, which was parked in the street and still running. The front doors flew open as they approached, and they dove in. Kurt pushed his foot down on the accelerator. The tires screeched on the asphalt for a moment before rocketing the car down the empty street.

It wasn't until they were several miles away that Kris finally relaxed, slouching down into her seat and turning to face out the windshield. Her chest was still burning. Her body and mind were exhausted from the fight, and she felt like she would just collapse into sleep at any moment.

Kris wiped a drop from her cheek, unsure if it was blood or tears. "I think we're safe. I don't think he's following . . ." Her voice trailed off when she looked over her shoulder to Kurt.

His face was ghostly white and his blue-gray eyes wide. His knuckles squeezed the steering wheel with such force that she worried he might snap it. His breaths came short and sharp, his entire chest heaving with each desperate gasp.

"Kurt? Are you—?"

He jerked hard on the wheel and slammed the brakes, then came to an abrupt stop on the side of the road. Kris slid forward and crashed against the dashboard.

She was still trying to process what was happening when he kicked open his car door, raced around to the front of his car, and dropped to the ground out of sight.

"Kurt?" Kris started to climb out, suddenly realizing she was still clutching the watch in a death grip. She set it down on the dash before sliding out, bracing herself on the car door as she peered over the hood. Kurt's head was visible just between the bright headlights.

Rounding the car, she discovered him sitting in the dirt, hyperventilating, his palms pressed into his forehead. He was gently rocking back and forth.

Kris said nothing while she slowly approached. She could hear each raspy breath over the rumble of the car engine as she crouched down beside him and tried to rest her hands on his arm.

He ripped his arm away. "No. No, don't." He hunched forward and hid his face as much as possible from view. "Don't look at me."

"Hey, hey, breathe," she whispered as calmly as she could despite her heart racing.

She talked Kurt through deep breath after deep breath, taking his hand and giving it a firm squeeze. Once he'd lowered his arm, Kris could finally see his face. It was wet with tears. The sight made her stomach twist.

It took several minutes, and many heartbreaking sobs, for Kurt to finally start forming sentences.

"Six years ago, I decided to confront Tynan. At that house. I don't know why I thought I could defeat him. I should have just left . . ." Kurt held out his arm, palm-side up, to display the large burn scar. "His beam did this when he tried to kill me. I barely escaped with my life."

Kris said nothing and traced her fingers over the scar. Eventually, she slid in closer, sat in the dirt right alongside him, and hugged his arm.

They both sat quietly for a few more minutes until Kurt's breathing was almost completely back to normal. He used the sleeve of his T-shirt to dry his face, and he stared down at Kris with a sad, crooked smile. "I'm sorry you had to see me like this."

"Don't apologize," she replied in a hushed voice. She nuzzled her forehead into Kurt's shoulder. "I'm just glad you're okay."

He tilted his head and rested his cheek on Kris's hair. After a moment, he cleared his throat and sat up straight. "We should go. Put more distance between us and that place."

As Kris lowered herself into the car once more, she picked up the watch from the dashboard. She examined it while Kurt buckled his seatbelt, then held it out to him. "Here," she said softly.

Even in the dark, the look of recognition in Kurt's eyes illuminated the entire front seat as he took the vintage watch from her hand.

"My father's watch," he mumbled as he traced his fingers over the edges. He became lost in staring at it for a long moment. Rubbing his thumb over the glass once more, he set the watch in the cupholder beside him and pulled away onto the street.

"You're welcome," Kris whispered, knowing he wouldn't be able to put the words together. As she leaned back in her seat, she felt the weight of the afternoon pushing down on her. Her head felt heavy and her eyelids continued to flutter shut.

"Get some rest. We have a bit of a drive ahead of us."

As Kris drifted off to sleep, she caught a glimpse of Kurt's soft smile as he changed his indicator.

Chapter 31

Fireflies

Kris woke to a gentle touch of her shoulder. She inhaled and looked around with squinted eyes. It took a few minutes for the haze to lift while she rubbed her neck and stretched her back.

It was dark outside the car, but she could tell they weren't at the cabin. Through the windshield, she could see the moonlight glistening on water not too far ahead.

"Where are we?" she asked groggily, grinding her fists into her eyes.

"Cade mentioned you've been missing this place," Kurt said. "And I wanted to do something to make it up to you."

Kris fumbled with her seatbelt and stepped out of the car. She was immediately greeted by fireflies buzzing around her. Her lips curled into a smile as she admired the insects spiraling through the air. "Lake Lampyridae?"

"I know it's not the same without your parents here, but I thought I would surprise you," Kurt said. He locked his car and walked around the front to meet Kris.

Her eyes were misted over as she gazed down the path toward the moonlight dancing on the water's calm surface. The night was completely still. No wind. No clouds. Just the icy-white moon, the fireflies, and the millions of stars staring down at them.

Kris wandered down the concrete trail towards the beach in silence, just marveling at the sight around her.

Kurt followed behind. "Are you . . . Is everything okay?"

About halfway to the beach, Kris whirled around with a huge smile. "This is incredible," she said in a hushed voice. She clasped a hand over her mouth as though to keep from crying. "I can't believe you did this." She grabbed him by the wrist and pulled him from the path into the woods. "Come on. This way!"

Kurt laughed, allowing her to drag him through the trees and shrubs. "Where are you taking me?"

Kris held a branch aside for him. "My secret spot," she replied, her voice filled with excitement. She climbed over a jagged boulder and rushed through the trees to a large rock that hung about five feet above the surface of the lake.

Kurt gasped at the view. The fireflies danced around the lake, their light reflecting on the water. "Wow. It's really something out here . . ."

His voice trailed off as she hunched forward and began to remove her sneakers and socks one foot at a time.

"What are you doing?" he said.

Her eyes were glued on the water below. "No way we came all the way out here to *not* go in." She gave Kurt a nod of encouragement. "Come on."

Though he was visibly trembling, he followed her lead, hesitantly pulling off his shoes and socks.

Kris peered over the ridge into the water and then backed up. "Ready?"

He crept up to the edge. "Is it safe? I mean, there aren't any sharp rocks or . . . ?"

She giggled and held out a hand to him. "Take a leap of faith."

Kurt took her hand as she offered him a reassuring smile. She could feel his pulse throbbing against her skin.

And then they were running. Their feet carried them right up to the edge of the rock, and they leaped off into the night.

Together they pierced the chilly water. Bubbles encircled them, trickling up through their hair. The refreshing, cool water seemed to calm Kurt for a moment, but then he panicked for air. Kris squeezed his hand and pulled him back up to the surface. Though the breath he took was deep, he was still smiling. He laughed as he swiped a hand over his face to remove the water dripping into his eyes.

Kris beamed and pushed strands of her own wet hair aside. "See. Not so scary."

Kurt looked up at the sky, and she did the same. Every star was clear and crisp against the black backdrop of night, and the soothing hum of crickets hung in the air.

"It's so peaceful out here. I get why you love it so much," he said.

She floated on her back, a serene smile on her face. "I just love floating out here. It's so quiet. I feel like such a small, insignificant piece in a vast universe. It's comforting." She raised her head out of the water. "It's cheesy, I know."

"It's not."

They smiled at each other for a moment.

"For the record, you'll never be insignificant to me," he said.

Kris blushed and pushed a hand across the surface of the water to splash Kurt. "You sap."

He chuckled, shaking the water from his hair and face. They both returned to staring at the stars, admiring the twinkling added by the fireflies around them.

"So . . . you were part of Tynan's cult, huh?" Kris asked, breaking the silence after several minutes of quietly floating.

He turned to face away from her. "He took me in after my parents—"

"I know. He told me." Kris swam around to face him. "Why didn't you just tell me?"

He shook his head. "How do you tell someone something like that? The things I did . . . Larsen doesn't even know."

"You don't need to be ashamed. You were a kid, put in a horrible position. And Tynan used your father's watch to literally control you."

"There's no rationalizing what I did."

She offered him a reassuring smile. "I know I got really angry earlier . . . but I guess what's important is who you are now. Who you want to be."

"You sound like Fia," he said, breaking into a grin.

Kris nodded toward the ledge where they had jumped in. "Come on."

They swam over to the cliff, and she climbed out using ridges, cracks, and roots that jutted out of the rocks and dirt. After she pulled herself over the top, she propped herself on her hands and knees to help pull Kurt up.

"It's kind of chilly up here now," Kris muttered, clutching both arms around herself.

"I'll make us a fire." He motioned for her to sit, and she obliged with a soft smile.

Kurt collected branches and brambles from the trees and formed them a few feet in front of her. She hugged her knees to her chest, unable to keep the grin from her face.

He formed a small fireball in his hand and held it against the branches until the dry wood caught. "There."

After he brushed his hands together to clear off the dirt, he lowered himself to sit beside her. She huddled up next to him as the flames began to grow and crackle. Kris rested her head on his shoulder and rubbed the goose bumps that covered her arms. Kurt wrapped an arm around her back, hugging her close.

"Thank you for coming back for me," Kris whispered after several minutes of watching the fire flicker against the night.

"I'm sorry I yelled. I didn't want you to leave."

"I'm sorry I snooped through your things. I should have trusted you."

Kurt brushed his fingers up and down her arm. "Can we just be done apologizing now?"

Kris chuckled. "Yes, please."

She could feel him looking at her, and after several seconds, she turned her body to face him. The fire reflected in his pale eyes as he gazed down at her. She could feel Kurt's heart pounding all the way down to his fingertips on her back.

No more second guessing. Kris leaned in and pressed her lips against Kurt's. It caught him by surprise, but after a deep breath, he relaxed into it. He clutched a hand around the back of Kris's neck, pulling her in closer while stroking her cheek with his thumb. She didn't feel cold anymore, but she was still trembling.

When Kurt pulled away, she could still feel his lips. Her cheeks burned and she had to turn her head away for a second to hide her grin behind her hair. He traced a finger across her forehead, moving a strand of damp hair and tucking it behind her ear.

He gently lifted her chin. "You're the most incredible person I've ever met," he whispered.

Kris giggled and bit her lip. "You're not so bad yourself." She then slid in right up against him so they could huddle up by the fire again.

Sparks snapped and fluttered up into the night as they watched the stars slowly drift across the sky. She didn't even realize how much time had passed until the horizon began to change to a pale yellow with the rising sun.

"We should get going," Kurt said. He held out a hand, and the flames died down into a small puff of smoke.

They both stood, now completely dry. Before leaving, he lightly cupped Kris's cheek and pulled her in for one more soft kiss.

"I think this was the best night of my life," he admitted, brushing his thumb over her skin.

"Mine too."

Chapter 32

The Dagger

"**Y**ou guys kissed?"

Kris frantically shushed Brie as she pushed the bedroom door closed and leaned back against it. She couldn't keep the smile from her face.

"How did this happen?" Brie pressed on. She bounced with excitement, her hands waving enthusiastically as she spoke. "First you insist that you're just friends, then you get in a huge fight, and now, what, Kurt's suddenly your boyfriend?"

Kris chuckled softly, able to feel herself blushing. "I mean, I don't know. We didn't really define what we are." She bit down on her thumbnail, replaying their kiss the night before in her mind. When she spoke again, her voice was barely audible. "I really like him, Brie. I've never felt like this before."

Brie grabbed her by the hands, pulled her away from the door, and danced around in place. Her energy was so contagious that Kris found herself jumping around too.

"I'm so happy for you," Brie said. "After all the crap you've been through these past couple months, you deserve to be happy."

~

"So, are you going to tell us what happened last night, or . . ."

Kurt was turning the dagger over in his hands, examining the newest clue they had found, but he fumbled and nearly dropped it at Cade's question. He set the blade down on the dining room table. "What do you mean?" He tried and failed to hide the smile on his face.

Cade grinned and pointed a finger at him. "I knew it. I *knew* it. The instant you walked in this morning with that big dopey smile and all this energy. You two finally kissed!"

"What?" Larsen twisted in his chair, setting his coffee aside to shoot Kurt a look. "You kissed Kris?"

Kurt shrugged. "I don't kiss and tell."

"Dude, your face is telling enough," Cade said with a laugh.

Kurt cleared his throat. "So—so you found the dagger encased in a tree?"

Larsen sat up tall, his shoulders tight as he rubbed his forehead. "No. Inside three trees. They were all twisted around each other."

"Oh sure, just change the subject," Cade said. "The dagger is only the second biggest piece of news around here."

"Cade, just drop it," Larsen said, slapping a hand down on the table. "Can we please just focus on the problem at hand and figure out where the next key is?"

"Fine, be a Debbie Downer." Cade picked up the dagger from the table and traced the garnets. "If you're so smart, why don't you just tell us what you've got so far?"

Larsen took a long sip of coffee from his mug and kept his head down. "Nothing you can't already discern on your own. It's steel, gold handle, encrusted garnets. It's a goddamn knife. It doesn't tell us anything."

Kurt looked to Cade quizzically as Larsen forced back his chair and stood in a huff, retreating to the kitchen.

Cade rolled his eyes up to the ceiling and shrugged.

"There has to be something here," Kurt said as Larsen returned with another steaming mug of coffee. "Don't worry. We'll figure it out."

Larsen dropped back into his chair. He glared at Cade and swiped the knife from his hand.

"Hey!"

"Just let me handle this," Larsen said. He used a clean kitchen towel to buff out Cade's fingerprints from the dagger.

"Fine." Cade scoffed, threw his hands in the air, and charged out the front door.

Kurt watched him leave, then leaned over the table to Larsen. "Is everything okay? You seem a little . . . off this morning."

Larsen sighed and rubbed his eyes. "Sorry, I'm fine. Just tired." He gave Kurt a quick glance from the corner of his eye. "I was up most of the night worried about you two."

"I should have let you know we were all right. I'm sorry." Kurt laced his fingers together as he rested on his elbows. After a long moment of contemplation, he said, "There are things about me . . . about my past . . . that I never told you. And I want you to hear them from me."

~

The purple orb that formed in Kris's hand sparked, spitting jolts and flickers of electricity as she tried to contain it between her palms. With fingers curled around the sphere, she slowly pulled her hands apart and concentrated the tingly feeling under her skin until the ball grew to be about the size of a softball. Once large enough, she grunted as she twisted her body and lobbed the orb across the field at the mannequin.

The electrical sphere struck it in the abdomen, and it toppled over into the grass.

"How was that?" She looked over her shoulder to Kurt as he approached.

"Your speed's improving. Make sure you mind your posture." He gripped her upper arms and pushed them back to square her shoulders. "You default to this hunch. Keep your body open. It will be easier for your energy to expand."

Kris stared into his eyes and couldn't hold back. She leaned in for a quick peck, then swatted him on the arm. "Quit distracting me. I need to practice."

"Me? You're the one who's distracting," Kurt said, backing away with a smug grin. "Flashing me those green eyes—the audacity."

Kris wrinkled her nose with a smirk. She shook out her arms, adjusted her posture, then turned back to the mannequin again as it raised out of the grass. *All right, keep your shoulders back,* she told herself as she clapped her hands together.

~

Larsen looked up from studying the dagger and saw Kurt and Kris kiss through the window. The smiles on their faces. The flirtatious twinkle in their eyes. The way Kurt's fingers brushed down Kris's arm. It all made Larsen's stomach churn.

He turned away in his chair and rested his forehead in the palm of his hands. *They do look happy, though . . .*

"Why are you being so salty lately?"

Larsen jumped, startled as Cade sat up on the couch. "How long have you been there? You nearly gave me a heart attack!" He clasped a hand over his chest.

"Seriously, you were irritating to be around before," Cade continued, pushing his hair from his face, "but now you're just a straight-up asshole all the time."

"Well, maybe it's just prolonged exposure to you." Larsen flung the dagger down against the dining room table with a loud clatter.

Cade climbed over the back of the couch and landed on his feet in the dining room. "Yeah, see, this is what I'm talking about."

"You're the one going around passing judgment on everyone else."

Cade shook his head. "Why are you even here?"

Larsen bit his tongue, then dropped his head for a moment. "Yeah, I've been asking myself tha—"

"Good morning!" Brie called as she exited the bathroom. Her damp blonde curls cascaded around her face, and her cheeks were perfectly flushed.

Cade nearly leaped forward, an oddly sincere smile on his face. "Hey."

Her smile quickly vanished when she read the tone of the room. "Is everything all right?"

"I'm just frustrated with this dagger is all," Larsen said.

Brie flashed Cade a smirk as she passed. "No leads on it yet?"

"We could try stabbing someone with it," Cade grumbled, leaning back against the couch.

Larsen sat up straight, thoughts turning in his head. "That's . . . not a bad idea . . ."

"I meant you."

He silenced Cade with a wave of his hand. "Yeah, I know what you meant." He picked up the dagger again, testing the sharpness of the blade with his thumb. "But some of that occult stuff has its roots in Witcan culture, so maybe . . ."

Larsen very carefully pressed his pointer finger into the tip of the knife until a small droplet of blood formed.

"Whoa," Brie said, stepping away.

Cade took a couple of strides towards Larsen before stopping. "Dude."

Larsen pinched his fingers together to stop the bleeding, then held the knife out. The drop of blood on the tip of the blade suddenly disappeared, dissolving into the steel. The three watched in amazement as tiny words scrawled along the dagger's sharp edge in dark scarlet.

"Kiss the sun?" he said.

Brie leaned over his shoulder. "What does that mean? Just, like, hold it in the sunlight?"

"I don't know," Larsen said with a shrug.

Cade snatched the dagger from him. "Let me try." He quickly disappeared through the front door.

Brie watched Cade, then flipped her wet hair back to shoot Larsen a look.

"Stop playing games, Brie," Larsen said, nodding to the front door.

She giggled nervously and fiddled with her hair. "Games?" She followed Larsen's glance out the front window, where they could see Cade on the porch holding the dagger out in the sunlight. When he saw Larsen and Brie looking, he spun away.

"Cade is actually being pretty sincere around you, so maybe you do the same."

She twisted around in her spot, biting her lip as they watched Cade trudge back up the steps with disappointment on his face.

"He likes you," Larsen said quietly. "So give him a chance to actually get to know you."

~

"Kiss the sun," Kris mumbled to herself as she squeezed the throw pillow in her arms.

Kurt sat on the living room floor in front of her and scribbled notes on a notepad.

"We tried sunlight. We tried high altitude." Cade counted off their attempts on his fingers from where he lay on the other sofa.

Brie propped her head up against her fist on the armrest, her eyes barely open. "Are these keys going to keep getting harder?" she said through a yawn. "Because I, like, already thought the riddle on the shield was pretty tough."

Kris slapped her hand against the pillow. "It can't be that hard. We must be overthinking it." Though she tried to fight it, Brie's yawn caught up to her.

"Like what?" Larsen asked. He was slouched against the coffee table.

"I don't know. Anyone kissed the thing yet?" Kris muttered, then let her head drop back on the couch. Her eyelids were only getting heavier.

Brie raised her hand weakly. "Tried it. Nothing."

"We're not getting anywhere tonight. Can we just go to sleep?" Cade said, finally yawning himself.

Kurt clipped the pen to his page as he rubbed his eyes. "No, we're so close. I can feel it. Did we try using a light sphere? Maybe it has to be Witcan light?"

Larsen held out a hand, palm-side up, and a small ball of white light formed in the air. He held it over the blade of the dagger, studying it for any changes, then waved the orb from existence. "Nothing."

"Maybe it's not the light we need to focus on," Kris said. "Maybe it's heat."

Cade raised his head off the couch and held out a hand towards Larsen. "Let me see that."

Larsen picked up the dagger. "Knock yourself out."

Cade walked over and grabbed it, then retrieved his lighter and clicked it open. Everyone watched as he held the small flame against the steel blade for a long moment. Disappointment overtook his face.

Kris let her head drop back into the couch again with a groan.

"Whoa, wait!" he said.

A small spark suddenly snapped into the air and circled around the dagger, and the group perked up.

"What was that?" Kurt asked, setting the notepad aside.

A second spark emerged. Then a third. They watched in silence as hundreds of sparks flicked into the air, spinning around as they slowly moved into formation to create a series of numbers and letters.

Kris read them off as she stood from the couch to see the code written in glowing sparks. Kurt snatched up his notepad again and rushed to write it down.

"Now, what does that mean?" Cade asked, shutting his lighter again.

"They're coordinates," Larsen said.

Kris fished through her pocket for her phone and started typing them into her internet browser.

Brie peeked over Kris's shoulder. "Coordinates to where?"

Kris smiled and held out her phone for everyone to see. "Mera, Arkansas. Quartz Cave State Park."

Chapter 33

The Mine

The bright green woods were lush with moss, which coated the trunks of trees and dappled the walls of rock all around them. The color was even more vibrant in the early-morning rain.

Kris breathed it in as she and Kurt descended the hill towards the hiking trail below. She held on to his arm with a firm grasp, carefully climbing down from the boulders. She wasn't going to slip and fall like she had back in Maine.

She noticed Brie clinging to Cade's sleeve just ahead, but she tried to pay it no mind. Larsen was already at the bottom of the rocky slope, peering left and right down the trail.

Two women in full exercise attire jogged by, shooting suspicious glances up the rock ridge as Kris and Kurt finally jumped down to the forest floor. One of the women whispered something to the other while they continued down the dirt path.

Kris eyed the women as they jogged away, then tugged on Kurt's sleeve. "I don't like the way they looked at us," she said quietly.

"Me neither."

Larsen waved for everyone to go to the left, away from the runners. "It's this way."

The five of them followed the trail in silence. The only sound was the rain trickling through the leaves overhead. It didn't soothe the anxious feeling in Kris's gut as she stared up at the ridge to their left.

Kurt brushed her hand with his fingers. "Don't worry. We'll be fine. In and out in no time."

Kris forced a smile. A drop of rain broke through the canopy and landed on her cheek. She wiped it away.

Just ahead, at the end of the trail, was a large opening in a tall rock ridge. It was pitch black inside, the hiking path sloping down into the earth's crust.

"That's the entrance," Larsen said.

Kris glanced over her shoulder. A hiker had stopped in his steps several yards away and was studying them. When he caught her eye, he backed away, then turned and headed the opposite direction.

Something doesn't feel right.

The way Kurt squeezed her hand let her know he felt it too.

"The mine's closed," he said, stopping to point to a red wooden sign a man was hanging near the entrance.

Larsen jogged ahead and waved to the man in the tan polo shirt and cap. "Excuse me," he called as he approached. "Is the mine closed?"

The man had a state park logo on the arm of his shirt, likely a park ranger. He turned to face Larsen and gestured to the sign he had just hung up. "Temporarily closed due to structural instability. A lot of rain this year." He eyed the group. "Didn't they tell you at the park entrance?"

Cade clapped a hand onto Larsen's shoulder with a forced grin. "Of course. *This guy* was just so eager to see it. He was hoping only part of the mine was closed."

The ranger looked between the two of them and shook his head, once again pointing to the sign. "Nope. Whole thing is closed. Sorry. Check our website for updates."

Kris's posture stiffened as the ranger studied each of their faces in uncomfortable detail, then shuffled by them to his ATV. He gave her a once-over before climbing onto his vehicle and speeding down the hiking trail toward the park entrance.

They watched him roll away, and once he had disappeared around the trail bend, Kris looked back to the mine. "We're still going in, aren't we?"

Kurt charged forward. "We should move. Before the ranger comes back."

Kris bit her lip and stole one more look around to ensure the coast was clear, then followed into the darkness. Kurt was less cautious, pressing on into the cave without hesitation. He created a small ball of light between his palms, which floated beside him as he dropped his arms and followed the trail farther into the mine.

Though small, the light from the sphere was enough to fill the void around them. The area at the entrance was wide, but Kris could see that the mine narrowed ahead. It made her anxious.

She followed Kurt's example and formed a light orb of her own, cradling it in her hands. Along the side of the trail were large spotlights, all powered off. Kris held out her light sphere to study the quartz crystals protruding from the reddish-brown rocks as she walked past. Their footsteps echoed off the walls of stalagmites. The various rock formations that surrounded them cast long, creepy shadows through the tunnel as they moved down.

A couple more light orbs formed behind Kris as Kurt stopped at a fork in the path. He held out his light to search both directions.

Kris felt a familiar warmth in her chest, just as she had back in Maine. She closed her eyes to find a soft, gentle glow pulsing far off in the distance. Opening her eyes again, she nodded to the path on the left. "This way."

"This place is creepy," Brie hissed. Her voice bounced off the stone and rang out through the cave. The sound sent shivers down Kris's spine.

"Agreed."

Kris touched her light orb with her fingertips. An energy passed through her skin, and the sphere doubled in size to cast more light around them as the cave got smaller. A ceiling of stalactites hung overhead, stretching down toward Kris as she walked beneath the sharp points.

In her mind, the light of the key was getting closer. Brighter. She put out a hand to stop Kurt mid-stride as her eyes settled on a thin crevice to the left of the trail. The space was only a few feet wide, and it made her stomach sink further into her gut.

Kurt followed her gaze before leading the way into the small space.

"Oh God," Brie grumbled from behind them. "I hate this. I hate all of this."

"You'll be fine," Cade whispered. "Deep breaths."

Kris kept a hand against the stone as they zigzagged through the crack. The cool surface of the rock helped calm her rising nerves, despite Brie's dramatic inhales just behind her.

The crevice widened and opened up enough at the end so the five of them could all stand together. Kris searched the walls, her heart pounding.

A glint caught her eye. There was something metallic protruding from the rock about an arm's length above her head.

"Is that it?" Brie asked. She squeezed up alongside Kris and pointed to a piece of silver against the brownish stones.

Kris closed her eyes for a moment. The light in her mind took shape, forming into an oval with a curved extension.

Without a word, Kurt slipped in front of her and extended a hand to rest his fingertips on the exposed silver. She watched as a handheld mirror slowly emerged from the stone underneath his hand. The back of the mirror was decorated to look like a blooming rose, with and bits of quartz crystals resembled dewdrops on its petals. It was like nothing she had ever seen.

No sooner was it completely free from the cave wall than Kris suddenly plummeted into a world of white.

What's happening?

She turned around and scanned the bright light that surrounded her. A tall, towering structure began to take form in front of her, like a thick fog slowly lifting, revealing a building with columns and statues carved in stone. She recognized it immediately.

This place again?

The ground emerged beneath Kris as she moved towards the building. Her footsteps echoed against the silver road as other smaller structures faded in around her. She studied them while she continued forward.

Each was carved out of gray stone and had windows and doors. Numbers were engraved in each.

They're houses.

Kris froze as the echo of footsteps grew louder. They continued even when she stopped. Approaching behind her were the silhouettes of six people walking in formation so that five surrounded one person in the middle.

The woman at the front of the formation was blurry, but Kris immediately picked out the object she was carrying in her hands: the silver mirror with the floral design and encrusted quartz crystals. The mirror key.

Only then did Kris realize that the man beside her had a shield strapped to his back. Even though she could only see a small section of it peeking over his shoulder, she recognized it.

The shield key. This is *Calosant . . . and these people must have all five keys.*

Kris stopped dead in her train of thought when she suddenly recognized the woman in the center of the crowd. Her black hair was tied back neatly in a long braid, and she wore an elaborate white and green dress decorated with beads and ribbons. It seemed to almost float around her as she walked, and her vibrant green eyes were glazed over as they stared blankly ahead.

Annona.

Kris could only gawk as Annona moved closer. She held her chin high, but there was something in the air around her that gripped Kris's heart, giving it a painful twist. She looked so . . . sad.

"Kris."

Her head snapped forward with an aggressive shake, and suddenly she was back in the quartz mine. Kurt released her shoulder when her eyes finally locked on him.

Kris wiped a hand across her forehead, glancing around nervously.

Brie was clutching the mirror to her chest with one arm, staring at her with wide eyes.

"What happened?" Kris asked.

"You were unresponsive," Kurt told her as he studied her. "Are you okay?"

She forced a laugh and pushed her hair from her face. "Yeah. Yeah, I'm fine."

"Let's get out of here," Larsen told them, pointing back down the narrow walkway toward the guided path.

"Please," Brie said. "This cave is freaking me out."

In a single-file line, Kris followed Brie and Cade, with Kurt and Larsen behind her. Cade stepped out onto the path first and held out a hand to help Brie as she stumbled over a rock jutting up from the ground.

"Did you see something?" Kurt whispered to Kris.

"I'll tell you later," she replied as she slipped out of the narrow passage to the trail.

Larsen linked arms with Kurt and extended an arm toward Brie, but Kurt's sudden head jerk caught everyone's attention.

"What is it?" Kris asked, following his gaze into the darkness.

His eyes went wide. "Get down!"

Before any of them could move, a gunshot rang out. The echo through the cave was deafening.

Everything happened so fast that Kris didn't even have time to process it. She could hear Brie screaming her name from nearby, but it felt miles away with the ringing in her skull. Kris slowly lifted herself to her knees and glanced around.

Larsen was on his back several feet away, a hand clasped on his chest. Cade was pulling Brie by the arms, twisting her away and ducking behind a large stalagmite.

Kurt had situated himself in front of Kris. He extended both hands until a glowing green force field began to form. It expanded outward, stretching from ground to ceiling. The barrier flashed and flickered with each bang.

Through Kurt's shield, Kris could see flashlights and silhouettes of men with guns.

"Surrender yourselves, and no one gets hurt."

Kris was heaved to her feet.

"It's an ambush!" Cade shouted. "We need to get out of here. Now."

Chapter 34

Ambush

Kris clung to Larsen's arm and dragged him deeper into the mine as the gunshots continued. "Kurt!" she called.

As she looked back, she saw Kurt still holding up a force field, slowly backing away as the beams of the flashlights grew closer. "Go! Get out of here. I'll hold them off."

Kris tumbled forward as Larsen suddenly collapsed.

"What's wrong?" she asked, checking for any blood. Aside from his pale complexion, he looked fine.

"They hit me with something," Larsen grumbled, and he pulled himself to the side of the path. He was panting hard.

Brie grabbed one arm and Cade the other, and they lifted Larsen back to his feet.

"It's a drug," Brie shouted over the hail of bullets. "They used it on me when I was arrested."

"Great, just what those jagoffs need," Cade muttered as they carried Larsen farther away.

"I can't teleport." Larsen's voice cracked. "We're trapped."

Kris glanced back again. She could still see Kurt around the bend in the trail. "What about Kurt?"

"He's a big boy," Cade said, scanning the cave around them. "He can handle himself."

That's what I'm afraid of. Kris remembered the way Kurt had reacted back at the NWDA facility. She hesitated, but followed Cade and the others deeper into the cave.

"We just need him to buy us some time to find another way out."

"How do we know there's another way out?" Kris said. "What if everything just loops back around to the entrance?"

"There's another way out," Cade said, despite the unsteadiness in his voice.

Flashlight beams came rushing around the corner toward them. Without a thought, Kris sprinted to the front of the group and threw her hands out. A telekinetic force extended outward, stopping multiple bullets only a few feet ahead of them.

More light hit her eyes, and she felt something whiz past her head.

"Kris!"

Brie's voice rang out from behind her.

"Stay back," Kris shouted at the NWDA agents closing in on her. "We're not going to hurt anyone."

More gunshots. A sharp pain fired across the side of Kris's neck. She cried out, clapping a hand over it as it burned. Her hand came away with droplets of blood, but the bullet had only grazed her.

"Kris, no!" Brie's voice continued to shriek as it got farther away.

"I said stay back," Kris yelled again, thrusting another telekinetic force forward. She could feel a rifle, and in her mind she wrapped both hands around the gun, ripped it away, and threw it aside. Over the commotion, she heard a loud clatter of a gun skidding across the cave floor.

Kris's hands began to glow, illuminating the space around her until she could make out the faces of the eight or so agents just ahead. Beyond their flashlights, beyond the various rifles and pistols, were angry scowls.

Another gunshot made her heart drop. She felt a sting just below her clavicle. She only flinched, keeping her arms up, but she could already feel the familiar tingle as the spot grew warm.

Kris raised her eyes to the stalactites hanging between her and the agents. Before she realized what she was doing, a ray of white light fired from each of her hands into the rock cones, breaking them from the roof of the cave and raining them down.

"Get back," one of the agents yelled. The group scampered backwards to avoid the falling rock.

Kris glanced back to where Cade was hiding in a crease in the rocks, and he waved her over. When she joined them, Brie instantly lunged at her and gave her a squeeze, eyes shining with tears. Larsen sat with his back against the stone. His eyes fluttered open and shut, his head bobbing with exhaustion.

"I'm fine. Mind Larsen," Kris instructed Brie, then stepped away.

Farther down through the jagged space, light pierced through the rocks.

"It looks like there's a way out up ahead," Cade said. "It's narrow, but we should be able to slip out."

Kris peered out to the trail. She couldn't see Kurt anymore, but she could still hear gunshots echoing from the direction they had left him.

"I'll take care of Kurt," Cade told Kris as he grabbed her shoulder and guided her back into the crack. "You need to clear us a path out."

Kris nodded. Her heart raced, her pulse roaring so loudly in her ears that she could hardly even hear his words. She leaned back against the rock for a moment and tried to catch her breath. Her knees felt weak and wobbly, like she could collapse any second.

A persistent pain continued to sting her skin at her collarbone, and she clasped a hand to it. She was startled to feel a cylindrical metal object stuck to her, only an inch long. Panicked, she ripped it away. It burned her skin as she did, and when she held it up to her eyes, she realized it was a dart. That must've been what they had shot Larsen with.

Brie looked up at her, and Kris hastily stuffed the dart into the pocket of her jeans. Still bracing herself against the cave wall, Kris moved deeper into the tight space.

We're going to get out of here. We have to get out. We will be fine.

She moved forward as quickly as she could, but she staggered to keep herself upright. She felt dizzy, a wave of fatigue washing over her, but she had to keep going. Had to power through.

In some places, the space was so narrow that she had to twist sideways to squeeze between rocks, and she scratched her arms against the rough surfaces. Over the distant gunshots, she could hear the rain as she got closer to the outside.

Not much farther ahead, there was a gap in the short ceiling of the cave only a couple feet wide. Roots dripping with rain jutted out into the mine, and beyond them Kris caught a glimpse of the greenery outside.

There! There's a hole. We're going to make it out!

Kris picked up her pace, fixated on the exit through her blurring vision. She was only steps from the exit when a force cracked the side of her skull, throwing her into the jagged rocks.

Head ringing from the blow, she was unable to catch herself as she slid down the stone wall to the ground with a quiet cry. The fall scraped her arms and back the whole way down.

An agent dressed in full SWAT gear stood over Kris with a handgun pointed directly at her. She pushed up onto her elbows, her chest heaving. The scratches in her skin stung, and the warm sensation didn't follow. *I can't heal,* Kris realized, her entire body aching.

Time stood still in those seconds as she stared down the barrel of the gun only inches from her face. When the gun didn't fire, Kris looked beyond it to the NWDA agent. She was surprised it was a woman. The agent's eyes were wide and unblinking with fear, and only then did Kris notice the gentle tremble of the woman's hands that teetered the gun side to side.

"D-don't . . . don't move," the woman said, squeezing the pistol's handle with both hands.

Kris breathed in deep and cautiously lifted herself up to sit. Her back throbbed with the motion.

"I said don't move," the agent repeated in a shaky voice.

"You don't want to shoot me," Kris said softly. She pivoted to a crouched position, then held her hands up by her shoulders. She maintained eye contact and gradually stood again. Her knees felt weak, but she did her best to stay upright, all while her head was still ringing from the blow the agent had delivered to her temple.

Tears whelmed in the woman's eyes as she stood her ground. She reaffirmed her stance, keeping the gun pointed at Kris. "You're one of them," she muttered.

Kris nodded back in the direction of the gunfire. "And right now, you're one of *them*. But you don't have to be." She took a tiny step forward. "You don't *want* to be."

The gun lowered ever so slightly.

Kris put a hand to her chest, her fingers trembling. "My name is Kristen. I'm not going to hurt you. We don't want to hurt anyone. Please."

"Walker," a voice called out not too far away. "Any eyes on them?"

The agent's head twitched with panic. Kris could see she was considering her options.

"Please."

After a brief standoff that felt like hours, the woman lowered her gun and stepped away. "All clear this way," she called to her team. "It's a dead end."

Kris released a heavy breath in relief, but remained cautious. She kept her eyes glued on the agent, who slowly backed away down another crevice and out of sight.

Once alone again, Kris clapped a hand against the rocks, hunching forward in a series of pants. She couldn't believe that had worked.

Focus. Get yourself together. You have to get us out of here before more agents show up.

A hand touched Kris's shoulder. She gasped and launched herself away, then whirled around.

"Hey, hey, it's me," Kurt said, hands raised.

Behind him, Cade and Brie were helping Larsen forward.

"Come on, let's go."

Kris let Kurt take her by the arm and pull her swiftly toward the hole in the ceiling.

"Tight fit," he said. He looked at Kris, making a cradle with his hands and grounding his stance.

Her mind was reeling, but she stepped into his hand for the boost. The water on the roots drenched her face as she clutched the dirt overhead to pull herself through the gap. She dragged herself out, mud and rocks coating her front until she finally managed to push herself to her hands and knees.

"Fresh air," Kris gasped, breathing hard.

She was sore all over, but she turned around to help Brie and then Larsen through the hole.

Her vision went dark for a moment after pulling Larsen out of the cave and into the forest. Kris felt herself collapse backwards, but she managed to catch herself before hitting her head. Through the blur, she could see Kurt heave her up again. Her feet were moving, carrying her downhill.

"We have to get away from here," Kurt was saying. His voice sounded so far away despite coming from right beside her. "We're surrounded."

"I think I'm good now," Larsen mumbled. "I can teleport."

All the pain in Kris's body and skull suddenly got much, much worse. Kurt wrapped an arm around her to keep her from falling as a howl of wind encircled them. Things became quiet and the distant echo of gunshots disappeared. All Kris could hear was the familiar sound of brushing grass waving in the breeze.

She could hardly open her eyes or walk, and instead she allowed Kurt to guide her forward to the cabin.

"That sucked," she said quietly.

"Not our finest hour."

Kris couldn't even make it inside, dropping to the front steps. Everything was still fuzzy, but she watched Cade help Larsen to the porch. Brie held the mirror out to Kurt, who set it aside and lowered himself to the step beside Kris.

No one said anything.

Chapter 35

A Night Off

Kris awoke on the couch in the living room, unsure how she had even gotten there. She sat up slowly with a grumble, then stretched her arms.

"You passed out," Kurt said, rounding the couch to enter the room. He held out a glass of water to her. "You all right?"

Kris scanned the room around her, dazed. Larsen was leaning all the way back in the recliner, a damp washcloth folded on his forehead. Cade and Brie were nowhere in sight.

Out the window, it was growing dark, the last few streaks of orange on the horizon.

"What time is it?" Kris muttered, twisting to plant her feet on the ground. She grabbed the glass from Kurt and took a long drink of water.

"Almost eight." He lowered himself to the couch and sat beside her. "You were out cold."

She rubbed her eyes. The pain in her back, arms, and head had finally lifted, but her mind was still spinning.

Kurt brushed his fingers down her forearm before gently taking her hand. He offered her a quiet smile. "I saw what you did," he whispered. "How you handled that agent."

The memory made Kris's heart sink. "I thought she was going to shoot me."

He shook his head and grinned. "No, you didn't."

Kris looked at him, confused.

"You knew exactly what you were doing," he said, squeezing her hand. "You *knew* she wasn't going to pull that trigger."

The sound of Cade's motorcycle grew louder as it approached. Larsen must have heard it too because he grumbled and slowly swiped the washcloth from his head.

"Hey," Kris said to him as his eyes opened just a sliver. "How are you feeling?"

"Like a failure." Larsen rubbed his eyes with one hand before pinching the bridge of his nose. "I could have prevented everything if I had just teleported faster—"

"It's not your fault," Kurt said, rotating to look at him. "I should have turned us around as soon as we passed those joggers. I knew something was wrong."

Kris leaned back into the couch and peered out the screen door. In the growing darkness, she could hardly see Cade stepping off his motorcycle. She turned back to them. "No ifs, ands, or buts. It's behind us, and we lived."

"Barely," Larsen muttered. The recliner creaked loudly as he leaned forward. His eyes settled on Kurt's and Kris's hands, their fingers still intertwined. He forcefully kicked the leg on the chair shut and stood up, hands on his hips. "Did you examine the mirror yet?" he asked Kurt.

Kurt shook his head. "I think we need a breather. We pushed ourselves pretty hard today."

Larsen dismissed the comment and strutted into the dining room where the mirror was on the table.

Kris released Kurt's hand and pulled herself to her feet. "Where's Brie?"

"She's doing something outside," Kurt said, standing as well. "I'm not sure. She and Cade seem to be up to something."

Kris crossed the living room to the window and peered outside. Brie was crouched in the grass far out in the field with her back turned. Cade was approaching her with plastic bags in hand. Brie stood and playfully swatted Cade's arm. Even in the dark, Kris could see the smile on her face.

"You should eat something," Kurt told her.

She followed behind him and peered over Larsen's shoulder at the mirror. The glass was perfectly clean, as though unaffected by its years embedded in the walls of the cave. The handle of the mirror was curved, embellished with silver vines, leaves, and small fragments of rose quartz. Between the designs was a series of letters.

Larsen was already scribbling them down in his notebook when Cade and Brie came in through the front door.

"Oh, Kris, thank God you're all right," Brie cried, launching forward to give Kris a bear hug. "You gave me such a scare."

Kris chuckled. "I'm fine, I promise."

Brie stepped back with a big smile and wiped a tear from her eye. "I'm glad."

"And that's why we've earned a night off," Cade announced, pointing to Larsen. "Put down that pencil and follow us."

Larsen shot him a glare and motioned to the mirror. "I'm in the middle of something—"

Cade stepped closer, grabbed the back of Larsen's chair, and pulled it away from the table. "And you can *finish* working on it later. Come on."

Larsen jumped to his feet and whirled on Cade, but Brie cut in. "We all had a rough day, and we deserve a break," she insisted, pushing open the screen door and gesturing for everyone to follow her outside. "So, whether you like it or not, we are *all* taking the night off, and we're going to have a little fun for a change. Now *let's go.*"

Kris approached her friend and gave her a skeptical look. "Okay . . . I'm trusting you."

Larsen shot Cade one final glare, but rolled his eyes and followed everyone outside.

Crickets and birds filled the evening air with a natural summer soundtrack. A sense of peace came with it.

Out in the middle of the field, a campfire burned. It was surrounded by blankets laid out in the grass. Brie plopped down on one of them, patting it insistently until Kris sat down beside her. Kurt and Larsen lowered themselves onto the second blanket, and Cade opened a red cooler.

Kris's heart dropped when he lifted out a beer and held it out toward her. She shook her head, her mouth suddenly remembering the burn of the tequila all those weeks ago. "No thanks."

Cade looked to Kurt, who also shook his head. "I don't think so . . ."

"I'll have one," Larsen said.

Cade recoiled in surprise, a curious smile twisting his face. "Really?"

"*Really?*" Kurt also said.

Larsen held out his hand. "I could have died today."

Cade beamed. "Well, all right." He tossed the can of beer underhanded to Larsen. "Kurt, you sure you don't want to join us?"

Kurt eyed Larsen as he snapped open his can and took a sip. After a moment of hesitation, he looked back to Cade. "Fine. *One.*"

"Hell yeah, man." Cade retrieved a second beer from the cooler and threw it to Kurt.

Kris watched in absolute fascination as Kurt opened his beer and took a tiny drink. His lips curled in disgust, but he said nothing.

"Never thought I'd see the day," Cade said as he dug through the ice. He pulled out another beer and set it aside for himself. "Lastly, for my wonderful cohost, as requested: something pink and sparkling."

He pulled a bottle of pink wine from the cooler and held it out to Brie, who twisted the cap off with a pop and took a swig. She grinned and offered it to Kris, who again shook her head.

"All right, Kris, since I figured you—and those two—weren't going to participate." Cade laughed and passed a can of lemon-lime soda to Kris. He then closed the cooler once more and sat down on top of it.

Brie looked around at the group. "Okay, we're going to play Never Have I Ever. Pretty self-explanatory game, but for those unfamiliar: When it's your turn, you say something that you have never done, and if someone else has done that thing then they drink."

"Right," Cade said, panning his eyes from one person to the next. "For example, I could say, 'Never have I ever . . . been on an airplane,' and if *you* have been on a plane, you would now drink."

"I don't know that I like where this is going, but okay," Kurt said with a coy smile, and he shifted around uncomfortably.

"I'll go first!" Brie said, raising her hand high into the air. She rocked back and forth and drummed her fingers on the glass bottle in a moment of contemplation before shooting Kris a sly grin. "Never have I ever been suspended from school."

"Really?" Kris scrunched up her face and took a sip of soda.

Kurt laughed. "You got suspended? For what?"

She rolled her eyes and forced a smile. "There was this girl on my volleyball team a couple years back. She was being really nasty to a girl on an opposing team, even made her cry, so I may have sort of . . . pushed her a little."

"She slapped her super hard across the face," Brie said, chuckling. "It was awesome."

Cade leaned forward. "You got suspended for a girl fight during a volleyball game?"

"It was brutal," Brie hissed to him, holding the back of her hand to her lips as though telling a secret, but loud enough for all to hear.

Kris shrugged. "I didn't handle it well. And I got suspended, and kicked off the team, *and* I had to attend anger management sessions."

"Well, those 'sessions' didn't help," Cade said.

"Excuse me, but why didn't *you* drink." Larsen pointed to Cade with a smirk. "What about that incident with Tom Branner in second grade?"

"Oh yeah," Kurt said, also looking to him.

"*Because* I was not suspended for smashing his stupid diorama." Cade sat up tall with a cocky grin. "I only got detention."

"All right, then," Larsen said. "Never have I ever received detention."

Kris and Kurt laughed as Cade fired a glare Larsen's way. "Oh, that's how you want to play this?" he muttered before taking a long drink of beer.

Kris was still giggling when she lifted her soda to her lips and took a sip herself. From her peripheral, she could see Brie take a swig of sparkling wine directly from the bottle as well.

"Two can play at that game. Never have I ever attended college," Cade said.

"Fair enough," Larsen said smugly into the can.

Brie nudged Kris in the arm. "You go."

She scratched her head, staring at the flickering flames as she thought. "Never have I ever . . . cheated on someone?"

"You sound so uncertain," Cade said before taking a gulp of beer.

Kris gasped when Brie took a sip of wine. "Brie!"

Brie shrugged as she lowered the bottle again.

"You cheated on someone? Who?" Kris asked.

She waved her hand casually. "Just a stupid fling at that stupid Bible camp my parents made me go to last summer."

Cade nodded towards Kurt. "Your turn."

Kurt lifted his beer into the air. "Never have I ever been drunk."

"A classic," Cade said as he, Brie, and Kris each took a drink.

Larsen stared down at his beer before taking a drink himself.

"What?" Kurt turned his whole body. "When?"

Larsen shrugged, his eyes fixed on his beer. "I was dragged to a house party in high school. It's . . . not a story worth sharing."

Brie stole another gulp of wine and cleared her throat. "Okay . . . umm . . . never have I ever had glasses."

Kurt and Larsen both erupted in a fit of laughter. Kris looked at them, confused, but the huge smile on Kurt's face was contagious. She couldn't keep the corners of her lips from curling.

"It's not funny," Cade grumbled, taking a long drink.

Kris pointed at him. "You have glasses?"

"*Had* glasses," he insisted, pouting as Kurt and Larsen continued howling with amusement.

Kurt wiped a tear from his eye. "He showed up to school one day with the most ridiculous glasses you've ever seen, and this kid in class just teased him *relentlessly.*"

"He punched the kid, and we never saw those glasses again," Larsen said, chuckling.

"Seriously?" Kris scoffed. "You need glasses?"

Cade set his beer down in the grass to retrieve a cigarette from the pack in his pocket. "I can see just fine without them."

Kris crossed her arms and squinted at him. "You care so much about maintaining this bad-boy image that you've been denying yourself proper sight for years?"

"I don't need them," he insisted again, clicking his lighter and holding the flame against the tip of the cigarette.

Brie shot him a big flirtatious smile. "I think you would look sexy with glasses."

Cade returned a small genuine smile, which quickly disappeared when Kurt and Larsen once again burst into laughter.

"He did *not*," Larsen said, slapping his knee.

"Oh, whatever."

"Okay, whose turn is it?" Kris cut in, trying to take the pressure off.

They went several more rounds. The campfire crackled as they played, keeping their little circle warm and illuminated.

Larsen finished his second beer, Brie's bottle of wine was nearly gone, and Cade was now sitting in the grass among his multiple crushed, empty cans. Kurt had inched to the edge of his blanket so that he was seated beside Kris. He had finished his first and only beer, but it was clear he was a bit inebriated.

"Never have I ever ridden on a motorcycle," Kurt said.

Cade laughed and slammed the last of his beer. "I'm starting to feel a little ganged up on." He squashed the empty can in his hands and chucked it over his shoulder.

Brie tipped her head back with the bottle and spilled down her shirt.

Kris took the wine from her. "I think I need to cut you off."

"Fine, but then *you* have to finish it," Brie said, trying to swat at the nearly empty bottle.

There were only a couple sips left, and Brie sat waiting for Kris to drink it. Kris put the bottle to her lips and poured the wine into her mouth. It was surprisingly sweet and fruity. Like juice . . . if juice burned.

Once Brie looked away with a smug, victorious grin, Kris turned over her shoulder and discreetly spit the mouthful of wine into the grass.

"There. Gone," Kris declared, wiping her lip and putting the empty bottle aside. She looked to Cade as he started digging in the cooler again. "You have a soda or a water for her?"

"I am *sometimes* responsible," he slurred. He retrieved a bottle of water and clumsily held it out to Brie, who fumbled and dropped it. Cade pointed to Larsen. "Another beer?"

He blinked hard and laughed. "Nah, nah, I should stop."

"Maybe we call it on Never Have I Ever before someone pukes," Kurt suggested, slipping an arm around Kris as she shivered.

"That's a brilliant idea," Brie exclaimed so loudly that Kris flinched and Larsen chuckled relentlessly. She drunkenly waved a finger around in the air and scanned the faces staring at her before pointing to Cade. "Cade, truth or dare?"

He sat back in the grass with a smirk. "Dare."

Brie's face glowed bright pink. "I dare you to kiss me."

"Brie," Kris hissed.

Cade crawled through the grass towards Brie, who shut her eyes and puckered up. To Kris's surprise, he gave Brie a peck on the cheek.

"Oh," Brie said.

That was . . . uncharacteristic . . .

Brie looked disappointed for only a moment, but then bit down on her bottom lip and brushed her fingers over her cheek with a huge grin.

"All right, so my turn." Cade's eyes set on Larsen. "Larsen, truth or dare?"

Larsen let out a deep breath and cocked his head in contemplation. "Truth."

Cade squinted, a serious expression suddenly taking over his face. He took a long sip before he spoke. "Have you ever kissed a girl?"

He stared wide-eyed at Cade, but dropped his head when Kurt turned to him. He fiddled his fingers around in his lap. "What . . . what makes you think—?"

"Just answer the question," Cade said.

Kris felt her heart sink deep into her chest as Larsen's face warped with pain. He hunched forward as though he were trying to hide inside himself.

"Cade," she warned softly with a stern shake of her head.

Larsen gave a long sigh. "It's fine," he said quietly. He didn't look up when he spoke. "No. I've never kissed a girl."

Cade leaned forward. "But have you ever kissed *anyone*?"

"You only get one question," Kurt said, stealing a quick glance at Larsen as he twisted away.

Cade raised his hands in surrender, and his grin dissolved briefly as he studied Larsen's face and posture.

"Okay, Larsen, so now you go," Brie blurted.

He rubbed the nape of his neck and peeked at Kurt. "Truth or dare?"

Kurt leaned back, pushing his hair from his face. "Truth?"

"Ooh, ooh, I've got a good one for Kurt," Brie said. She raised her hand and looked to Larsen for approval.

"Oh God, this isn't going to be good," Kris muttered as she picked up her soda can from the grass and took a sip.

Larsen held out a hand toward Brie. "Go ahead."

"Is Kris a good kisser?" Brie asked with a wicked smile on her face.

Kris's face burned beet red. "Brie!" She smacked Brie across the shoulder with the back of her hand.

Kurt blushed and let out a small chuckle. "You know what, I think I'll take 'dare.'"

"Oh good," Larsen said with a smirk. "I dare you to play us a song on your guitar."

"What? No." Kurt shook his head. "No, I can't."

Cade leaned forward. "Nah, that's a good dare. You gotta do it."

Kris gave Kurt a big smile. "Come on, play for us."

Kurt shook his head again.

"Please," Brie said, clasping her hands against her chest.

"You don't want to hear me play."

Larsen disappeared from the spot where he sat and reappeared a moment later with Kurt's guitar in his hands.

"Come on, we hear you practicing every night," Larsen insisted, forcing the guitar into Kurt's hands.

Kurt looked to Kris, and she offered him a reassuring smile. "Okay . . ." He adjusted the acoustic guitar in his lap and rested his fingers on the frets. He glanced at Kris from the corner of his eye. "Please don't laugh."

Kurt stared down at the strings as he started to play a soothing rhythm. The melody made Kris's heart soar.

"A villain's mask, a liar's crown. An empty shell sleeps on the ground. Cocooned outside the gates of hell," Kurt sang softly while he plucked at the metal strings.

Each word punched Kris in the chest, and she became completely lost in the song. The field, the fire, even the others, all faded away. All she saw was Kurt's lips moving ever so slightly as he sang out the most intoxicating lyrics she had ever heard.

"Wake from my slumber and set out in quest. Reaching for virtue and forget the rest. Abandon the hurt, the shattered and broken. Finally sing all the words I left unspoken. Be patient until then. When we can bring me back again."

Kris's eyes welled with tears as Kurt gradually grew more confident. By the time he reached the final chorus, he was belting out the words, a gentle tremble in his voice.

His eyes flicked up briefly to meet Kris's gaze. Her chest burned as he sang.

"Waters rise and the tides wash at my feet. Drowning in dread but I do not retreat. Pinch my nose and jump in. Maybe you can bring me back again."

Kris pressed her fingers against her lips. Her hands were shaking as Kurt strummed his thumb across the strings one last time, letting it ring out. He kept his head down.

"Christ," Larsen breathed, waking Kris from her own little world. "Kurt, that was . . ."

"That was amazing," Brie gushed. She held her hands to her heart.

Cade laughed in disbelief. "Dude, you *wrote* that?"

"That was so beautiful," Kris whispered.

Kurt rested his hands on top of the guitar. He still refused to look up, but Kris could see how red his face was.

"Damn, I guess I have to learn guitar," Cade snickered, and everyone laughed.

Kris looked around the group at all the smiling faces. She met Kurt's eye and they beamed at each other.

A weird, little family.

Chapter 36

Don't Wait Up

Kris stopped in the hallway, out of sight, at the sound of voices in the kitchen. The smell of coffee instantly filled her nose.

"I'm sorry about last night," Cade was saying in an oddly sincere tone. "I shouldn't have called you out in front of everyone like that."

"No, you shouldn't have," Larsen said. The sink faucet turned off and was followed by a sigh.

"You were never going to admit it on your own."

"Oh, don't pretend you were trying to help me." Larsen's voice was hushed and rough. "You asked for *you*. Your own selfish curiosity. You just *had* to know."

"You're right. But I still don't think you should hide it."

"Well, it's a good thing it's none of your business."

Kris finally took her weight off the wall and stepped forward, peering into the kitchen. Larsen was drying a bowl while leaning back against the kitchen sink. Cade was twisting an orange around in his hands.

They both turned away from each other when she came in.

"I guess I did bag on you a *lot* about your glasses, so whatever," Larsen muttered.

Cade fake-laughed. "Yeah. Yeah, the glasses jokes *never* get old."

Larsen poured himself a mug of coffee and took a sip from the steaming cup.

"Where's Brie?" Cade asked, peeking down the hall. "She said she wanted to start training today."

"Training?" Kris crossed her arms. "To use magic?"

"Yeah, she didn't tell you?"

Kris frowned and glanced quickly down the hallway, then back at him again. "No. I didn't think she wanted anything to do with it . . ." She let her voice trail off and cleared her throat. "Well, at the moment, Brie is hungover and demanding bacon."

Larsen looked around the kitchen. "We don't have any."

"I'm on it," Cade said, instantly throwing the orange in the fruit bowl on the counter and digging his motorcycle keys out of his pocket.

Larsen scoffed as he watched him hurry to the front door. "I don't know what kind of spell your friend has him under, but it's creepy."

"It's weird, right?"

"Terribly unsettling."

Kris followed him as he rounded the wall to the dining room. The hand mirror was still on the table alongside his notebook from the night before.

"Are you okay?" she asked, leaning over the back of the chair beside him.

Larsen laughed softly to himself as he traced his finger around the rim of his coffee mug. "I'm fine."

She lowered herself into the chair and touched his shoulder. "Hey, just know that I love you. No matter what. And if you ever want to talk about it, I'm here."

~

"What's a Caesar cipher?" Kurt asked, lowering himself onto the couch closest to Larsen.

Kris stood over Larsen and braided her hair as he created a grid of letters in his notebook.

"A Caesar cipher is essentially a way to encode text by shifting the letters of the alphabet by a fixed amount," Larsen explained, scribbling a line of text on the page. "What I need to figure out is how much that shift is."

Kris twisted the strands of hair around each other and watched Larsen scrawl out another line. He shook his head in disappointment.

"At least this code is shorter than the one on the shield," she said.

Larsen half laughed. "Yes, this is true."

Brie's giggling from outside distracted Kris from whatever Larsen said next.

Tying off the end of her braid with the band around her wrist, Kris tiptoed over to the front door. Cade and Brie were both sitting at the top of the steps shoulder to shoulder. And Kris could see Cade's lighter hovering in the air just in front of them.

"You were actually a cheerleader? Schools still have those?" Cade laughed.

He nudged Brie's arm, and the lighter teetered but remained in the air.

"I *was*, and I was good too," Brie bragged, raising her hand to telekinetically lift the lighter higher. "Like, I could have led the team to State. But when my parents saw the routine, and the uniforms . . ."

"Strict parents?"

Brie groaned and threw her head back. The lighter dropped to the steps below. "You don't even know."

Their eyes met, and the softest smile enveloped Cade's face.

Both heads turned to the screen door as Kris stepped out onto the porch.

Cade sprang to his feet. "Hey. How's it going in there?"

Kris looked at Brie with a smirk. "Can I borrow Cade for just a minute, Brie?"

"Sure." Brie flashed Cade a grin as she slowly stood. She tucked her hands into her back pockets and went inside.

Once the door closed, Kris looked back to him. "What are you doing?"

Cade motioned inside with his whole arm. "We were just train—"

"Oh, come on, I'm not stupid," Kris blurted, then lowered her voice. She took a couple steps forward, a scowl on her face. "You've been hitting on Brie for weeks. Are you trying to groom her like one of your dimwitted conquests?"

Cade's eyes widened and he recoiled. "No! No, I'm not. I swear."

"You *promised* you weren't going to make a move on her." She crossed her arms. "I love Brie, but she is too naive for her own good. And if you think you can just exploit that and take advantage of—"

"Kris. Kris, stop." He held up a hand and glanced inside before lowering his gaze back to her. "I like her, okay?"

"You like her?"

Cade jammed his hands into his pockets and shifted his weight. "Most people might write off a gorgeous, doe-eyed blonde with legs that go on for miles—"

"You're supposed to be changing my mind."

Cade's eyes danced around as though he were searching for the words. "I don't know . . . She's smart. She's funny. She gets my messed-up humor. She has the biggest heart of anyone I've ever known. You should hear the way she talks about you."

Kris gave him a skeptical expression and cocked her hip. "Why don't I believe you?"

"Because I tend to go out of my way to avoid taking things seriously." Cade pulled a face and turned away.

"So . . . what? You want to date Brie?"

Cade leaned forward with his elbows on the porch railing and smiled to himself. It was odd to not see his usual smirk. "Despite what you might think, your friendship is actually important to me. So if you say no, I'll back off. I swear."

Kris glanced inside to where Brie was chatting with Kurt and Larsen. Her cheeks were bright pink, her eyes glowing. She looked so happy.

Kris stepped up beside him, slapped her hands down on the railing, and let out a long sigh. "Understand this: If you ever, *ever* hurt her . . . I will destroy you."

Cade did his best to hide the big smile that broke out across his face. "I would never hurt her."

~

"You never told me why you decided to take up training,"

Kris grumbled, twisting her pocketknife around in her hands. She was sitting cross-legged on the bed while watching Brie pick through her wardrobe.

"Does it matter? I'm ready to learn." Brie held up a striped pink blouse against her torso and examined herself in the mirror beside the dresser.

"You were so against it before. I'm just curious what made you change your mind. Or *who*." Kris smirked, watching Brie cast the shirt aside and try another.

"What do you mean?" Brie held up a pale blue tank top. "Does this make my eyes pop?"

Kris stood up, tucked the pocketknife into her back pocket, and chuckled. "Not that one." She dug through the unfolded pile of clothes in the dresser drawer. "Be honest, did you only start learning as an excuse to spend more time with Cade?"

Brie shrugged and fidgeted in place. "I mean, that was a bonus, but . . ."

Kris selected a flowy chiffon top from the drawer and held it out to her. "Try this one."

Brie's eyes lit up and she promptly pulled the shirt over her head and twirled around in front of the mirror. Her cheeks glowed bright red. "Good choice."

"You want to borrow my earrings? I have those dangly ones with the stars that you like."

"No, better not. We're taking his motorcycle, so with the

helmet, probably shouldn't wear earrings."

There was a knock on the door and Kris opened it. Cade looked right past her to Brie, his motorcycle helmet clutched under arm.

"You look beautiful," he said.

"Thank you." Brie fluffed her hair as she bounced over to the door. "You clean up nicely yourself."

Kris forced an awkward laugh before slipping past Cade into the hallway.

"I can't believe you're letting Cade take Brie out. On his bike no less," Larsen said, not looking up from his notebook as Kris entered the dining room.

"Am I a bad friend?" she asked, half joking. She leaned back against the table between Larsen and Kurt.

"I think they're sweet together," Kurt said with a shrug. "They bring out the best in each other."

Kris snorted. "I'll remind you that you said that when this ultimately blows up in their faces."

Kurt gave her a crooked smile and sat back in his seat with crossed arms. "Why so cynical?"

"I have plenty of experience watching Brie rush headfirst into relationships that always implode, and Cade doesn't have the best track record either."

"She's not wrong," Larsen said, still keeping his focus on the page in front of him as he continued writing.

Cade escorted Brie down the hall and held out the helmet to her. "We're heading out. Don't wait up."

"Please be safe," Kris said, taking her weight off the table as they passed.

"No drinking and driving," Kurt added.

Cade laughed as he held the door open for Brie. "You two are like an old married couple."

Larsen's head perked up at that comment.

"Bye," Brie said, waving before stepping outside.

Kris crossed her arms and shifted her weight in a long moment of contemplation. "Well, I think I'm going to go take a bath since the two bathroom-hogs will be out for the evening." She turned on her heels and strutted back down the hall again.

~

When Kris opened the bathroom door and shook her long, dark hair free from the bun on top of her head, she found the cabin was strangely quiet. And dim. Except for some orange light coming from the dining room.

"Kurt?"

She sniffed the air and immediately recognized the smell. She was still adjusting her hair as she crept into the dining room.

There were three lit candles and two place settings side by

side at the table. And on the edge of the table were two stacked pizza boxes.

"Filipelli's," Kurt said as he came down the hallway in a button-down shirt and jeans. "A deal's a deal, right?"

"You remembered?" Kris couldn't contain a smile as she nervously fiddled with her hair.

He pulled out a chair and motioned for her to sit. "One pineapple, and one pepperoni for when the pineapple pizza is *inevitably* disgusting," he said, laughing.

She sat down, allowing Kurt to move the chair closer to the table. "Prepare to be pleasantly surprised," she said with a grin before glancing down the hall, confused. "Where's Larsen?"

He sat down beside her. "He went to his apartment for the night. He needed to clear his head. And didn't want to feel like a third wheel." He opened the boxes of pizza, serving each of them a slice of pineapple. After his first bite, he turned to Kris with a straight face. "I don't understand how this works . . . Why does that work?"

She chuckled and took a bite of hers. "Told you."

After they finished eating, Kurt picked up the boxes of leftovers and brought them to the fridge while Kris cleared the dishes. They paused and stared at each other in the kitchen. Neither could stop smiling.

"You should play your guitar for me again," Kris finally said, biting her nail.

"You liked it that much?"

She inched closer and nodded. "Please?"

Kurt brushed his fingers down her arm. "Uh, okay. Sure. I'll go get it."

Kris sat in the living room and waited for him to return. Her entire body trembled, and she had to clasp her hands in her lap to control the shaking.

He returned with his guitar and sat beside her, then cleared his throat. "I've actually been working on something that I think you'll like."

He placed his fingers for the first chord and, after a deep breath, strummed his thumb over the strings. Kris recognized the song after the first few notes.

"Try my best with you tonight. But words never come out right," Kurt sang softly, his eyes fixed on his strings while he played.

She pulled her legs up onto the couch and curled up with a huge smile as she watched him. Each note resonated. Made her heart burn.

Kurt turned his head ever so slightly to look at her during the chorus. "'Cause you are all I need. You're in all that I see. All that I do. Everything is for you."

She knew the words inside and out, but hearing them from Kurt was like the first time she had ever heard the song. Kris bit her lip as he strummed the final chord and turned to her.

"I love that song," she whispered, blinking away the tears. "But you made it a million times better."

Kurt laughed and pushed his brown hair from his eyes. "I don't know about that."

"No, seriously, I *love* Breathing Oceans. But when you sing . . . I don't know. It hits harder, I guess."

Kurt beamed and held the guitar out to her. "You want to try?"

She giggled, waving her hands in front of her. "No, no. You don't want me touching your guitar."

"Come on." He gently forced it into her lap. He leaned in close, taking her left hand and guiding her fingers. "There, now strum."

Kris dragged her thumb over the strings, which made an annoying buzz.

"Press down harder," Kurt instructed, touching her hand to push her fingertips down on the strings.

Her fingers were burning, but when she strummed again, it sounded clear. Beautiful.

"Okay, now put this finger here." Kurt rearranged her hand and had her strum once more. He then showed her another chord. "There," he said with a big smile. "You now know the three basic chords to any pop song."

Kris laughed and turned to face him. His blue-gray eyes were gleaming. Magnetizing. She couldn't keep from planting a firm kiss on his lips.

Kurt took the guitar from her and set it aside. They leaned back into the couch, his arm around her as he hugged her close.

"The day . . . the day before Tynan killed Sofia and Jacob," Kurt said quietly, breaking the silence. His voice cracked when he spoke. "Sofia tried calling me. She had a feeling something was about to happen. But I didn't answer her call . . ."

Kris could hear the weight in each word. The dread. The fear. The pain. Like something he had held on to for far too long and it had begun to eat away at him.

"I was hiding out, wallowing in self-pity," he continued, and she could feel his pulse racing.

Kris craned her neck to look up at him, but his eyes were shut in concentration.

"Nina died," he finally said, another break in his voice. "The NWDA found her, and they killed her."

She said nothing, letting Kurt take his time to get it all off his chest.

"She had called me, asked me to come pick her up in St. Louis, but I didn't. I was too scared to leave. Too scared to get hurt again. I didn't know what had happened until weeks later when I saw it on the news."

Kris stared across the room at the TV as the realization suddenly formed in her head. *Nina was Shay's sister.*

Kurt took several deep breaths. She could feel his posture

relax.

"Had I picked up Sofia's call, maybe I could have saved them . . ."

Kris gave his hand a squeeze. She couldn't get Shay off her mind. She had never told Kurt about any of it. About him coming to the cabin. About him kidnapping her and trying to persuade her to leave. About him taking her to Tynan's home.

She opened her mouth to speak, when she heard footsteps stomping up the stairs on the porch. She had been so absorbed in her thoughts, in Kurt's confession, that she hadn't even heard Cade's motorcycle pull up outside.

A moment later the screen door swung open and Brie charged inside. Her mascara was smeared under her eyes, and she had an angry scowl on her lips.

"Oh no, what did Cade do?" Kris asked as she jumped up from the couch.

Brie's eyes locked onto her, and she pointed a shaking finger. "You kissed Cade?"

Chapter 37

Stay

Kris stood up from the couch, her brow crooked in confusion. She almost laughed, but did her best to contain herself given Brie's anger.

"What are you talking about?" Kris managed to get out.

Cade came rushing inside and tossed his helmet onto the couch. "Don't blame Kris, okay? It was completely my fault."

"What?" Kris held her arms out, looking between them. "I have *never* and *would* never kiss Cade."

"See," Cade told Brie as he held a hand toward Kris. "I told you she doesn't even remember it. She was blackout drunk."

"Oh my God," Brie shouted, clasping both palms over her eyes and charging down the hall toward the bedroom.

Kris hurried after her. "Wait, Brie." She pushed Cade from her path.

Brie was flopped over on her bed, bawling into her pillow.

"Brie, I have no interest in Cade," Kris started as she slowly approached. "If I did kiss him, I have absolutely no recollection—"

She sat up abruptly and wiped tears from her face, which smeared her makeup even more. "God, why do you always get *everything?*"

"What?" Kris took a tiny step away.

"Everyone always likes you better. Guys always like you better." Brie sobbed, snatching up her pillow and hugging it tight.

Kris laughed. "Are you kidding? I was invisible. *You* were the one everyone was always talking about—"

"Oh please. *All* the guys liked you. You were just too obsessed with Ian to ever notice."

"That's ridicul—"

"You always had everything, Kris. Even now. Even as a Witcan, you still have everything."

A knot formed in Kris's throat, and she couldn't keep the thought from bursting forth. "My parents are dead, Brie!"

"I lost them too, Kris." Brie whimpered for a moment, and Kris waited as she struggled to get through her sentence. "Your parents were my family. My parents reported me to the NWDA not even an hour after I finally confided in them and told them I was a Witcan."

Kris stepped away. Her eyes were welling with tears.

"Do you know what it's like to be screaming and crying for your parents to save you?" Brie wept, burying her face into the pillow again. "Begging them for help and they can't even look at you? I asked Cade to train me because I was terrified of losing you."

Kris inched forward and reached out to take her hands. "You could never lose me." She knelt on the floor in front of Brie.

Brie's sobs were deep and painful. "I thought you were going to die. Back at the cave. And I was powerless to save you."

Kris gave her arm a squeeze and offered a small, forced smile.

"And it still always comes back to you," Brie mumbled, twisting away and flopping onto the bed to face the wall. "Because everything is always about you."

"Brie."

"Just go."

Kris stood, uncertain for a long moment. Her heart was thudding in her chest. Her eyes were burning, and her throat felt tight. Finally, she backed away to the hall.

Kurt slowly approached. "Are you okay?"

"You all knew, didn't you?" Kris said, chuckling through her tears. She shook her head and clutched her arms around herself.

Kurt stuffed his hands in his pockets and looked away with a small nod.

"I'm sorry, Kris," Cade blurted, shifting around in the hallway. "I had to be honest with her. I didn't know she would take it this hard."

Kris pressed her fingers over her eyes and backed up until she was against the wall. Her head was still reeling. She felt dizzy. Brie's muffled cries made her stomach turn.

I can't believe I kissed Cade. I can't believe everyone but me knew about it. And now it's hurt Brie. God, she looked so broken. And it's my fault.

"I'm going to be sick."

Cade was saying something, but she couldn't hear him anymore through the pounding of her head.

Kris let Kurt guide her into his room and sit her on the edge of his bed. His voice was calm and soothing, but it didn't make her feel any better. She looked up at him with a heavy breath.

"I ruin everything," she mumbled in a broken voice.

Kurt sat down beside her and squeezed her hand. "She's just upset. Give her some space."

Kris swiped a fist under her nose and sniffled. "You should have told me."

"You're right. I'm sorry." He brushed a tear from her cheek.

Kurt rubbed her back and allowed her to cry, and they sat there in silence for a while.

"You should get some rest," he finally whispered to her, then started to stand. "You'll feel better in the morning."

"Wait."

She grabbed his arm with both hands, hardly able to see him through her blurred vision. "Stay. Please?"

Through the haze, she could see him nod slowly. "Okay."

Kris buried her face in his chest as he sat back down, and she wrapped her arms around his waist. He smelled like citrus. Kurt embraced her and rested his chin on top of her head.

Kris's eyelids were getting heavy, and she found herself sinking down into the bed. He remained seated, running his hand over her hair.

When she was barely still conscious, he brushed the bangs from her face and kissed her cheek. "Good night, Kris."

Chapter 38

The Mirror

Down the hall, Kris could hear Cade knocking on the bedroom door again. It was the fifth time that morning.

"Brie, please let me in." The doorknob jiggled with another attempt to get inside the locked bedroom.

"He's not very good at reading a room, is he?" Larsen said as he wrote out another line of text in his notebook.

Kurt rubbed his eyes in exhaustion. "He's just stubborn."

Kris didn't look up as they spoke. She instead kept her head down, her forehead cradled in the palm of her hand and her elbow rested on the tabletop. "He's just stupid," she muttered, shutting her eyes.

"He did the right thing, telling her," Kurt replied, seated beside her at the dining room table.

"He could have done it better."

All Kris could hear was Larsen's pencil scribbling across the paper. The loud scratching echoed in her mind and rang through every corner of her skull. She just wanted it to stop.

Footsteps approached, pausing a few feet away.

"Kris, can I talk to you?" Cade asked.

She kept her eyes closed, relieved when the pencil noises stopped. "You're talking now, aren't you?" she said.

"Privately?"

Kris groaned and rolled her head to scowl up at Cade, who stood at the entrance of the dining room. He looked disheveled. His long blond hair was a tangled mess, and he had bags under his eyes.

"Please?"

She dragged herself from the chair. "Fine."

She followed him into his bedroom, and he closed the door behind her. Kris found it hard to meet his eyes as she leaned back against the dresser and crossed her arms over her chest.

"I'm sorry I didn't tell you about that night, all right," he said, pushing his back against the wall by the door. "You were drunk and vulnerable. You made a move on me, and I should have stopped you."

Kris wrinkled her nose. "Ugh, can we just . . . can we not talk about it anymore? I don't want to think about that night. Any of it."

Cade fiddled with his lighter. "Is she going to forgive me?"

She shrugged, looking down at her bare feet.

"How do I get her to forgive me?" His raspy voice seemed extra rough.

"I don't think it's very appropriate for me to get involved. You know, seeing as how I *am* involved . . ."

Cade took his weight off the wall and stepped closer. He squeezed his lighter in his hands. "Kris, please? I want to make it right."

Ugh, he sounds like Ian.

She rubbed her eyes for several seconds before finally looking up. The broken expression on his face was telling enough, and it made her heart sink deep into her chest.

"Brie tends to forgive too easily. Just let her get there on her own." Kris turned to the door, but paused with her hand on the knob. "And maybe some pink lilies when she starts to calm down. They're her favorite."

She reentered the dining room but didn't sit. Instead, she leaned on the back of her chair, staring at Larsen's notes.

"Everything all right?" Kurt asked.

Kris gently shook her head with a small shrug and jutted her chin toward Larsen. "You got something?"

"Sessilia's declaration," Larsen read off as he put down his pencil. He looked between Kurt and Kris.

Kurt leaned over to read it off the page himself. "What does that mean? Who's Sessilia?"

"That sounds familiar." Kris dropped her head, squinting to herself.

Larsen reached over to his laptop and flipped open the lid.

"Sessilia's declaration?" Cade repeated as he wandered over and stared over Larsen's shoulder.

Kris looked up to the ceiling, still racking her brain. "Sessilia. I know I've heard that name before. Where did I hear that name?"

"Because I told you about it last year."

All four jumped at Brie's voice and whirled around to her as she charged past them and snatched the mirror key from the dining room table. Her hair was in a messy bun and makeup was smeared down her face. She looked like she hadn't gotten a single ounce of sleep.

Brie held up the mirror in front of her, studied her reflection, and cleared her throat. "My truest beauty lies fathoms below. In my blood and in my soul," she said, her blue eyes filling with tears.

The glass of the mirror glowed white. The four huddled in close to see what was happening.

The light faded into an image of a wide river that cut through a thick forest and forked in different directions. Between the fork was a tall tree with yellow-and-orange flowers. At the base of the tree, the dirt began to fall away. It crumbled down into the earth as a small hole formed, exposing a white light below the soil. The light burned bright and illuminated the mirror once more before dissolving back into Brie's reflection.

Brie took a deep breath and blinked with a look of surprise, then shook her head. She set the mirror back down on the table, keeping her eyes cast down.

"'The Tale of Sessilia' is an ancient Roman short story," Brie explained quietly. "It's about a woman who is left broken because of love, and has to learn to love herself and see her own beauty."

She looked up and shot Cade a glare. No one said anything, but instead they all watched her in stunned silence as she stomped away back to the bedroom.

Kris hurried after her before she could lock the door again. She closed the door behind her. "Brie, I'm so sorr—"

"Please don't apologize, Kris. I'm the one who's sorry," Brie said with a sigh. She sat down on the edge of her bed, twiddling her fingers. "I shouldn't have taken any of it out on you. I know you didn't do anything wrong."

Kris crossed the room and sank down into the mattress beside her. "I feel so embarrassed . . ."

"How do you think I feel?" Brie whispered, a crack in her usually chipper voice. "I fell for that jackass. You tried to warn me about him, and I didn't listen. And then I, like, took it all out on you. God, I thought he was different."

"He's not a jackass, Brie. He's a mess, but he . . . he cares about you."

Brie snorted, brushing her fingertips underneath both eyes to wipe away the droplets that had formed.

Kris released a heavy breath and shifted around on the bed. "He didn't have to tell you the truth. He could have lied. He could have hidden it. But he wanted to be honest with you."

"Yeah. Yeah, I know. I just . . . like, I can't get the image out of my head."

Kris shuddered.

"I'm so sorry I snapped at you, Kris." Brie turned towards her, clutching both hands against her chest. "Can you forgive me?"

Kris smiled sadly; her lips pursed as she fought the tears in her eyes. "Of course I forgive you, Brie-bear," she replied, her voice breaking. "You're my best friend. You're my sister."

Brie wrapped her arms around Kris and buried her face in her shoulder, her tears dampening the sleeve of Kris's shirt.

"And for the record, *I* was always jealous of *you*," Kris said, laughing through her sobs.

"You're such a sap."

Kris hugged her. The ringing in her head was finally beginning to lift.

The moon was barely visible through the cloudy night sky. The air, humid but still chilly, sent goose bumps up and down Kris's skin. She and Kurt stood together on the front porch. They stared out into the darkness and listened to the crickets sing their summer song.

"So, Larsen says the key is in Tennessee?"

Kurt nodded. "He identified the type of tree and the location of the river."

"He didn't want to go tonight? Get it over with?" Kris turned toward him.

"We figured it was better to hold off until tomorrow. Let the dust sort of settle, so to speak."

"How do you feel? Being one step closer to Calosant, I mean?"

He leaned forward with his elbows on the railing. "Honestly? A little nervous. You?"

"Same," she said, nodding. She copied Kurt's posture. "Feels like something ominous is lurking just around the corner."

Kurt gave her hand a squeeze. "Everything is going to be all right. We're going to get the next key tomorrow. And then find the last key, and before you know it, we will be in Calosant. We'll destroy the Mina Ring and, with it, all temptation for Tynan—or anyone—to use its power for evil."

"It still won't stop him from killing."

"I know. We will just have to find another way to stop him once we ensure he can't use the ring."

The house was silent. Larsen had already gone to bed, Brie was still in her room, and Cade had left a few hours earlier without a word. The house was in shadows except for the yellow light that spilled out of the kitchen into the dining room.

Peace and quiet. Just me and Kurt again.

Kris lifted her eyes to look up at him and opened her mouth to speak. She immediately shut it again with a sigh as Cade's motorcycle sped into the meadow. The headlight washed over them as he skidded to a halt a few feet away and clumsily jerked down the kickstand with his foot.

"He's been drinking," Kurt said, releasing Kris's hand and letting his arm drop to his side.

While fumbling to remove his helmet, Cade tried to step over his bike. His foot caught the seat and he flopped into the grass.

"Jesus."

Kris and Kurt both hurried down the steps to where Cade remained on his back, still struggling to pull off his helmet.

"Goddammit, Cade," Kris grumbled as she gripped either side of the blue helmet with both hands to slide it off.

His eyes were only half open, and he forced a goofy smile. "Hey, guys . . ."

"Come on, get up." Kurt grabbed one arm and tried to pull him up, but Cade made no effort to move.

"Half-off whiskey tonight at that crappy bar, the Red Eye?" Cade slurred, waving a hand around in the air. "It was a good deal. I feel so much better."

Kris put his helmet on the motorcycle's handlebars and waved the smell of liquor from her face. She grabbed Cade's other arm, and with her and Kurt's combined effort, they managed to pull him to his feet. He stumbled around in the tall grass and flashed them each a grin. "Iloveyouguysyou'rethebest," he mumbled as though it were one long, incoherent word.

"Jesus Christ. How much did you drink?" Kris exclaimed, still holding his arm to keep him from falling.

Kurt turned Cade's head to force eye contact. "Be honest with me. Did you take something tonight?"

Cade scrunched up his face and shook his head. But after a moment, it changed to a nod and a look of disappointment.

Kurt let out a drawn-out sigh through his nose, then dropped his eyes to the ground.

"I'm sorry. I fucked up," Cade muttered as they guided him up the stairs.

"It's okay," Kurt said. "You're going to be fine. Come on." Kris could tell that he did his best to mask his distress, but she could feel the hurt in each word. "I'll go put him to bed," he told her quietly as she pulled open the screen door. "You shouldn't have to see him like this."

Kris said nothing, simply nodding as she watched the two of them go inside. Kurt fought to keep Cade on a steady course as he staggered with his heavy feet. There was a physical pain in Kris's chest while she watched Cade struggle to keep himself upright.

"Well, you and Kye have gotten quite chummy lately, haven't you?"

Kris's voice caught in her throat as she spun around to the swing.

Shay rocked back and forth, a smirk on his face. "Glad to see you listened to me."

"You shouldn't be here," Kris hissed. She fired a glance inside, but Kurt and Cade were already out of sight.

"Neither should you. That guy is going to get you killed. I need you to see that."

"And *I* need you to leave."

A look of surprise crossed Shay's face before he turned his head away with a smug smile. He chuckled and looked back at Kris. "You haven't told him anything, have you? He has no idea you and I are talking."

"I wouldn't say we *are* talking. If anything, I would say we *have* spoken."

"And yet you're keeping that fact hidden. Why?" He took a step closer, cocking his head.

Kris stole another glance inside, but Kurt was still in the bedroom. "That—that's none of your business."

"You haven't told him anything because, deep down, you know I'm right," Shay said, arms crossed. "You know he has a dark side. You've seen glimpses of it, haven't you?"

She glared up at him and clenched her fists at her side. "Kurt is a good man. He's made mistakes, but he has a good heart through and through. Which is more than I can say for you."

He chuckled, leaning back with an arrogant expression. "Me?"

"At least Kurt stood up for what was right and left Tynan's stupid little cult." Kris jabbed a finger into his chest. "Last I checked, you're still groveling before your master. Still serving in his name. So who's really the bad guy here?"

Shay held up both hands in defeat and backed away into the shadows of the porch. "You can tell yourself that crap all you want."

Kris heard the familiar creak of the floorboards in the dining room. She spun around to the screen door just as Kurt stepped outside. Looking back, she saw that Shay had disappeared, and she did her best to disguise the look of panic on her face.

"What's wrong?" Kurt asked.

Kris glanced over her shoulder to the spot where Shay had been standing. She grabbed a strand of hair and twisted it around. "I just . . ."

Now isn't the time. Kurt has enough on his mind.

She straightened her posture. "Is Cade going to be okay?"

He sighed, then stepped forward to plant his palms on the porch railing and dropped his head. "He's going to be fine."

Kris continued to fiddle with her hair as she stepped up beside him. "You're not going to kick him out . . . are you?"

"He had a setback. I'm just going to have to help him through it again."

She put a hand on Kurt's back. They locked eyes before embracing each other. With her ear to his chest, Kris could hear his pulse. It was pumping hard, thudding loudly against his ribs.

"You have a good heart, Kurt," she whispered to him, stealing one last glance to the corner where she had last seen Shay. She opened her mouth to speak, but promptly shut it again. Instead, she closed her eyes, lost in Kurt's heartbeat and the lemony smell of his cologne.

Chapter 39

Down The Rabbit Hole

"Are you sure it's a good idea, leaving Cade behind?" Kris asked as she tied her sneakers.

"Trust me, the aftereffects are going to kick in soon, and you will see a little piece of evil," Larsen grumbled, swiping a hand over his face. "You're not going to want to be around that."

Kurt was silent while he laced up his shoes, but the pained look in his eyes said everything.

He had another sleepless night.

Kris stood up and lightly brushed a hand over his shoulder. He looked up at her with a forced smile.

Brie, still in her pajamas, wandered down the hall towards them. "You won't be gone long, right? I don't know what to do if he starts freaking out."

"He'll be fine. Just leave him to sleep," Kurt said.

Larsen slung his backpack over his shoulder. "We shouldn't be gone too long."

Kris gave Brie's arm a pat. "Be safe."

"You too."

"Ready?" Kris said to the other two.

Larsen straightened. Kurt put a hand on one shoulder and Kris the other.

"Be back in a flash," she told Brie with a wink.

She nearly didn't feel the effects of teleporting, besides the quiet ringing in her head and the sudden shift to warmer, humid air.

The sound of roaring water was all around when they arrived. Kris dropped her arm to her side, turning her attention from the rushing river in front of her to admire the yellow-orange flowers in the nearby tree.

"This is the spot," Larsen said. His eyes panned around to study the woods.

Kris smirked. "This might be the easiest one yet." She turned over her shoulder to look at Kurt.

But Kurt's expression was one of disappointment. "I don't think this will be as easy as you expect."

Larsen and Kris followed Kurt's line of sight to a mound of dirt near the base of the tree. Just beyond the mound was a hole several feet wide and about three feet deep. They crept up to it slowly and quietly, then peered in.

Kris cocked her head, eyebrows furrowed. "It's a . . . book?"

Larsen lowered himself to the ground, extended his arm down into the pit, and lifted out the paperback novel from the soil. He turned it over in his hand to view the cover: *Fahrenheit 451.*

"Is it another clue?" Kris asked hesitantly, looking up to Larsen, whose face had gone pale.

He squeezed the book in both hands, then abruptly jumped to his feet. Larsen kicked at the dirt.

"Whoa, whoa, hey." Kurt took a couple of cautious steps towards Larsen, who kept his back turned. "What is it?"

"It's goddamn Alex," Larsen shouted over the rush of the river. He threw the book to the ground and scanned the woods around them.

"Alex, your-old-friend-who-is-currently-working-for-Tynan Alex?" Kris felt her heart stop for a brief moment. Her blood ran cold.

Kurt spun back to the hole in the dirt, searching for any clues. "How would he have found this place? How could he have known where the key was without the mirror?"

"I don't know. I don't know," Larsen growled as he paced back and forth on the riverbed.

Kris turned her attention to Kurt. "Do you think . . . Do you think Tynan already has it?"

"Alex didn't give it to Tynan," Larsen said. He snatched the book out of the dirt again. "He's using it to mess with me."

Kurt frowned. "How do you know th—?"

"Because he left *this* here," Larsen violently shook the book around in the air. "He wants me to know he was here. He wants me to know that he took it."

Kris stepped closer to him, reaching out both hands to try to calm him. "Hey, it's okay," she said with a reassuring smile and nod. "We're going to find him. We're going to get it back."

Larsen planted his hands on his hips and shook his head. "No . . . No, this is something I have to do on my own."

~

Kurt set down a glass of water in front of Kris and slipped into the chair beside her. "I've never seen Larsen like that before." His eyes moved across the table, taking in the shield, the dagger, and the mirror.

"He's pretty worked up," Kris said, taking a sip of water.

He noticed the tremble in her hands and reached out to lightly touch her wrist. "Everything is going to be fine."

She pressed her lips together and bobbed her head in a subtle nod. But when she turned to face him, he could see the doubt in her green eyes. "What if Larsen is wrong?" She set the glass down on the table and traced her fingers over the condensation. "What if Alex gives the key to Tynan? What if he already has?"

Kurt brushed his fingertips across the surface of the shield in quiet contemplation. He'd been wondering the same thing. "Larsen is hunting Alex down as we speak. I'm sure we will know soon enough."

He could hear Cade grumbling from the bedroom down the hall. He hadn't left the bed all day. It left a pain in Kurt's chest and a tightness in his throat.

"Do you really think we're going to find anything new here?" Kris said, picking up the dagger and twisting it around in her hand to examine all sides.

Kurt shrugged. He slid the shield closer and turned it around on the surface of the table. "Difficult to say . . . but right now, it's all we've got."

~

Larsen took a deep breath as he strolled through the grass of the darkened park. He looked back over his shoulder at the school behind him. At this hour of the night, it was quiet. No movement.

He turned his attention back to the tree in front of him, his eyes fixed on the initials carved in the bark: *A + L*.

Larsen traced the engraving, his jaw clenched tight. "You led me here. So where are you?" he muttered to himself, drumming his finger on the tree trunk. He flipped through the copy of

Fahrenheit 451 and stopped at a page where the same initials had been doodled in the margins with black ink. With a long, sad sigh, he turned to scan the park again. "Where the hell are you?"

The park was silent, and Alex was nowhere in sight.

"Of course you're not here," Larsen said, leaning back against the tree in defeat. "This is all just a wild goose chase."

He slammed his fist behind him against the bark, and something dropped from the branches above him to the ground. Larsen jolted, then clasped his chest with a breath of relief when he saw it was just another book.

He picked it up and turned it over a few times. *Romeo and Juliet.*

A green sticky note poked out of the top of the book, and it opened to a highlighted phrase.

"'These violent delights have violent ends,'" Larsen read aloud.

He stacked both books in his hands and looked up into the branches. *Alex is leading me down the rabbit hole, and he knows I have to follow.*

Larsen removed his backpack and slid both books inside. He made sure the coast was clear while zipping his bag shut again.

I'm going to find you, asshole.

And he disappeared.

Chapter 40

Addiction

"Did Annona create Calosant?" Kris asked, turning away from the vegetables in front of her to look back at Kurt.

"The Elders created Calosant long before Annona existed," Kurt said as he seasoned the pork loin on the countertop. "It used to be on the surface, but humans kept attacking us, and us them. So the Elders hid Calosant away under the earth, below the surface."

Kris set the knife aside and leaned back against the kitchen counter to listen.

"And then one day, Annona just . . . appeared. The Elders presented her to Calosant. This enchanting goddess, sworn to protect them. Able to sense and stop humans from reaching the city. Able to heal anyone if the humans should ever attack." Kurt sighed, staring down at the pendant around his neck. "They must have felt so lost when Annona disappeared . . ."

"Can you be any more irritating with that crap?" Cade's rough, agitated voice came from the bedroom and stopped Kurt in his thought.

"You shouldn't even be here," Larsen retorted. "Kurt should have kicked your sorry ass out after you decided to jump right back off that wagon again."

Kris and Kurt exchanged looks, and he quickly washed his hands in the kitchen sink.

"Not again," Kurt mumbled as he turned off the faucet.

"If you have such a problem with it, then why don't you just leave?" Cade shouted.

"And leave Kurt to deal with your soul-sucking behavior on his own? We can't all be as selfish as you."

Kris and Kurt rushed to the bedroom. Cade and Larsen were both standing in the middle of the room, chests puffed up and shooting glares at each other.

"Oh, *please*," Cade said. "You've been selfishly enabling Kurt to keep hiding from his problems all these years because you don't have the balls to face *your* own issues."

Cade thrust his hands into Larsen's chest. Larsen stumbled back but maintained his balance. He tried to charge back at Cade, but Kurt quickly inserted himself.

Kurt grabbed Larsen by the shoulders and moved him back. "Hey, hey, cool it."

Kris inched into the room, clutching her arm as she looked between the two.

"Maybe you cause enough problems for all of us, Cade. You ever consider that?" Larsen shouted, trying to push past Kurt.

"Larsen, stop," Kurt insisted.

"Keep talking and you will have yourself a problem." Cade closed the gap between them.

Kurt slammed one hand against Cade's chest and forced him back. "Cade, step off."

Cade scoffed and shook his head. His blue eyes flashed, but he raised his hands in surrender and turned away. "Whatever."

Kris jumped back, her spine against the doorframe, as Cade marched past her to the front door. Kurt jutted his chin toward him, suggesting she follow.

She found Cade slumped forward over the railing, his hands trembling as he clicked and clicked his lighter. When it couldn't hold a flame long enough to light the cigarette in his lips, he hurled it out into the night with a grunt. Kris approached slowly as he removed the unlit cigarette from his mouth and held it in his hand.

"You, uh . . . You're coming down hard these past couple days," Kris said, minding her distance.

Cade rubbed his eyes and leaned forward on the railing again. "Four hundred days, Kris," he mumbled. "Almost four hundred days battling this addiction, and I cracked . . . destroyed everything I worked so hard for."

She took a few hesitant steps closer. "Not everything. You still have us."

He scoffed, casting his eyes out across the black meadow. "I betrayed his trust again. There's no coming back from that. Not really." Cade put the cigarette in his lips again and held out his hand. After a failed flicker, she realized he was trying to create a fireball.

Kris sighed. "Here." She unfurled her palm as the heat from her fingertips formed a small orb of fire. She held it out to Cade, who touched the cigarette to the flames long enough for the tip to glow red.

His hands were still trembling as he took a long drag. "Thanks."

Kris waved her hand, and the fireball vanished from existence.

"Do you believe in karma?" he whispered, releasing a cloud of smoke.

She leaned against the banister, leaving some distance between them, and faced forward. "Sometimes."

"Well, all the bad I've put out in the world the past several years is coming back around to me again."

"You made a mistake. Your life isn't over."

"Brie won't talk to me. She won't even look at me." Pinching the cigarette between his fingers, Cade motioned towards Kris. "You're disappointed in me, too. I can tell." He took another long drag. "I don't know . . . Maybe it's time to just accept the fact that I *am* a piece of walking, talking garbage. It was inevitable."

"You're not garbage." Kris finally turned herself completely to face him. "This is just the withdrawal talking. It's messing with your brain chemistry."

Cade chuckled. "I wish I could believe that." He peeked over at her for just a second before looking away again. "Thank you, though . . . for trying."

She looked over her shoulder to her closed bedroom door and sighed. *He really needs to talk to Brie. It would make him feel so much better.*

She touched his arm, keeping her eyes cast down. "You're going to be okay, Cade. We're here for you."

She walked back inside and entered her bedroom. Brie was lying on her stomach across her bed, using her forearms to hold open a hardcover book as she read. She didn't look up when Kris came in.

"Brie, I'm really sorry to play this card, but I need you to talk to Cade."

"Why would I do that?" she replied in an uncharacteristically flat tone. After a moment's pause, as though finishing a paragraph, she looked up.

Kris twisted her hair through her fingers as she crossed the room. "Because he's coming down hard, and no one can get through to him like you can."

Brie shook her head and turned back to her book. "He's having withdrawals because of his own stupid decision to do drugs. It's not my responsibility to talk him down—hey!"

Kris pulled Brie's book away, tucking her thumb in the crease to not lose the page. She held it away as Brie reached out to grab it back.

"You made me talk to Ian when I wanted absolutely nothing to do with him," Kris reminded her, pointing a finger. "You forced me to have to face him after he hurt me, and to talk it out because you said both he *and* I were hurting."

Brie twisted around and sat up on the edge of the bed.

"Well, Brie, I know *you* are still hurting." Kris motioned with her free hand towards the door. "But Cade is hurting worse."

Brie pressed her lips together and turned her head away. "Okay, fine. I'll talk to him," she said, holding her hand out for her book. "Just let me finish my chapter first."

~

Kurt squeezed Larsen's shoulders to try to move him away from his desk. "You're starting to scare me."

He swatted Kurt's hands away. "I need to find Alex before he does something stupid, like give the key to Tynan, or destroy it, or use it to find Calosant himself." He shoulder-checked Kurt as he charged past to his laptop.

"This isn't about the key, or Calosant. This is about Alex. You've become obsessed."

The words hit hard. Larsen's chest felt tight, but he kept his jaw clenched, pulled out his desk chair, and sat down. He flipped open the paperback copy of *Romeo and Juliet* to the flagged page and ran his finger along the lines as he read. After a few lines, he started typing some numbers into his laptop's internet search engine.

"Larsen, please listen to me. You're poisoning yourself."

I have to do this, Larsen kept telling himself, ignoring Kurt's desperate pleas as he continued to work.

Finally, Kurt gave up and left the room.

I can't let Alex best me.

Larsen rubbed his eyes and stared at the highlighted line in the book. After a moment, he sat up taller, noting the numbers on the left side of the page. Each corresponded to the line of text.

Could the line number be an address? But what was the street?

He tapped the character's name. *Lawrence.*

His heart raced as he turned back to his laptop and typed in "1440 Lawrence." He scrolled through the options listed and stopped, recognizing his hometown.

Larsen clicked the address and pulled up the street view. He pushed back his chair, stared at the location on the screen, and grinned. *Got you.*

~

Kris didn't even have to ask when Kurt returned to the kitchen. He kept his eyes down, his posture hunched forward. He leaned over the sink with a deep breath.

"Any luck with Cade?" he asked.

She shrugged and continued chopping the carrots. "I got Brie to agree to talk to him, so that's . . . something?"

Kurt hesitantly turned back to the stove and adjusted the temperature of the oven.

She put the knife aside once she finished cutting the vegetables, then pressed a hand against her forehead. "How did we get here?"

Behind her, Kurt was still quietly futzing around with the oven settings. Quiet.

Kris chuckled under her breath and rested her back against the counter. "I thought . . . I don't know . . . I thought we were a family. But it feels like that's starting to fall apart."

"Families fight too."

"I know."

Kurt glanced over his shoulder. "Done with the vegetables?"

"Yeah." She carried the cutting board over to push the carrots and potatoes around the roast in the baking dish. She sank back helplessly, watching Kurt cover it all with foil and place it into the oven. "What's going to happen to us when this is all over?" she finally asked, fidgeting with her hair.

He closed the oven door, keeping his back to her. "What do you mean?"

Kris bowed her head. She could feel her pulse racing all the way down to her fingertips. "After Calosant . . . what happens next? With us?"

She could see the strain in Kurt's shoulders. He was aching to speak, but remained silent.

She forced a small smile as she inched around him to meet his eye. He seemed to instantly relax. "Wherever I go, whatever I end up doing . . . I want you with me."

Kurt lowered his head again with a subtle grin. "Is that really what you want? This awkward recluse weighing you down?"

"I know I'm young," Kris said, nudging his shoulder. "And I know we've only known each other a few months, but . . . it feels like there's something here. Something real. Right?"

He reached out and touched her hand, then leaned his forehead against hers. "My heart is yours for the taking."

Kris snickered. "You should put that in a song."

"Maybe I already have," Kurt said with a smirk. He turned away, setting the timer on the stove. "It should be ready in about an hour. Can you turn the oven off when it's done?"

She deflated as Kurt picked up his keys from the bowl on the counter. "Where are you going?"

He brushed a thumb over her cheek and gave her a tender peck on the lips. "I need a new capo for my guitar."

There was a brief look in Kurt's eye as he turned to the door that made the hair on Kris's arms stand on end. She couldn't identify it, but as he laced up his sneakers, she could sense something was wrong.

"I won't be long," he said, giving her a reassuring smile. "Keep an eye on Cade."

Kris pressed her lips together and nodded, but said nothing.

~

Kurt turned off the engine but remained seated in his car for several minutes, his eyes fixed on the small house across the street. Light came from behind closed curtains, but he could sense there was no one actually inside. Finally, he stepped out into the night and crossed the road.

He kept his hands in his pockets as he wandered around the side of the red brick house to the flower garden in the backyard. Small lanterns illuminated the stone path that cut through the roses to where an older man sat on a bench with his back to Kurt.

He had long gray hair that hung off his shoulders, and he didn't move as Kurt approached.

"It's been a long time, Kye," the man muttered in his rough, raspy voice. Every word felt like a strain.

"I don't go by that name anymore," Kurt replied quietly, stopping a few feet away.

He gave a harsh laugh. "Maybe not, but you will always be Kye to me."

Kurt nodded and looked down at the white roses beside him. "It's good to see you, Fox."

The man rotated; each movement was stilted as though his joints were rusted with age. He gave a large, wrinkled smile. "I could report you to Tynan, you know."

Kurt smirked and sat beside him on the bench. "We both know you won't."

Fox chuckled, which led to him coughing into a handkerchief. He stared dead ahead, clearing his throat loudly.

"How have you been?" Kurt's leg bounced nervously as he peered at Fox from the corner of his eye.

"The NWDA roughed me up pretty good," Fox rasped, using the handkerchief to dab sweat from his forehead. "Unfortunately, that wasn't enough to get away from Tynan, so here I still am. A slave in my own home." He stared up at the night sky. "I should have never shared with him my vision all those years ago. I created this monster. And now it will destroy me."

Kurt remained silent, admiring the flowers of the garden around them.

Fox eyed him curiously. "I hear you're hunting for Calosant. Always thought you were running from that destiny."

"I was . . ."

Fox grinned. "Have you come to learn your fortune again, young Kye?"

"I'm not here for me," Kurt whispered.

Fox's irises disappeared as his eyes glowed solid white. He turned his face up towards the sky once again. "Then tell me what it is you seek . . ."

Chapter 41

Violent Ends

Larsen had been standing outside staring at the yellow house for what felt like hours. It was dark inside. No movement in the windows, or in the street. The neighboring houses were far away, also quiet at this hour.

Finally, he took a few steps forward.

Alex is in there. I know he is.

Hands glowing a pale purple, Larsen thrust his heel into the front door with such force that it swung open and slammed against the wall behind it. He stormed into the house, swiftly shutting the door behind him again.

"Alex," he bellowed into the darkness.

A light clicked on just beside him, and Larsen jumped. He raised his glowing fists to the lamp on his right, but the living room was empty.

"It took you long enough to find me."

Larsen whirled as Alex stepped out from behind the wall to his left. His arms were crossed, and he had a smug grin on his face.

"Did you like my clues?"

Larsen kept himself grounded and waited for a surprise attack as he took a small step forward. "Where's the key?"

Alex raised his hands and motioned for him to relax. "Nothing to say about *Fahrenheit 451* or *Romeo and Juliet?*" he asked, stepping back into the dining room. "Did you even notice that those are the actual copies you had back in high school? Do you have any idea how long it took me to track those down?"

"Where's the key?" Larsen asked again through clenched teeth, hesitantly moving closer. Even he could see that his hands were shaking.

Alex motioned to the table behind him, where a small gold box rested. Engravings of leaves and aquamarine gems embellished it, with a keyhole in the front.

Larsen lowered his guard as he approached it, eyeing the decorated box the whole time.

"Beautiful, isn't it?" Alex said, reminding Larsen of his presence.

Larsen raised his fists again and sized up his opponent, who stood casually to the side.

"I couldn't get it open, but I figured that would be no problem for that big brain of yours."

"How did you find it without access to the previous keys?"

Alex moved to block Larsen from the table, separating him from the locked box. "Your drunk friend had been spotted at that dive bar a couple weeks back, so I've been there waiting for him to return." He ran his fingers along his temples with a smirk. "A little bit of ketamine lowered his inhibitions enough to take a peek without him realizing."

Larsen's brow twitched. "You drugged Cade?"

Alex laughed, leaning back with his palms against the dining room table. "Oh please. I hardly mentioned that I was carrying, and that addict jumped at the opportunity—"

Larsen jolted forward with his fist, but stopped inches from Alex's face. He didn't even flinch. Larsen grunted and backed away. "Why go through this trouble to drag me out here? What do you want?"

Alex stood up straight, his hands still tucked behind his back. "We can do this ourselves."

"What are you talking about?" Larsen looked down at the box again. He sank away as Alex moved in closer.

"You and me. We can find Calosant on our own. Find the Mina Ring. We would be unstoppable."

Larsen scoffed before realizing the expression on Alex's face was serious. "What about Tynan—?"

"Fuck Tynan," Alex said, waving his hand to the side. "Forget him, and forget those so-called friends of yours. We don't need any of them."

It was a moment before Larsen even realized he had completely dropped his guard, his hands now at his sides. His heart was pounding in his chest.

Alex crept forward again, his eyes shifting ever so slightly as he studied Larsen's face. "Your brains, my brawn. An unbeatable team."

"I . . . I can't do that. I don't want to hurt anyone." Larsen's lips quivered when he spoke.

Alex reached out and squeezed his shoulder, giving him a gentle shake. "You don't have to. I'll take care of the dirty work. You can keep your hands clean."

Larsen carefully removed Alex's hand and shook his head. "I'm never going down that rabbit hole with you. Ever again."

"The universe brought us together," Alex said, holding his hands behind his back. "Time and time again."

"The answer is no, Alex." Larsen's voice was firm, and he nodded towards the box on the table. "I'm here for the key, and nothing more."

Alex's expression darkened. His jaw clenched and his brow furrowed. "If you know what's good for you, you will reconsider."

Larsen sneered and stepped around to get to the box.

Alex lunged at him, jabbing him in the side of the neck with a syringe he produced from behind his back.

Startled, Larsen grabbed the needle and pulled it from his skin, then tried to wrestle it away from Alex. The two slammed against the wall, struggling with the syringe. Larsen's arms felt weak, and he immediately recognized the fatigue he had felt back in the quartz cave when the NWDA had shot him with their sedative.

I'm not going out like this.

With a grunt, Larsen twisted the needle around and forced it into Alex's shoulder, then pushed down the plunger to inject the last of the serum.

Alex cried out. He ripped the needle away and threw it to the side. "At least it's a fair fight now," he muttered, glaring at Larsen.

Larsen's mind was clouded. He felt dizzy, and he braced himself against the wall with a few deep breaths as he tried to focus. "I'm not going to fight you, Alex."

Alex stabilized himself against the back of a dusty dining room chair, panting hard. The wicked look in his eye was fixed on Larsen and nothing else. "Then only one of us will be leaving this place alive."

The punches came at Larsen so fast that he hardly had time to deflect them. He raised his arms, frantically blocking Alex's fists and backing away.

"You don't have to do this," he pleaded as he grabbed Alex's wrists to hold them away.

Alex grunted and smashed his skull forward into Larsen's nose. Blood spewed from Larsen's nostrils as he stumbled back and clutched his face.

"Quit stalling and hit me," Alex shouted, rushing him again.

Too weak to teleport, Larsen wasn't able to escape the blow to his cheek. He crashed into the wall, then shuffled away with a hand clasped beneath his nose. His head was ringing, and hot streams of blood continued to pour down his face.

"I'm not going to fight you," Larsen said again, leaning away from a right hook and ducking into the living room.

"You're a coward!"

Alex's eyes flashed as he grabbed the front of Larsen's T-shirt and swung him around, throwing him to the floor. The back of Larsen's head thudded against the carpet, which immobilized him for a few seconds. He desperately tried to scurry away as Alex approached and delivered several kicks to his gut.

"Get up," Alex shouted with each kick.

Larsen coughed, rolled onto his side, and clutched his stomach.

"Pathetic."

Alex was on top of him, pushing him onto his back. He clasped both hands around Larsen's throat and slowly constricted his grip.

Tears spilled from Larsen's eyes as he gasped for breath. He slapped Alex's arm, begging to be released, but the hands around his throat only got tighter. Through his misty vision, he could see the pain that clouded Alex's eyes. His face was twisted and twitching as he fought to contain his cries.

Larsen lowered his arms so his hands rested on top of Alex's, and he softly nodded. "Just do it," he managed to get out.

He could feel the tremble in Alex's arms. Feel the crack in the anger. He lightened his grip for a second—only a second—before squeezing down harder again. "I'm sorry."

Larsen's vision was fading in and out as he wheezed for air. *I never imagined it would end like this.* His eyes fluttered shut.

The hands suddenly let go and Larsen choked for oxygen, rolling to his side as he searched the blurry room.

Someone was struggling to overpower Alex. It took several seconds of the two smashing into the adjacent wall for Larsen to recognize that it was Cade.

Cade managed to get one of Alex's arms pinned, but Alex threw him back with a sharp punch to the jaw. Larsen's heart sank when Alex shot him a feral glare and rushed at him, but Cade tackled him with a grunt.

Alex's skull collided with the corner of the coffee table. His body immediately went limp.

Cade gasped, scrambled to his feet, and backed away as a red pool filled the carpet around Alex's head.

Larsen panted as he crawled across the floor over to Alex. "No. No. Alex . . . Alex?" He didn't even realize he was crying until his voice cracked.

He rolled Alex onto his back. A huge gash split his forehead and his hairline, and his face was coated in blood. He slowly focused on Larsen as his chest heaved with labored breaths.

"Violent ends," he murmured. His eyes fluttered shut with his last few pants.

Larsen squeezed Alex's hand and pushed his forehead into Alex's chest. His pulse was getting weaker. "I forgive you."

And then his heartbeat stopped.

The house was quiet except for Larsen's broken sobs, but finally Cade rested a hand on his shoulder.

"We should get out of here," Cade said in a gruff, shaking voice.

"It should have been me," Larsen whispered, sitting up. He stared down at the blood on his hands.

"Come on."

Trembling, Larsen let Cade pull him to his feet.

"Is this it?" Cade asked, moving into the dining room and picking up the box from the table.

Larsen nodded.

"Good. Let's go."

Cade guided him to the front door and out to his motorcycle.

With head lowered, Larsen tried to steady his breathing. "I can't believe he's gone."

Cade slipped the box into one of the saddlebags, retrieved the helmet from the handlebars, and held it out. "Best not to dwell on it. Let's just get out of here."

Larsen took the helmet but didn't put it on, instead teetering weakly from side to side. "It should have been me."

Cade cleared his throat, but when he spoke, his tone was still harsh. "I know how hard it is when your feelings aren't reciprocated. When someone doesn't love you like you love them—"

"Don't pretend to know what I've been through."

"Not personally, but I *know* . . ."

Larsen peeked up. Cade's blue eyes were strained, shoulders hunched forward, as he fought to hold himself together. When Larsen met his eye, he nodded.

Larsen laughed sadly to himself. "I'm not naive, okay? I know things never would have worked out with him."

Cade clapped a hand on his shoulder and gave it a comforting squeeze. He gestured to his bike. "Come on," he whispered.

Larsen managed to pull on the helmet. His arms felt heavy, weighed down by the sedative, and he was barely able to step over the bike.

"You're going to be fine," Cade said as he started his motorcycle. "Just hang on."

Chapter 42

Omen

Kris and Brie both stood as Larsen came into the house, a small gold box clutched in his blood-covered hands. His head was down, and his feet dragged heavily across the hardwood floor.

Kris took a step towards him. "Larsen?"

Despite the warm feeling she felt in her bones that immediately told her the box he carried was in fact the newest key to Calosant, she was far more concerned with the broken, vacant expression in Larsen's eyes and the dried blood smeared across his face. She watched him pass, trudge down the hall to his bedroom, and close the door behind him.

She and Brie looked outside to Cade. He stood in the grass at the foot of the steps, his face hidden by his long hair.

Kris could only stare as Brie went outside to him. She couldn't hear what was said, but in an instant, Cade's head collapsed into Brie's shoulder, his muscles heaving with each strenuous sob.

Brie wrapped her arms around him, doing her best to comfort him, and Kris couldn't even call upon her feet to move from the place she stood rooted. Her chest burned, ripping at the seams, as she watched Cade fall apart.

~

Hours had passed. Everyone else had gone to bed, but Kris waited on the couch in the dark until she saw the headlights of Kurt's car pan across the ceiling of the living room.

She rose to her feet as he came in, her heart thudding in her chest and roaring in her ears. The looks on Cade's and Larsen's faces when they had come home were still fresh in her mind.

Kurt jumped when he found her awake. He offered her a smile, which quickly vanished. "What's wrong?"

Kris approached, immediately noticing that he was empty-handed, but she ignored it. "Larsen and Cade retrieved the fourth key tonight . . ."

Kurt pushed the front door shut behind him and locked it, then eyed her curiously. "That's good news . . . isn't it?"

She swallowed hard. "They had to kill Alex for it."

"Oh." He leaned back against the door and gazed past Kris, down the hall to the closed bedroom doors. "Is Larsen . . . ?"

"He's a wreck. So is Cade."

"Jesus."

Kris bit down hard on her bottom lip with a deep breath

before lifting her eyes. "There's something else. Something I've been meaning to tell you for weeks."

He stood up straight and waited.

Thank God it's dark in here so I won't have to see Kurt's face . . .

Kris released a sigh. "Weeks ago, when I disappeared in the middle of the night . . . when I told you I was sleepwalking? I lied."

Kurt cleared his throat and shifted his weight.

"One of Tynan's men found me and took me out into the woods," she said under her breath. She squeezed her arm as goose bumps covered her skin. "He tried to convince me to leave. That you were dangerous, and that he was trying to save me."

Kurt lowered his head and took a long pause before speaking. "That's why you went digging through my room?"

She nodded slowly. "I was afraid that he'd be right . . ."

He scoffed and shook his head. "I guess he was, wasn't he?"

Her lips pinched together. "There was a time in your life when it may have been true, but not anymore."

Things were still. Seconds felt like hours before Kurt finally spoke again. "Has he been back here?"

Kris nodded. "A couple times."

Another long pause. But this time it was broken when Kurt stepped forward, put his arms around her, and hugged her close.

She stood still, confused by his reaction at first, but eventually slipped her arms around his waist.

"Thank you for being honest with me," he whispered, and rested his chin on her head. "I know it couldn't have been easy for you."

She buried her face into his chest, taking in the intoxicating smell of his cologne. "I thought you were going to be angry with me."

"I'm not a hypocrite. I know I haven't been the most open person either." He kissed her forehead. "I'm just glad he didn't hurt you."

Kris breathed a sigh of relief. *No matter what Shay says, I'm not going anywhere. I belong right here. With Kurt and my weird, broken little family.*

~

Kurt's bedroom door was closed, as it had been for the majority of the past few days with him hiding away inside.

Kris kept telling herself that maybe he was finally getting some sleep. When she put her ear to the door, she could faintly hear his guitar. Thanks to the amateur soundproofing of his bedroom, it was difficult to eavesdrop.

Maybe he's just writing a new song, she convinced herself, returning to the dining room where Larsen sat staring at the fourth key. The box was turned upside down. A series of Vs, Ls, Xs, and Is were engraved between the decorative gold leaves on the bottom.

Larsen sat slouched forward, his cheek resting on his fist. His brown eyes were empty. Emotionless.

Kris used her chin to indicate the empty coffee mug beside him. "More coffee?"

He stirred as though waking up, then gazed around confused before his eyes zeroed in on her. He pushed a smile. The effort looked painful. "No. Thanks, though."

Before taking her seat, she glanced outside. Across the meadow, Cade and Brie walked along the edge of the woods. They were too far away for her to get a read on their facial expressions. *At least they're talking again.*

Larsen pulled up a grid on his laptop. There were numbers along each axis, and letters in the cells between them.

"What's that?" Kris asked, lowering herself into the chair beside him and sliding closer to see the screen. "Is that going to decode our roman numerals?"

"It's a Polybius square cipher," he replied quietly. He started typing in the series of numbers into a text box. "Should have an answer soon."

She leaned back in her seat and eyed Kurt's bedroom door. "How are you holding up?"

Larsen lifted his fingers off the keyboard and sighed. "I see his face every time I close my eyes. Even when I blink . . ."

"Maybe that's why Kurt's such an insomniac," Kris said under her breath, twisting back around to face Larsen. "It's not your fault what happened to him. You were only defending yourself."

Larsen rubbed his eyes and returned to typing. "And yet I still feel soul-crushing guilt."

Kris fidgeted in her seat, glancing back yet again. She longed to ask about Kurt's odd behavior, but given Larsen's fragile state regarding his own emotional crisis, she opted to keep her mouth shut.

Larsen struck the Enter key and leaned back in his chair, waiting for the results to load. Once the page refreshed, he and Kris both inched closer to the screen.

Kris tilted her head. "Virgampa? Are you sure you entered all the numbers correctly?"

"Positive," Larsen said flatly, but he held up his notebook to verify the numbers again anyway. He then set it aside with a sigh. "Yeah, it's all correct."

Once he started typing their findings into the search engine, they both had the same "aha" moment.

"Virgam, Pennsylvania." Larsen selected the search result. "It's a small, unincorporated town. Not a lot of ground to cover. We should be able to find the last key pretty quickly." He pushed back his chair and his shoulders hunched forward. He looked at Kris with a sad smile. "I guess we'll go get the last key tonight."

~

For the first time since the incident at Quartz Cave, they all left together. And despite the silence between them, it made Kris feel stronger. United.

Virgam was nestled peacefully where the cool evening fog collected between the tree-studded hills. Far in the distance, Kris could hear cars on the interstate, but the unincorporated town, which consisted of one age-damaged road lined with out-of-business shops and restaurants, was empty. No cars. No people.

The lit streetlamps guided them down the road to a median at the end of the block, where a stone statue stood. Kris cocked her head, studying the statue as they moved closer: a woman in a long dress, hair slicked back in a thin braid down the length of her back. Her hands clasped a silver scepter. The top was twisted up into a point, like a flower bud prepared to bloom.

"Are you okay?"

Kurt's words shook Kris from her daze. She brushed the tear from her cheek.

She forced a laugh and held out her hands flat in front of her. Her fingers were trembling. "That's so strange," she mumbled.

She looked up at the staff again. There was no doubt in her

mind that it was the key. The final piece of their puzzle.

Kris's heart was racing as she stepped up the ledge, staring into the eyes of the statue for a long moment before resting her hands on the staff. The metal felt hot against her skin.

She wasn't startled this time when her vision went white. She found herself teleported through time and space, now looking up at the tall white building on the ancient streets of Calosant once more.

The structure was closer now, closer than it had ever been before. Her eyes panned across the statues that lined the front of the structure. Men and women, holding a shield, a dagger, a mirror, a locked box, and the scepter.

Kris ascended the steps towards the entrance and gaped up at the towering columns. Beyond them, she could see open windows on the upper floors, one of which had a rope dangling down from the windowsill to the silver and gold tiles of the vacant first floor.

What was up there?

Visions rushed by in a flash. Annona, standing from a lounge chair and racing to the window as a dark and shadowy figure climbed in. But she wasn't startled. She was beaming. Her hands clasped around his neck, and she pulled him in for a passionate kiss.

Then the man slipped back out the window again, holding on to Annona's hand as long as he could before disappearing down the rope.

Then the window was sealed shut, latched with metal and locks.

Then Annona sat up tall in the lounge chair. She stared forward, eyes empty. Blank. Just as they had appeared in past visions.

She's lost . . . trapped . . .

Despite seeing Annona and looking directly at her, Kris felt that she and the woman were one. She could feel everything. The fear. The doubt. The loneliness.

Annona's lifeless body, crumpled in the field, flickered before Kris's eyes. A cruel reminder of the fate that awaited her.

Kris took a deep breath in. She was in Virgam again, clutching the staff out in front of her. Kurt was holding her arm and helping her down from the median.

Her mouth hung open, her jaw quivering. Kris whipped her head around to the statue behind her, recognizing it as one of the ones she had seen in her vision, and somehow knew the woman's name. Lady Patina, an Elder of Calosant. A creator of this key . . .

Kris twisted the silver staff around in her hands. It was still warm to the touch.

Larsen was talking, but it was miles away.

She clasped a hand over her chest. *I can still feel Annona.*

Brie pinched Kris's shoulder and gave her a firm shake. "Hey, snap out of it. You're freaking me out!"

"Sorry," Kris muttered, blinking hard. She did her best to focus as they huddled into a small circle in the empty street.

"Well, guys, we did it," Cade said, disbelief resonating in his raspy voice. "We found the final key."

"Part of me never thought it was possible," Larsen admitted as he glanced around them.

Kurt gave Kris's hand a gentle squeeze. "We have all the pieces. Now we just need to put the puzzle together."

~

Kris lay on her back, long blades of grass extending around her up towards the gray above. The weeds rustled as a gust pushed the clouds across the sky. The air suddenly got colder.

"Not so tough now, are you, Goddess?"

What?

Before Kris could sit up, a man stood over her. He grabbed her by the wrist and jerked on her arm. She shrieked in surprise, realizing at that moment that her hands were bound tightly with rope.

She fought against the man, but he squeezed harder, crushing her bones. He clasped a hand around her finger and ripped something away. Kris yelped, the skin on her finger burning.

Was that . . . the Mina Ring?

The man was holding the silver ring in his hand, holding it up to his eye before glaring down at Kris again.

This is my vision. Annona's death.

Kris twisted to her knees and fumbled with her tied wrists. A group of men encircled her, all with wicked scowls.

But I'm Annona now . . .

A sharp, cold pain pierced Kris's side. It throbbed through her entire body, immobilizing her. She collapsed into the grass and curled into a ball. She panted, trying to breathe through the pain.

Another hit.

"Stop, please."

Kris was struck in the head. Her ears rang, and her vision blurred. The ache in her skull dulled the rest of the pain as the men continued to strike her.

"You brought this on yourself."

That voice . . .

Clasping her tied arms to her chest, Kris twisted around in the grass to the man crouched in front of her.

But, no . . .

It was Kurt, a cruel grin on his face. He was holding her father's pocketknife and pointing the blade at her.

"Kurt—"

He didn't let her finish and instead stabbed the knife forward directly into her chest.

With a harsh gasp, Kris shot up in her bed. She pressed her open palm to her chest, but there was no wound. Breathing hard, she leaned forward and rubbed her eyes. The room was dark, and Brie was still fast asleep.

That had felt like a warning.

Kris left the room and knocked gently on Kurt's door, but she opened it and peered inside before getting a response. "Can I come in?"

He hastily ripped his earbuds out and slammed Larsen's laptop shut. "Hey," he said, sliding back his chair from the desk.

She slipped inside and closed his bedroom door again. Hands behind her back, she took a few steps forward.

"You okay?" Kurt asked. He stood up and rubbed her arms.

She eyed the laptop on the desk. "Can I show you something?"

He tilted his head with a curious little smile. "Sure?"

Focusing on the vision she had seen of Annona's death, Kris lightly rested the tips of her fingers against Kurt's temple. She kept her eyes open and watched his face as it dropped.

"That's . . . Annona."

Kris nodded. "I saw that the day we met. When you brought me here."

"You're shaking."

She dropped her head and shrugged, then moved past him to sit on his bed. "I dreamed I was Annona. And I was the one getting killed."

Kurt sat down beside her, and she peeked at him through her hair.

"It felt like an omen," she said. "I think something bad is going to happen when we go to Calosant. I think I might meet the same fate as Annona."

He clenched his jaw and sternly shook his head. Cupping Kris's cheek, he turned her face. "I would never let anything like that happen to you."

Kris blinked away tears and turned her eyes up to the ceiling. "I'm scared," she said under her breath. "The closer we get to Calosant, the more I feel . . . not like myself."

"What do you mean?"

She frowned, struggling to make sense of things. "Like . . . Annona is taking over. Like she's trapped inside me and she's fighting to get out. I don't know how to explain it."

"You don't have to go to Calosant. You don't have to destroy the Mina Ring. It's not too late."

Kris chuckled and looked away. "You know I can't."

"I know," he said, laughing quietly. "It's just one of the things I love most about you: your borderline annoying, unwavering moral code."

Heat rushed to her cheeks. "Annoying?"

Kurt nudged her arm and flashed her a smirk. "*Borderline* annoying."

"What about you and your constant condescension?" she said, punching his shoulder.

"Condescension?"

Kris pushed him. "Yeah, you're condescending. All the time."

Kurt squeezed her sides. She squirmed and threw herself against him. Before she realized it, they were lying on the bed, his arms wrapped around her.

Kris's dream was the furthest thing from her mind as she gazed into his blue-gray eyes. She inched closer and pressed her lips against his.

"Kris, I—"

Her heart skipped a beat. Panicked, she put her finger to his lips, cutting him off. "Don't say it."

"Why not?"

She propped up on her elbows and started twirling her fingers nervously. "I don't want to say it too soon."

Kurt brushed her hair from her face. After a moment, he sat up and snatched his old, portable CD player from the desk. He leaned back again and Kris took the earbud he held out to her.

A crisp electric guitar strummed a slow, soothing rhythm, and when the verse started, Kurt sang along quietly. "Lost in the dark, shadows surround. I call for help, but can't make a sound."

Kris laced her fingers between his and sang the next lines. "The storm blows in, thunder around. But there's a warm light I've found."

As the chorus started in a beautiful harmony, she looked up to the ceiling. "Annona wants me to set her free," she whispered. "I don't know how, but I need to get to Calosant to somehow release her spirit." Kris pressed her eyes shut. "But if I set Annona free, how much of me will be left? How do I know where I end and Annona begins?"

Kurt twisted his head and kissed her shoulder. "Annona may be guiding you, but she isn't you." He was quiet for a long moment before speaking again. "I have a sense of presence—it's what I was trained for—and while I can tell there is something else in your mind, all I feel in your heart is you."

Chapter 43

The Scepter

Every breath that Tynan drew was sharp and cold, his dark eyes narrowed and fixed on the old man who was kneeling before him in his rose garden.

"We freed you from that prison," Tynan hissed, grinding his boots into the rose bushes by his feet. "I extended my hospitality, my resources, to liberate you from that NWDA hell, and this is how you repay me?"

Fox kept his hands clasped in his lap, his head down. He eyed the petals that now littered the soil of the flower bed. "The NWDA might have put me in chains, but it was less a prison than the one you've kept me in."

Red, who stood behind Tynan, took a step forward and began to remove his brown leather gloves, but stopped when Tynan raised a hand.

"I am our savior," Tynan said. "I am the one to deliver our people. To save us from the darkness." He loomed over Fox for a long, heavy moment. "Isn't that what you showed me all those years ago?"

Fox bowed his head and took a deep breath in. "If I had known then what was truly to become, I would have left you none the wiser."

Tynan scoffed. "My loyal disciples had warned me not to trust Kye." He stomped down into another rose bush. He was adamant to crush every flower, every leaf, ensuring that the old man watched it all. "They have also always expressed distrust in you. Perhaps I should have listened."

Fox fought to keep a straight face as he winced with the destruction of each rose. "You will get no repentance from me," he croaked weakly.

Tynan struck him across the face, which threw him to the stone path. Fox cried out with each blow, hit after hit.

Finally, Tynan stood again and wiped blood from his face. He stared down at the old man as he wheezed, clinging to each dying breath.

"It would appear there was more than one weak link in this chain," Tynan muttered to Red without looking back. He stood there and waited, watching the life drain from Fox's eyes.

"Bring Shay to me," he said once the old man was silent. "I think it's time I reevaluate *his* loyalty."

~

"Let me try." Kurt gently took the scepter from Kris's hands and twisted the dials of letters along the bottom.

Kris pressed her palm against her forehead, leaning her head back on the couch. "I'm telling you, it's not in English," she grumbled. "It's just like the French riddle on the shield all over again."

Larsen took a sip of his coffee and watched over the rim of the mug as Kurt fidgeted with the cryptex. "I think Kris is right."

"I don't think it's French." Brie leaned forward with her elbows on the back of the couch, motioning with her hands as she spoke. "I futzed with that thing for, like, an hour this morning. Some similar roots, though."

"Might be Latin," Larsen pointed out. He set his mug down on the coffee table and crouched beside Kurt to examine the cryptex.

Kurt dragged a coaster across the coffee table towards Larsen but said nothing, waiting for him to relocate the placement of the hot mug.

"Nothing like using a dead language for the most important riddle in the world," Cade said, glancing back over his shoulder at Brie.

Kris noticed their eyes lock and the subtle smiles before they turned away again.

"Wait, wait, wait, hang on." Larsen reached out suddenly, pulling the staff closer and adjusting the dials. "Lumine. It *is* Latin."

"And you know Latin?" Kris asked, sitting up straight again.

Larsen scoffed and shook his head. "I'm familiar with some Latin roots in the English language, but other than that, no. Not really. But it's a good thing the internet does." He handed the staff back to Kurt and hurried out of the room.

"It's so weird, right?" Brie said, twiddling her fingers with a dramatic shrug. "That this is almost over?"

Kris cleared her throat and shifted uncomfortably in her seat. She studied the faces around the room, but she could tell their smiles were as forced as her own. Even Kurt, who had once been so giddy about finding Calosant, had a somber air about him as he shuffled back to lean against the couch beside her.

She was hit with a melancholy jab. Without so much as a thought, she found herself running her fingers through Kurt's tangled brown hair in an attempt to soothe the looming feeling in the pit of her stomach.

Larsen set his laptop down on the living room table, took another swig of his coffee, then turned back to Kurt for the staff. "Let me see that."

They were all quiet as they watched Larsen twist the cryptex dials.

Cade craned his neck and looked up at Brie. "Have you given any thought to my offer?"

"What offer?" Kris asked, adjusting her position on the couch.

Brie shrugged, avoiding Kris's stare. "Cade wanted to know if I would consider moving to Indiana," she said quietly. "To mend and build our relationship."

Kris's heart sank. She swallowed the selfish thoughts and tried to maintain a happy expression. "Wow. That's huge."

Brie waved her hands. "I haven't accepted. Just considering it. I mean, I'm only seventeen. It's not like I would be able to, like, rent my own place. Plus, the NWDA and, you know . . ." She shot Kris a fleeting glance.

Kris forced a smile. "Brie, if that's what you want, then I think you should do it."

Cade's face slowly lit up, and he turned around on the couch to face Brie.

Brie blushed and stared down at her fingernails as she continued to wriggle. "Like I said, I'm just considering it. I'm not making any decisions right now—"

"Trabem," Larsen blurted. He lowered the staff and glanced around for his notebook. "Is anyone writing this down?"

"I got it," Kris said, tearing her eyes away from Cade and Brie. She lunged across the couch to snatch up Larsen's notebook and pencil from the far armrest. "Trabem . . . and lumine . . ."

Kurt pulled himself to Larsen's laptop and typed both words into the translator. "*Trabem* means 'beam,' and *lumine* means 'light.'"

Larsen's eyes lit up for the first time in weeks. "I got it."

He turned over his shoulder towards Kris and read out the letters. As he did so, Kurt typed them into the computer.

"Beam of light illuminate jeweled shield," Kurt read.

One by one, they all stood, turning their attention to the other keys on the dining room table.

"I'll hold the shield. Kris will create the beam," Kurt said.

"What?" She whipped her head to look at him as he charged forward into the dining room.

He picked up the shield and didn't respond to her surprise, instead motioning for everyone to follow him outside.

Kris's chest felt tight. She hurried after him and stopped him in the grass at the base of the porch steps. She traced her fingers over the scar on Kurt's forearm. "I can hold the shield," she offered.

Kurt twisted his head and gave her a crooked smile. "I trust you."

"I don't," she muttered. She turned her back to the porch as the others came outside, then dropped her voice to an intense whisper. "Remember what happened last time?"

He clasped her shoulder and gave it a reassuring squeeze. "Don't worry. You've got this."

She watched Kurt in disbelief and he confidently stepped out farther into the grass with the shield. Though her heart was still racing, she shook out her arms to limber up as she followed Kurt's lead.

Cade, Brie, and Larsen all stood back on the porch. Waiting. Watching.

Kris's palms turned sweaty. She took several deep breaths in, exaggerating her exhales as she stared dead ahead at Kurt. He gave her a firm nod and raised the shield in front of him.

It didn't take much effort to summon the fiery feeling in her heart. It filled her body in seconds, and once Kris's hands began to glow, she thrust her palms forward with a grunt.

The white beam tore across the space between them and struck the face of the shield.

Kris gasped. Was he okay? She couldn't see beyond the beam. Couldn't see if anything was happening or if Kurt was all right. After a moment, she swung her arms out, ripping the force away, and the light dissolved.

Panting, she hurried over to Kurt, who slowly lowered the shield. His eyes were wide with panic as he tried to steady his own breathing.

"Are you okay?" Kris asked. She could hear Larsen, Cade, and Brie approaching behind her.

Kurt grinned with a soft laugh of relief. "Yeah. I'm—I'm good."

"What happened? What did it do?" Cade asked as they stopped beside her.

Kurt motioned to the inside of the shield. "It was instructions to activate the staff. It said a tear can make the flower bloom."

Larsen disappeared from his spot and reappeared with the staff in his hands.

"A tear?" Cade said, turning his attention from the staff to Kurt with a look of skepticism.

Kris gave Brie and Cade a coy smile. "Well, you two are pros at manipulation. Can either of you cry on cue?"

Brie laughed, apprehensively taking the scepter from Larsen. "I mean, I can try." She squeezed her eyes shut in concentration, and Kris couldn't keep from giggling. Brie opened one eye a sliver. "Don't laugh, I'm trying. And don't look at me." She whirled around to face the opposite direction.

"This might take a while," Cade jeered, cracking a smirk. It was good to see him getting back to normal.

"Kristen."

Kris's spine stiffened. The voice behind her made her heart stop.

She saw the fear in Kurt's eyes before she turned and looked over her shoulder.

Shay was clutching his shoulder and limping through the tall grass toward her. There was a slash through his shirt sleeve, tarnished with fresh blood. His brown eyes were wide and focused only on Kris.

His warning was chilling: "Tynan's coming."

Chapter 44

Warning

It happened so fast, Kris didn't even have a chance to stop it.

Kurt rushed at Shay and struck him down with a green fist from several yards away. "You are not welcome here," he shouted.

"Kurt, stop," Kris yelled, hurrying after him.

Shay, still clutching his injured shoulder in the grass, forced a palm in Kurt's direction. The telekinetic push was enough to knock Kurt back, but it didn't keep him down long.

"Stop!"

Kurt grabbed Shay's arms, trying to pin them down, but was hit in the nose with a defensive elbow.

"I came here to warn you," Shay shouted as he struggled to his feet again. He looked past Kurt to Kris. "You need to get away from here. Now."

"You don't make decisions for her," Kurt spat, brushing blood from his nose and squaring up again.

Shay shot him a glare. "And neither do you."

Larsen suddenly appeared beside Shay and took a swing at him, but Shay teleported away and reappeared behind Larsen.

"Haven't you people been involved in enough violence?" Shay grunted, jabbing a palm into Larsen's gut and throwing him down into the dirt.

Kurt moved in front of Kris. "Only because of you and *your* people."

"Stop it!" She yanked back on Kurt's shoulder, then pushed her way forward, blocking Shay as he approached. Her eyes panned from one to the other. Kris had to physically push her palm against Shay's chest to hold him back as he pointed at Kurt.

"Tynan knows you're here," Shay growled, his eyes flashing. "He's on his way, and if I don't get her out of here, then you're going to get her killed, *just* like you did Nina."

"What did you just say?"

Kris shifted her energy to hold Kurt back as he tried to move around her.

"Nina's dead because of you—"

"How dare you—"

Kris grabbed Kurt by both shoulders and forced him back. "He's Nina's brother!"

Kurt looked down at her in disbelief, then back at Shay. His shoulders relaxed slightly, but he maintained his scowl. "You're Brendan?"

"And you're the asshole who used my little sister," Shay shouted, pushing forward again. "The NWDA only found her because she tried to call you when she was scared and alone—"

"I didn't use her, she used *me*," Kurt countered.

Cade took Kurt by the arm and pulled him back, allowing Kris to focus on Shay.

"Either way, Nina's dead and I'm sorry," she said, "but you two screaming at each other isn't going to bring her back." Kris slammed her hands against Shay's chest. "I'm sorry."

He stumbled and maintained his glare at Kurt for a long moment before dropping his eyes to Kris. He clutched his bloodied shoulder. "Tynan jumped me. He read my mind. He found this place, and he's heading here now, so please, *please* just come with me. I can't leave you here."

Kris shook her head, her jaw clenched tight. "I'm not leaving."

"Tynan's going to kill you." He waved his arm at the others. "He's going to kill all of you."

"All the more reason for me to stand here and protect my friends."

Shay clasped a hand on her shoulder and gave her a shake. "This isn't a time for heroics," he hissed under his breath.

Kurt jolted forward. "Get your hand off her."

Shay paid him no mind and stayed focused on Kris. "You need to get out while you still can."

"If what he says is true, he might be right," Cade said to Kurt, then looked back at Brie. "Live today so we can fight tomorrow."

"We're already out of time," Kurt muttered.

Kris followed his stare across the meadow, where Tynan now stood in the tall grass, two of his followers behind him. Four more appeared.

Her breath caught in her throat as the small, ominous crowd started towards them. The late-afternoon sun suddenly disappeared behind the clouds, casting the field in darkness.

Kurt cleared his throat. "I guess we fight today."

Chapter 45

Out Of Time

Kris's hands quivered. Her eyes were fixed on Tynan and his six followers as they gradually made their way through the tall grass. She recognized Night, Red, and Flint, but the other three she hadn't encountered before. Two of them, a man and a woman, looked almost identical with gangly limbs, curly brown hair, and narrow eyes. The third, a young man with a buzz cut and full beard, had tattoos covering every inch of his exposed arms and neck.

Kurt stepped up, holding an arm back to protect Kris. He turned his head over his shoulder, but kept his eyes forward.

Larsen stood on one side, now holding the shield. On the other side, Brie was still clutching the scepter against her chest. Cade motioned for her to stand behind him.

"It's not too late," Shay hissed under his breath as he moved forward and took a defensive stance like Kurt. "We can still run."

"Excellent work, Shay," Tynan shouted with a wicked grin, stopping with his line of supporters a few yards away. "Thank you for leading us right to them."

"Don't talk to him like he's one of your slaves." Kris tried to push her way forward, but both Kurt and Shay raised their arms to block her path.

Tynan turned his gaze to her with an amused expression. "You think you can trust this man?" He nodded towards Shay.

"Don't," Shay warned with a stern jerk of his head.

"Who do you think gave us your mother's name?" Tynan laughed, crossing his arms.

Though Kris felt the hit emotionally like a punch to the gut, she maintained her poker face and held herself tall.

"You weren't supposed to kill her," Shay yelled. His voice echoed through the meadow.

Kurt's shoulders hiked up, and Kris could hear his heavy breathing as he tried to keep himself collected.

"Get the hell out of my home," Kurt growled at Tynan.

But Tynan just chuckled, completely disregarding the warning. "I always knew you were an asset, Kye. I'm grateful that I didn't kill you. You did all the heavy lifting for me." He eyed the shield that Larsen still held. "Hand over the keys."

"Fuck off," Cade said, adjusting his posture as though preparing for battle.

Tynan took a couple of steps forward and cocked his head as he looked down at each of them.

Kris's stomach felt uneasy while she sized up the followers behind him. They were outnumbered, and Tynan's group definitely wouldn't show the same level of restraint.

"There's no reason anyone has to get hurt here," Tynan continued, pausing only a few steps away. He looked between Kurt and Kris, grinning. Waiting.

Kris clenched her fists to cease the shaking. "We're not giving you *shit*."

He narrowed his dark eyes and stared into her soul. It shook her to her core, but she lifted her chin high anyway.

"I'm not scared of you anymore," Kurt said, taking a powerful stride forward. "So let me say it again: Get off my property."

Tynan scoffed and glanced back over his shoulder. "Lev, Lex . . . fetch."

The twins disappeared from behind Tynan. Brie cried out a second later as the man grabbed the scepter and tried to pull it from her grasp. Cade took a swing at him, throwing him off, but the teleporter was quick to fire back.

Larsen grunted and struggled behind her, and Kris whirled around. The second teleporter, the woman, was clasping the sides of the shield, so Larsen rammed the shield forward and knocked her to the ground.

The rest of Tynan's followers charged forward with a battle cry, fists glowing.

"Protect Kris," Kurt yelled to Shay as he formed a giant purple orb that sparked between his palms.

Red charged past Kris, grabbing Larsen's wrist. She instinctively jabbed an illuminated fist in his direction. Although Red was out of arm's reach, Kris felt her fist telekinetically connect to his gut, which caused him to stagger and gave her time to throw another punch.

Shay raised an arm, a turquoise shield materializing just in front of them. Kris jumped back as a large fireball collided with the force field, burst into flames, and burned out. Had Shay not stopped it, it would have struck her directly.

Ahead, Kurt was fighting Night. She delivered a red fist across his face. He stumbled back but remained on his feet, throwing a few punches in her direction as well. They were shouting at each other, but Kris couldn't hear them over the turmoil.

Cade was jumping around, doing his best to defend Brie. One of the men managed to knock him to the ground, but before he could hit Cade again, Brie swung the scepter at the cultist's head, allowing Cade enough time to stand.

Flint grabbed Shay's injured shoulder and gave it a brutal jerk back. Shay cried out but managed to still swing. Flint deflected it, and before Kris could interfere, he formed an ice sphere and hurled it at her feet. The ice sphere broke over Kris's shoes and solidified. She waved her arms out as she fought to keep her balance, unable to move her feet.

Flint had Shay on the ground, violently striking him again and again with a glowing fist. Kris cringed at the blood smearing across his face and spilling into the grass.

She frantically forged a small fireball and tried to square up to throw it at Flint, but with her feet frozen in place, she nearly toppled back. She instead held the flames against the ice in a rushed attempt to melt it.

When she looked up again, Shay had teleported and was now standing above Flint. Shay subdued him with a telekinetic force that sent Flint spinning through the air.

Kris had finally freed her feet when she felt an arm wrap around her throat from behind, squeezing tight. Panicked, she sank her teeth into the person's flesh and slipped away.

Kurt had Night pinned against the ground, and the woman suddenly morphed her appearance. Kris instantly felt sick when she saw her mother's face.

Despite his better judgment, Kurt hesitated. While still wearing Sofia's face, Night rammed her skull up into Kurt's. He clutched his head and glared at her as he backed away to collect himself. Even from where she stood, through the chaos around her, Kris could see the flicker of rage in his eyes.

Night thrust a fist forward, a red beam of light firing in Kurt's direction. Kris's heart sank.

"Kurt!"

But he had already created a beam of his own, the green light surging through the air and crashing into Night's.

"Watch it!" Shay yelled.

Kris narrowly avoided Flint's punch by twisting away. Shay appeared behind Flint, wrapped a thin chain around his throat, and jerked back on it. Flint instinctively grabbed at the chain, coughing as he struggled to free himself.

"Stop," Kris said, grabbing at Shay's wrist. "You'll kill him!"

He looked at Kris with confusion, but he obliged, instead throwing Flint down into the grass.

Night's scream made Kris's blood run cold. She just barely caught sight of Kurt's green beam consuming the last of Night's red light. The woman shapeshifted rapidly in a last-ditch effort, but she returned to herself as Kurt's beam struck her in the chest, the force of which sent her sailing several yards through the air until she crashed back into the dirt.

Kris could still hear fighting all around her, but she stood frozen, staring at Night's body in the grass. In her peripheral vision, she could tell that Kurt was also stunned and unmoving.

Tynan approached Night, an odd look of sorrow in his eyes. He lowered himself beside her, taking her hand and tenderly stroking her cheek. They were whispering to each other until Night's head dropped back. Once her body was motionless, Tynan rose again, a monstrous glare focused on Kurt.

"No!" Kris screamed.

The moment came to a halt; the seconds passed painfully slow as Tynan punched two fists in Kurt's direction, launching a ray of deep blue light.

Kris extended her arm and darted toward Kurt, but each step felt like it took hours. As she helplessly watched the beam jolt forward inch by inch, she knew she couldn't possibly reach him in time.

But she didn't have to.

When the beam was only a foot away, Shay suddenly appeared in its path, outstretched arms blocking Kurt. The blue light hit him directly in the chest and threw him back into Kurt. They both fell into the grass.

Things paused for a long moment in which nobody moved, until Kurt pulled himself to his hands and knees. He crawled over to Shay. "Why the hell did you do that?"

Kris dropped to the dirt beside them, panting. "Shay?" she whispered. Her voice caught in her throat.

His brown eyes opened only a sliver, searching. When he saw Kris, he offered her a faint smile. "I'm sorry, Star Eyes . . ."

"You're going to be okay," she managed to get out.

Kris rested a hand on his chest. His skin was growing cold, even in the warm summer evening. She concentrated hard to drive the glow in her chest to her fingertips, but her magic didn't go anywhere. She could feel Shay fading. She could feel the pain. And it was unlike any injury she had ever encountered.

There's nothing to heal, she realized, her eyes filling with tears. *It's irreversible.*

"Beams destroy the soul, Kris," Kurt reminded her quietly. "You can't fix this."

Shay's clouded eyes turned to Kurt. "Take care of her . . ."

Kris sucked in a sharp, broken breath. She gave him a gentle shake. "Shay?"

"Enough of this." Tynan's voice pierced the silence. There was a waver in his words, but he sounded more irritated than heartbroken. "Lex."

Kris looked up when she heard Brie shout. The male teleporter appeared beside Tynan, squeezing Brie's upper arm. He flung her to Tynan, the scepter still in her hand.

Kris jumped up to her feet as Tynan grabbed either end of the silver staff and pulled Brie in front of him like a shield. He yanked the scepter up into her throat until she was balancing on her tiptoes to maintain contact with the ground.

"Tell me the location of Calosant *now*, or she dies."

Chapter 46

Surrounded

Cade charged towards Tynan, shouting while he drew back his fist. But before he could make contact, he froze mid-swing. He grunted as he tried to force himself forward to strike Tynan, but was inevitably yanked backward.

Red caught Cade and wrapped both bare hands around his throat. He constricted his grasp as Cade fought to break free, his eyes glued on Brie just ahead of him. But it didn't take long for him to sink to his knees.

Kris raised her hands to her shoulders in surrender and took a small step forward. "Stop. Please."

"Don't give him anything, Kris," Brie said, squirming to keep her feet on the ground.

Tynan jerked the staff higher, which lifted Brie completely off the grass for several seconds. Kris winced at the sounds of her friend desperately choking for air.

Kris took another step closer. "Please don't hurt her."

Brie grabbed at the scepter, trying to pull herself up to relieve the strain on her throat. After a few seconds of struggling, Tynan lowered her back to her feet.

Kris locked eyes with Brie, and a hot tear spilled down her cheek. "I'll give you whatever you want, just let her go."

Tynan loosened his grip just enough for Brie to take a big gulp of air. "Good girl," he murmured. "Where's Calosant?"

Kris looked back and bit her lip. The woman teleporter, whom Tynan had called Lev, had Larsen pinned to the ground underneath the shield and was pressing the rim down on his arm. Cade was on his hands and knees, coughing as Red finally released him. Flint was standing over Shay's lifeless body and clutching Kurt's arm, which was twisted behind his back to hold him in place.

Kurt's chest heaved with a big sigh and he gave Kris a gentle nod. *It's okay*, he insisted silently.

Kris turned back to Tynan. "We don't have Calosant's location yet. I need the staff." She held out a shaking hand as she approached him.

He squinted, studying her cautiously, before finally lowering the staff. He held on to Brie's arm and kept her close as he extended the scepter to Kris. "Don't try anything stupid."

She shook her head and pressed her lips together.

Brie, still coughing, gripped Tynan's hand as she tried to free herself. She continued to pull away from him, but he effortlessly clung tight to her elbow.

Kris's eyes were still clouded. She squeezed the staff tightly with both hands and clutched it close so the curved tip rested against her cheek.

The metal felt as though it were buzzing underneath her fingers, but it didn't provide the same sense of security Kris had felt in the past with the keys. Her breaths were short and sharp as she tried to compose herself.

A tear rolled over her lashes and down her cheek until it met the staff.

The scepter almost instantly burned hot. Kris gasped and moved it away, but she held on despite it smoldering in the palms of her hands.

The tip of the scepter unfurled like a budding flower to reveal a large polished emerald and a small gold key that remained suspended between the two twisted silver petals.

Kris gently plucked the key from the air with her fingers. It had to be for the locked box.

Stealing a glance over her shoulder, she could see that Red had planted a foot on Cade's back and pushed him down into the dirt. Lev still had Larsen pinned, and Flint was forcing Kurt forward.

She turned back to Tynan. "Call off your goons," she demanded, standing tall despite the tremors in her knees.

Tynan held her stare for a long moment before smiling smugly. "Release them."

Lev groaned but took her weight off the shield so that Larsen was finally able to free his arm. He rubbed his wrist as he slowly stood. Flint hesitated, then kicked Kurt behind his knee to force him to the ground before releasing his arm. Kurt took the shield from Larsen as they both helped Cade to his feet. Cade shot a glare at Red, who backed away with a chuckle.

"What's the key for?" Tynan asked Kris.

She closed her hand around the key and held it against her chest. She bowed her head with a deep breath in. "It will open a locked box."

Tynan nodded to Lev. "Retrieve the other keys from the house."

Kris watched Kurt wipe blood from his nose as he helped stabilize Cade.

In her mind's void, she and Kurt stood face-to-face. Despite there being no barrier between them, Kris raised her hand out in front of her. Kurt did the same, pressing his palm against hers. He offered her a reassuring smile.

Don't worry, he said to her softly, leaning his forehead against hers. Their fingers interlocked. *No matter what happens, everything's going to be all right.*

Lev appeared beside Tynan in the field, carrying the dagger, the mirror, and the box in her arms.

"Give me the key," Tynan instructed Kris, holding out his free hand while still clinging to Brie's arm.

Kris clutched the small gold key against her chest. "Give me the box," she countered.

Tynan smirked and shook his head. "Do you really think you are in any position to be giving me orders?" He yanked on Brie's arm, and she whimpered as she tried to pry his hand off her.

Kris bit down on her lip and breathed in sharply. She remained quiet and finally raised her gaze back to him. "The box," she demanded again.

Tynan chuckled, then reached out to take the scepter from her hand. "You can deny it all you want, but you would have been a valuable ally to my mission."

"Never," Kris insisted under her breath, allowing Tynan to rip the staff from her clutch.

He snickered and turned to Lev. "Give her the box."

The woman paused, flipping her brown curls from her face and staring up at Tynan with an expression of pure irritation. But finally, she held the gold box out to Kris.

Kris's hands were shaking so much that she couldn't get the key in the keyhole. Her fingers trembled as she forced it in, and she stole one last glance back at Kurt before twisting it.

The lid of the box immediately snapped open. She cried out in surprise as it jolted, and a bright light erupted from inside.

Kris watched in awe as a projection of Earth formed in the air above. Kurt made a sound of surprise behind her. He held the shield out in front of him, and the smoky quartz crystals were the first to illuminate, burning bright until the entire face of the oblong shield began to glow.

Lev jumped back, dropping the dagger and mirror in the grass as they also burst into light. And then eventually the scepter in Tynan's hand.

As each key activated, the translucent projection of the world narrowed, first zooming in on North America, then the east side of the United States. As it zeroed in on the location, details became clearer until finally Kris was gazing up at a rock cliff that stretched high up above the surrounding treetops.

Tynan's grip on Brie's arm loosened as he gaped. "After all my years of searching . . . of sacrifice . . ."

Brie took the opportunity to rip herself away and stumbled over to Kris. She latched on to her friend's arm, panting hard. It didn't take long for Kurt, Cade, and Larsen to crowd around her as well.

Without warning, the projection shrunk back down inside the box, and the lid slammed shut with such force that it thrust into Kris's gut.

She glanced around as the cultists closed in and surrounded them. Tynan closed his eyes and took a long, deep breath, and a peaceful smile settled on his face. When he opened his eyes again, he was looking at Night's body, his jaw clenched.

"Kill them," he said flatly.

"No!" Kurt shouted.

"Wait!" Kris cried. She kept her eyes on Tynan, twisting only her body to shove the box into Larsen's hands and taking a step forward. She stretched her arms out in front of them protectively.

Tynan gave her a skeptical look.

"You need us," she said.

Her heart was racing, and she was confident Tynan could tell, but she fought to keep a straight face. She looked down at the dagger and mirror on the ground near Tynan's feet, scrambling for an idea.

"The—the keys. They have imprinted on each of us," Kris stammered. "You need us to open the gates."

Tynan squinted. He stepped over the mirror and dagger to close the space between them. His dark eyes burrowed into her, staring into her mind and soul, but Kris held his gaze. Her chest heaved with each breath and she flinched when Tynan suddenly shifted the staff towards her. Kris hesitantly took it from his hand.

"Sir, you're trusting *them?*" Red shouted, making no effort to mask his frustration.

Tynan looked past Kris to Kurt, a wicked flicker in his eyes. "What have we got to lose? We kill them now, or we kill them later."

Kris crouched down, keeping an eye on Tynan while feeling around in the grass for the mirror and dagger. She carefully held them back out to Cade and Brie as she stood up again.

Tynan grabbed her by the arm, jerking her forward and lowering himself to whisper directly in her ear. His voice was hushed but menacing as he eyed Kurt over her shoulder. "I wouldn't try to pull any funny business if I were you."

A shiver ran up her spine, but Kris nodded. She tried to step away to rejoin Kurt, but Tynan maintained the grip on her arm and held her in place.

"Lev, Flint, you're with me," he instructed. "Red, Lex, and Jay, you take the leftovers."

We're going to Calosant. We're actually going to Calosant. With Tynan.

Kris couldn't breathe. The gravity of the situation dawned on her in that instant and *she couldn't breathe.*

She reached out, trying desperately to grab Kurt's hand, but the meadow around her was already changing, twisting and warping into a dense forest. The sky above the trees was orange and pink, the clouds glowing in the bright colors, but everything felt much, much darker for her.

Tynan tugged on her arm and turned her to face a towering white cliff that loomed ahead of them. The ridge extended high beyond the canopy of the trees, just as they had seen in the box's projection.

"This is the entrance," Tynan mumbled, squeezing Kris's elbow as they took a step towards the cliff. But he jolted back as a deafening snap echoed through the trees and a large crack fired up from the ground through the rock like a bolt of lightning.

Kris could only stare silently, awestruck, as the crack in the cliff branched outward and broke off small sections of rock. The pieces crumbled to the ground and rolled away into the darkness behind it. Each one that was removed exposed a little more of the tunnel in the cliff that plunged down into the earth.

A rush of emotions hit her all at once. She was lightheaded but energized. Her heart burned in fear, but was also eager with anticipation as she gazed into the darkness. Something was calling to her. An invisible force beckoning her like a siren's song, guiding her inside.

Tynan dragged Kris toward the tunnel once the entrance was complete and no more rocks were falling. She stumbled. Her feet couldn't move, as though her body was pulling away while her mind was drawing her in.

Over her shoulder, she saw the others appear. Flint had a firm hold on Kurt's arm again, forcing him forward to follow behind Tynan and Kris.

"Eyes front," Tynan hissed to her with a jerk of the arm. "This is the place of our ancestors. Show some respect."

The hair on her arms stood on end as they crossed the threshold. Once her feet touched the stone, tears poured from Kris's eyes and her skin went numb.

This is it. All the training, all the searching, all the riddles . . .

It has all led to this.

Chapter 47

Calosant

"**A**re you afraid?"

The temperature was dropping rapidly with the sunset's light disappearing the farther they descended down the tunnel. And Tynan's hushed words sent an extra shiver up Kris's spine.

She swallowed hard, her eyes darting around the darkness. She could feel the goose bumps rising on her skin. After a moment's hesitation, Kris nodded. "Yes."

"There's no need to be afraid. You are giving your life to save our people. To save thousands."

Kris was shaking so violently that she stumbled. Tynan loosened his grip.

"You don't have to kill us," she muttered. "You can let us go—"

"You'll never stop fighting." He gave her arm a yank. "It's the only way I can trust that you won't interfere."

The tunnel echoed with footsteps, and several light spheres formed behind her. Kris watched from the corner of her eye as

Tynan effortlessly created his own with a single hand. He cradled it between his fingers and held it out in front of them to illuminate their path.

Her head throbbed, and her vision momentarily blurred. She felt dizzy. Kris glanced over her shoulder to look at Kurt, but there was no one there. And the world beyond the exit was in shadows. No more orange light crept in.

"Keep up the pace," a voice told her.

Looking ahead again, she saw that two men were leading her down the tunnel. She recognized them immediately from the statues she had seen in her vision.

Lord Ruben, Kris somehow knew. Her eye caught the glint of gold on his hip. It was the handle of a blade, decorated with garnets: the dagger key. She looked at the other man. Lord Dustan.

"Our people will be eager to learn that the cavern entrance has been secured," Lord Dustan was saying. "The enchantment is sure to keep those filthy humans from sniffing around."

Am I . . . Annona?

Kris was wearing a floor-length black cotton dress laced up with a red ribbon. She turned her hands around in front of her, surprised to find she wasn't wearing the Mina Ring.

There was a jerk on her arm, and in a blink, Lord Ruben and Lord Dustan were gone.

"Keep moving," Red's voice said from behind her.

Over her shoulder, behind Kurt and Flint, she saw Cade collapse. Red reared back a fist as though preparing to strike him.

"No!" Brie cried. "Stop!" She tried to pull away from her captor but failed.

Kurt tried to tear himself free, but Flint gave his arm a violent twist behind his back. Larsen slammed his elbow into Lev's chest, forcing her away and jamming the box into her hands. He then grabbed Red's bare wrist with both hands, stopping him before he could hit Cade.

"Leave him alone," Larsen said with a sneer. His brow twitched as he flung Red's arm away, panting hard.

"That's enough," Tynan roared.

Kris twisted away from his booming voice, which left her head ringing. Larsen helped Cade back to his feet and shot Red a glare. Tynan jerked his head forward, motioning for everyone to continue, allowing Larsen to escort Cade himself.

From the shadows ahead, a shape faded into existence. A woman in a white dress.

A man stood with Annona, the same hooded man Kris had seen crawl through Annona's window. He was holding her hand and pulling her towards the exit. They both had huge smiles on their faces.

Annona giggled and glanced back. "I can't believe I'm doing this."

She's wearing the Mina Ring this time, Kris noticed as they ran past her.

"Hurry on, my love," the man said. "Before those old fools make wise."

Kris's head pounded. Still clutching the scepter, she pressed the butt of her palm to her forehead. Her feet were aching and her knees weak. It took all the strength she had to keep moving despite being unable to catch her breath.

"Gate up ahead."

She raised her eyes as they approached a stone wall. Just before it were five pedestals in a V formation.

Kris squeezed the scepter in her hand as they stopped in front of the middle platform. The white cylinder was made of stone, with elaborate spiral carvings along the sides, and on the top were two staggered prongs.

For the staff.

She looked down at the object in her hand and took a deep breath. She held the silver staff out to set in place, but paused. Keeping her eyes on the key, she whispered to Tynan, "Once we do this, you're going to kill us?"

"Yes."

Kris winced, her blood running cold. She pressed her eyes shut with another deep breath. Her throat was closing up, but she fought with all she had to keep calm. "I surrender," she said, keeping her voice barely above a whisper, afraid Kurt might hear. "I will pledge my allegiance—my life—if you spare them."

Tynan was quiet, but Kris could tell he was considering her offer. "You would give your life for them, but not the thousands of Witcans dying at the hands of the NWDA?"

Kris held her tongue. Instead, she dropped her head with a gentle nod. "Do we have a deal?"

She waited, her arm still extended with the staff inches from the pedestal. Her heart was pounding.

Tynan released her arm. "Don't ever say I am not merciful," he whispered directly into her ear.

Kris turned her head away to hide the tears that flooded her eyes. Her lips pinched as she sucked air in sharply through her nose. Finally, she set the scepter in its cradle.

The spiral carvings around the pedestal lit up, illuminating the cavern. Kris kept her head down, unable to look at Kurt as he stepped up to the pedestal beside her to place the shield. She could feel his eyes on her, willing her to look up, to make eye contact, but the pit in her stomach kept her sights on her sneakers.

As the cavern grew brighter, Kris knew all the keys had been put in place. There was a hum in the air as the rock wall before them gradually faded into a thick veil of smoke. A foggy barrier.

"Bring them," Tynan instructed his followers, gesturing for Kris to continue on.

The veil was cold when she passed through it. She wrapped her arms around herself to keep from shivering.

On the other side, the cavern opened up. They were standing at the top of a hill, looking down over a deserted city illuminated by glowing shards of crystals that projected out of the rock walls and ceiling high overhead. Like stars.

Calosant.

The city was no less than a mile across. From the vantage point on the hill, Kris could see all the winding streets lined with small stone houses, and at the center of it all down below was the towering white structure she had seen in her visions.

In her mind, the ribbons of light reached out from the building and spiraled towards her. Called her. Even though she was trembling, the light warmed her and eased her fears.

"The Temple of Annona," Tynan said, gesturing to the structure. "That's the capitol building. That's where the Mina Ring is kept."

They moved forward, but a few steps down the hill, Tynan abruptly stopped and looked back at his followers. "I will go on from here alone," he said, taking Kris by the arm again.

"But, sir—" Flint protested.

"Keep the prisoners here until we return." Tynan's raised voice and glare silenced Flint.

"Wait," Kurt said.

His voice forced Kris to finally turn back. She gave a small yelp as he lunged forward and wrapped his arms around her and hugging her close. Kris buried her head in his shoulder and fought to hold back the tears.

"I'm sorry," she whispered to him with a crack in her voice.

Kurt gently shushed her, stroking her hair. Kris could feel his heart beating hard in his chest, and she knew he could feel hers too.

"No matter what happens, I just want you to know," he said softly to her. "I love you."

She forced a smile as a sob caught in her throat. "I love you too."

Kris stepped back. Kurt's pale eyes were filled with tears as he brushed his thumb across her cheek. Behind him, Brie's expression was begging Kris for an explanation, but she gave her nothing. Just a nod and a faux smile of encouragement. Cade hung weakly off Larsen's shoulder. He was trying to speak but couldn't get a sound out.

Larsen studied her sadly. "We believe in you," he murmured. "You'll be okay."

Without a word, Tynan pulled on Kris's arm again and they started down the hill. She watched her friends over her shoulder as long as she could, desperately holding Kurt's gaze, until they disappeared behind a line of houses.

Things were quiet for a long while, their footsteps on the silver stone streets the only sound. The silence, coupled with the deserted city, made Kris anxious. She caught herself peering into the windows of the houses around them, but there was nothing but darkness inside.

She peeked up at Tynan. He was focused on the temple, but his jaw was clenched, his mind clearly lost in thought.

"I'm sorry about Night," Kris finally said, eyeing his reaction.

He released her arm with a gentle fling but said nothing. There was an almost undetectable twitch in his brow, but he kept his stern expression on his face.

"You loved her, didn't you?" she pressed on.

Tynan sneered. "You think you know what love is because some boy you just met swooped in to white-knight you?" His words were oozing with contempt and he made no effort to hide it. "It's loyalty. Devotion. A willingness to die for each other."

"Would you have died in Night's place?" Kris asked, distinctly remembering his lack of participation during the fight.

He quickened his pace, his arms swinging aggressively with each stride. "You know nothing of love."

Kris frowned. "I would have said the same about you."

She hugged her arms around herself, pausing for a moment when she caught a glimpse of Annona walking towards her up the street. Her heart skipped a beat, but the vision faded almost as quickly as it had come.

Tynan scoffed, still fixated on the temple as they approached it. "It's so easy for you to write me off as evil, isn't it? Cast me as the bad guy? But we're not so different, you and I. I'm just willing to make the hard decisions and do what needs to be done to protect our people."

"Violence isn't the answer," Kris whispered, more to herself than to him. Her mother's words played over and over in her head.

"Violence can't be fought with daisies in gun barrels," he retorted, shooting her a quick glare.

Kris stopped dead in her tracks and stared down a street to her left toward a house at the end of the road. It looked identical to the other homes on the block, with gray and white stones covering the walls and roof, but something about it called to her.

She found herself standing in a crowded street. She jumped as children ran past her, laughing and giggling. People were walking up and down the narrow road. Talking. Reading. Carrying sacks over their shoulders. And at the house at the end, a young girl with matted black hair sat on the front steps, staring directly at Kris.

"Can you see me?" Kris called to her.

The little girl didn't move, but her eyes shifted slightly as though she were studying Kris. A woman appeared in the doorway behind her, causing the young girl to spring to her feet and dart inside.

Then in a blink, the street was empty again.

Was that Annona? As a child? Could she see me?

Kris took a baby step towards the house, staring at the windows and door as though waiting for someone or something to appear.

"Keep moving." Tynan bellowed, then looked over his shoulder at her with a scowl.

She glared at him, opening her mouth to speak, but promptly shut it again. She had chosen this. For Kurt. For Brie. For Larsen and Cade. Instead, she pinched her lips and nodded, following behind him once more.

Not far down the street, beyond the houses and shops of the main road, Kris could see the entrance to the temple. The towering statues of Calosant's Lords and Ladies. The columns at the front bracing the upper floors. The steps leading up to the open ground floor. Even after years and years of neglect underground, the building still appeared to glow white in the light of the cave's crystals. Beautiful and serene.

A man stood at the top of the steps and looked down at a crowd. He held his arms out, trying to calm them. Kris glanced up at one of the statues in front of the temple, then back at the man. As she approached the base of the silver steps, she recognized him as Lord Azule.

"We have taken Annona to the surface and scouted a nearby village. The humans were hostile and violent. Fortunately, Annona, our goddess, was able to protect us. We have increased security at our borders."

"So when can we open the gates? When can we go to the surface?" a man in the crowd asked.

Lord Azule straightened and stood up tall. "Annona does not feel it is yet safe for us above."

There was outcry. The crowd turned on him, arguing, until Annona herself stepped through the mob. Each person she bumped became silent and shrunk away, until the city street was quiet and she stood in front of Lord Azule. She looked around at the faces, pausing when she caught Kris's eye.

Kris jolted, taking a step back. *Can she see me too?*

Annona held her stare, and it was weirdly calming. Like she was watching over Kris from beyond.

"The surface is not ready for us yet," Annona finally said, breaking the silence and looking away from Kris. "As long as we remain here in Calosant, I can protect you."

Kris's head snapped back, and once again Annona was gone. *She definitely saw me.*

She quickened her pace to follow Tynan. At the base of the steps, she stared up at the temple. It looked just as it had in her visions, aside from the cracks and fractures in the stone.

"The Lords and Ladies of Calosant," Tynan said, scanning the five statues on either side of them as they climbed the steps.

The first floor was open besides the many stone pillars that supported the upper floors. The tiles, though covered in years of dust and dirt, still gleamed in the light of Tynan's orb.

He stopped in front of a statue in the middle of the floor. The figure towered over them, stretching all the way up to the ceiling. "And there's Annona."

Her arms were outstretched and her face turned up to the sky. The intricate detail carved into the dress she wore took Kris's breath away and made her forget her plight for a moment.

Tynan motioned to a staircase to the right. "This way."

She froze at the bottom step as Annona and the man came rushing down. They were giggling and darting from pillar to pillar.

"Hurry. Come on," the man kept saying until they disappeared down the steps outside.

Kris felt physically ill as she followed Tynan up the stairs to the second floor. Her head was clouded. Her hands shook. The knot in the pit of her stomach tightened with each step.

She eyed Tynan's back. He was distracted. Unsuspecting. *I could probably do it. I could strike. I could defeat him* . . . Her hands glowed white, but with a sharp breath she shook her head. Violence was not the answer.

At the top of the first flight of stairs, Tynan stopped before a red door with decorative gold lining, then looked back at Kris with a smug grin. "You truly impress me. You had the shot. You had opportunity. Yet you didn't take it. Why?"

Kris pressed her lips together and held her chin high as she marched up to the landing. "Because no matter what you say, I'm *not* like you."

"I've had no shortage of opportunities, but you're still here. I've let you live."

"In exchange for slavery. You're not exactly benevolent. I'm just a tool to you."

She grabbed the doorknob and gave it a twist, but it didn't turn. Kris slammed her shoulder into the door. It didn't budge.

"You have the heart of a lion," he said. "It's threatening, but admirable."

Kris froze before ramming the door again. She studied his sincere expression, and goose bumps rippled up her spine.

Tynan lightly touched her shoulder and she lunged away, jerking her arm with the motion. With a single ram, he crashed through the door. He held the doorframe to keep from stumbling, then stepped aside to allow Kris to enter first.

She eyed him skeptically and side-stepped into the room, but the instant she looked around, her breath caught in her throat.

The room from her vision. Annona's room.

The dusty queen-sized bed. The shelves littered with books and loose pages. The empty vanity and mirror buried under centuries of grime. Kris took it all in as she crossed the room to the sealed-up window and traced her fingers over the metal. Despite the temperature in the room, it felt warm to the touch.

"You are *never* to see that boy again," someone said behind her.

Kris turned. The five Lords and Ladies were blocking her from the door.

Lady Patina, who stood at the front, held the Mina Ring in her hand. "You are a symbol of hope for this city. For our people," she said sternly, squeezing her fingers around the ring. "And we will not let you squander that because of some childish romance."

Kris nodded slowly. "I will never see him again," she said in a voice that wasn't her own. "I'm here to serve you, and only you."

Serve?

She jumped at the sound of shattering glass, returning to the present where Tynan stood in front of a wardrobe. Fragments of the glass door clattered to the tile floor.

Her chest burned as she slowly approached. She knew it even before she could see it.

The Mina Ring.

Standing beside Tynan, Kris stared down at the silver ring for what felt like ages. Everything in her body was yelling for her to back away, to leave it be. But she couldn't fight the energy drawing her in.

"My life's work has led me to this," Tynan murmured.

Fingers trembling, Kris reached towards it, and he didn't stop her. The instant she touched it, images flashed around her so rapidly that she had little time to digest what she was seeing.

She was outside the house she had seen in the city. The young girl was sitting on the front steps and darted inside as the five Elders approached.

In the house, the girl hid behind a young couple. They were crying.

"A deal's a deal," Lord Dustan said to them, and he set a small sack down on the dinner table. It jingled against the wood.

"Mama, no," the girl cried, clutching her mother's dress. "I don't want to go. I want to stay with you."

The mother and father crouched down and hugged her. "We're sorry, Anya," the father said.

"They can give you a better life," the mother added, brushing tears from the girl's face.

The girl screamed as Lord Ruben pried her away from her parents. "No. Mama. Papa. I don't want to go. I don't want to go!"

Kris was in the temple's bedroom again. The young girl, now a little older, was sitting in a chair at the window. She stared out into the city as Lady Roetta approached.

"Lord Dustan says you can have your ring, only if you behave," Lady Roetta said in a condescending tone. "Can you behave like a good little girl?"

The girl turned and nodded, holding out her hand. "I'll be good. I promise."

Lady Roetta withdrew the Mina Ring from a pouch on her hip and gently set it in the palm of the girl's hand. A few white granules dropped from the woman's fingers.

The girl was older now. A teenager, standing at the window. A large crowd of people outside shouted in outrage.

Lord Azule stood behind her. "Go out there and tell your people that it is too dangerous to leave Calosant. That you would be unable to protect them out there."

The girl chuckled and shook her head. "The only thing I should be protecting them from is *you*."

Lord Azule scowled. He lurched forward and ripped the Mina Ring from her finger. She cried out in surprise, swiping through the air in an attempt to grab it back, but she missed.

He stuffed the ring into the small pouch at his side and glared at her. "Let's try this again: Go out there and tell our people that they cannot leave Calosant."

The girl's eyes glazed over and she nodded. She looked almost lifeless as she moved towards the stairs.

She was older again, a young woman now, sitting cross-legged on the bed as she traced her fingers over the Mina Ring. A man slipped in through the window.

The woman shot to her feet, her fists glowing white as she took a defensive stance. "Who are you?"

The man jumped, startled. He backed up against the wall. "I . . . I didn't think anyone would be in here."

They stared at each other for a long moment.

"I've never seen you up close before," the man whispered. He stepped away from the wall with a soft smile on his face. "You're beautiful."

She lowered her hands. "What do you want?"

"I'm Rolf," he said, touching his chest. He approached her, and she backed away. He chuckled as he raised his hands in surrender. "I didn't mean to scare you. I can leave . . ."

She looked away, but took a step towards him. "I'm Anya."

The room became dark, and Rolf burst through the door. Anya jumped up from her bed, running to him for an embrace.

"I thought I'd never see you again," she said through sobs. "Lord Dustan said you were to be killed."

He stepped back and squeezed her hands. "Run away with me."

It didn't take much convincing. With the Mina Ring on her finger, she didn't even hesitate, and she ran down the stairs with him.

They were in a forest outside the cave. Her eyes twinkled in the dancing sunlight that escaped the canopy.

"I'm free," she breathed. But when she looked back at him, Rolf was no longer smiling.

"I'm sorry," he told her.

Before she could say another word, she was grabbed from behind.

And then she was in the meadow. The infamous scene Kris knew all too well.

The group of men stood around her and beat her. They took the Mina Ring from her hand. And the last man to step forward for the killing blow was none other than Rolf.

"You brought this on yourself," he hissed before thrusting a blade into her chest.

Kris gasped through ragged breaths, clutching her chest. She stumbled and backed away until she was up against the wall. The Mina Ring bounced against the floor.

She replayed the vision in her head, piecing it together.

The Mina Ring wasn't a weapon. It wasn't a powerful item created for Annona. It was used to control her.

Chapter 48

The Mina Ring

Kris's head reeled. The cold stone against her back helped calm her breathing.

Tynan bent down and picked up the Mina Ring as it rolled away from Kris. "What did you see?"

Her eyes were fixed on the silver and emerald ring in Tynan's hand. She jutted her chin towards it. "The Mina Ring has no power," Kris mumbled, glancing up into his dark eyes.

His brow twitched. "This is Annona's ring. It contains her power."

She shook her head and stepped away from the wall with timid steps. "It was her mother's ring. The Elders used it to control her. Make her their puppet to manipulate the people of this city."

Tynan squeezed the ring in his hand, his eyes flashing. "You're lying."

"They used that ring just like you use your pledge trinkets." Kris held out a shaking hand for him to give her the ring.

"But Annona's ring . . . It has the power to save our people," he muttered to himself as he stared down at the silver in the palm of his hand.

"That's what the Elders wanted us to believe, but the ring is still tethered to Annona," Kris whispered, taking a small step closer. "She's trapped, Tynan. I need it to free her."

His fingers slowly closed around the ring again as his face wrinkled with rage.

"Please." She kept her guard up while she approached. "Help me do the right thing."

"You're lying!"

A glowing blue fist whizzed just past her face as she stumbled out of the way.

"I'm not lying, I swear," Kris said, dodging his second punch.

The energy was still radiating from the ring in Tynan's hand, calling to her. Without a thought, she grabbed his wrist in a feeble attempt to pry the ring free.

"Rat!" He rammed his forearm into her throat, forced her back into the wall, and pinned her in place. "I should have known better than to trust you," he hissed, spit spraying from his lips and dark curls of hair coming loose with his furious head movement.

Kris pushed against his arm, trying to free herself, but he held strong. "Please," she wheezed.

He pushed harder, and her neck burned under the pressure. She was unable to even cough.

Panicked, Kris whipped open her father's knife from her back pocket and stabbed it into Tynan's shoulder. He cried out, lumbering away with a hand clutched to his shoulder, the knife still protruding from it.

She was on her feet, coughing for air, but the sound of metal clattering against the floor made her look up. She dove for the Mina Ring, which was rolling away from Tynan. Her fingers scratched over the stone as she frantically cupped the ring in both hands.

A piercing pain erupted from Kris's foot. Tynan had hurled her knife with such telekinetic force that it punctured through both her sneaker and her foot, then embedded itself into the stone floor, pinning her in place.

"You will not take this away from me," Tynan roared, forming a flickering ball of fire with his hands as he approached.

Kris tried to move away, and the knife cut deeper into her foot. She shrieked, tears spilling down her face and blood pouring from her shoe, covering the floor.

Tynan flung the ball of fire towards her. Unable to move away, Kris pushed an open palm forward. The energy extended outward to form a curved, translucent shield just in time. The flames crashed into the force field and burned out.

From the corner of her eye, she could see the familiar blue glow from his hands. With that surge of adrenaline, Kris grabbed the pocketknife with one hand and ripped it free from her shoe just in time to roll away from the blazing beam of blue light.

Tynan's beam blasted the floor, and the entire building rattled. Kris stumbled, her foot slipping in the blood, and she crashed back down to the tile.

"Give me that ring!" he yelled.

Kris clumsily pulled herself to her feet using the vanity as he charged her. Her heart was pumping and her foot throbbed, but she didn't have time to catch her breath.

"I'm sorry," she whispered, and she squeezed her hand tight around the Mina Ring.

Kris didn't hesitate, summoning all the strength she had into the palm of her hand. The ring burned hot as the white glow grew brighter and brighter. Every muscle in her body contracted. Her knees felt weak. Her foot ached, but she kept her focus on the ring.

At that moment, it felt like Annona was there beside her, her hand on Kris's hand. Lending her strength.

Tynan's eyes widened in horror as he dashed forward, his arm outstretched.

The light from Kris's hand filled the room, and with a grunt and a blinding flash, the ring shattered and crumbled into fragments in her sweaty palm.

Squinting through the light, Kris saw a face—a young woman. A small smile curled the woman's lips as she met Kris's eye.

At long last . . . I am finally free. Thank you.

Her light dissolved.

Kris took a deep breath in as she slouched back against the vanity. Her smile was serene. Calm. Accepting.

But it vanished in an instant as the floor suddenly gave way beneath her feet.

Her voice caught in her throat as she fell, fractured stone surrounding her. She waved her arms frantically in an attempt to twist through the air.

Two arms suddenly caught Kris before she hit the ground.

"Kurt!" she cried.

He dropped to a crouch and raised an arm in the air, catching a large slab of stone a few feet above them. The temple was coming down on them.

Kris gasped. She tried to stand, but the pain in her foot forced her to her knee. With both arms raised, she reached out telekinetically as the walls of the floors above began to cave in. She pushed back against them as best as she could, but her arms trembled with exhaustion.

"I can't hold it," she said, panting. In her peripheral vision, she could see Kurt sinking to a knee as well.

"We'll be okay." He waved his arm to fling a collection of stones and debris away.

Kris's vision faded in and out as one of the walls fractured and started to fold in towards them. *Breathe*, she reminded herself, and she shifted to put all her energy into the crumbling wall.

"Look out!" Kurt yelled, lunging forward as a blast of blue light fired towards Kris.

The beam struck Kurt in his arm and singed his flesh, but he had shielded her. He cried out in anguish and didn't move until the light faded away.

"Kurt!" She turned towards him as he dropped to the ground. He clutched his arm, but a chair crashed down beside her, reminding Kris to focus on the collapsing building.

From the corner of her eye, she could see Tynan pulling himself from the rubble and staggering forward.

"You! You ruined *everything*," he shouted at her.

"Tynan, please," Kris said, clutching a chunk of fractured rock and flinging it away.

Kurt sat up, his injured arm held tight against his chest. He said nothing as he extended a hand in Tynan's direction, throwing a short blast of green light.

"No!" Not even a thought crossed her mind as Kris formed a shield in front of Tynan just before Kurt's beam could strike him. The magic reflected off the surface of the force field and blasted through some falling rubble.

"Kris," Kurt warned as he slowly stood.

"He doesn't deserve to die," she said, grunting while stopping a chunk of upper floor from crushing them.

Kurt feebly threw another beam at Tynan, which Kris scrambled to deflect with another shield. "You can't save him," he insisted.

"Both of you," Tynan growled. "You destroyed everything I have ever worked for." He fired a blue beam towards Kris.

Tears poured down her face and her arms shook as she extended one hand to hold back another section of wall, and the other to deflect Tynan's beam.

"Tynan, stand down. Please," Kris pleaded, her voice cracking like the temple around them.

"Kris," Kurt said. He shuffled to the side in an effort to hold the crumbling walls back. "Not everyone can be saved. Just trust me . . . please."

"You have doomed our people!" Tynan screamed.

Kris dropped to her knee again, panting to keep from sobbing. She wanted to give up. Her body was telling her to give up. But she couldn't let go.

She could hear Kurt grunt as he forced another large slab of stone away.

I can't . . . I can't.

Her hands glowed white . . . but the hue slowly changed, fading through multiple colors before settling on a pale purple.

Kurt cried out as he threw both palms forward. The green light pierced the air, raging in Tynan's direction, who did nothing to stop it. Instead, Tynan just fired one last beam at Kris.

Pushing up to her feet, Kris released a battle cry. All her energy burst forth, extending around her and throwing every remaining piece of debris away into the city that now surrounded them. At the last moment, she threw out an arm and formed a flimsy shield. Tynan's beam collided with the force field and veered off.

Kris dropped to her knees and watched Kurt's beam strike Tynan and throw him onto his back. Her throat tightened as she saw his chest rise and fall, a little slower each time.

"You did this," he muttered.

And then he was still.

She sank to the floor, panting. Her jaw quivered as she fought to keep herself composed.

"Kris." Kurt's wavering wheeze made Kris straighten and look back over her shoulder.

He was crouched with his injured arm clutched against his chest. But his chest was also burned.

Her heart sank into the pit of her stomach. "No . . ."

Kris dragged herself through the rocks over to him as he collapsed to the ground. She rolled him onto his back so his head was in her lap and she could study the wound on his skin.

"No, no, no, Kurt, you're going to be fine," she whispered, gently resting a hand on his chest.

He winced. A tear spilled down the side of his face as his blue-gray eyes zeroed in on her. "It's okay," he said. "You're going to be okay."

"No. No, we're not doing that. We're not saying goodbye," Kris cried, her voice cracking. "I'm going to get you out of here. I can fix this."

Her hands glowed with familiar warmth, but once again, she felt that it had nowhere to go as Kurt's body was rapidly growing cold.

Kurt subtly shook his head. "I'm sorry."

"Save your strength. Just stay with me." She sat him up and hugged him tightly. "You're going to be okay. We're going to be okay, remember? You promised we were going to be okay . . ."

"So stubborn," he mumbled with a weak laugh. It quickly changed to a cough, followed by wheezing. His attempts to speak morphed into painful gasps. He rested a hand on her jaw and traced his thumb over her cheek. "I . . . love . . . you . . ." he managed to get out.

"I love you, Kurt. Please don't leave me," she whimpered. "Please don't go. Please."

His hand slipped down to the floor. And when Kris couldn't hear his tortured breaths anymore, she knew she was once again alone.

Chapter 49

Haunted

Three mounds of fresh dirt lay side by side in the grass, a wooden cross placed in the ground above each grave.

It was another cloudy day. No wind. No sun. No rain. Just dry, still air.

Kris stared down at the middle grave with puffy, red, unblinking eyes. She didn't look over as Cade stepped up beside her. He reached out toward her but then dropped his arm back to his side.

"He deserved better than this," she managed to get out in a wavering, broken voice.

Cade nodded to the center grave. "*He* didn't think so."

The world was silent. The birds weren't even singing.

Finally, he held out a small black thumb drive. "He left this for you."

Kris averted her eyes, staring out into the trees. She shook her head. "This place is haunted, Cade."

When she turned to him, his blue eyes were filled with tears.

His jaw was clenched, but he slowly nodded.

"I can't be here anymore."

~

A big wooden sign had Salman Sanctuary painted across it. Beneath that was a map of the reservation, which labeled apartments and houses, as well as the community garden, school, library, shop, and cafeteria. The obligatory "You Are Here" arrow showed that Kris stood by the administrative office.

She studied the map until she heard Brie sniffling behind her.

Cade had both arms wrapped tightly around Brie, her face buried in his chest. Her shoulders jerked with sob after sob.

He met Kris's eye, and she instantly looked away again. *I told her not to come. I told her to stay with Cade. To go to Indiana.*

Up the steps, Larsen was talking to a plump, middle-aged, olive-skinned man with short, curly black hair outside the office building. When Larsen caught her attention, he waved for her to come up.

Kris clutched the strap of her messenger bag and started up the stairs, but paused as she stared down at her sneakers. They were perfectly intact. No stab wound or blood. Like Tynan had never pierced her foot with her pocketknife. Like it had been a dream.

Like it had *all* been a dream.

"Miss Hanwel, I must say, it is an honor to meet you," the man exclaimed, pushing an open hand at her. He had scarring all the way up his arm. Straight lines, one on top of the other.

Kris reluctantly gave his hand a shake and returned to twisting the strap of her bag.

"It's so wonderful to meet another healer," he babbled, motioning with his arms as he spoke. "Our healer support group will be thrilled to have another member. It's only been two of us this past year."

"So, you can heal yourself, too?" Kris mumbled, more so to herself. *And only yourself?*

"Kris, this is Mattias Finkleman," Larsen said. "He's the housing manager around here."

"Oh yes, sorry. Where are my manners?" Mattias rambled on. He reached out and patted Kris's shoulder. "I was so sorry to hear about your mother's passing. Many of the Witcans who have come through our door only made it here because of her. You should be proud."

Kris nodded halfheartedly and peered over her shoulder where Cade and Brie were slowly climbing the steps, hand in hand. They both looked so tired. So weak. So broken.

There's a lot of that going around lately.

"Kris?" Larsen's voice broke through her train of thought.

"What?"

"Would you like the tour, or would you like to get settled in your apartment first?" Mattias asked.

"Just to my apartment," Kris said quietly.

~

Mattias opened the door and held it for Kris and Brie to shuffle inside. "Not a lot of vacancies lately, what with the NWDA activity spiking nationwide," he said.

Kris clutched her bag close, scanning the small kitchen and bar in front of her. There was a living room just behind the kitchen, furnished with a single blue couch, coffee table, and the world's smallest television. Immediately to the left of the front door was a bathroom, barely bigger than a closet.

Stepping past the kitchen, she peered into the two small bedrooms just off the living room. Each had a full bed and a tall, narrow dresser.

It was simple. Basic.

And lacked the charm of the cabin.

"All the paperwork you need to fill out is right here," Mattias said, setting the keys down and patting a small stack of papers on the bar separating the kitchen from the living room. "Just get this filled out and bring it down to the office tonight, then we can talk to Tammy about academic enrollment." He fanned out the papers on the counter. "I've also left you a pamphlet with a ton of information about our facilities, rules, hours, our healer support group, all that fun stuff. Otherwise, if you need *anything* at all, let me know."

Kris leaned against the doorframe and stared at the folded blankets and sheets at the foot of the bed.

"Thanks so much for your help, Mattias," Larsen told him before the door closed.

"This place is . . . nice," Brie said quietly, stepping up beside Kris to look into the second bedroom.

"You should go to Indiana with Cade," Kris whispered, unable to look at her. "It's what you really want."

"Kris, stop it, okay?" Brie tossed her plastic bag of belongings onto her bed. "I'm not leaving you. You need me more than Cade does. I need *you* more than I need him. End of story."

Kris cracked a small smile. She knew it was a lie.

"If you want, we can grab a quick bite at the cafeteria," Larsen offered. He was doing his best to maintain a positive energy, but Kris could hear the breaks in his voice.

Following Brie's example, Kris slipped her bag over her head and set it on the bed in front of her. "Sure."

Chapter 50

Time

The leaves had already changed from green to the bright colors of autumn, and the late-afternoon sun was shining rays of orange light into the dimmed room.

Kris lay on her back and fiddled with the thumb drive Kurt had left her. She opened and closed the USB, biting down hard on her bottom lip.

The apartment door opened, and there was shuffling in the entrance. Kris clutched the flash drive to her chest and rolled to face away from her open bedroom door.

"Skipped classes again today?" Brie asked, her voice moving into the adjacent bedroom.

Kris remained quiet.

Brie's footsteps returned to the doorway. "Cade's coming to visit this weekend," she said softly, a flare of excitement in her voice.

"I'll be scarce and give you some privacy," Kris replied without turning. "I don't want to bring you guys down."

It was quiet for so long that Kris had to twist her head to see if Brie was still there. Her once blonde hair was now dyed bright pink and styled in perfect curls. Her eyebrows warped into a look of sympathy as she forced a smile.

"It's been weeks, Kris," she said quietly. "Stop playing with the flash drive and just see what Kurt left."

~

The library was empty at 11:00 p.m. except for the young girl at the front desk. But even she had her headphones on, mindlessly scrolling through the news feed on the reception PC. She didn't look up when Kris came in.

Kris snagged a computer room near the back of the building. The chair creaked loudly when she sat down, and it echoed through the racks of books. She stared at the computer desktop for a long time, but finally took a deep breath and inserted the thumb drive into the USB port.

The contents of the flash drive opened up. There was a video file called "For Kris," as well as a few audio files.

She pulled her sweater around herself. Her chest was already aching at the thought of what she might find inside. Hands shaking, she plugged in her earbuds and apprehensively clicked on the video file.

She started to cry almost immediately when a video launched of Kurt sitting in his room at the cabin. Kris lightly touched his face on the screen.

"Hey, Kris," he said quietly with a sad smile. "If you're watching this, then it means we're either laughing about how dramatic I can be, or I didn't make it home after Calosant . . . probably the latter."

Kris clapped both hands over her nose and mouth, doing the best she could to suppress her sobs.

"The truth is, I know what fate awaits me. I've been on borrowed time basically ever since I left Tynan's cult. I spent so long running from death that I never really lived. At least not until I met you. This beautiful, forgiving, understanding . . . *adorably* stubborn girl."

Kris dropped her head with a small laugh.

He twisted in his chair and lifted his guitar into his lap. "I'm sorry I can't be there for you, but you're never alone. You, Larsen, Cade, even Brie . . . I need you to promise you'll look after each other when I'm gone."

Kris ferociously wiped the tears from her face.

"I love you, Kris. And I wish I had the power to change things for you. I would go back in a heartbeat and fix everything if I could." He drummed his fingers on the belly of the guitar for a moment while he composed himself, then lifted his pale eyes directly into the camera. "This song's for you."

Kris closed her eyes as Kurt strummed the guitar and sang her a beautiful, heartbreaking ballad. When it was done, she rewound the video to listen to it again. And again.

The chair creaked as she sat up and sniffed the air. She scanned the small study room and the area of the library outside. It was empty, but the smell of lemon filled her nose. "Kurt?" she whispered.

"No matter what happens, Kris," Kurt said in the video, "I will always be with you."

Chapter 51

Once More

The first snow had fallen, covering the hill in a thin, pristine layer of white. The midday sun shimmered off the surface, and Kris took it all in.

She sat on a bench at the top of the hill and gazed down to the greenhouses below. Through the fogged-up glass, she could see the workers rummaging through the garden to pick ripe vegetables. It brought a small smile to her face.

Kris removed her earbuds and stuffed them into her coat pocket, when she heard footsteps crunching through the snow toward her. She didn't look up.

"Brie said I'd find you here," Larsen said. "May I sit?"

She shrugged, but shifted over anyway, her eyes still fixed on the gardens below. "Free country."

Hands in his coat pockets, Larsen sat down and released a heavy sigh, visible in the chilly air. "Happy birthday."

"Not until midnight," Kris mumbled, clutching her phone in her lap.

It was quiet for a moment before he tried again. "Cade

mentioned you're going to be speaking at the Coexistence rally next month."

"If you're here to talk me out of it—"

"I'm not. I think it's great. The Witcan community couldn't ask for a better representative."

They were both quiet. Kris fidgeted with her phone and frowned.

"How have you been?" Larsen asked.

She scoffed. "You know, living the dream. Therapy. Classes. Work. The whole nine yards."

"Mattias says you haven't attended his healers group in weeks."

She shrugged ever so slightly. Her throat felt tight. "I'm not like them," Kris finally said. "They can only heal themselves. Their guilt isn't actually their fault . . ."

Larsen lightly brushed his fingers against his neck. He was silent for a long moment.

"The night Alex died, he nearly killed me," he said softly before clearing his throat. "I got a short glimpse of the other side."

Kris slapped her arms down in her lap. "Where are you going with this?"

He took a deep breath and pivoted to face her. "There have been studies claiming that people who have near-death experiences are able to communicate with loved ones who have passed on—"

She whipped her head around and glared at him. "Is this about Kurt?"

Larsen raised his hands. "I'm getting to that—"

"Goddammit, Larsen." Kris sprang off the bench, took a few steps away, and buried her face in her hands. After a deep breath she whirled back to him, motioning as she spoke. "*This* is why I can't talk to you. I can't do this again. Every time you come around with another half-baked idea to bring Kurt back—"

He stood and pointed to the ground. "This time is different."

"I'm not doing this again."

Larsen took a step forward, jabbing a finger in her direction. "Kurt would *never* give up on us, so how can you give up on him?"

"It's not giving up, it's moving on," she shouted. "Kurt is dead, and you can't change the past, remember?"

"Maybe we can, but I can't do this without you."

Kris spun away, breathing hard. Her palms were sweaty as she stared down at her phone, where Kurt's song was still playing. As she turned off the screen, her sad eyes reflected back at her.

"Kurt deserved better. You said so yourself," Larsen continued.

"You could have teleported," she said quietly, her jaw clenched.

He paused. She could hear his feet crunch through the snow as he took a step back. "What?"

Kris pressed her eyes shut and took a long inhale through her nose. "In Calosant. When you saw the temple coming down, you could have teleported to us and helped."

Larsen scoffed. "And you could have just listened to him and killed Tynan," he scolded before muttering under his breath. "Happy birthday."

His footsteps got fainter as he walked away, and a tear spilled over onto Kris's cheek. She knew she shouldn't have said that.

The words from Kurt's video kept repeating over and over in Kris's head. *"I would go back in a heartbeat and fix everything if I could . . ."*

Kris put a hand to her chest as the familiar warm feeling started to burn.

Why?

Her head was pounding. She pressed her fingers to her eyelids until the feeling passed. When she opened her eyes again, she was sitting on the bench once more.

"May I sit?"

Kris jumped. Larsen was standing over her, motioning to the bench.

Her mouth opened and closed. "It's a . . . free country?"

Larsen offered a small, sad smile and twisted to sit beside her.

Déjà vu?

Kris blinked, confused, gazing down the hill at the workers in the greenhouses.

"Happy birthday," Larsen said.

She chuckled and shook her head. "We already did this."

It was quiet for a moment, and when she finally met Larsen's eye, he looked amused and perplexed. "Did . . . what?"

Kris rubbed her eyes again. "You came to ask for my help recreating a near-death experience in hopes of seeing Kurt."

Larsen jumped up from the bench and backed away. He was saying something, but Kris couldn't hear his words.

How did I do that?

Kris closed her eyes, calling the fire in her heart once more. Could she do it again?

"May I sit?"

She laughed in disbelief and sprang to her feet. She grabbed Larsen by his arm and spun him around. "I can manipulate time," she blurted.

Larsen chuckled with a tilt of his head. "You can manipulate time?"

Kris nodded emphatically. Her mind was racing and she didn't even realize she was rambling. "That's why my sneaker is undamaged. That's why I was able to restore those flowers at my parents' grave. That's why, when I heal, I don't scar like Mattias does."

He took a little step away. "You're serious?"

She clasped her hands to her mouth as tears of happiness filled her eyes. "I would go back in a heartbeat and fix everything if I could . . ." she whispered to herself.

Kris met Larsen's brown eyes with a stern nod. "I'm going to fix *everything*."

About The Author

After nearly twenty years writing and rewriting her first novel, Sarah Chayer finally published *Incandescent: Magic Unknown* in 2022. She has since published *Moon Rise*, a collection of original poems and illustrations about her personal struggles with mental health. Her other works-in-progress include future young-adult, urban fantasy books for the Incandescent series, as well as a second, separate series.

She graduated cum laude with a Bachelor of Arts Degree for Communication emphasis in Journalism from the University of Wisconsin - Green Bay and has won awards for her work in fiction, poetry, and English.